KOHAN KILLETZ

Seven Times and Seven Times I Bow

A TALE OF REBELLION, LUST, BETRAYAL, AND WAR IN ANCIENT CANAAN

Contents

II TABLET TWO: BONDS FORGED,
BONDS BROKEN

Acknowledgement

This work is dedicated to Morty Segal, the *Man of the Beginning.* Without him, the work would not be possible.

I

TABLET ONE: THE VIRGIN LANDS

1

Chapter 1: Donkey Caravan

What could be said for a donkey? A donkey is a much-maligned creature. If you want to call someone an idiot, you say they are "Kama Ḥimari" like a donkey. You could say they were "Binu Ḥimari", son of a donkey. But donkeys, despite their purported stupidity and stubbornness, are remarkably hard-working creatures. They will carry a fat man on their back, despite their small size. They can carry about five hundred deben's weight in goods for miles with little rest. Despite their utility, they endure nothing but abuse and whipping. By the standards of asses, Gubu was a fortunate one. He was ridden by a boy, not a man, and not a large one either. The boy, Upuzu, was a kind and gentle boy to his animals; much unlike his father, Abi Rashpu. They were quite different in appearance. Upuzu was short for his age, ten, had a small button nose and eyes twinkling with the curiosity that youth endows in great measure. His father, a merchant, was tall and fat, with a scraggly black beard, a beaked nose, and a tendency to speak at length about haggling. Abi Rashpu was a man who had found his true calling as a trader. He had been in bazaars from the magnificent Hundred-Gated Thebes, city of the Pharaohs, to Susa, the dazzling capital of the enigmatic Elamites, but he never struck off beyond that.

"Whenever you haggle, request twice the price you're willing to sell for", Abi Rashpu said.

"As if there was someone who'd fall for that old trap." Upuzu picked his nose, until his father rode up to him on his own donkey and smacked the boy's hand.

"Disgusting. You'll get snot on the merchandise!"

"As if you don't scratch your butt and then sniff it…". He flicked the booger in the direction of his father. It hit his hapless donkey.

"Ya'ani… I got a boy who is snotty and unmannered. Now about the trade… Did I tell you about the haggling? You should always tell them you bought the product at the price you're willing to sell for. And — that you only do it for them. Also, you can add some worthless garbage as a free gift… make them think they are getting a good deal. "

"I know, father. Tell me something about Egypt." That was their destination; the ancient and mythical land of Egypt. Not only that, but it was for Upuzu his first journey away from home and his mother in Qaṭna. His eyes widened when he thought of the tales of his uncle, who spoke of the stupendous palaces, imposing temples to queer animal-headed gods, and golden tipped pyramids that seemed to almost kiss the clouds. That is, if a cloud was ever to be seen in the land of Egypt. It was a land alien to the Canaanites; where rain never fell and the Nile alone provided great bounty. It too was the land they bowed to in supplication, seven times and seven times was the formula. It expressed complete obedience to the mighty rule of Pharaoh; for there was only complete obedience or the fires of revolt. And the God-Kings of Egypt looked down on their Canaanite subjects in the best of times. When they revolted, Pharaoh's armies would be merciless.

Upuzu grabbed his father's brilliant multi-colored tunic to get his attention. Dyes were big business in Canaan, so Merchants that dealt in it wore colors so bright it would dazzle a peacock. It was a sort of advertising, and in those days, also the peak of fashion. Abi Rashpu scratched his itchy beard, thinking of something to say. He was not a learned man. Finally, after thinking for what seemed like an age and a half, he decided to just say the first thought that came to his mind.

"Ah. It is very green beside the rivers, oh, and there are many fine products! A few cubits of cedar wood will get you..."

"No, something interesting! Like the pyramids of the Pharaohs. I've heard that inside them the ancient kings live for eternity, feasting on offerings brought by the living"

"Pu! That's foolish nonsense and womanly talk. You should know, my dear boy, that dead is dead is dead is dead. Once you pass the eternal threshold, there is no return." He playfully gestured with his hands his own decapitation, much to his beloved boy's amusement.

Upuzu was thrilled by the speech of his father, his heart racing and beating like the war drums of Pharaoh's Kushite Soldiers. He imagined his death, not with fear but with awe. Would he pass into the Field of Reeds, to face monsters and demons with magic spells, as his Uncle told him? Would it be a gray and dark abyss, where he would eat dust and drink muddy water, as his mother warned him of? Or would he rest, eternally, in a deep dreamless sleep? That thought both comforted him and disturbed him. But not knowing, with his youthful curiosity, that was gnawing at him like the ticks that were feasting on his young supple flesh.

There was a rustle in the bush by the road, a rather queer road to be sure. On the west side there was some light greenery in abundance, and on the east, a barren, scrubby desert. The path just bisected the borders between the domain of life and the realm of death. The donkey caravan was kicking up a lot of dust, so the merchants could hardly see their greedy hands in front of them. Furthermore, the clatter of donkey's hooves, their braying along with the idle chatter of merchants drowned out the faint footsteps, just out of sight, just inaudible, just approaching; running with the speed and agility of a caracal.

But, children seem to have a third eye. Something was wrong, and with the force of a small calf, Upuzu jumped off his donkey, catapulting directly into his father's ample paunch. This knocked Abi Rashpu in turn right off his donkey and

6

sent them both careening. They wound up piled on the dusty ground. Just before the father could raise his fist to severely chastise his child, an arrow whizzed by sounding like the hum of a bee. Its trajectory was such that it would have hit him had he been seated on the donkey, likely piercing his liver, dooming him to a miserable death. Before his mood could change from anger to gratitude, more arrows flew. Merchants, who had been his dear companions and drinking buddies for most of his adult life, started falling like hunted deer. Their cries of anguish drowned the air in fear and sorrow.

Into the dust cloud emerged figures, in white, blue, and orange kilts. There was one thing they could be. Ḥabiru: the terror of the countryside, the scourge of cities, bandits and mercenaries devoted to a life of pillage and worse. The south of Canaan was lousy with them. Brutally, they started slaughtering the whole caravan, sparing neither man nor beast. Abi Rashpu told his son, in a hushed whisper, "Take this arrow and cover yourself in the blood of asses. If you play dead, then you can escape when they turn away from us."

Abi Rashpu and Upuzu held arrows upon their bodies and hid as best they could amidst the slain donkeys. This fooled many of the low-level Ḥabiru, getting drunk on stolen wine. But not Abneru. That bastard could hear any sound, it was said, no matter how faint. He often joked that he could hear a flea sneeze from a mile away. And the breath of Abi Rashpu did not escape him. Abneru was a funny man, it was said. He was captain of this group of Ḥabiru and was so accustomed

7

to death that he made constant japes. Besides that, he was highly regarded as a warrior. He was rich, too, for a Ḥabiru. He wore bronze scale mail, and in his mouth, the gaps in his teeth from fights caused by his jokes were filled with golden surrogates. His beard was full and round, and the hairs of his head were long and curly. His nose was crooked from being broken so often, and he always smiled.

"Mutba'alu, looky-looky, beneath these donkeys there are some more donkeys, some smart asses that think to fool us by playing dead."

Abneru grabbed the arrows the father and son bore, and with arms as strong as a bear's and at least as hairy, he pulled them to their feet.

"You merchants thought you were so clever hiding in the dust like insects. Don't you know that insects get stomped?" Abneru threw a rough punch right into Abi Rashpu's heavy paunch. The victim reeled, falling backward. A blow like that was hard to take, and he was not accustomed to being beaten. The last time he took a really good beating was when he sold a Hittite soldier some dye that he claimed was purple but was so adulterated it was almost brown. Then, justice, now, injustice. Abneru laughed at the wheezing noises his victim made as he attempted to catch his breath.

"Spare my life and that of my son and I will amply reward you! I am a very rich man!" said Abi Rashpu, weeping.

"A good father I see! I'm in the mood for mercy now, see, I'm

8

not such a monster! I'll spare your life, rich man, or that of your kiddo, one or the other, you decide!"

"Take my life, so that my son might live! He is a good boy! He has no faults that demand you spill his blood! I've been greedy, I've cheated men before! Kill me and spare him!" Upuzu looked at his father, at once feeling grateful, sad, and guilty. His powerful father would sacrifice his own life for him? He wasn't lying about cheating people, so might he be truthful about his sacrifice?

"A good father! You passed my test! I'll spare both of you!" Abneru grabbed the fallen father by his arm, pulling him up. The relief was so palpable on the tearful faces of both father and son. Their joy was such that neither immediately noticed that Abneru had slipped a long, thin, straight akinakes sword right between the ribs of Abi Rashpu. The smile on the face of the father turned a mouth retching blood. The sword had pierced his lungs. That was a death sentence. Abneru pushed the dying man back onto the ground, fiercely cackling.

"Mutba'alu, the boy has turned yellow!" said Abneru, wiping the blood off his sword with a handkerchief.

"Hahaha. And he's pissed himself." Mutba'alu replied. Mutba'alu was a prince. Not a traditional virtuous heir from the stories, but a more bellicose figure. He had a shadow of a beard, covering most of his head and neck, and two massive oversized front teeth like a rabbit's. He was not like a rabbit. He was vicious and wicked of spirit, his heart as black as the charred remains of the houses he burned. The ghosts of the

9

men he killed just five minutes prior could attest to that.

"Mutba'alu, when are you going to get us a contract from your daddy?", said Abneru. In fact, despite consorting with Ḥabiru bandits Mutba'alu was the son of a local King; Lab'ayu of Shechem. Shechem, the thorn in Pharaoh's side.

"We're mercenaries." replied Mutba'alu, "he'll hire us when there's a war."

"We'd better start one then." Glancing over at little Upuzu who was restrained, cowering in fear in the arms of two burly, hairy Ḥabiru mercenaries. "Run off little boy, go, run! Your mama is lactating just for you!"

Upuzu was released by those who had bound him, and he made haste to the north. He knew that the Ḥabiru men were skilled archers, so he ran by an exceedingly twisted path, such as a serpent makes. As he ran, the arrows flew true and swift, never too far from where he had once been. So far they had all missed him, but he couldn't run forever. Men were chasing him, leaping over the carcasses of man and beast, splayed on the roadside. They were fast, but their life wasn't in danger. Upuzu was well ahead of them, and certainly well out of bow's range. He thought so at least. He stopped a moment to breathe, but a sudden pain in the back thrust him to the ground. An arrow had embedded itself in his spine. It was an arrow Mutba'alu had loosed. The mercenaries were all joking about the boy's pathetic fall and congratulating Mutba'alu on his magnificent shot. Upuzu crawled on the ground, trying to get up, but he couldn't move

10

his legs. Finally, a plump Ḥabiru man with a stout bronze-headed mace kneeled over him, laughed a jolly cackle, and cracked open his skull like it was an earthen pot.

"Look at this!" said Abneru, holding up a cylinder of stone with engraved carvings. It was the seal of king Milkilu of Gezer. The man who carried it must have been one of that king's most trusted men. Now he was dead, at the hands of the Ḥabiru.

"If this doesn't start a war, I don't know what will!" said Mutba'alu, "My father hates that pimp Milkilu and his two filthy brothers. Let's be honest, all of Canaan does. Let's send this seal back to Milkilu, shoved up the ass of the man who bore it!"

"That" said Abneru, "Is true comedy. I can't wait to see how Milkilu likes our little joke."

"He'll be beating his belly with laughter... and his wife!" Mutba'alu inserted the seal into the dead man's rectum. "A donkey! Bring me a donkey to carry this ass!"

Somehow, Gubu, the lucky donkey, had survived the massacre. Abneru grabbed the beast's nose ring, leading him towards his friend. "Too bad you killed the boy. Could have led the donkey to Gezer."

"No need! All donkeys know the way to Gezer!"

2

Chapter 2: The Pimp of Gezer

"I feel a drink is warranted!" Yapahu raised a silver rhyton, "Oh mothers of Canaan, hide your daughters, for the sons of Zimredda will do their business..."

"And Pharaoh will have his fun!" Addadanu poured yet another draught down his thirsty gullet.

Three brothers, born of three mothers, stood in the courtyard of the palace of Gezer. They drank wine from rhytons of Gold, Silver, and Electrum. They were rich beyond measure, for the Egyptian yoke was not harsh for all her subjects. Some made a fortune, peddling the flesh of their country's women to the wealthy of Egypt. No one in the Two Lands had such a big appetite for flesh as the Pharaoh himself, Amenhotep III. Not any woman would do for him, he desired beautiful virgins, and for that, he would pay a premium. Premiums that could cover the floors in rich woolen carpets, bodies in the finest dyed and embroidered robes, and walls in murals painted in bright colors by masterful artists of Kaphtor.

Milkilu, King of Gezer, and his two half-brothers, Yapahu and Addadanu were Pharaoh's conduit to the prettiest girls in Canaan, and by pimping, they reaped the rewards of wealth and favor. Their mutual father was not a king at all, but a native Canaanite minister to the Pharaoh. A promiscuous man, he sired three sons by three different women, Milkilu by a Nubian, Yapahu by a proper Egyptian lady, and Addadanu by a wild woman of Libya, his bed slave. Milkilu was a natural leader and a favorite of the Pharaoh. He was placed upon the vacant throne of Gezer despite his bastard birth and complete lack of royal blood. His two brothers, who were as near and dear to him as a full brother would be, were employed by him as his procurers. Each took after their father in different ways. Milkilu was charismatic and virile as his father, and handsome despite being very dark, whereas while Yapahu was not handsome, being balding and big-nosed; he had his father's eloquence and intellect. Finally, Addadanu was the most handsome of them all, fair-skinned and bearded, with mighty shoulders and breasts. Yet it was as if God had not spared a shekel on sense when he designed the poor boy. Yapahu would always do the talking. Addadanu was to merely flex his muscles and look enticing. Through this strategy, scores of women and girls were procured to feed the lusts of the now elderly Pharaoh.

"It was difficult, but we have had success. The virgins, all twenty, are on their way to Pharaoh! And did we scour the land for them!" proclaimed Milkilu. Virgins were becoming increasingly difficult to find in these days of libertines and Ḥabiru set on rapine.

13

"Indeed! Let's drink to that!" replied Yapahu. They had already had quite a lot to drink, but with them, there was no limit to the drinking and merriment after a challenging but highly rewarding venture. Yapahu was content. *Wine in my belly and brothers by my side. Free to enjoy the fruits of our labor, what is better in life?*

"To Pharaoh, pretty virgins, and whatever- gods forbid- he does with them." toasted Milkilu. Milkilu dealt in flesh, yet he was a traditional man. He was no libertine. The innocence he possessed stood in harsh contrast to the vulgar nature of his trade.

"I can think of a few things he can do with them!" butted in Addadanu. Oh, the 'Peacock' could indeed think of more than a few things. He was rather familiar with the depravity of the Pharaoh. After all, he participated in these hedonistic orgies himself. Addadanu was a seducer of the highest order. He had been chased out of the houses of other men's wives more than he could count, both in Egypt and in Canaan. From that, he learned to be a quick dresser and an even quicker runner. His athleticism in escaping the clutches of the cuckolds only made him more appealing to their wives.

"With twenty of them? I only have one wife and she savages me!" Milkilu, contrary to what a pimp may be expected to do, had behaved more like a Canaanite king than a depraved pharaoh. His wife, the daughter of Tagi, King of Ginti, was a political match. She was a beauty no doubt, but there was nothing beautiful in the way she felt about her situation. Nothing Milkilu could do would ever cheer her up. His jokes annoyed her, his embrace hurt her, and his awkward combination of low birth and ostentatious wealth made her despise him. *It's not my fault I'm not a descendant of some mythical king who never even existed!*

At that moment, the most powerful man in Canaan walked through the gate. He was Hanya, the Commissioner of Archers. His duties included maintaining order, commanding the infantry, and now, paying for Pharaoh's virgin obsession. That he would often come to call on Milkilu and associates in the city of Gezer stressed both the city's importance and the all-consuming desires of the Pharaoh for Canaanite flesh. "Peace to you, Milkilu!" bellowed Hanya, with eyes so black they could neither reveal happiness nor distress in his expression.

"Peace and health! What brings you to Gezer, my friend?" replied Milkilu, instantly ascertaining the possible answers. *Tribute payments, must be tribute payments.*

"I bring a message from the Pharaoh himself." Hanya handed Milkilu the clay tablet, written as always in Akkadian, the language of diplomacy.

Milkilu read it, and read it again. His smile dropped to the floor, followed by the tablet itself. At last, he cried, "Devils take me!" The tablet was hastily rescued by Hanya, who dusted it off. Luckily, the carpets prevented the pharaoh's precious tablet from shattering.

"What does it say?" asked Yapahu in silent disbelief. It was

15

not like Milkilu to react like this.

"The core of it is we have to get Pharaoh another forty concubines."

"Forty? That can't be done!" gasped Addadanu.

"Don't worry! For the acquisition, Pharaoh sent many fine things. Gold, ebony, garments, uh... turquoises. Silver too... " Hanya said with a smile on his face that made him look very untrustworthy. His men brought in the treasures of Egypt. Magnificent though they were, no treasure surpasses the lovely virgins of Canaan. Pharaoh stole them away from their mothers and fathers, their dear innocent sweethearts, and discarded them like a spent arrow. And Milkilu was his conduit. Milkilu was loved by Pharaoh almost as his own son.

"Would you sell your daughter for any of these things, Hanya?" asked Yapahu.

"No, but..."

"Exactly. And didn't we just send twenty lovely virgins?" said Addadanu, "Good, fine virgins with the tastiest breasts you ever seen. I could of just eaten them up!"

"Ah, if so, they never reached Egypt."

"I know what happened." Milkilu clenched his fist, "It's that dog Mutba'alu, son of Lab'ayu. He is with the Ḥabiru. His

16

men robbed and killed a caravan that among other things was carrying my goods for sale in Egypt. And I wouldn't have known if he hadn't made himself known by sending my man back to me, dead, with my damned seal shoved up his backside!"

"With those girls killed, Gods forbid, and raped too no doubt, how could we go and recruit more? We've pretty much cleared the land of good looking virgins." Muttered a bitterly agitated Addadanu.

Meanwhile, Milkilu was in deep thought. Finally, he found his solution. "Mutba'alu, son of Lab'ayu committed this raid."

"How would I know?" said Hanya.

"Then we'd be justified if we recruit virgins in Shechemite territory. I once had this girl from Shechem. Oh mama, she was a tasty morsel!" Addadanu smacked his lips, trying to remember the taste of the girl's nether regions, "But her father, oh mama, and her mama, oh baba, they were some mean folks. If they caught me, I'd have been hung by my balls!"

"Addadanu is right. It's risky. Lab'ayu is a dangerous and unpredictable man. Much like those testy parents Addadanu speaks of", said Yapahu.

"We should do it anyway. Pharaoh will protect us! What can Lab'ayu that ill-tempered man do against Pharaoh and his archers?" Milkilu said, eyes filled with anger and the thrill

17

of getting revenge.

"We'll drink to that!" shouted Addadanu. They raised their shining vessels and drank the sweet white wine. A new mission has begun. Slaves loaded ox-carts with Egyptian treasures. It was now time for the brothers to do their wicked business. They would celebrate the Marziḫu in the country of Shechem.

Milkilu's thoughts turned to his beloved father. *Would he be proud of his son, now a king?* Milkilu thought so. Even if his business was dirty, Gezer was strong, and rich. *The people,* Milkilu thought. *The people. They will soon be honoring their beloved dead in the afterlife. I will feed the people on good meat, and make offerings to god. The city will be prosperous, and safe. Father, the city will not fall under my watch.* Milkilu drank. Wine always tastes sweetest in the mouths of the prideful.

3

Chapter 3: Remembrance — Part One

Though the autumnal breeze blew like icy daggers, the warmth of oil lamps fended off the chill. This was a night when the shades of the dead were said to walk among the living. Needless to say, death caressed the families of Qadesh like the veil caresses the faces of the virginal brides. It shrouded the city in nostalgia and inebriation. In death, we are all equal. The Marziḥu bridged the divide of rich and poor, male and female, even living and dead.

Nothing is as sweet as a celebration, and nothing is as bitter as death, particularly that of a loved one. If so, what can be made of the celebration of death, the Marziḥu. The Canaanites might say to a curious foreigner that it was not truly a celebration of death, but an annual remembering of the dead and a commemoration of life. Marziḥu was traditionally celebrated by a society, to honor the memory of one or more of its members. In this particular case, it was celebrated by the royal family of Qadesh, a city at the

19

headwaters of the Orontes in Syria. The tables were decked with a traditional feast, however, not as large a feast as you might expect for kings. There was a roast of Lamb, seasoned with cumin, garlic, and wine, dates, grapes almost blue in color, fresh green figs, ḥummus with vinegar, lentils, and flatbread of the ovens. A large vessel of white wine was held by Sura'ata, wife of the King. She began her invocation. "Hereto, on the Marziḫu, I pour wine to bless the shade of the king, dwelling in the Netherworld." The wine she poured into a shining bowl. "May he be well. May the gods in their mountains bless him, and may they be well. May the gods bless us, and make us be well".

The king referred to was not to be named, for he was a rebel. By order of the Pharaoh of Egypt, Amenhotep III, *Damnation in Memory* was placed on his name, so it may be forgotten forever. King Sutarna's mind filled with a frenzied frolic of death when he remembered the end of his father's days. His normally quite swarthy face had become paler, though still, he was tanner than anyone in the room. Contrary to the melancholy of the King, the princesses of his loins were not in turmoil but were devouring the food with great gusto. Despite being royal by birth, kingship meant less than one would think in the Canaanite world. Each city had a king, though they were more a mayor than a king, and bureaucrat too, and each hill had a walled city. As such, kings were not especially rich, often poorer than the wealthy merchants that plied their trade between north and south, east and west. Sutarna's youngest, Gulati, was a pale and sickly child. No one had expected her to live so long as she had but were glad of it, for she was amiable and sweet, a child of twelve. Her hair, like all of her sisters', was long and curly and black. The eldest was Tiwati, Priestess of Ashtartu. She was a tall and outspoken girl of nineteen, with her father's handsome face and a colorful reputation with men. She was devout though, and would not see gods or ancestors get less than their due, "Mother, you must fill the vessel all the way."

"Tiwati, always the priestess. Hubby, would you say a few words?"

"Peace to him..." Of all of them, he was the only one that knew his father and saw his fate first hand. A fate he determined he should never allow to happen again.

"You must say more than that," said Tiwati, "He was your father after all!"

Sutarna placed his handsome face into his hand. He hated Marziḥu. His father's death, his uncles' death, and those of countless others. The men, women, and children were chopped, stabbed, and shot by the Egyptian soldiers, at the order of the Pharaoh. The same Pharaoh to which he has sworn undying loyalty.

"Must I?" said Sura'ata "Well, there are warriors, then there are heroes, then, only then: there is my father-in-law. With indefatigable courage, inhuman vigor, and unshakeable honor, he raised the soldiers and the chariots in defiance of Pharaoh..."

"He lost his head. Qadesh burned." The small fire upon the

21

altar couldn't help but remind him of the inferno that once engulfed the city in his boyhood. But there was distraction too. Sutarna found new comfort in his animal companion. His mighty Canaanite dog, as clever and as strong as a wolf, sat at his lap, breathing in that friendly way that dogs do. Sutarna had no sons so he called his dog that, Binu, which meant son in his language. Sutarna loved Binu just as much as he loved his favorite daughter, the conspicuously absent Shisita. Sutarna fed Binu on the roast meat of his table.

"Would you like to speak of him? Remember, it is bad luck to speak ill of the dead." Sura'ata glanced at him, eyes slightly agitated with annoyance. Then she found an excuse to scold him. "Stop wasting meat on the stupid dog!" She chided him on it, even though she knew it wouldn't do a damn bit of good. He would always feed the dog, and she would always scold him. That was the nature of their marriage. It was the most petty power struggle in the history of kingship. Sutarna wasn't really much of a king.

"The dog is wiser than he looks. He knows not to bite its master. He's a good dog!" Sutarna rubbed the dog on the head and scratched his lupine ears, gave him a juicy slice of meat, and sent him off, smiling; for his dog brought him joy like no man nor woman besides ever could. Sura'ata despised that dog with the jealousy of a scorned woman, for though long ago the couple had been very much in love, it was not to last. Not since Gulati's troubled birth had Sutarna laid with her, nor kissed her large and puffy lips or said one word of affection. She knew he loved her no longer, which would have been fine with her if she had ceased loving him,

22

or he even gave her cause to. He never had intercourse, nor masturbated, nor even looked at a woman with the faintest lust in his eye. He was true to her in body, but his heart was with that stupid dog. *If only I could have given him a boy, he would have loved me forever*, she often thought.

Suddenly a wizened old man, hoary of beard, walked into the room. He was the magistrate in charge of trade. His skin was orange of hue, and he had a large black mole on his cheek. Though he was decrepit, his eyes were always smiling. "Sorry to interrupt your conversation, but emissaries from Gezer say that the caravan that went through our market last week was robbed and slaughtered by the Ḥabiru, in Canaan."

"There was a boy with them… is he safe?" asked Gulati, a child too innocent and empathetic to live in this world.

"Can I tell her? " asked the magistrate, turning his head to Sutarna, who nodded his head. He didn't mind frightening his youngest daughter a little, the more to scare her off going south like Shisita.

"The Ḥabiru make a point of leaving no survivors." finished the official, "I suppose if they did, they wouldn't be Ḥabiru!

"Papa, Isn't that where Shisita is fighting?" Gulati remembered. Sutarna sighed when he heard her name. And of course, Gulati was right. Hearing her name was enough to push Sutarna over the edge into the realm of silence.

"Papa, is that where my sister is fighting!?" This was too

23

much to hear. Sutarna walked out of the room. It is one thing to have a masculine daughter, to be a child of fierce 'Anat the war goddess, but for her to disobey him and run off to fight and perhaps die? She was the darling of his eye, how could she? She was his favorite and he did not know if she was alive or dead, if he would ever see her again.

Gulati looked into her mother's eyes, with an expression that told much more than the words on a clay tablet ever could.

"I know, Gulati. He is upset that Shisita disobeyed him and ran off to fight in Canaan. As for me, good on her! I wish I had those kinds of eggs when I was her age. I wouldn't have married a limp noodle of a man like that one, then! May Ba'alu bless him, but I swear there is more man in our daughter than in him. More man in you, little one, to tell you the truth."

"There was a time," said the Official, "that a burning passion ruled in his heart. In his youth he was spurred to action by…"

"Yes, I hear him muttering in his sleep. Lab'ayu, Lab'ayu…" Sura'ata wiped a tear from her eye with a dirty handkerchief. She then noticed the food smearing her face, and she took a clean cloth and wiped that.

"Who is Lab'ayu?" asked Gulati to her mother.

"Who indeed!"

24

4

Chapter 4: Remembrance — Part 2

Sutarna walked through the city of Qadesh with only the stars and moon for company. Two months had passed from the observance of the Marziḥu. That festival struck him worse each coming year. As the herald of the winter, it kindled memories from the darkness... memories of flame. The thin Syrian snow seemed much like ashes to the King. He remembered how, some thirty years past, ashes blanketed the streets of Qadesh like so many snowflakes. When his breath condensed into fog in the air, he could almost smell the scent of smoke. The winter chill burned his skin, like the flames that still roared in his mind. He remembered.

Sutarna again was a boy, a boy not ten years old. He stood in the palace of Qadesh. Activity and speech rang through the halls like bells on bridal garb.

"My king, I think we cannot hold out any longer. Stocks of food have run low, and the people have grown restless. Soon they'll be after your head." said the Vizier.

"Those fatuous people! When we said we would fight Pharaoh, and be rid of oppression, did they not cheer, did they not rally!" Sutarna's eldest brother raised his spear above his his head, "If they are after heads, let them chase Pharaoh's, he is just outside the gate."

"I have advised you my king for a great many years, have I not?" the Vizier placed his hands comfortingly on the shoulder of Sutarna's father, "The war is lost. The better part of the troops died in Canaan... my condolences for Ammatanu. He was a dear, dear loss."

Sutarna remembered how as a boy he didn't understand death. He thought if he prayed enough, someday his brother Ammatanu would enter the cedar door and play the game of twenty squares with him again. Instead, he would find brothers exiting the cedar door but never returning.

"Durusha stood, looked Pharaoh in the eye, and defied him!" said the heir.

"I don't know what nonsense you've been reading, boy, but when Durusha saw all hope was lost in Megiddo, he bent his knee to Pharaoh. He saved the city, the people, himself. Now look, my king, I have spoken to emissaries of the Pharaoh. They say he tires of fire, bloodshed and death! Do not allow Qadesh to be flamed, do not allow the people to be slaughtered. Think of your young son, Sutarna. Do you want him cut to pieces by the enemy? Do you want him tossed between the soldiers to satisfy their carnal lusts? Give over the city, if but for the sake of the innocents, like Sutarna..."

"So you've been colluding with the enemy, eh?" the heir drew his bronze akinakes sword and thrust it towards the vizier's throat, "You want me dead so Sutarna can have MY throne, and be a puppet you can rule over! I should have your head!"

"ENOUGH!" said the King, "We will have no discord in our ranks. When I make my decision, it will be final. Send Sutarna out of the room. He should not be forced to be a pawn in our struggle. He should not have to see the fate of his father. Vizier, take Sutarna, and bring him to Pharaoh as a hostage. Take gold too, to secure his life. Go!"

The vizier dragged Sutarna from that hazy room of memory, those giant, overbearing pillars of his past. As if no time had passed at all, Sutarna was standing in the midst of the Pharaoh's tent. The face of the Pharaoh was seared into his memory, far more so than his father or brother. The prior memory was like a dream. This was as real as life.

"So this is the son of the rebel king?" asked Amenhotep III. His size was massive, his muscles raw, his gold glittering, his beauty horrifying. The youthful Pharaoh towered like a grand monument surrounded by houses.

"My king! This is Sutarna, son of…" the Vizier said.

"Do not speak the name of the rebel in my presence! I am the son of Amun!" Amenhotep III crashed his royal staff into the metallic floor of his royal pavilion. It resounded, like the roar of a bull. "I ask, does the dam's presence here mean the father is ready to give up the city?"

"Regrettably not, great king. He means to spare his innocent son the horror of his fate. Please, take him with the hostages so they may learn the values of Egypt... wisdom, truthfulness, duty, obedience to Pharaoh."

"He shall be inducted into my hostage chamber. As for learning the value of obedience to Pharaoh, let the lesson begin now..."

Sutarna was again swept away by the passage of thought. He was returned to Qadesh. It looked not unlike the Qadesh in the moment of his remembering. In fact, the dream and reality had intersected. It was transitioning. But it made his memory no less vivid.

Sutarna was restrained by the arms of the Pharaoh's soldiers. Wounded, emaciated, nude, Sutarna saw his family led in front of him. Their bodies were as black as sky, with the only features on them being red blood from their many wounds. The flames raged behind Sutarna's sire and his dam. The sounds of women screaming gave hints to the violence done that Sutarna in his youth could not understand.

"You should see, Sutarna, what disobedience to Pharaoh brings." Pharaoh clapped his hands, and one by one, the family of Sutarna was slaughtered before his young eyes. His uncles, his brothers, and at last his father, were dispatched expertly. Their faces in the moment of their death flashed before the eyes of Sutarna. These faces, bloodied, beaten, a moment before death, would be the sole faces Sutarna would ever remember of his loved ones.

28

"Remember" said Pharaoh, "Like this for you if you ever betray me."

Sutarna jolted awake.

"Oh, good gods. I'm looking for you all over the city, and guess where I find you! Asleep in the mud and snow, in a puddle of your own piss!" Sura'ata helped her husband up. "Thank the gods for me. If I didn't exist, you'd be in dreamland all day pissing yourself!"

"My head hurts," said Sutarna.

"You and me both. If you are going to sleep, at least sleep in a nice warm bed and not in muddy pissy snow!" She glanced at the mud on his fine royal robe, "I will have the slaves draw you a bath. You can get washed up, and then no one will say, 'why is that disgusting drunken beggar wearing the king's robes?!?' "

In his wife's arms, Sutarna felt even more alone.

5

Chapter 5: The Ants

"Where are you heading to now, prince?" asked Issuwa, the old general.

"He's heading to the brothel no doubt. Look at that smile on his face." Dadua, son of Issuwa slapped his knees, choking with laughter at his own joke. After a long pause, Mutba'alu replied to Issuwa.

"I'm going to the palace to speak with my father."

"I spoke true! He is going to the brothel! You'd never see such a den of harlotry in all of Canaan as the palace of Shechem. No where else do you see the children of Canaan so whored out to Pharaoh!"

"It's that bad, Dadua?"

"That bad or worse. Egyptian officials and opportunistic lickspittles dwell there, feasting on the carcass of our dignity, honor, and having their way with our..."

"Then it seems right that I have a few words with the king."

"May your words move mountains" said Issuwa, "Mine never have."

"Pity. Good thing you know your way around a sword." Mutba'alu entered the palace, maintaining the airs and grace of a noble prince. His accustomed tunic was long since swapped for the robes of state.

Mutba'alu laid his sword, a shining bronze Khopesh, at his feet. With true affection he approached his father the king Lab'ayu. Lab'ayu was a somewhat curious looking man. In his appearance, as with his personality, he seemed almost mundane and ordinary. But it was unmissable; his common appearance seemed almost to add to his greatness. In his banality anyone could look and see a relatable figure, a fatherly archetype. His face was angular and manly, with a big black beard, light tan skin, a pointed triangular nose, and large eyes and thick eyebrows. He was quite refined and perfected by his aging. He looked better as a forty five year old man than he even did as a youth. His wrinkles only gave his face more character. His palace complimented the refined beauty of the king with the stones' ancient texture and the pillars' lofty majesty. There was no ostentation at work in either the king or the palace. Simple and straightforward was the fashion kept by Lab'ayu, and the city of Shechem followed in his wake. Colors there were not garish, nor overly muted. The nobility of Shechem was so well known, that, unlike

Gezer in its extravagance of color, Shechem could be satisfied with the beauty of bare stone.

"My son. Good to see you have found your way home. Please, tell me about your travels. Don't neglect the details that make such stories truly interesting!" said Lab'ayu in a voice that was sweeter and smoother than honey.

"Nothing much of interest there, just dusty roads and lonely nights," replied Mutba'alu.

"A pity. You best be careful. Dangerous Ḥabiru abound in Canaan."

Mutba'alu fought hard to resist laughing at the irony, before replying, "Father, you worry too much. What is troubling you?".

"Milkilu, the Pimp of Gezer has sent his brothers to OUR country to carry away girls. It is loathsome enough that he serves the lusts of Pharaoh with the innocent women of his country. To then go to my country and dishonor those under my protection is a provocation of the highest order! Somehow or other, I'll get even with them."

"Hush, hush, father! Do you not see these eyes upon you, sense the listening ears in this room? These are the eyes and ears of Pharaoh, and what you speak of is not far from rebellion." whispered Mutba'alu.

"Then let's go somewhere where no one can hear or see us. I

know just the place! We shall retire to the privy!" whispered Lab'ayu.

The two men, father, and son retired to the hall of the limestone thrones. They lifted the hem of their garments and sat their naked bottoms on the privy. These were fine high-end toilets of kings, smooth ones that didn't give you splinters in your bottoms and balls like the wooden stools used by the lower classes. As they pretended to release their stool, they spoke now more freely.

"Milkilu has done wrong. That is a matter of which there can be no debate. How we shall proceed should be considered carefully." said Lab'ayu.

"War with Milkilu means rebellion against Pharaoh. Are you ready to take that risk? He won't hesitate to send his Pitati." Lab'ayu couldn't help but gasp a little at his son's mention of Pharaoh's deadliest warriors.

"When an ant is struck, does it not fight back and bite the man that struck it!" exclaimed Lab'ayu, "I know the risk. Do you see the ashes of my father's palace, stones marred with soot? Do you know that my father does not rest in a tomb, but was picked apart by jackals for his crime of daring to strive for freedom! But if we do not rise together and make ourselves a strong united country, we will be no more than slaves for Pharaoh's empire."

"Now, the thing about ants is they have an army. If you deign to lead your little insurgency you will need one. Your paltry force shall not suffice."

"And how to find one dear son? I don't suppose you have one hidden up your sleeve?"

"In my sleeve no, but on the foothills of Mount Gerizim, you will find I have one. Skilled and experienced, though a little rough around the edges. All are willing to fight for a share of the plunder. And Gezer? She is the ripest fruit south of Megiddo."

'You are suggesting I use mercenaries, the cruel Ḥabiru who ravage and rape the whole land, to rebel against Pharaoh and his ministers?!"

"It is you who is suggesting rebelling. I am only suggesting the Ḥabiru." Mutba'alu smiled, revealing his rodent-like front teeth. "Should I inform the men you mean to make war?"

Lab'ayu sighed. "We will call a meeting of the assembly. All the officials, magistrates, nobles, anybody who is anybody in Shechem must come. They will take solemn oaths; to never betray the cause of freedom in Canaan. Milkilu will fall. If they send Pitati against us, the Pitati will fall. Pharaoh comes against us, he will fall. We will build a new nation of free men and women who are not subject to the will of Pharaoh and his dogs!"

"Truly rousing. I will take as needed for the advance payment for the Ḥabiru. As I am trusted among them, they agreed to fight for you at a considerable discount. After all, plunder is sure to be got."

"Do as is required. I will open the gates to them, and rouse the Shechemite youths to arms. I am prepared to meet my father and my gods as either a liberator or a martyr!"

Perhaps both, thought Mutba'alu solemnly. What a grand revolution they were plotting from the potty. There was one hiccup though; a person Mutba'alu's thoughts turned to as he thought out his plans of war. A nemesis. *But now, with Lab'ayu's gold, his prestige, his name, would she ever stand a chance against me?*

6

Chapter 6: The Finger Taker

"So, men" said the Lady of the Lions, Shisita, "Kill those damned bastards, but spare their captain. I want to get a little heehaw from that ass."

"He will be heehawing," her lieutenant said, "Or my name isn't Yassib the Finger Taker."

Shisita and Yassib, and their little army of seventy men peered out from behind the vine-straddled garden wall of a rural village house. They saw the Ḥabiru coming, japing, eager to catch the bait. An insecure place, such as this one, the unwalled town of Gina, was easy pickings for Ḥabiru raiders. They barely needed to bring a whole unit, only a small raiding party to terrorize the locals into giving them all they wanted and having a good old time ravishing whatever woman or pretty boy might be there. Leading the party was Huzziya the Baby Lover. Rumors of the activities that earned him such a name had traveled far.

Huzziya was the target of Shisita, the righteous, the daughter of 'Anat. Actually a daughter of the craven Sutarna, not the war goddess, but still. She and Yassib, a young noble of Ugarit, had gone south to answer a call by the Queen of Egypt: the guileful and mighty queen Tiye. Tiye had seen Shisita and Yassib when they had been in Egypt. "Go to Canaan, Lady of the Lions, brave Shisita, and rid the land of these dreadful Ḥabiru!" Tiye ordered. However, only about a hundred fighting men were willing to follow Shisita and Yassib. Brave, rugged, if a little foolish, they had all been bereaved by the evils of the Ḥabiru in some way. But even among Canaanites, fear is greater than ferocity. Tiye greatly underestimated the numbers of the Ḥabiru. Canaan didn't. To fight them is madness. But Shisita and her mad hundred would fight. Thirty had died since. Now reports were trickling in through Shisita's informants that the Ḥabiru were amassing. She needed to know why, and where. The chance to kill a condemned criminal? That's just honey on the cake.

The denizens of the village were ordered to go about their lives as normal, even though they knew the Ḥabiru were coming. This they would do for no man. They did it gladly for the Lady of the Lions, for this Shisita. She was their only protector. They tried to act normally as they were bid, but they soon saw the cruel faces of the Ḥabiru. They ran for the roofs of their houses after blocking their doors and pulled up the ladder. That was all they could do as the fierce Ḥabiru came down the streets, bows, swords, and spears ready. They were in bliss to see a village that had made no effort to prepare for them. Gina hadn't hidden grain, wine, and oil, nor gold and silver. Everything was for the taking. They were already filling their bellies with stolen wine when Shisita attacked.

Charging, beating, dispatching… that was the rhythm of combat. Serpents can get under the fat bellies of bulls. Shisita threw an over hand blow from her ax, catching a hapless Ḥabiru on the fat of his cheek, brutally cutting the better portion of his face off. Before he could retaliate, he was put out of his misery by a ruthless backhand severing his grotesque faceless head. It was cast into the face of the hapless man's fellow, distracting him. This allowed the opportunity for Yassib to avoid an ill-placed blow and land his own. His spear penetrated the guts of his target, exiting the back of the mercenary just to the right of his spine. Yassib then yanked the spear backwards, allowing the back of his spear blade to carve a new path out of it, shedding a fair amount of blood before the dance of death continued. The victim of Yassib lay on the ground in agony, slowly dying but grateful. He clenched his gaping hole, as if to prevent any organs from escaping it. He died, smiling.

Before long, the dusty streets were moistened by blood. The Ḥabiru lay like sheeps killed in honor of God. The only one who was spared the clean and merciful death was Huzziya the Baby Lover. Such was the skill of Shisita and company that he was wounded in such a way that he could not escape their clutches. He was now on the ground, moaning and clasping a slight gash across his belly as if he feared his guts would spill out. Shisita and Yassib crouched over him. He laughed and spit his vile saliva in their faces. Thus began his interrogation.

Shisita was far too honorable to interrogate properly. As she was a woman, respect among the Ḥabiru could not be gained through deeds of barbarity. Yassib had his purpose. He stuck his spear in the soft earth by its butt and drew his dagger; Fingertaker. That was his technique. Ḥabiru warriors did not fear death, only dismemberment. They could not serve their blood god Yahu missing any part, even a finger. It was seen as a fate worse than death.

"Where is the Ḥabiru army!" demanded Shisita, "How many of them are there!".

"You think I'll tell you, dog! Why would I! You may kill me or not. Doesn't matter to me! My life is for the kingdom beyond!" Cursed Huzziya.

"You like fingers? Such marvelous things! Such dexterity, such magnificent utility! Such as you can use to hold a sword, or draw a bow, or even stroke your spear. Though I assure you mine is far longer than yours." threatened Yassib.

"Bastards! I'd have ended the both of you if we met on fairer ground!"

"How many fingers does a man even need? The full number is ten, but I suspect the third or fourth finger could be safely done away with. But the First and Second, and the Thumb surely it would be hard to make do without. Whether in this world or the next."

39

"Just kill me and be done with it!"

"That we intend, but first tell us the number and location of the Ḥabiru army. Until that time, I would be happy to start adding to my collection."

Yassib took out his little satchel. It was filled with finger bones. He shook it. The deathly rattle chilled the cowardly captain to the bone.

"That's enough, damn you! We number three-thous men, growing daily. We are rallying arms to Mount Gerizim to serve Lab'ayu of Shechem."

"For this I dearly thank you. Shisita, he is all yours."

Shisita raised her Khopesh, and swung it backward, piercing the left temple of his head with the spike on the back. He died instantly, smiling. No part of his body was separated from its brother.

"Go now to your god, Ḥabiru. Pray he is more merciful than you or I," said Shisita. "Men. We are now hopelessly outnumbered. You don't need to be a scribe trained in arithmetic to know that three thousand is too much for seventy. We will go now, to the court of King Sutarna my Father. I pray he brings with us men, stalwart men to fight this new menace and restore peace, in the name of Ba'alu and the Pharaoh!"

The men cheered. The villagers cheered. Even the mooing

of the cows seemed like cheering. The daughter of 'Anat set out to see her father. Perhaps she alone could mold his soft clay into the shape of a man. And if not? She was more than confident she could lead an army of any size herself.

7

Chapter 7: Pimps and Virgins

"Addadanu, can you help me load these beauties into the cart?" Yapahu shot his brother a loving but stern glance, "Hands off the merchandise!"

"Yapahu, they are not merchandise... They are people!" Addadanu laughed, as if what he said was absurd.

"People who are our merchandise, our tribute to Pharaoh. He wants virgins."

"Oh, come on, Yapahu! We like your brother!" said a virgin, "What harm will a few kisses do?"

"Make sure it sticks to kisses," said Yapahu, "The cost of every deflowered virgin will come out of your cut."

Yapahu and Addadanu set one last eye to those pristine lands, those virgin hills and valleys of Samaria. With them came their valued prize, their hard-won plunder. Forty beautiful maidens without blemish or defect, who had never known the embrace of a man, followed them under guard. They sat in cushioned carts to not despoil their precious hymens. Yapahu of the silver tongue and Addadanu of the stunning looks rode astride the carts in magnificent chariots. If any man could be found with the wit and charm of Yapahu and the beauty of Addadanu, the world would be his, along with the forty virgins. Yet, the forty in the carts were for Pharaoh. Yapahu and Addadanu did of course enjoy the company of women who had known men, but the virgins were for Pharaoh alone.

One of the virgins who stood out among these goddesses of beauty and virtue was the astounding Emminat. She was comely and stately, like a proper queen. She hailed from a house well-moneyed in past days that had fallen on hard times. Her father was slain in battle and their lands pillaged and desecrated by the Egyptians. The mother, a stern and foul-mouthed but courageous woman, possessed the only thing that was holding her family together; a house, once majestic, now dilapidated for want of repair. Yapahu made sure she was duly distracted before Addadanu made off with her prize jewel. Emminat.

Emminat, as it happens, was the intended bride of Mutba'alu, and her mother hoped that marriage into the royal house of Shechem would grant a little class and dignity, and more than a few shekels into her ailing house. Yapahu did not wish to be around when she found her home bereft of the one thing of value she had left; her maiden daughter. In return, only forty shekels of silver, a few linen garments, and an

43

ebony chair. All poor consolation for an ailing mother with visions of grandeur. She didn't know if she'd ever see her daughter again.

Heading to the southeast through the rugged Samarian hills, Addadanu and Yapahu were careful to light additional campfires each night. This was to give the impression their party was bigger in number than they were. This served to avoid harassment and potential banditry. All this of course was Yapahu's idea. Addadanu, in his *infinite* wisdom, found it an unnecessary precaution. After all, they had tablets marked with Amenhotep's cylinder seal, so if they were approached, anyone would have to leave them unmolested or face the wrath of Pharaoh's ministers. Yapahu won out of course because the guards thought avoiding danger would be best for them getting home safely and being paid. Addadanu did grumble a few obscenities under his breath when he was outvoted. Resentment simmered. Hatred of one's kin; the sin of the ignorant.

Finally, they had passed through to the end of hostile territory and arrived in the "friendly" town of Ginti, a settlement ruled by Tagi, father-in-law of Milkilu. It was not much of a wonder, with a wall that was only stone at its base but had ramshackle mudbrick the rest of the way up. Even that was not very high. Tagi was a king in name, of ancient and prominent birth, even claiming descent from Enmerkar, Lugalbanda, and Gilgamesh in mighty Uruk, but his only possession of value was his pedigree, nothing else. He was enriched somewhat however by his association with Milkilu and Gezer, but their relationship was little more than

44

transactional. It would only be slightly an exaggeration to say that Tagi of Ginti had sold his beautiful but depressive daughter to Milkilu for drinking money, a fact she was only too aware of even if he'd pretend otherwise.

As the brothers, Yapahu and Addadanu went by, the young girls went scurrying back into their houses. They knew well what Yapahu and Addadanu did. Other ladies lifted their garments to show their nethermouth fully unflowered, shouting, "Not a virgin by the grace of the Gods and my lover!" Women in Ginti began living lives of licentiousness to protect themselves from being sacrificed to the thirst of Pharaoh. As for their mothers, they thought it better they be deflowered here in Canaan by their sides than ravaged in far off Egypt where they'd never be seen from again. Virgins in Ginti were notoriously scarce, even at shockingly young ages. Men from around Canaan flocked to Ginti's brothels, which performed excellent services at affordable prices. Knowing a profitable venture when they see one, many of the brothels of Ginti were owned by the brothers Yapahu and Addadanu. This tied Ginti to Gezer with ties more powerful than politics or family. The power of money bound the cities at the hip like a lover's embrace. Even if, at times, the embrace was rougher than Tagi would have liked.

"Where is King Tagi?" whined Addadanu, "He should greet us at the gates to welcome us for a proper meal. His absence smells of treason!"

"Peace, brother," replied Yapahu, "I am certain he must be hard at some important task to not divert himself for our welcome. And I assure you, he is under no obligation legally to treat us as overlords, whatever custom may have become. So I suggest you respect him, with no provocation, for this is his city."

"I wish dearly brother you were not so spineless."

"And I wish conversely you were not so foolhardy!"

Addadanu puzzled for a long moment, not knowing what the word "conversely" meant. The awkward silence between the brothers was broken, as a slave from the palace emerged. He was clothed in the tufted Gunakku kilt that had not been in style since the days of Sumerian greatness one thousand years hence. Making his slaves wear such outdated garb was Tagi's way of asserting his mythic pedigree. They hated it. It was itchy. The slave spoke, "Yapahu, Addadanu, my sires! Tagi expresses his humble regrets that he was unable to meet you at the gates! He surely respects you, oh yes!"

"He has a funny way of showing it; sending a slave!" grumbled Addadanu.

"An unexpected and honored visitor, of highest birth and honor, has been passing through. Tagi, my sovereign, is having all the big men of the city attend to this visitor."

"And who may he be? Not Lab'ayu, gods forbid."

"Not him, never!"

46

"Hanya?" asked Yapahu, "Or perhaps his subordinate, Re-anap?"

"It's a maiden, not a man! Come meet her, and see for yourself. Sup with the king!"

They entered the halls of the palace of Tagi, king of Ginti. Fine couches were laid out with costly damask coverings embroidered with samite and Tyrian purple. Such luxuries are displayed only for the most honored visitors. The disdainful Addadanu was expecting to curse the woman who had stolen their welcome but was stopped in his tracks when he saw the beautiful Shisita sitting in the place of honor. She was of uncommon habits for a maiden, eating and joking with the men. They knew her well. She was the Lady of the Lions, with the cylinder seal of queen Tiye herself. Of all the virgins in Canaan, she was the most eligible, suitable, sought after... but unavailable. To anyone, king or commoner.

Tagi greeted the two pimps with a smile less fake than usual. "Yapahu, Addadanu, what a pleasant surprise! Do you have any news of my daughter, Ramashtu in Gezer?"

"Ramashtu is hale like the sun, gods be thanked."lied Yapahu (tastefully).

"I present to you Shisita, lady of the lions!"

"She needs no introduction for us," said Yapahu.

"But I'd still appreciate one anyway!" quipped Addadanu,

who could not conceal infatuation in his speech, nor ever tried to.

Tagi laughed. He had grown used to suffering the foolishness of Addadanu and the deceits of Yapahu. And he was in a fine mood, drinking wine with a notable beauty. Forty more notable beauties just entered his hall and all forty-one of the beauties were virgins. He felt like he was Pharaoh for a day. As he was a little flustered, he spoke no longer.

"I'm very glad you are here, Yapahu, Addadanu. I have a matter I wish to speak of that concerns Milkilu and Gezer, that he must hear of straight away." said Shisita.

"Fetch clay and a stylus," Yapahu grabbed a slave by the hem of his kilt. "I will take dictation."

"I wrote it already," said Shisita, handing the tablet to Yapahu. It was marked with the seal queen Tiye gave her. Yapahu looked at the tablet in disbelief. It was written neatly, not scrawled, in perfect Akkadian. He was quite impressed at this quality of scribal work no matter who was responsible, but from a girl not sixteen years old? He was shocked. He was so caught up in the girls' genius that he almost missed the message the tablet contained. Then it hit him like a ton of bricks.

"What does it say, Yapahu?" asked Addadanu.

"It bodes war. Between us and Lab'ayu. And he has the Ḥabiru on his side."

48

"If it's a war he wants, then let him taste the stinging of Pharaoh's Pitati." Addadanu mimed the shooting of bows, taking aim at invisible Ḥabiru and making absurd noises to mark their deaths.

"I shall go to my father in Qadesh. He will bring aid from the north. Just hold out until our reinforcements arrive!" Stated Shisita.

"Bless you, Shisita. I kiss the ground of every step you walk to Qadesh. But hasten! Tagi will provide swift chariots." Addadanu ordered.

"I will?"

"Please sir, for your safety and that of Canaan!" said Yapahu.

"For you, anything," said Tagi, awkwardly stroking Shisita's lustrous curly hair. Lost in drink, lost in beauty, his heart sang paeans to Ashtartu. Only after the beauties dispersed to the four winds did Tagi regard the song of 'Anat, the chant of war. In the city of whores, the virgin is queen.

8

Chapter 8: The Tents at Gerizim

"Son, I am happy to provide strong oxen to pull the cart…" said Lab'ayu.

"No! I shall pull the cart myself, as a show of strength to the men! I am a warrior and a real man." Mutba'alu flexed his young muscles. Killing people is good exercise.

"That… has its merits! I see what you are going for! Go forth! Inspire the men with the heroism of our cause. This is no ordinary war. This is for the liberation of Canaan. I'll accept nothing less."

Mutba'alu grasped the heavy yoke of the cart in his hands, placing the weight on his strong shoulders. *Look father, does Ayyabu perform feats like this*, thought Mutba'alu. *This is why I should be heir.*

He went down the hill for a while so the going was relatively easy. He felt powerful. But soon he was pulling it up the mount, and he was blistered and worn. The night was warm that time of year, and sweat dripped down his brow, feeling like freshly spilled blood. He entered the camp of the Ḥabiru, earning the cheers and jeers of the different sorts. Ḥabiru men called him ass, ox, and horse, but their comments only made him fill with forlorn pride. He was performing a feat, such as is talked about with respect and pride for posterity, even if mockery was the initial outcome.

He went by some men playing the game of twenty squares. One of the players was clearly winning... he had all of his pieces in play, and many were approaching the finish. The losing player, who counted himself a master strategist, was stymied by the dice. He just couldn't get his pieces into play.

"You've rigged the dice!" said the loser.

"Nonsense! We are playing with the same ol' knucklebone we always play with. Maybe you are not so good at this game as you say!"

"I'm a master strategist. I've just had some bad rolls"

"Bad rolls my ass! If you want to win, play for real! Beating you is almost too easy."

"Your mother was a toe-licker!" cursed the loser, toppling the board off the cedar stump they had been playing on. The pieces were flung far and wide.

"My mother was an angel!" said the son of a toe-licker,

51

pummeling the loser with his fist, "Your mother ate grass and bore loads. She was a donkey!"

They began to quarrel, and were soon on the floor wrestling and beating each other's skulls. Mutba'alu greeted them, and they waved, before biting each other's fingers like brothers do. Finally, Mutba'alu reached the tent of Abneru, who was waiting for him.

"As you can see Abneru, I am as stubborn as an ass and as strong as an ox!"

"Perhaps you are dumb as an ass and as spayed as an ox. But I see you brought us a cart full of our pay."

"Have a look at the fine things my father gives you. Did I not tell you we'd make a killing in the killing business?"

Abneru ran over to the cart, giddy like a child about to receive a sweet. But when he looked inside, his joy turned to mild dejection, and he sighed.

"I see there is some gold in here, a little more silver, but what I mostly see are weapons. You know, you're my friend. I'll work with you for a discount. But my men… they need to be paid! Soldiering is expensive!"

He brandished a mace and a sword in his hands.

"They are good weapons Mutba'alu, but we want gold!"

"Gold you will have when we meet and defeat our foe."

"And who will that foe be, Mutba'alu?"

"Does that even matter to you?"

"In principle, no."

"It is Milkilu of Gezer."

"To Gezer it is!" Exclaimed Abneru, "That's a fat enough hog for me!" he clenched his brand-new sword, then remembered, "But what about Pharaoh and his strong, manly son?"

"Let us pray to the gods that the Pharaoh is as much a liar concerning his heir as my father."

"Everyone's a liar" said Abneru, "But knowing your brother, Ayyabu, Pharaoh's son would have to be pretty pathetic to match him."

"May Prince Thutmose be like my idiot brother, or, barring that, may he just die or something. That can go for both of them."

"I love you..." Mutba'alu's perturbed reaction caused Abneru to shift tone, "You are a real Ḥabiru. I love THAT."

Mutba'alu slapped Abneru's firm buttocks, "I know you love me. I'm a warrior and a real man. So don't you be getting any ideas. "

"Don't flatter yourself. If I wanted to sodomize a virgin I would start with your betrotrothed."

"Ah, sweet Emminat. I almost feel sorry sending her to the clutches of the Pharaoh. I mean, I feel sorry for the Pharaoh."

"Let's drink to the Pharaoh's health... may it be as strong and as sturdy as a fart."

"And as enduring." They drank. "What's in this wine? It tastes like piss."

Abneru laughed. Sometimes the jokes of men conceal a sorrow as great as the tears of women spurned.

9

Chapter 9: A Fool, a Woman, and a King

The prince was dead. The heir was dead. The hopes of the Pharaoh were dead. THUTMOSE, who was meant to be the fifth pharaoh to bear that most esteemed name, was dead. Amenhotep III was filled with dread, sorrow, and pain. Queen Tiye and their second son, also named Amenhotep, stood by his side. Thutmose was the perfect prince, handsome like his father. He was beloved by all. The only son left to the bereaved Pharaoh was the ugly and deformed Amenhotep IV. He had a long chin, potbelly, elongated feet, and hands. His sight was unfit for a Pharaoh, both loathsome and almost girly. He was a boy who should not be Pharaoh. His head was filled with delusions about the sun god Aten. *The boy should not be Pharaoh. The boy cannot be Pharaoh. The boy... will be Pharaoh. But first, he must learn. Now shall not be the time of weeping, it shall be the time of teaching.*

"Son" addressed the Pharaoh to his prince of the same name.

The young prince did not turn around, for his father had never addressed him as a son before.

"Son, I've addressed you!" said the father.

"He's dead, father. He won't be quick to respond to you."

"I addressed you, boy!"

"Well, that's a first…"

"Don't be a spouter of water, boy! You are to become a Pharaoh someday, but you must learn wisdom first."

"All true wisdom," said the son "as all good things do, emanates from the true sun. The Aten,"

"Wisdom 'emanates' from living, and from the old to the young. You must learn the ways of Pharaoh, and to become the god you are… apparently destined to be. Emanates… a fine word, a godly word. Son, let me learn you… teach you! You must study."

"Study is indeed required, but is it not an ill-chosen time for it?" Queen Tiye asked. "We've lost a son and he lost a brother. Can it not wait?"

"It has waited far too long already! He will learn now."

Pharaoh ordered the tablets from Canaan brought in and handed one off to the prince. The boy looked over the clay tablet, briefly running his long finger over the strange markings.

"Read!"

"It is not like anything I've ever seen. Doesn't make a bit of sense to me."

The Pharaoh knew his son so little that he didn't even know his son was untrained in Akkadian. Trying to grasp patience from the jaws of anger, he decided to explain.

"This is Akkadian: the language of Babylon and Assyria. The Asiatics all use it to send us messages to provide us with knowledge about what's occurring where they are. Usually, they are requesting troops for their petty squabbles, and it is hard to know which king is in the right. But you must know. And you must exercise good judgment in where to send troops to maintain order. You may even be forced at times to lead armies there yourself. You must never let them grow too unified or they will become a threat. Do not allow them to become too divided or the Hatti will take them as easy pickings. Everything is about balance. You have to keep all the plates spinning just so. That is the way of being a Pharaoh."

"Nothing you said interests me." the Prince pointed up to the horizon, then continued, " Aten is the one true god. He is the same for all lands. If he means for there to be order, there will be order. Petty conflicts with stinking, lice-covered Asiatic vassals are no concern of mine. Now, the temple of Karnak...

"

"Should be left to the priests of Amun. Do not interfere with the priesthood. Along with the Pharaoh, the Vizier, and the Army, the priests are the fourth pillar that holds Egypt. If you enter into conflict against them, Egypt will be delivered unto her enemies like a lamb to the... Don't do it."

"Interfere I will, father. And Egypt will be better for it."

"I need to go now. If I cannot conceive another son by my loins, Egypt is doomed." Whispered Amenhotep to Tiye.

"By all means make love. Remember though, my son is my only choice for an heir. Don't worry about him. I'll guide him rightly! And if harm comes to one hair..."

"He's bald."

"I don't make idle threats, husband. I am the cane by which you stand. You do well to remember that."

Amenhotep barged out of the room, muttering antiquated and confused obscenities about leaving Egypt in the hands of a fool and a woman. Now maybe it is time to fool around with a woman. He slipped a wizened hand into his kilt and felt the member therein. It was still more than ready to do the business Pharaohs like best.

10

Chapter 10: Listen Much, Speak Little, Record Everything

Emminat and the rest of the forty virgins Pharaoh sent for had arrived in the morning, but it wasn't until after dinner that they met their new master. Until then, those poor girls had done what innocent girls do when they are confronted with luxury; they get sucked in like barley beer through a straw. Of course, there was beer aplenty, and wine, in the Harem. Soon, the girls became intoxicated and frivolous, playing all manner of games. Their immature frivolity soon turned the disdainful eye of some of Amenhotep's foreign brides. Gilukhepa of Mitanni was the main she-hawk, but other wives from Arzawa and Babylon turned their heads. They were royalty in the country of their origin and were *supposedly* queens here too. More frequently than they liked, a new batch of unrefined girls were led in the harem chamber to satisfy the Pharaoh's 'manly vigor'. Emminat looked different from the rest. She did not act like common chaff did in the Harem, but sat respectfully and surprisingly forlorn, despite the luxury; cushions and sweetmeats. Gilukhepa was cautious at first to obtain this gem as an ally, but her eagle's heart would not allow her to cower. She was a princess of Mitanni, and she would do her duty to her father the king.

"Do you speak the tongue of the Egyptians?" asked Gilukhepa in Canaanite.

"I do, and many others besides" replied Emminat, "Akkadian, Canaanite, Hurrian, Hittite, and even a little Sumerian."

"What a prodigy. However, here, the ignorant reign among the harem. If you wish to earn the confidence of the Pharaoh, speak only in Canaanite. Pretend you are not wise. Listen much, speak little, and I will record everything."

"There's a price for my ears" said Emminat, "I have a fiancé in Canaan. He is Mutba'alu, son of Lab'ayu. It was his notion that I am taken here to Egypt to provide him with valuable gossip. The two of them must receive the messages I deem necessary, and in exchange, I'll be your ally and assist you. I know you and I can be good friends. And both you and I know I will be the girl most favored by the Pharaoh." Emminat brimmed with the arrogance of the aristocracy. She had calculated her prideful attitude would not sully her relationship with the equally proud Gilukhepa.

"Of that, I have no doubt. You are a beauty among beauties, and Pharaoh has a very discerning eye for those things. Believe me, you are powerful. For all the talk of manly this, and vigorous that, we women can make a place for ourselves here, and even a little power. But beware of Queen Tiye. She is as wily as me and as jealous, but far more powerful."

"I shall take your words as sound counsel. And now I shall play the role. Pray, tell me if I play it well or ill; I intend it to be a showstopper."

And then the room, so full of giggles and levity a moment ago, fell silent, when two old men, reeking of drink, garlic, and overpriced perfume ambled in.

"As I said, the harvest of Canaan has done well this year, despite all of Milkilu's excuses" proclaimed Aperel, pharaoh's jowly and wrinkled Vizier. "The fruit, as you see, is ripe, but not spoiled." He touched the face of a young beauty, who recoiled from him, visibly disgusted. When she had come with the handsome Addadanu and the charming Yapahu, this was not what she bargained for.

"They look very firm," said Pharaoh, "But soft in all the right places. But this one..." gesturing to Emminat, "is the best. She looks to me almost like a noblewoman. Her bearing, her complexion, her lack of frivolity, all this conveys to me that she alone needs no training. I can tell she knows what I need from her. It is what she was born to do. I will have her in my private chamber."

"As you will, sire. Should I fetch the perfumes? Asiatics have, as you know, the most offensive stench."

Pharaoh sniffed the hair of Emminat, her armpits, her loins, her backside, increasingly lustily. "That will be unneeded.

She is perfect as she is. The scent, looks, the sound of her heartbeat! She reminds me of one of my conquests, many years ago when I was in Retenu."

The old, but still surprisingly strong and dashing pharaoh lifted Emminat in his arms like a baby, carrying her through the beautifully painted bas-relief-adorned rooms of the palace. Chariots charging, crocodiles seizing oxen, and images of her people being killed and subdued. She knew what was needed of her. She was ready. Her war would be in love and hate.

She was gently placed down on a soft, comfortable and lavishly gilded bed, adorned with amber, lapis lazuli, and turquoise, along with red carnelian. Her hands brushed his face as he removed her light linen tunic. If she was a beauty with clothes, then she was a goddess without, and few men had ever seen that sight. It is good to be the Pharaoh, sometimes, thought the King as he lay heady kisses on her virgin lips. She did not resist, did not kick, did not scratch and bite like the wilder girls he had known. She had the beauty of a swan and the timidity of a mouse. Yet she returned his affections, surprising him. None had done it, not in many years. She was trained, it seems, by her mother, he thought.

How did Milkilu ever come by such a gem, for just forty shekels of silver? Her lips were the most pleasing thing he had ever felt in his life, and by kissing them his royal crook became stiff and straight, like an obelisk. He had a desire in mind, but how can he express it? She seemed to understand no Egyptian, and being a woman, her speaking Akkadian was out of the question to him. Now that was a good thing. Anything he said to her would be in confidence, but how would he get her to put his penis in her mouth? He had tried to act it out before with different girls. They usually misunderstood and laughed at him, and a proud Pharaoh does not, or at least should not get laughed at or misunderstood. Especially about something as simple as fellatio! But with Emminat here, he would dare risk it. Whilst being subtle, he pointed to his erect phallus, then to her, then to her lips, and made a subtle little sucking sound. He finished it off with an Akkadian word Maqasha, meaning to suckle, and hoped she knew what to do. Akkadian and Canaanite are both Asiatic languages after all!

He was in luck, he was in the hands of an expert. She laid him gently on his back and did as she was bid, suckling the spear most pleasingly. Relaxed and alert, and more than a little bit intoxicated, Pharaoh began to let slip his mind, in Egyptian, of course.

"I have a few troubles that I have to get out of my head. Best you can't understand. My chief wife has her spies everywhere... Her son is an abomination... unworthy to bear my name."

She picked up her pace and quietly pricked up her ear. He was already shedding secrets, secrets that Mutba'alu her master deeply needed.

"I lost a son... an heir. No one outside the palace yet knows about his death. Even my other wives do not know."

Emminat was a multi-tasker, carefully listening word by word, recording it in her memory like a clay tablet. Meanwhile, she lashed his two eggs with her wicked tongue. His already firm and long obelisk seemed to raise another inch or so, and wept tears of serene joy.

"I fear my wife… she has spies everywhere. She favors her youngest. The abomination, the heretic. Maybe she killed Thutmose… maybe she'll kill me too. Stop. I have a job to do. I must save Egypt. Egypt cannot be ruled by a mad man and a poisoner. "

Pharaoh pushed his lover onto her back and held her legs pronely. She had known fellatio. She had been trained well in it by her Fiance Mutba'alu. But what he was going to do… this could only happen once, and there was fear, even for Emminat. She put the comb she had brought in her mouth like Mutba'alu instructed her. Then the old man, the pharaoh, the virile bull, the god on earth, the source of secrets, prepared to mount her. The first moment was the worst. Amenhotep had deflowered virgins by the myriads and had no patience for their comfort. It was, of course, his favorite pastime, the last true joy in his life now that he distrusted Tiye and Thutmose was gone.

This time was a little different. He forced himself inside her, while she tried not to scream, the fearful sounds muffled by the biting of the comb. Her hymen, relatively thick but not too much so for the ruthless Pharaoh, gave way almost

64

immediately, and a little blood came out. At that moment, a sharp pain, a chill, fiery heat, and sublime pleasure shot up Emminat's spine. It was like dying, she figured. If that was the end of their rutting, it would have changed her for life, but it kept going. The pain dulled with time and the pleasure got more pronounced. She could see the beauty in the old man's black eyes, the love she felt she won from him. Did she love him? It would be possible. He was handsome for an old man, after the fashion of Ilu himself.

When he was young he must have been a beauty, far better than her betrothed Mutba'alu. And a combination of Pharaoh's talent and many decades of experience almost made Emminat forget about her mission, her secret harvest. She could allow herself a few minutes rest, but now it was time to get serious. Both because she loved him and thought he deserved it, and partly because she still wished to betray the Pharaoh's secrets to Shechem and the Mittani, she gestured that she was ready to take the lead, to mount him, and bring him to climax with the rocking of her hips. It took a while, and some coaxing to get this stalwart lover off of her, but she succeeded. She knew he was too focused on humping her to let slip any more secrets. She would need to relax him. This would be the greatest challenge she had ever faced, for Amenhotep was slow to climax, and a vigorous man. Many pharaohs like him had sired sons and daughters by the score, but Amenhotep had only ever had two sons and four daughters, relatively few. This was not from lack of trying.

This time, it would be different, Amenhotep thought. He had

often tired himself out, humping women. This time, this one will do the work herself! This time it just might work. He said a prayer to Bes, to Heqat, to Mesenet, to Min, and before he was even done reciting the names of fertility deities, she was on top of him. Experience, it is said, often counts in these matters, but talent is not something to be sneezed at, nor persistence, nor insistence. She was as eager to take his seed as he was to give it to her. Her lips on his, he tasted for the first time his own manhood; and liked it. She was a delicious morsel, every bit of her adding to the pleasure he felt, and the beer and wine he drank loosened his lips a second time. What's the harm? She speaks no Egyptian anyway!

"I fear my son ... if he truly is my son, and I have more than cause to doubt" he muttered, "Will lead Egypt to chaos. Our Asiatic empire will crumble with my death, gobbled up by Mitanni or Hatti or Assyria. He will push through religious reforms that will alienate the Priesthood and the commoners, probably all of Upper Egypt. No one outside the palace knows this, but he means to deface the sanctuary of Amun at Karnak. If that happens, there will be a civil war. Egypt will lay prone and desolate, ready for the jackals. Nubia, Libya, and Canaan will come like a flood from three directions, and Egypt is doomed"

This was exactly the sort of information Emminat wanted to hear. This was exactly the information Mutba'alu, Gilukhepa, Mitanni, and all Canaan wanted to hear. But it saddened her a little, to betray the old man, the great lover, who brought peace between all nations for so long by the power of his loins. She became eagle-eyed. *If I can free Canaan peacefully, it will be with the son Pharaoh gives me.* So she worked at it and rocked her hips, and lo, when she thought she could go no longer, and the morning sun began glancing over the Nile, she took his seed. And he was happy beyond measure, for he knew, once this part was done, a child would be born. And by Amun, the sun god of Thebes, it would be a boy. It had to be. The gods themselves depended on it. Emminat collapsed in his arms, seeming almost dead from exhaustion, seed and blood dripping in equal measure from her nethermouth. Amenhotep, as a token of his newfound love and deepest respect, let her sleep on his bed. He washed in the Nile, then dressed. As fit as a well-tuned lyre, he went about the business of the day. *Sometimes, it is good to be Pharaoh. At least better than being a damned peasant!*

11

Chapter 11: The Maxims

Hanya set to work with his company of Archers. He had reached the nome of Khenty-Aabti, the *Easternmost Land*. He decided that before he left the lands where the Nile flows for Tjaru, he would gather the rich clay of the Delta. In the arid desert along the *Way of Horus*, scarcely any good quality clay could be found for tablets. Hanya dug with his men, and loaded the red clay upon carts he had previously used for the conveyance of virgins. The men then wrapped the clay in moist linen towels, to preserve its malleability. Hanya looked upon his men as equals: good, strong Nubian Pitati, vigorous Egyptians and hearty Canaanites. They labored without complaint, for Hanya was a generous master. Unlike others they labored under, he labored.

"Men, you have loaded enough for one day!" Hanya wiped his brow. "Let us bathe in the cool water, for it may be our last opportunity to do so for some time."

Eager to cool their bodies in the water, the men each stripped nude. Hale men and boys splashed in the water. Their activities attracted the attention of the local people. In these parts, the makeup of the land was not unlike that of Retenu... the Delta could be called a Canaanite province even as much as Canaan could be called an Egyptian one.

The noises of play in the water, the catcalling of the girls, the clay between his toes... all gave cause for the memory of Hanya's youth to reignite like a flame in a clay oven.

"Hanya, come in for study!" his mother called for him.

Hanya remembered being a boy seven years of age. He ran from the river where he, along with his numerous brothers, uncles and cousins dug into the black mud. They were clearing the irrigation channels from the annual flood. Year after year, century after century, millenia after millenia, it was the same routine for the Egyptian peasant. Akhet (Flooding), Peretor (Emergence), and Shemu (Harvest) passed in turn. The calendar was tuned to the agricultural cycle, and the vast majority of Egypt's population, peasants, followed the cycle of seasons like spokes on a wheel. Not so for Hanya's father. He was a social climber.

Hanya remembered how his father spoke; it was at once poetic and profound. His father had learned as a boy the story of The Eloquent Peasant. He decided the only way to escape the backbreaking labor of planting, digging, watering, and harvesting was through education. He would spend every idle hour in chat with whatever learned man he could find. Whether it was a scribe, priest, artisan... he always would engage with them. They quickly took to the boy. He was not a common spouter of water. "If he who listens listens fully, then he who listens becomes he who understands." he said, when asked why he spoke so much less than the other boys, and listened so much more.

"And only speak when you have something worth saying," said an old scribe, "This boy has learned the *Maxims of Ptahhotep* by heart, and at such a young age. He is a prodigy."

The learned men, moved by the plight of the clever boy were at last moved to pay for him to attend scribal school. Before long, he had gone from an illiterate reciter of wisdom to an articulate reader and cunning writer. His tutors had recommended him to the Pharaoh's service. The boy was ecstatic.

There was another boy who was studying in the scribal school, a lad known as Qenna. He was the son of Userkare, the landlord who owned the land Hanya's family lived on, and all but owned them. Though they were not slaves in name, in deed, they were little higher.

Qenna was envious of Hanya's father, and he set in motion a plot to topple the peasant's rise. One day, Qenna broke his own tooth upon a stone. He ran, weeping, keen to tell his father of the wrong done him by his rival. This was the only straw, but it was the last straw. Userkare came to the house wherein dwelt Hanya's father, and dragged him out. Then, with his brothers, nephews, sons, and cousins, they beat Hanya's father. They had intended to beat his twelve year

70

old body to death. They had succeeded merely in breaking his back. Though Hanya's father would never walk again, and could only lift his arms and speak with great difficulty, he would live. In those moments of agony, in his hour of distraught lonesomeness as he waited for his family to cease cowering and attend to him, he remembered the story of his youth. *The Eloquent Peasant.*

Hanya remembered how his mother told the story of his father's courage. He spoke, though marred in agony, with such eloquence, that each magistrate took him to their superior, from the Overseer, to the Nomarch, to the Vizier. Until finally he reached the ears of the Pharaoh, Thutmose IV. Pharaoh heard the case, and judged it summarily. The property of Userkare and his family would become the property of the eloquent peasant, and his son, or any male of his family he so chooses, shall enter the service of the Pharaoh. To that effect, Hanya's father was given papyrus documents and Thutmose's golden scarab.

Hanya recollected now how he as a boy was made to cease his work in the field early. He was the envy of the other boys in those days. He would retire from working just past noon to study. He would study late into the night, by oil lamps once the sun fell. It was well past midnight before he would be allowed to sleep, and then he would wake again at the crack of dawn to work again in the field. He remembered how his father, in a voice quaking and hoarse, would recite for him the *Maxims of Ptahhotep,* "All conduct" he said, "should be so straight that you can measure it with a plumb-line."

Hanya remembered how his father lived. He was a man of principle. He never sought revenge, never mocked, never cursed, and never blasphemed. In his judgement he always sought the righteous case, and no punishment ever came without a lesson, "Punish with principle," he would say, "teach meaningfully. The act of stopping evil leads to the lasting establishment of virtue."

When Hanya came of age at thirteen, it was to be the time of sundering in his young life. He had anticipated that milestone with both anticipation and some degree of dread. He was sent away from his home, the house by the Nile he had never left before. In the company of Ani, a ranked official, he was transported, papers and scarab in hand, by boat, to the new Palace of Malkata, called *'Per-Hay'* (house of rejoicing). The boy was met by officials, priests and slaves as he disembarked. It was a world unlike any he had seen before. Opulence, color, sensuality and people from exotic lands were abundant.

"Make him ready for the sundering of Ra," commanded the chief priest to his acolytes. Hanya was taken, washed, anointed with precious oils, then sent to a dark chamber. An old priest, whose responsibility was for the matter of sundering, took Hanya by his male organ. In his other hand, he cut with two exact and swift strokes. The kiss of the knife, of precious meteoric iron, did not feel anything but cold as they severed the roof of his foreskin. However, a sharp burning pain soon agitated Hanya's loins. "The ointment is to make it acceptable," the old priest applied the soothing substance, "Hold him so he doesn't fall!" With those words recited, and the deed done, Hanya became a man.

Hanya, as he bathed in the river, recalled the pain far less than the joy. He was taken into a large feast hall. Music rung out on the harp, the lute, the lyre, and the pipes, all played by beautiful women wearing little else but jewelry and a girdle around their waists. Foods of all types were laid out. Duck, goose, ibex, gazelle, hare, fish, refined bread, beer, and wine. Hanya had hardly tasted the flesh of a beast before that night; he knew only rough bread, lumpy beer, onions, jute leaves and fish if he was lucky. Now, he ate and ate.

The next morning, play gave way to work. He soon found the education more strenuous, and punishments more liberally given by his instructors. He was always Hanya, the peasant boy. The other students, all of lofty rank, incessantly mocked him. He was the whipping boy of choice for teachers as well. When a student needed to be made an example of, it was always "the Eloquent Peasant" that was chosen. Instead of regarding his beatings as injustice, Hanya remembered them fondly. These thrashings drove him, pushed him to extend the limits of his knowledge and merit. Soon, the appellation "Eloquent Peasant" was given to him by his teachers and peers less with jeers than with deep respect. Hanya was soaring. He remembered the day he met the Pharaoh for the first time.

"So this is the 'Eloquent Peasant' you so often praise" Pharaoh said to Ani.

"Most certainly! Would I deceive such a man as you!" Ani said, "As I always say, be careful to avoid the mistake of lying. It will prevent you from fighting the evil inside yourself."

"He looks hale and swarthy. Like a peasant, or a PHARAOH… " Amenhotep smiled as Ani winced, "Are we men all not cut from the same fabric? When death comes, it embraces the Pharaoh even as the peasant."

Hanya was told not to speak by his master, Ani, but he couldn't help it. He was so transfixed on the virtuous and wise Pharaoh. "May gods guide the Pharaoh. Those who the gods guide cannot get lost…"

"And those they forbid passage will not be able to cross the river of life." the Pharaoh laughed, with all the jollity of a man who is satisfied in the heart. "If all men lived by the teachings of Ptahhotep, there would be peace in the home, in the palace, and in the foreign lands. Come, Hanya… I have a task for you. A task that befits such a man as you… learned, indeed, but more importantly, a man of morality."

So, at the age of just sixteen, Hanya's lot went from being a student of teachers to being a teacher of students. He remembered the day he saw his students for the first time. Milkilu, Yapahu and Addadanu, sons of Zimredda, overseer of the Harem. They were strong boys, made of honest common stock. Hanya could not help but see in them a little of himself. Not to mention, they grew up speaking refined Egyptian. Now, in his class were such children as Hanya regarded less fondly. Lab'ayu, son of Ba'aluya of Shechem was a hot head. Even before he came to understand the spoken tongue of Egypt, he would speak loudly and angrily, in a tone reminiscent of gossip and accusation. By his side was always Sutarna of Qadesh, who was always glum-faced and lazy. Hanya had no respect for people who do not labor in the pursuit of knowledge. Education was a gift worth more than gold to him. Needless to say, he often made Lab'ayu and Sutarna's backsides red with the reed cane. They had a third member, this gang of lofty thugs. Shalimazaru of Jerusalem was harder for Hanya to hate. He was quiet, like Sutarna, but he was not lazy. He was, by all measures, a good student. Hanya often spoke to Shalimazaru, encouraging him to keep better company. Hanya remembered, and shed a little tear.

One day, when the boys were bathing in the river, a dispute broke out between the gang of Milkilu, called the *Arising Ones,* and Lab'ayu's gang, called the *Old Guard.* From what he could gather, the conflict began, as many do, over a woman. Shalimazaru had been laying with a low-born slave girl, and had made something of that coupling that was not there. He believed in their love. So when he caught his lover lying with Addadanu, conflict ensued. Soon, war was waged on the river. It seemed almost innocent at first, but Shalimazaru had lifted a cane to beat Addadanu's head. Milkilu, in a passionate rage to protect his dear brother, threw a smooth river stone at the assailant. It struck Shalimazaru on his temple, and he collapsed bleeding into the river. *The boys were so shocked at what happened, they called for me,* Hanya thought, *but it was too late.* The boy, sole heir to Jerusalem, had perished in the Nile. After that, the boys never fought again, as long as Hanya had them. Pharaoh was pleased with his work. Hanya looked down into the water that he was bathing in. Life and death, love and hate, sang in the rushing of the brown water. Hanya resolved to be a protector of the innocent, a man of justice.

12

Chapter 12: Virgin 'Anat's Daughter

"So, when you meet my father," said Shisita, "don't show him your bag of finger bones. He is a sensitive man, and he may find it uncouth."

"What sort of man is your father? I've scarcely heard you speak of him. I don't know a lot of girls, but those I do know always mention their fathers. Besides you." Yassib grinned mischievously.

"To his credit, he is compassionate. Who's ever heard of a king taking a little beat-up puppy off the street, then nursing it back to health, feeding it better than he feeds himself?"

"He sounds precious to me," said Yassib.

"Like a demure princess!" said Shisita, "He doesn't speak a lot, and he mainly keeps to himself, as far as being a king will allow. Everyone in the family, let's face it, everyone in Canaan looks down on him. For what? He's not a killer. He just wants to live a simple, quiet life."

"Seems rather the opposite of you."

"I'm my mother's daughter."

"A pity we have to drag him into war."

"For all his 'cowardice' he is King of Qadesh and the last male descendant of Durusha. That means something, especially the *male* part. Men usually want to follow men. But Sutarna, he will follow me. Then all those men will follow him, and we'll win the war.*

A noon sun shone on the passing chariots of Shisita and Yassib, turning their bronze armor into a gleaming gold for all to see. Swift mares whinnied with wet air escaping their blaring nostrils. Their swift movement indicated one thing to the people; war was coming, and from peasants, they would be made soldiers. After her they followed to the great tel of Qadesh. It had the appearance of a large hill but there was nothing natural in its structure. It was the ruin of city after city, going back two thousand years at least, rising on the horizon like the sun in the morning, embraced by the swift-moving Orontes river. It was, without a doubt, the most strategically important city in all Syria, perhaps all Canaan. It sat directly midway between the lands of Mighty Hatti, Cultured Babylon, and Golden Egypt. All trade going north, south, east, and west passed through the gates of "Holy" Qadesh. So too passed the company of Shisita and Yassib, through the high limestone walls to the great Souq where king Sutarna, Sura'ata, Tiwati, and Gulati stood to greet them on a great pavilion made of fine cedar wood. A crowd had gathered there. The call of war attracts the ignorant masses like a flame attracts moths. Their fates are much the same, even if some manage to loot a little gold along the way. As for those who want glory, revenge? Their ignorant, flammable moth bodies is what feeds the flames of war that burns up so many, innocent and otherwise.

"At your feet seven times and seven times I bow, father" Shisita stated firmly and prostrated herself. The men in her company did so as well, like the passing of a wave onto the shore. Sutarna lifted his daughter's head by the chin, with a tenderness he reserved as yet only for her.

"No need to do obeisance for me, my beloved daughter, my moon, sun, and stars! It is enough that you are home, returned from your long wanderings! I am so glad to see you in my presence again, not not in my dreams alone. And I see you have a handsome young man with you. I do hope you'd await my blessing before choosing a husband."

"I'm not her husband!" said Yassib, "I am Yassib, her sword brother. Together we battled Ḥabiru around Canaan on behalf of Queen Tiye. We gave them a little taste of the wrath of 'Anat."

"A man of Ugarit, if my ear for accents is still good. But the Ugaritic speech is unmistakable. How did you come to be acquainted with my virgin daughter?"

79

"It was a chance meeting, in Thebes. I had gone to Egypt to register with the Pharaoh's army as a spearman, a common Maharu of Syria for the army. But among the recruits, Shisita called out for volunteers to fight the Ḥabiru in Retenu. The southerners among us, the majority of our number, dreaded the Ḥabiru and dared not go with her. But I, among ninety-nine others who possessed hearts of lions, went forth. As for me, I agreed to fight because I am a northerner. Hatti is our neighbor, far fiercer than any Ḥabiru. So I was eager to go, and since she took a shine to me, I became her second in command."

"What a deeply inspiring story! Surely, you are the pride of us Syrians. What brings the two of you to Qadesh on such short notice?"

" Father, it is a matter of great urgency that we have hastened to you to seek, well, men..."

"Is one not enough, sister?" Tiwati flicked her tongue, mocking Shisita. Shisita had more important things to deal with than a jealous sister.

"Only you would know!" dsaid Shisita, shushing her sister's petty spat.

"It is a matter of troops, my lord" said Yassib, "and a king to lead them. Chaos is brewing in Canaan. Lab'ayu of Shechem has mustered a force of Ḥabiru numbering three thousand, perhaps four thousand strong. He intends to wage war on Gezer. It is only a matter of time, till all Retenu is burning and desolate, and Pharaoh will wreak his vengeance on all Canaan, regardless of guilt. If we can quash Lab'ayu's rebellion before it grows out of hand, many lives will be saved."

This was exactly too much for Sutarna. His eyes glazed, his heart beat fast, and cruel visions raced through his mind. The burning, the corpses of his brothers, his father, his uncles. Even the women were not spared. He was then taken to the land of his family's killers, to learn to be obedient, to be a good subject, a king subordinate to a greater king. In that time he had one friend; the boy Lab'ayu, an orphan of war, like him. Lab'ayu alone had protected him from all the evils and slights wrecked by pharaoh's favorites. Now they must battle? For the sake of Pharaoh? Sutarna collapsed. His wife Sura'ata helped him up. She was actually gladdened by the prospect of war. Anything to man up her feckless husband was good in her book.

"As you can see," Sutarna dusted off his blue robes, "I am not a warrior. I do the calculations as to when to put in the crops. I preside over religious ceremonies. I manage the royal expenditure and make sure Pharaoh gets his due, but I am not a warrior." Sura'ata rolled her eyes.

"Your father was a warrior. His father too was a great warrior. And before them, your ancestor Durusha was a warrior. How can you not be a warrior?" chided Shisita. "It's in your blood. Look at me! Even I, a woman, can be a warrior! Qadesh is strong! We will triumph over any enemy!" She raised her weapon into a position well known to all Canaanites as the 'smiting pose'. Her power was rooted in Canaanite religion. The tales of goddess 'Anatu showed women can be warriors. Even so, it was a rarity.

The peasants cheered their Princess; they did not know what war brings. With the hearty cheering of the masses, Sutarna acquiesced. He may love Lab'ayu, he may hate Egypt, but he feared the burning of his youth more. A quick war, to save Canaan from a great one. There was nothing left to do but to arm the men and sway the gods to their side. The beating of drums shook the ground and the heart of the king. If my daughter can be brave and strong, he thought, so can I. He looked at his people. They were all eager, all ready to follow him. He never had such acclaim.

Like the moth, he beat his wings, and drew closer to that flame. In the south, the flame glowed hot and bright, with all the fury of a bull who just became an ox.

13

Chapter 13: Springtime for Battle — Part 1

"Offer in the earth war, Place in the dust peace. You must hasten! You must hurry! You must rush!" Lab'ayu misquoted the Canaanite scriptures of Ba'alu. All the while the crosses rose, like summer wheat. Blood watered the ground.

It was springtime, time for birth, time for fertility, planting, lovemaking. Time for war. Lab'ayu, king of Shechem gathered his two sons, Mutba'alu and Ayyabu, his Uncle Issuwa and Issuwa's son Dadua, and numerous Ḥabiru under the command of Abneru and his cousin Yishaya the Dog Hater. The time was right for war. The king had vacillated over the point all winter long; a decision to invade Gezer, the wealthiest city in the south, and rebel in all but name against Pharaoh himself… it could not be taken lightly. The coming of Mutba'alu and the Ḥabiru had tipped the scales. The war party in the end had their way. The other leaders, hostile to the plan, were rounded up. Their crucified bodies lined around the city wall of Shechem as a grisly reminder of what loyalty to Pharaoh purchased from Lab'ayu.

In actuality, Lab'ayu wanted all these men spared, but Mutba'alu warned him that they would endanger the war by spreading true information about their councils to the enemy. Mutba'alu got his way, and dozens of the most prominent men of the city, magistrates, judges, merchants, and the entire Egyptian garrison were nailed each to a cross and used as targets for archers and slingers, and to test newly made blades. Flies buzzed around their wounds and their eyes and mouths hung open, frozen in horrific positions of agony. With all questioning of the course purged, the final spur to action was when the messenger from Egypt arrived bringing a secret tablet from their spy. Pharaoh was aging, losing control of his kingdom to his wife, and his heir was an incompetent religious lunatic with no desire to maintain hold of Canaan. Lab'ayu needed no more urging, and they set off, expecting to celebrate the Akitu within the walls of Gezer.

There was some debate over whether to first attack Tagi's stronghold of Ginti due northwest of Shechem and then to march on Gezer. It was considered unwise to leave a foe in the rear, to support Milkilu from behind. On the other hand, time was of the essence, and they needed to enter Gezer before Pitati archers were sent from Tjaru. Reluctantly, the decision was made to divide the forces, the majority going with Mutba'alu, Abneru, and Lab'ayu to attack Gezer directly, and a smaller force led by Ayyabu, Issuwa, and Dadua to tie up Ginti with a siege. Abneru sent his cousin Yishaya the Dog-Hater to go with Ayyabu.

As the Shechemite youths set to marching, along with their Ḥabiru brethren, their speech turned to gossip.

"I heard Yishaya hates dogs so much because they bit off his balls!"

"Do you see that beard on his face? That man has all the balls he needs. No, Yishaya needs no reason to hate dogs, he just does! I heard he just goes out in front of the Ḥabiru column and leaves dead dogs for his comrades to find!"

Yishaya, who was within earshot, heard the gossip. He was blessed, but also cursed with sharp hearing. When he heard his name, his ear pricked up. When he heard about the nonsense about dogs, his blood started to boil with rage.

"Excuse me, young men, I couldn't help but overhear you were talking about me."

"Oh, shit, he heard us"

"I just want to clear up some misconceptions," said Yishaya, "I don't actually hate dogs. I actually rather like dogs. It's people I can't stand. Especially people who spread rumors about me regarding dogs…" he toyed with his bronze dagger, threateningly.

"Oh yeah… if you like dogs, why are you called Yishaya the Dog-Hater."

"It's my damned cousin, Abneru." Yishaya spat in disgust,

"This all started during a particularly long siege. We were with the army of Abdi-whatever trying to take one of his rebellious cities back for him."

"Boring..."

"Do you want a mouth full of teeth when I'm done with the story, oh youths? Pay attention. So it came to the point where the men were eating dogs. That donkey, Abdi— screw him, don't even remember his name, well he didn't feed us good. I mean, there was bread, and water, but, well, we were eating dogs."

"Yes, you said that already."

"Ah, ah, ah! But I wasn't eating dogs! That's why I'm called the dog hater."

"I don't get it."

"I wouldn't eat dogs. First of all they are an unclean animal. They lick their own balls. Secondly... Like I said, I like dogs. They are nice. Much better than that old Abdi-whatshisname. So my cousin, like the monkey he is, started telling people I hate dogs! Then, he started killing dogs and blaming me!"

The youths laughed. It was a mistake. Yishaya punched each of them in the face. The soldiers around the youths had long since taken notice of the amusing dialogue between two young fools and an old fool.

86

"A man's reputation is his greatest treasure," said Yishaya, "especially for us soldiers. He must guard it with his life."

The soldiers around cheered.

"Know this. That if any man dares to spread rumors or joke about my appellation, he shall soon find himself... "

"Lectured." said one of the youths, who had recovered enough from the punch to stand up.

"Dead." Yishaya stuck his dagger through the fool's eye. He found it tiresome. After all the people he killed, it was still the name Dog-Hater that stuck.

Ayyabu, Issuwa, Dadua and Yishaya's force was the first to arrive at their target. To their surprise, the walls were guarded by stout defenders.

A contingent of Shisita's men, the Lions of 'Anat, had been left with the king Tagi. They numbered around thirty. They soon imparted their martial skills to the citizens of Ginti, most of whom had never held a sword or spear or shield before.

After Shisita's hasty departure, the Lionmen gathered among themselves to elect a new leader. They picked Apapa.

"Gather, people of Ginti!" said Apapa, "Your city is under dire threat. Who will come forward who will defend the people of Ginti with their life and arms!"

Silence reigned. Silence, until Rimatu spoke.

"Pathetic! Look at these 'Men of Ginti'. Indeed, look, I cannot find them anywhere! Are they hiding under their beds? These men, foreigners, strangers, have pledged their lives to protect us, and you 'men' remain coy and silent when they call you to arms. I think I speak for all of us whores in the city of Ginti when I say, if there is no man in the city, let us take up arms! We will fight for Ginti, to protect the precious innocent boys who are too busy having a wank to fight for themselves!"

The whores rushed forward, and stripped naked in full sight of everyone. They entered houses and took from it male garb, kilts and tunics. They dressed themselves, and girded themselves with cuirasses. They took up all the armor and weapons that they could. Needless to say, the men were shamed. Apapa got his army. That was the army that faced the Shechemites. That was the army that built up the defences of Ginti to be an equal for any fortress in Retenu.

Tagi looked out over the ramparts of his city. He looked at the rough army of Lionmen, Levies, and Lascivious Ladies his city possessed. He stood alone, thinking, with no one to talk to. The madams of the brothel now had more power in his own city than him. He knew, to hold out, he would need reinforcements. Reinforcements from Milkilu. His fate was in the hands of the Gezer Brothers. Oh, Ramashtu, he thought. If only I married you to a man who possessed only

88

the normal amount of evil in his heart. He sighed. Pharaoh is fortunate, he thought. He can marry his own daughters.

14

Chapter 14: Springtime for Battle — Part 2

Milkilu was cheerful that day, for the first time in a long time. He had long been filled with consternation at the thought of leading his city to war. He confided in Yapahu that, "War is life on the edge of a dagger." Yapahu did little to dissuade him of his fear. Milkilu had dreaded that Sabbatu meeting when he would say to the people, "War has come".

The people had gathered at the temple of Ilu the Patriarch for the Sabbatu sacrifice. They were none the wiser of the news Milkilu planned to disclose to them. The ritual of Sabbatu was performed in the same fashion that Milkilu always had, at least to begin with. Five fatted cows, ten sheep, fifteen goats and fifty pigeons bled upon the altar. Then, they were grilled upon an open flame. It was one part gory religious spectacle, one part all you can eat barbecue. Each denizen of Gezer from the lowliest slave, to Milkilu himself would partake in the beef, mutton, goat, buffalo, pigeon... whatever meat was available on the market. Milkilu would inform people of the news concerning the state of Gezer. None dared to look away from him; those who stayed attentive were rewarded with gold. But this speech was not typical.

"People of Gezer!" Milkilu coughed awkwardly, "People of Gezer. God has smiled on us this week. Great wealth was gained... oh... People of Gezer! I cannot conceal from you what is troubling... igniting my heart! The king of Lab'ayu... The king of Shechem, Lab'ayu has made groundless accusations against me... against Gezer! He has designs on OUR city so that he may pillage it, and take the good things I have obtained for you. He has bought and paid for an army, an army of Ḥabiru. That means one thing. War! Though I made..."

Applause. Applause and cheering. It was as if the whole city was clapping, shouting appraisal, whistling and whooping. Milkillu had never had his words met with such approbation. He had expected boos and taunts. Instead, the people of Gezer rose like a mighty wave before him. He felt like a sorcerer summoning green flame from salts and sand.

"War!" said Milkilu.

The people cheered even louder. It was as if he cast a magic spell on them.

"WAR!"

The people were clambering. Their enthusiasm was deafening. Milkilu's spirits lifted. The people wanted a Warrior

King. When it came time for the 'Gold Dole' the people turned away the gold in a show of civic pride.

"Put away that gold, oh king, save it for the war chest!"

"Give us arms! Spears and shields, helms and cuirasses! Let us fight like our fathers!"

The procession carried Milkilu and Yapahu away, from the temple to the armory. The people grabbed weapons long dusty from disuse, and outfitted themselves. Gezer was again a city of soldiers. As they sang and chanted old war songs, Milkilu was moved to tears. His people would fight for him, he thought. He shouted to his people, "I would die for you, oh Gezer of my bosom!" They then made it a song.

I would die for you, oh Gezer of my Bosom,
Put a spear in my hand, in my left hand a knife
Give me a shield to defend my fellow's freedom
With my honor, my courage and my life!

Milkilu was humming as he walked through the colonnade peristyle of his palace. His mind was abuzz in the stratagems of war. He passed, by chance, his wife. She smiled. In this moment of his mirth, he didn't immediately regard what she was smiling at. He waved at her tenderly. She didn't notice. It was not for him that she smiled. That glance caused Milkilu's eye to wander towards the target of her affection. He just caught the man for a moment, the curly hair, an oxhide sandal. His mind turned from mirth to suspicion. Addadanu was the object of his scorn. There was no proof, but Milkilu did not

92

recall seeing him at the Sabbatu gathering, neither him nor Ramashtu. Malice crept into his plan, like ants into a nest filled with hatchling peacocks. The ants must devour the birds when they are chicks, or else be devoured themselves in time, he thought. Soon he had formulated the plan and sent his brothers off with enthusiastic soldiers in tow.

Milkilu would stay put. Though he trusted in the height and strength of his walls, and in the water supply from the spring under his palace, he knew his place was to guard the city of the king. No defenses are strong without the will to guard them. He had assumed that before attacking Gezer, Lab'ayu would first have to attack Ginti, and then go through Muhazzu, the fertile agricultural hub of Gezer's territory before attacking the city of Gezer proper. He sent one third of his army with Yapahu to reinforce Ginti, another third he left with himself, just in case, and the smallest third he sent under Addadanu to Muhazzu. Milkilu thought about his youngest brother. Was that foolish attitude real or affected? Either way, it was dangerous. As for his wife's possible liaison with his brother? There was no proof yet; but there was no need to wait for it to be too late. He will be loyal and fight the Ḥabiru on the front lines and guard the supply routes, or he betray me from a distance, and then there will be time for action, thought Milkilu.

As Milkilu suspected, enemies arrived at Ginti first. They wasted no time surrounding the city and taking everything of value that wasn't nailed down from the surrounding countryside and farms. The men and women on the walls were not going to budge. Any thought of negotiated surrender or assaulting the city with ladders or rams was quickly scrapped. The citizens of Ginti were not going to give up without a fight. "Fine," said Yishaya, "Now they'll soon find out how much they like to eat dogs!" Being in on the joke, Ginti's defenders began releasing hounds from their front gates, laughing hysterically. Morale was high among the Gintites, as Yishaya just let each and every dog sent to him go as it may, this way or that. Soon they were a constant nuisance in the Ḥabiru camp. Nonetheless, Yishaya had given orders not to harm them. He was eager to remove his embarrassing nickname. He also liked dogs... a shameful thing to admit.

Meanwhile Addadanu was completely oblivious to the lack of trust his brother held in him, even though he was humping his wife. How could he not have her? She was beautiful and lonely and only seemed happy when he was inside of her. He thought, in our line of business, who can be too touchy on who humps who's wife. I'd let him hump my wife too, if I had one, and she was interested! Of course I have no interest in wives, after all, the bachelor's life leaves me with no shortage of partners! He set his men to work fortifying his stronghold of Muhazzu as a base of operations and a strong defensive position. Meanwhile, he indulged in his favorite pastime. He eventually turned nearly the whole male populace, anyone who had a wife, sister, daughter or mother into his enemy by his aggressive sexual conquests among the women. But for now, the soldiers did their duty, and the citizens stayed in line, because of Addadanu's cylendar seals; now two. Both the grand one of Pharaoh and the smaller one from Milkilu. Little did anyone notice, much less the

94

distracted and illiterate Addadanu, that his seals both had the words, "Void, not a valid seal" written on them in bulky cuneiform script. The Peacock was lucky that peasant girls and common soldiers had no ability to read.

Addadanu's corruption festered in the heart of Gezer's cohesion. Though he was too ignorant to know it, his brothers wrangled with it in a game of cruel candidness and ignominious ignorance.

15

Chapter 15: Springtime for Battle — Part 3

While Addadanu was engaged in rutting and strutting, Yapahu, the Mizrite, was marching his army north to Ginti along the coastal road. Night was the cloak of movement for the army. The coolness of it allowed the men to make faster time, and in the day, they rested. In those sleepy days, he was lost in wandering thoughts. Although his life was less stressful with the Peacock miles away, he pined for his brother, the one who had been his companion over so many travels and his wingman over so many beauties. They had enjoyed so many women together, and Yapahu knew they were better as a team. When Milkilu ordered his forces divided, Yapahu begged Milkilu to let him go with Addadanu and send another man to go to Ginti. But the King's word was final, and at least he knew he was in his brother's trust. He knew about Addadanu's affair, and worried nightly over the fate of his brother should he ever be caught. No amount of sweet talking could save him from that. One day, under the cool shade of an olive tree, wizened and grey with age, the Mizrite debated with himself.

"What will I do! If I do not act, Addadanu will be done away with by Milkilu."

"If I act in his defense, I may be cast into suspicion along with Addadanu, and I fear the whole house of our father will fall. Maybe it is better to implore Addadanu to come clean about his adulteries, and blame it all on the wife's promiscuity."

"But if I did so, then she will surely be treated harshly, and that would spoil the alliance with her father Tagi!"

"What if I warn Addadanu to stay away from the woman, telling him he is suspected."

"But Addadanu is like a crocodile, once he grasps his prey he never releases it."

"Maybe I can play the ignorant, and plead for my brother and the woman out of necessity."

"But Milkilu will not let them off the hook, he is vengeful."

"But what if I prove my valor through a great victory, will not Milkilu heed my advice out of admiration?"

"More likely any success I gain in battle will diminish my value, not add to it, for in victory I become the threat while in deadlock I remain indispensable."

His thoughts raged like the storm and the sea, subsiding only when dreary sleep overtook him with sweet dreams. That was his respite, drooling and napping in the spring sun, his mind refueling for the battle ahead. Furthermore, the battle was not with the enemy, but was with his kin. Only in dreamland could Yapahu adopt the indifference that brought such catastrophe and joy to the family of Addadanu.

16

Chapter 16: Springtime for Battle — Part 4

Milkilu sat strong in his city surrounded by strong walls. The granaries were filled with ample supplies. In the barracks more than enough soldiers camped to repulse any potential attack. He had faith in his brother Yapahu as well. If Yapahu was not a warrior, then he surely was an adaptable, cunning man. He would strike Lab'ayu, putting him between two armies like grain between a mortar and pestle. And even if the enemy took Ginti, Addadanu would have more than enough men to finish Lab'ayu off. In the city, no one even seemed to notice anyone was at war. Spring was in the air, and pleasure was on the mind of every citizen of Gezer. Food was consumed heartily as quickly as it was brought in from the countryside. Wine was drunk, and sacrifices were made in the honor of the gods; notably, not asking for victory in battle, but the typical Gezerite supplication asking for bountiful harvests and plentiful trade.

Milkilu knew Lab'ayu as a youth, had fought him as a boy,

and in their contests always won. It was not from mere brute strength that Milkilu bullied Lab'ayu as a child. It was the power of numbers. Three brothers, more than enough to create a clique that could challenge any boyish gang. Milkilu, the oldest, took pleasure in tormenting the hostages Pharaoh sent to his court. He was never chastised when he beat the son of the king of Qadesh, or Shechem, or Jerusalem. Even after the heir to the throne of Jerusalem died from his beatings, having been struck on the head by a rock and drowned in the Nile, the Pharaoh didn't reprimand Milkilu. The Pharaoh always took his side. Without any rebuke to Milkilu, he simply installed the son of a Hurrian footsoldier as king of Jerusalem. This loyal lackey, Abdi Heba, ruled the powerful city even now. Milkilu felt as safe as an elephant in a fortress. Supremely confident, Milkilu took this opportunity to try to make up with his wife, the beautiful but sullen Ramashtu.

He came into her chamber by night, unexpected, unannounced, as usual. As normal, she was afflicted with melancholy. She stared out her window longingly in the direction of Muhazzu. In her sensual way, she traced her ring-bedecked, manicured fingers along the intricately carved stiles that in their crisscross pattern separated the domestic world to the public one. As a light spring breeze blew through the gaps, she smelt the air of the market. Scents of cumin, garlic, onions, and coriander from the market, and the smell of urine, feces, and decaying fish from the latrine. To her, the distinction between pleasant and unpleasant odor meant nothing. Both teased her nose with the desire she could never obtain. Freedom, from her husband, from childbirth, from boredom, and the cruel pleasure of loneliness. It meant going into the beautiful yet harsh world she knew only from the tales of her one true love, Addadanu.

"I know what you are here for. Take it quick and leave me. I don't have the will to fight you tonight. You are too strong. I'm just a weak pathetic woman. Use me how you like and please go before I start weeping and wake the children."

"I have not come for that, wife." Milkilu scratched his short beard, "Nor to fight. Not with words, your weapon, or fists, mine. I've come to apologize. I've been no good to you. I've taken it too personally, your sadness, as it is a sickness. I hope someday to find a cure, so you may love me, as I have always loved you."

"Love you!" She almost raised her voice in anger, "It would be hard not to hate you. You keep me here, far from my Mother, my Father, like a pretty bird in a cage meant only to breed you some heirs. And I have to watch them, one by one sicken and die, or worse, take after you. It is more than this woman can take."

Milkilu put his strong, thick hand around her slender shoulders. She knew those hands better than any part of him for their beatings, for their gaggings, for them holding her from resisting when he took his husband's right. Can hands like that comfort a suffering soul? She couldn't help but weep. He wiped her eyes with his dark, monstrous hands.

"I can not take back the things I've done. But once I've defeated Lab'ayu, and my need for your father is over, I'll divorce you, like you always wanted. You can go back to Ginti, or marry whoever pleases you. But remember that, until that day comes, you are my wife and my wife only. If I ever catch you committing adultery, I'll have you and the man responsible stoned in the marketplace, regardless of the objections of your father. I've honored this marriage and known no other woman but you, but by God's beard if you ever betray me your life is worth less than nothing to me!"

Ramashtu was relieved to hear Milkilu was back to acting like himself again. The date syrup sweetness only served to make her uncomfortable. She undressed, and let him have at her, saying a quiet prayer to the gods to aid Lab'ayu and kill Milkilu; yet spare Addadanu. She smiled at her husband for the first time tonight. Thinking the night a capital success, Milkilu returned to his quarters for drink, song and merriment. Ramashtu slept, hoping she would not get pregnant again. She didn't dare to pray for it. If God was real, he could only be evil for granting her such pain. Prayer to him would be like informing your greatest enemy of your most vulnerable weakness. She would keep her secret, even from God.

17

Chapter 17: The Heretic Prince

Amenhotep the Prince rose from his bed in the morning, put
on his kilt, and painted his eyes with Kohl. Those were the
last normal things he did that day. To the east gate of the
palace he hastened, giddy with delight. It was the time of the
spring equinox, and he was eager for days to get longer and
summer to blast its heat like the blare of golden trumpets. He
stood outside the palace, as was his habit on such occasions,
to greet the sun. And he stood there, hour after hour, gazing
at the sun, not looking away from it's grandeur, singing
words of praise. Egyptians took religion unusually seriously.
Whether he was called Ra or Amun, the sun god was honored
by all Egyptians. Despite this, most saw the behavior of
the prince a little extreme, and quite worrying. They loved
prince Thutmose, a strong boy who looked just like his father
Amenhotep III when he was young. But they saw no more
Thutmose, and they were seeing more and more of this other
prince, and they wondered what happened to their favorite.

But by the passing of the suns and moons, Amenhotep the

prince began to attract a following. The poor, the slave, the scarlet woman saw a generous patron in him, and they greeted the sun with him every morning, collecting lavish gifts in the process. Soon people's curiosity and greed outweighed their orthodoxy, and he began attracting a crowd. As more and more people joined the game, believers started to appear. Before it was a mad boy who happened to be a prince making a mockery of the gods, but now with these crowds? He must be a true prophet. He was ugly, true; but was not also Sobek, the crocodile god? His soul was pure. Many people began seeing him as a worthy successor to his father. Many became pious fools.

The priests of Amun, however, were not willing to be spat at in the face. They had kept the alliance strong with the Pharaoh as long as the eighteenth dynasty ruled, but they feared the worst from this deformed heretic. Daily, he gave them much to revile. He told the poor tenants on the priests' land to cease paying their rent to the temple. He began speaking of devoting the complex at Karnak to his one god, Aten, and how he intended to ban the worship of all other (false) gods. Needless to say, Amenhotep III spent many days of his gray years with the Amun Priests begging at his feet, pleading for him to do something, anything, about his mad son. But there was nothing to be done. There were no other sons. And then, Smenkhare was born to one of Pharaoh's concubines. Some suspected Smenkhare was born a girl. Naturally, they said, Amenhotep chose to disguise this fact for obvious political reasons. Now Amenhotep had an heir, and a spare and he meant business. He wasn't talking to his once beloved wife Tiye much anymore either.

Since her son's religion started spreading like wildfire, she had wholeheartedly endorsed her son's prophecy. She was becoming more and more the most powerful person in Egypt. Amenhotep III was seen now as being older, weaker, and never a particularly impressive pharaoh to begin with. His glory days were long forgotten by all but the oldest and most orthodox.

Amenhotep III had one last plan up his sleeves, albeit a risky one. It was time for a Sed Festival and royal jubilee. Commemorating the thirtieth year of Amenhotep's reign, it would remind Egypt of the virility of their old king. An artificial lake was built for Queen Tiye, along with a new temple at Malqata. He would visit each of Egypt's forty-two Nomes, performing an ancient and carnal ritual. He would knock at the door of the temple, mace in hand, followed by his Queens and royal daughters (There was some overlap between the two). Then, the king would perform a manly feat to affirm to all Egypt his divinity and masculinity. It was a rare enough thing to have a Sed festival; no one alive remembered the last one, under Hatshepsut. Amenhotep would have to run alongside the Apis bull to demonstrate his divine ageless power. He would perform this feat in each nome, from the far south of Upper Egypt by the border of Nubia, to the Delta. Throughout Upper Egypt he performed well, after all, the Apis Bull was as fat and tired as he was. Then, he came to the city of Avaris. It was the former capital of the Hyksos, a Canaanite people that once ruled the north of Egypt. There lived the Canaanites of the Delta, a people who amalgamated Egyptian and Canaanite culture into one. It was in their city, the city of Ba'alu in Egypt that the Pharaoh... stumbled.

The ceremony was performed in the local temple, all according to custom. The burning incense stung the kohl-painted eyes of Egyptians and Canaanites, and the smoke of savory sacrifices induced hunger in the crowds. This meat was not for the hungry. Once the gods took their fill, it was the plump priests that ate the leftovers. Once the priests were certain the gods were sated with the burning of animal flesh, the Apis bull was brought forth. It was a bull of immense girth. A lifetime of having it's face stuffed with bread, cakes, meats, honey, and dates made it a portly beast. It lumbered irregularly as if in a divine trance. This was the result of it being intoxicated with enough beer and wine to blur heaven and earth in a mucky haze.The poor animal was prodded and goaded to run, to chase the Pharaoh who in his age had a worthy opponent in the corpulent inebriated beast. Pharaoh had not neglected exercise at any point of his life. Archery, chariot riding, wrestling, footracing and javelin throwing were all as much of his daily routine as governance and sex. But the bull, crucially, did not understand that it needed to let the Pharaoh win. That was the genius of the Sed festival. It confirmed, with no bias, whether the Pharaoh in his old age was worthy or not worthy to continue to rule Egypt.

The bull was set loose, it's black eyes reflecting the heat of fury almost as if it were a proper bull and not a pampered idol. The rolls of fat heaved left and right like the jiggling breasts of a harlot. Stirred by the coming bull, Amenhotep III ran. He was confident, and sure, and then he stepped on his foot wrong. Pain shot up his leg, bringing the powerful but aged Pharaoh down like the toppling of a gazelle shot through the breast with a swift arrow. If he had stayed on the ground, he could have made a show of courage by halting the bull with the intensity of his stare. But he chose again to rise, then he stumbled. He rose again, then fell flat on his face like a sack of barley. The Canaanites of the Delta, who hated the Pharaoh, laughed like hyenas at the ailing king. They goaded the Bull...

"Come on, Apis, finish off the pretender! We'll make a stew out of his balls!"

"Though it wouldn't make much of a meal!"

Amenhotep's prestige was recovering, but with one little embarrassing trip and fall, it all came crashing down. Egypt was abandoning him for his son, whom he was forced now to make Co-ruler. A man of many successes, great deeds done in the name of his country, was hobbled by a twisted Achilles heel. He would never be great again. The wool was pulled from the eyes of the people, and the myth of divinity was shattered. Egypt would look to a new leader now.

18

Chapter 18: The North Gathers

The kings of Syria were shocked when they received messages in the name of Sutarna, King of Qadesh. This was a man they thought they knew well, broken by the fire and blood of the Pharaoh, so long ago. But there was no arguing with his dictate. Sutarna was seen as weak and craven. If even he was to march south, there was no leeway for the other northern kings not to harness their chariot-steeds. Sutarna's arguments hit the nail on the head. If there was chaos in the south, the trade routes to Egypt would be disrupted. No one in Syria could afford that. Trade was the lifeblood for the Syrian kings, and any disruption would be a disaster. Furthermore, rumors of a mad prince, the new heir, had reached as far as Syria. "Perhaps he will kill us and take our cities, not knowing friend from foe" wrote Sutarna. The north relied on Pharaoh's protection as a deterrent to prevent Hatti from attacking. Loyalty to Pharaoh was rote, regardless of what the kings may have thought in private.

"We must maintain the power of Pharaoh in Retenu, or else

we will have war on our soil!" declared Sutarna. Heeding his call, an army of kings, some of cities and royal lines a thousand years old marched behind Sutarna of the Sudden Sword. Maybe Qadesh was a city of warriors again? Idanda, the king of Qaṭna had taken up the call with his intensely fatalistic son Akizzi. Their loyalty to Egypt was unshakable, as they were the ever vigilant guards against the Hittite menace. Akizzi was a man who best embodied the traits of a falcon. His eyes were vivid and dark, his nose beaked, and his scorn for enemies of Pharaoh was as intense as if he had been Pharaoh himself. Akizzi lived far too close to Hatti. Qaṭna would never forget what Hatti had done to Aleppo not three hundred years ago. Three centuries of living on a knife's edge bred loyalty to Qaṭna's protectors.

Sharrupshi was much the opposite of Akizzi in many ways. As a son of Addu-Nirari, the wealthy king of Nuhhashe, he was more fond of lavish fetes and extravagant gowns than battle and slaughter. His father sent him south to man him up. Petulant, Sharrupshi was only persuaded to leave his whores after his mother spoke to him about the lascivious women of Gezer. He needed no more convincing.

Alongside those from Nuhhashe and Qaṭna, magnates and potentates from up and down the Orontes river valley gathered. The shimmering bronze plates of the soldiers' scale armor scattered the sun's rays like so many mirrors. The lightly armed troops appeared like a host of heaven in its multitudes. This was a force that appeared to all as a force of rebellion. Instead it was the army of the King, Pharaoh of Egypt, loyal if not in soul, then in pragmatism.

Passing along the river paths, a song was sung by the Lions of 'Anat that the rest of the army picked up as they marched along the way. The brave percussion of marching feet and brash lyrics caused many farmers to join their army along the way.

"When the Bronze Sun is setting, and the iron moon is rising,
It is time for weapons to rise by the score.
Whenever your enemies commit heinous crimes without
punishment,
You have a perfect excuse to wage a war.
It's time to gather strong men, great soldiers,
For these will be bloody wars, and brazen.
The gods are watching from their mountains,
Don't dishonor yourself by being craven!"

Along the way, more and more people in the army forgot the original purpose of the army. Wishful thinking led to the belief it was a grand army for the freedom and unity of all Syria and Canaan. When Shisita informed her father of this fact, he dismissed it saying if misinformation was good for morale, it was good for him. Akizzi suggested they may be able to fool Lab'ayu into thinking they had come to join him, and cut the head off the enemy at a feast. Sutarna didn't like this idea one bit. Shisita took note.

Their path took them through the Cedar forests of the Lebanon mountains, where they began to encounter smaller armies of the West Canaanite cities, particularly the Amurru raiders of Abdi-Ashtirta and his son Aziru. Abdi-Ashtirta was known as the Old Ram, and his son Aziru as the Blood

Lamb. They were engaged in a life-and-death battle with Rib-Hadda of Gubla. Rib-Hadda was well known throughout the Egyptian court. He had sent hundreds of tablets begging for Pharaoh to aid him against his enemies in Amurru. He became known as Rib-Hadda the Pleader.

Pharaoh would periodically send a few troops here or there, just enough to impose continued loyalty from Rib-Hadda, but never enough to deal with the Amurru problem. Rib-Hadda had since resorted to hiring Sherden mercenaries to fill his depleted ranks. He figured that they, being foreigners in the land, would not grasp the hopelessness of his situation before being thoroughly invested in his cause. This was despite the advice and pleading of his younger brother Ili-Rapih that the business of mercenaries was war; they surely would come to understand the truth of the matter and then betrayal was certain. Rib-Hadda had no other options. He couldn't even spare men to bury his dead at the Adonis river. The Adonis river was said to run red every year, due to the death of its namesake the god Adon, but this year it ran red entirely out of season! The dead were left as carrion, unable to enter the afterlife, forced to wander the earth as shades until their bones could be given proper rites. Rib-Hadda had concentrated what was left of his forces in the city of Gubla, but sent his sister and her children, his heirs, to the island city of Tyre for protection.

The carcasses of the Gublaite dead littered the ground by the myriads, their bodies stripped of everything valuable. Their decaying penises shuddered in the wind for want of robes. The piteous sight moved the men greatly, and so Sutarna commanded a halt to properly bury the dead. The soldiers dug, with even some of the leaders lending a hand after Sutarna grabbed a shovel and started digging. The priests who had accompanied the men said the proper prayers, and the dead were finally laid to rest, given back to the gods.

"We have done good Sadiqa today" said the priest Kohan Benel. "Surely the gods and the souls of the slain will guide us to righteous victory in battle."

As if they were ghosts summoned by sorcery, the emissaries of King Rib-Hadda arrived, bearing fine gifts. Blue glass, carnelian, fine linen garments and silver were offered. Then, they declared a message. " May the king, my lord, know that Gubla , the maidservant of the king from ancient times, is safe and sound. The war, however, of the Ḥabiru against me is severe. Our sons and daughters and the furnishings of the houses are gone, since they have been sold in the land of Yarimuta for provisions to keep us alive. For the lack of a cultivator, my field is like a woman without a husband. I have written repeatedly to the palace because of the illness afflicting me, but there is no one who has looked at the words that keep arriving. May the king give heed to the words of his servant."

"That" said Sutarna, "Is for Pharaoh's ears only. And I am not he!"

"You, Sutarna of Qadesh, are our last hope. Abdi-Ashtirta has made war on us besieging us in Shigata and Ampi! The chaos is such that the field is untended, and if it goes on like

112

this, the cities of the king will be lost!"

"How can we fight this war?" asked Sharrupshi, prince of Nuhhashe, "What's in it for us? We are not Ḥabiru, to accept gold as a price for blood. Among us are many Amorites, how can we make war on our brothers? "

Then a dark, silent hooded figure on the periphery of the delegation laid down his hood in anger and disgust. It was Rib-Hadda himself.

"I was resolved to do this the right way. To offer bread and oil, however short in supply on our side, to your great army. Prepared to offer terms of fraternity with your people, and to provide ships to carry grain from north to south for your troops. Our enemies are one and the same, what better is it to fight Lab'ayu's Ḥabiru in the South than to fight Abdi-Ashtirta's Ḥabiru here in the North? If you intend to have clear supply lines north to south for your army, you need the path clear and with Amurru controlling the countryside, that would be impossible."

"Perhaps we should make terms with Amurru instead!" balked Sharrupshi.

To keep the peace, Sutarna butted in, "Rib-Hadda, in a gesture of friendship and piety we buried your dead in full honor. We have neither quarrel with you, nor with Amurru. To ensure the supply lines, north to south, we are prepared to allow you to take one third of the produce sent from Nuhhashe to feed your people. Furthermore, we will negotiate with the King of Amurru on your behalf, so he may honor a truce. You will, in order to purchase the peace, give over to Abdi-Ashtirta the city of Ampi. Your people will be evacuated peacefully from the city which will not be given over to rapine and plunder."

"Why do you expect I will give in to those terms!" spat Rib-Hadda.

"Because you have no choice," Shisita stroked her chin as if she was a man with a beard, "it is your best option. You were to lose Ampi anyways, and now you will no longer lose Gubla and your own head as well."

"Take my plight as an example, Sutarna. See what loyalty to Pharaoh will grant you. I have forever honored my vassalage to Pharaoh, and he left me, bereft of friends to be devoured by the wolves!"

"You expect Pharaoh to serve you. The duty of us mayors is to always serve Pharaoh loyally. If you had done your duty, no trouble would befall you." said Akizzi.

"When trouble befalls you, Akizzi, remember how you said this to me." replied Rib-Hadda. "When your enemies are near, and friends are few, remember you did not aid your fellow."

19

Chapter 19: Weapons Raised in Anger

The forces of Milkilu, under the strong arm of Yapahu had made their way to the north following the road of Horus. They took pains to light extra fires along the way, increasing in number as they got closer to Ginti. His intent was to make the relatively small army appear decisive in number, and deter the forces of Lab'ayu from fighting. The greatest victory, after all, is the victory gained without bloodshed. If Lab'ayu could be made to leave the lands of Gezer and her allies without fighting, that would be perfect. Men do not grow on trees, especially warriors. However, little to the Mizrite's knowledge, the bulk of Lab'ayu's army was nowhere near Ginti, but to the south and the east fast approaching Muhazzu. Lab'ayu's army had used shepherds' paths, through the rough terrain most kings would say is unsuitable for an army. Shechem is a land of hills so Lab'ayu chanced to use the terrain to his advantage.

Yapahu's army was well equipped. His force mostly consisted of heavily armed and armored Na'arun infantry and Maryannu chariotry. Each fighter was clad with a coat of overlapping bronze scales and bronze helmets domed like onions to a point. For arms, they possessed khopesh swords, duck-billed socket axes and long spears, with richly painted shields in their left hands to act as a bulwark against the ferocity of the foe. Yapahu surveyed the men, shining in their splendor in the sun. These were the weapons of Gezer, the salvation of the brothers. But it had been so long since Gezer had ever fought anyone, so how well will these noble sons fare? Yapahu banished the thought of defeat from his mind. Such thoughts were unfitting of a General of Gezer.

Meanwhile, in the camp of Ayyabu, Issuwa, Dadua and Yishaya, an argument had broken out among the leaders. There was some disagreement over who was left in charge. Ayyabu, Lab'ayu's eldest, who had been given the leadership role by merit of his birth, had taken sick. It was rumored that his illness was pure fakery. The oldest son and heir of Lab'ayu took more young females as visitors in his tent than men of the medical profession. In the power vacuum, Issuwa attempted to claim seniority because he was the eldest. Yishaya contended that because he had the most men and the most experience, the command should be his. Dadua didn't have much of a basis for his claim to leadership, but he still continued to blather some sophistic argument that he should be in charge. The conflict came to a head over the "treatment of the enemy dogs". Yishaya the Dog Hater was feeding the dogs that the enemy had released, wasting good food in some vain attempt to remove his nickname. Issuwa was mostly unconcerned, as he was aware that their food supplies were more than ample, but his son Dadua was apoplectic. "Instead of feeding these enemy dogs, we should eat them, and post their heads on stakes to intimidate the enemy!" said Dadua.

"Listen here, Dadua, Issuwa, that it would be no boon at all to kill these Ginti hounds. Their masters released them believing that I would do exactly such a thing. What if, instead of eating these dogs, we feed our enemies to them? Our scouts report that Milkilu sent an army of green boys, under the pimp Yapahu, to relieve Ginti. I suggest we release the dogs on the army of Yapahu, and in the confusion, make kibbe of them. Then with Yapahu's head on a stake instead of mere dogs', all hope will be lost inside the city. It will fall without a fight, either by surrender or by betrayal."

"What is this nonsense? Have you been drinking spoiled goat's milk, dog-man?" said Dadua.

"What's gotten into youths these days! I swear by Rashpu's bow that when I was a young man we had respect for our elders!" Issuwa struck his son on the back of his head, and added, "Yishaya, your plan has merit. Let us grown men partake in the blood of the vine and plot the battle plan. As for you, Dadua, go chop down a tree. At least your anger can boil us a pot of chickpeas!"

With the course of war resolved by the elders and the wood gathered for the chickpea pot, the plan took effect. In order to conserve food resources and create ferocity in the hounds, the army began kidnapping local villagers and feeding them live to the dogs. Not only was it effective at feeding the hounds, but it proved both entertaining for the army and intimidating for the besieged. Many of them had loved ones that failed to flee from the Ḥabiru onslaught, and had to watch them get ripped apart and devoured by their own hounds. Talk of surrender was in the city, but the militant prostitutes and the Lions of 'Anat silenced all talk on the matter. Tagi himself was eager to surrender the city but he had long since lost control of the situation and the city. Tagi would not give up his brave attempt at cowardice so easily…

On a beautiful spring day when the seeds would have been planted if not for the war, Yapahu blew the ram's horn and attacked. His chariots, gleaming in the sun like fiery stars, were let loose. The sound of the horses' gallop was like that of a great earthquake. Of course, the Ḥabiru were fully prepared. They had dug pits in the ground in front of the camp, filled them with sharp spikes doused in excrement, and covered over the top with some branches and turf. The horses, thundering like the roar of war drums, charged headlong into the trap. They fell face first into the deep pits. Horse meat was made into instant kebabs, seasoned with their own blood and the feces of men and dogs. The charioteers, the best and most experienced warriors in Gezer, were thrown from their chariots. Most lay, mangled on the ground, bitterly broken. Ḥabiru warriors rushed to them, and the charioteers expecting to be rescued and sold for ransom put out their hands and cried out for aid. To their surprise, they were brutally dispatched. This was not a petty war of prisoners and genteel captors. This was Ḥabiru war.

118

Then the Ḥabiru began looting the dead and wounded for their armor and superior weapons. Yapahu, believing the enemy thoroughly distracted, sent in his infantry. As they passed around the pits, Yishaya released the hounds towards the enemy from the rear. The hounds bounded in like hungry wolves, and leapt upon the Gezerites from all directions, pushing many infantrymen into the pits where the dead and dying horses lay. Some men were impaled, others still were kicked to death by dying steeds. Some had their throats ripped out by hungry dogs. This was too much for the denizens of Ginti. They sallied out, much to the surprise of the Ḥabiru, and cleared a path to the city of Ginti. Seeing their opportunity to save themselves, many Gezerites fled into the safety of the city. Hundreds of soldiers were killed trying to enter Ginti, either trampled underfoot by the pressure of their comrades or slain by the enemy striking them from behind.

"Men!" shouted Yishaya, "Let's take the initiative, and the city!"

The Ḥabiru charged ahead. Those beautiful cedar wood gates were open to them. Soon they would open the legs of the legendary courtesans of Ginti... and not even need to pay for the privilege.

"The ugly sons of donkeys are coming" said Rimatu, a militant madam, "Normally I say, open the doors to them and just raise the price. Pu!" She spat, and it flew over the ramparts and dampened the helmet of a Ḥabiru beneath her. "If I can shoot my spit and hit the sons of shoes, surely you can give

119

them a taste of their own medicine," She grasped a javelin and a bow and arrow, "With these. Poke them good!"

The Ḥabiru were having a grand old time killing Gezerites who were trying to escape into the city of Ginti. At least, until they started to suffer the slings and arrows of outrageous whores. They were used to penetrating... not being penetrated. Bracing themselves behind shields, they ran off to kill easier prey. The whores had won their skirmish. However, Gezer sorely lost the battle.

Seeing his force in haste either cut to pieces or fleeing like cowards, Yapahu followed the example of the latter. He set out back to Gezer, barely escaping with his life. As he sped away with as much haste as his horses could manage, the cacophony of screams pursued him. Even when he was clear of the sound of the battle, he still heard the pitiable cries ringing in his ears. This was a true defeat. Though he had considered losing intentionally, he never could have predicted what losing would mean. The wounds, both of body and spirit, would sit long in the memory of the survivors. Now when Yapahu slept, there could be no more rest.

Yapahu had regrouped with the survivors a few miles outside Ginti. Trying his best to instill order, Yapahu insisted they march home in disciplined order, same as how they came. In truth, the men shambled more than marched. Once, along the road, a small yappy dog came to the army with its owner, an eight-year-old boy. The boy had come to sell food and drink to the men. His dog's bark, though that of a petite lap dog not a fierce hound, reminded all the men of the defeat they suffered. Morale was harmed. So Yapahu, as fatigued as any of his men, ordered the dog be killed. It was intended to be a merciful killing, a simple clean cut across the nape of the neck with a dagger. Instead, the beleaguered troops took out all their fury, their frustration, their martial savagery: on a puppy. The dog suffered kicks, stabs, cuts. Its bones were broken, and its eyes torn out. The dog was mutilated, mauled, and manipulated as a puppet. They took up the crushed and bloody body of the dog upon their spear and called it "Yishaya". Needless to say, the boy was shocked; he didn't understand. His beloved family dog did the soldiers no harm, he thought. But he knew not to question Yapahu. He could be killed as dead as the dog. Silence dawned at last on the sons of Gezer. They had offered their blood to the earth. Will the goddess of war ever be sated?

No, Virgin 'Anat will never, ever, be sated.

20

Chapter 20: The Seduction

Now that the unclean dead bodies were disposed of, the virgin Shisita needed to bathe to rid herself of the filth. Or so she told Yassib. Despite being a virgin, and the value of that in her society, she had desires; as do all men and women. Yassib was meant to glimpse her nakedness, and deflower her in the cool waters of the Adonis river so she could take him for a husband. Was it love, or the desire for a family, or mere lust that swelled in her? Even she didn't know. Her ambition, if it could be called that, was as ill-formed as the Pharaoh's son. No one told him of her ambition. He did come to the river, and bathed alongside her, in the cool water, but he did not take notice of her beauty, or even raise his manly spear. She was a little put off; she wanted him, yet he seemed totally unaware of her desires. She decided to be a little more explicit.

"Would you wrestle me, oh Yassib, and test your manly vigor?" She touched his breast with her strong hand in a coy way. He batted her hand away, laughing. She had hoped that that referencing his manly vigor would spur him to manly action.

"I would, and if I don't throw you I'll be a monkey in a kilt!"

Shisita was surprised to find his wrestling entirely firm, and not seductive. She had no hatred of the pain of being thrown, for she wrestled many times. He was likewise surprised that her touch was too gentle. He was perplexed, but happy to be beating her. It must be a cunning strategy, he thought. Then she changed her strategy, and threw him with all her strength. Yassib landed on his back prone in the shallow water. There was little time for Yassib to react before Shisita mounted his waist, expecting the warm feeling of her wet nethermouth against his skin would at last raise his spear. But instead of that, he laughed and clapped.

"At last you are fighting worthy of your strength! Now get up and I will beat you in the next bout!"

"I will not! You will stay here till I am through with you!" and she started kissing him. Her kisses gave herself pleasure, she loved feeling her lips against the body of her victim. If he was nearly any other man, he would have either fainted of pleasure or returned the kisses heartily. But he was Yassib, and his way was... different.

"What a peculiar tactic! What do you mean by this?"

"Love" she said, "And my passion"

"I have a lover" he cried, "And what would they think of this

123

shameful display?

"A lover! Who is this whore! I'll have at her!"

"Not a she... I'm in love with your father"

Stunned totally, Shisita leapt up and beat a hasty retreat. What in the name of the gods is going on? Questions circled her head like eagles ready to peck out her liver. She didn't stop running until she was all alone in the forest. She was unsure whether to weep, laugh, or curse the gods. So she did what frustrated people do when they don't know what in the world is going on. She masturbated. Once her itch subsided, she would think of Yassib no more. As for Yassib, he would not soon forget this assault, even though he dared speak of it to no one. It was shameful enough to be a receiver, but to spurn the advances of the most beautiful and eligible woman in Canaan? He decided it was best not to speak to anyone about the incident; and pray Shisita does likewise. They could bear the load of shame like two chariot horses. They would gallop on, as if nothing ever came between them. But their friendship was over. Yassib's epithet, 'The Finger-Taker", once so manly, took on a whole new meaning.

21

Chapter 21: Ants Bite the Peacock — Part 1

"What do you think the gods up there are thinking of us right now?" Tamar bit Ammunapi pointed at a silvery cloud illuminated by the full moon. On the roof of her house, the two lovers could see each star, each planet with great clarity. Such was the smallness of Muhazzu, the lack of light there.

"What gods?" asked Addadanu, "I don't see anyone in the sky. Nothing in the sky to distract me from your beauty on earth."

"You are kindly, good and handsome…" Tamar kissed her lover's cheek, "but try to at least think of something they could be thinking, those deities of stars, moon and planets…"

"They are probably thinking of coming down here and kissing those perfect breasts themselves!" Addadanu suckled at his lover's nipple, "But hands off gods, these bosoms are mine! Anyway, why don't we have another taste of the halwa..."

"Oh, Addadanu, you never tire! We are going at it like Enkidu with Shamhat..."

"Who-du and what-hat?"

"The Wildman, Enkidu, and the Harlot, Shamhat... from the stories of Gilgamesh?"

"Oh, Tamar, why do you try to impress me with words when you have beauty for it?"

"I don't mean to make you feel like a fool, Addadanu." Tamar kissed Addadanu's forehead.

"I'm not a wild man... I shave from my neck to my toes..." Addadanu pulled his loincloth up, "see my perfectly smooth eggs!"

"Oh, what I would give to be the mistress of those eggs..." said Tamar, "But your eggs answer to no one. Or everyone."

Addadanu was enjoying his time governing the town of Muhazzu, despite the war. While he put the men to work erecting passable stone and mudbrick defenses, he took company with their wives and daughters. It became an enjoyable if mundane routine. Monday: Irqati, the young and beautiful (but dreadfully dull) daughter of the miller. Then Tuesday: Amat-Shurrupat, the experienced and well sexed wife of a local landlord. She had been playing the adultery game long before Addadanu came along, and played it well. Then Wednesday: Qamarti, the naughty little slave girl that liked to play rough and knew how to use her teeth and nails to her advantage. Then Thursday, back to Irqati for a palette and wound cleanser.

Finally, Friday, Saturday and Sunday was spent with the one who was by far his favorite, Tamar bit Ammunapi, the bastard daughter of a local Egyptian official. She was the person who was the de facto ruler of Muhazzu; she was as clever as Addadanu was foolish. Meaning to say, she was very, very clever. But he cared not for her wits, but for another of her assets. She had the largest, most pronounced and luscious breasts and the narrowest and most slender waist, tapering into hips that sailed ships… and docked phalli. Especially for a shallow and stupid man like Addadanu, these surface details won love even while her better virtues were ignored. She was not blind to the effect his courtship of her had on the jealousy of the populace. They whispered, and Tamar's spies heard, that Addadanu should be given over to the Ḥabiru when they come. He would be dealt with rightly (as the cause of this baneful war) and the town would be spared the deprivations of a siege.

On a verdant and sunny day on the fifth day of the spring month of Nisanu, a merchant entered the town of Muhazzu.

"You poor folks, I'm telling you, I really feel for you. Better get out now when the getting is good, no?"

"What is the matter? Tell us, do not leave us in ignorance!"

"Well, you all know that Milkilu sent an army up to Ginti to relieve them from their siege."

"And?"

"I got a good sight of them, though I must say the smell hit me before I could get a good look. Those poor boys, now they take after Kibbe more than living men. A pity on their mothers, I must say. If you have any sense at all, I'd suggest you don't be here when Lab'ayu comes through. As for me, I'm going to make straight for Egypt without stopping to sell along the way. I'm not taking any chances in Gezer."

The townspeople of Muhazzu decided in secret to put on a good show of resisting Lab'ayu before they would surrender and turn over the city and Addadanu to him. A month, they thought, was enough time that they would have a fair excuse to give up; food would be low and their honor would be mostly intact. But to their utter surprise and horror, not one week into the siege Addadanu had absconded from the city and no one knew where he went. They then discovered his note, scrawled incomprehensibly on an ostraca, saying, "I left the city to get fresh troops from Tjaru. I'll return soon. Until then, Tamar bit Ammunapi is in charge" and a badly drawn stick figure smiling and winking with a crudely drawn erect phallus.

"What shall we do now?!" bemoaned the village elders.

128

"Addadanu was our bargaining chip! I'd have gladly handed him over to Lab'ayu, but now, who could we hand over to the enemy? Tamar? Gods forbid!"

"Perhaps we could wait for him to return with the Archers?" Suggested Irqati.

"Perhaps we should jump on daggers and burn ourselves alive too!"

" 'The Peacock' is not reliable. We need to find a way we can surrender. Do any of you have any handsome slaves that could pass for him." They spent hours trying to find a surrogate.

"If I had a slave like that bastard, I would be pimping him out and make a fortune" said an accosted slave master, "and I would not have to live in piteous little Muhazzu."

Outside the city, in Lab'ayu's camp there was another story entirely.

22

Chapter 22: Ants Bite the Peacock — Part 2

"Lab'ayu, Mutba'alu! It is as I said, they made this nut tougher to crack!" explained Abneru, "We may have underestimated Addadanu."

"How will we take it? Time is of the essence!" asked Lab'ayu.

"We can throw men at it, with ladders, and rams, but there is always a better way. Sometimes we can trick them into coming out and fighting us, and slip in when they retreat. Or we can send in infiltrators, they can bribe or slaughter the guards and open the gates for us. The latter is risky to the spies we send but it is the plan that bears the best hope of speedy success, with least loss of life. Well, at least on our end. The enemy is properly minced." Abneru winked, mouth slightly drooling from the thought of eating tasty Kibbe. He found his mind often turned to thoughts of food when he contemplated violence.

"Who should we send to take the city?"

"I'll have five picked men, each a strong climber and skilled with tongue and sword, and inconspicuous to boot. I will have them dressed as common farmers, and I'll have them enter in the dead of night. They will have the gate opened, and then our men will go through and that will be that. Sha-shu, qa-qu." Abneru flourished his hands as he made onomatopoeia of the sound of slashing and puncturing weapons.

"I will go." Insisted Mutba'alu. "I am fit for what is required, and I am eager to taste Gezerite blood. Those bastards suckle at the cock of Pharaoh like piglets at a sow's teet."

"Blood will be plentiful," replied Abneru, "When the city is breached. But what we would find most advantageous, is to secure the gate bloodlessly. It would be too great a risk to use the bronze sword when the weapon suited for it is the golden tongue, and the silver shekel."

"Will you object, father, saying I am your son and heir and too valuable to risk?"

"I shall not! If I see my son possess that most noble of virtues, courage, how can I reprimand him! You Mutba'alu, are valuable as a hero; that is what makes you my heir! Let your ancestral gods guide you, and do your duty rightly!"

Night fell, and Mutba'alu and his five inconspicuous picked men clothed themselves in the humble garments of farmers.

They hitched an ox to a heavy cart full of barley, onions, oil, wine, and cheese concealing some shining nuggets of gold. Mutba'alu guided the ox with a farmer's crook, bidding it go forward to the gate. The guards, seemingly easily fooled, allowed them in with hale and hearty hellos, bidding them peace, and thanks. Huzziwanda of Hanigalbat, a Ḥabiru who had some charisma, at least according to Abneru, hailed the captain of the guards. He then displayed the gold for their bribe.

"Harken, guardsmen, for rich men you shall be if you do as we bid you, and dead you will be if not, if not by our hands than at the hands of Lab'ayu our master! Better get rich and be away now than suffer the slings and arrows of unkind fate!"

"You think us fools, Ḥabiru, that we would have not noticed you to be infiltrators? We are, as a city, inclined to surrender, peaceably. Milkilu's appointed commander, Addadanu, the arch-scoundrel, has made off in the night without our prior knowledge, willing to sacrifice us to our fate. We will open the gates, and save Lab'ayu time and men taking the town. We only ask that our city be spared the rapine, arson and cruel sword that comes with a city's downfall. Will you now return to Lab'ayu, and carry out the request we bid you? We have, as a town, more quarrel with our overlord Milkilu than with any of you."

Huzziwanda pondered the idea. It seemed fair in his mind, and he caught no whiff of a trap. In truth, there was none. But unlike him, Mutba'alu had a nose that was keen at sniffing

132

out treachery, both real and imagined. He deemed this was not what they wanted at all. Certainly, it was not what he wanted at all. He wanted rapine and murder and arson to come to pass because those were the things his adolescent mind found both fun and especially manly.

"We accept your proposal" lied Mutba'alu, "just let us up on the wall so we can give the a signal that would convey your instruction to our men."

"Come on up, my good lad! You make your country proud." said the Captain as he lowered a rope. However, once Mutba'alu and his men were atop the wall, he seized the grizzled veteran by the scruff of the throat, and chucked him right over the wall. Mutba'alu then engaged the stunned and shocked guardsmen, who, with Mutba'alu's ferocity, cunning, and sheer heroism were overcome one by one. A little chop-chop to the left, a little stabby stabby to the right, and of course, the mother of all attacks, the skull-cracking back-spike blow that made the Khopesh a notorious weapon. Some guardsmen dropped their weapons and begged to be spared. They were the ones most easily slain. The other four Ḥabiru, the perplexed Huzziwanda excluded, made their heroic deeds apparent as well, killing many men and opening the gates, then sounding the signal to attack. Huzziwanda asked Mutba'alu, "Why did you do such a thing? The city was in our hands without blood!"

"You should know! It is for your death they shall suffer!" shouted Mutba'alu as he beheaded his cowardly comrade. "Let us avenge Huzziwanda. He died to take this town. Let's go kill them all!"

Then the army of Lab'ayu, stirred in the heart by the great signal, flooded into the city like a swarm of ants. Flame glew brilliant red-yellow, on the torches, then on the buildings. The cries of the men who were slain and the women who were raped resounded in the night air. Once the men of Shechem were near at hand, and the Ḥabiru besides, Mutba'alu had plunged sword first into the carnage. He had heard that among the Muhazzites there was a notable woman, the daughter of a Pharaonic official, and a lover of Addadanu. He wanted to take his personal revenge for his people, the Canaanites of Shechem for their slaying and raping at the hands of Egypt.

This woman would do nicely as a scapegoat. She was found by Mutba'alu in the governor's palace, bow and arrows in hand, dead Ḥabiru at her feet. Mutba'alu saw he was not the first of his men to have the idea. But he would ensure that her insolent resistance to their righteous revenge would not be suffered willingly. She shot at him with arrows, but Mutba'alu proved a faster runner and better with his shield than his groaning and dead colleagues. He was soon upon her and bashed the bow out of her hands with his shield, causing her to roughly fall to the floor, painfully spraining her ankle. Crying out in grief and pain, she struggled to stab him with her arrow and reach for salvation, her dagger. But both proved impossible in the grasp of the furiously jubilant Mutba'alu, who had never had such fun in his life.

He wrested the arrow from her hand and snapped it. He took

hold of the dagger first, and used it to cut away her beautiful garments like they were ears of wheat. He took precisely no care to avoid cutting her skin while he removed her clothes. Stinging wounds covered her body, her sensitive parts, and all she could do was wait, hoping for death. Death didn't come soon enough for her taste. Mutba'alu was, in point of fact, actually a virgin when it came to the carnal arts. He had been instructed by his mother to save himself for marriage to the beautiful woman he was betrothed to and loved in his adolescent days. Passion overcame his mother's prudence.

This woman would be a worthy start to a long campaign of spearing across Canaan and hopefully Egypt too. She was full breasted, which he had appreciation for, and it was not unknown to him that she had been a lover of Addadanu. *If I can take Addadanu's woman for his own, then I am surely a man of valor!* He became verile and hard at the thought of crushing Addadanu's skull with a bronze headed mace, and began penetrating her. She was actually absolutely paying no attention to the raping, but was dead-eyed, trying to ignore the pain of her bleeding cuts. Some were deep, and all were cloying with their bite.

"So how do you take to the spearing of a real man!" Mutba'alu slapped his victim in the face to get her attention.

"I take well to it! I am the lover of Addadanu, and he is a *real* man." she spat her blood and broken teeth at her assailant in defiance, "Oh, when he lays a hold of you scrawny boy, you are in for a world of pain..."

"Addadanu will do you no good!" when he lay his fists upon her body and wounds upon her honor she appeared as one unconcerned.

That was no good for Mutba'alu, he wanted to be noticed, and screamed at. Her uncanny lack of concern for his manly spear made him ashamed of it. He decided instead to do a deed so forbidden, only fabled libertines among women would allow it. He resolved to sodomize her. She genuinely was not expecting that, and screams of pain were not far from her lips as her flesh ripped in the back to make room for Mutba'alu's average length but quite thick organ. This was more than pain, this was more than death, this was an insult to her and she would not lie and take it! She fought with her teeth, her claws, but this indeed made Mutba'alu happier. This was what he wanted, not resigned surrender. The scratch on his face, the bite on his hand made Mutba'alu climax, but if Tamar thought this would save her, she was mistaken. He wanted now to cause her greater physical pain, in recompense a thousand measures more cruel for every drop of his blood upon her teeth and nails.

He used her own dagger to remove, one by one, her finger-nails from her flesh. This was beyond mere cuts to her, she wished for death, she begged him for him to place the dagger in her heart, or slice across her throat. But as her bleeding nailless fingers crossed her lovely breasts, Mutba'alu had a sinister idea for a dish he would serve to Addadanu when the man was in his power. He used his knife, efficiently and coldly to sever each one of her perfect, oversized mammaries. *I will preserve them in fat and salt, then have his beloved present*

136

her own mutilated and cooked body parts to him. Mutba'alu desired the Peacock sup on them, the first of many cruel tortures for that cowardly pimp.

In the midst of the chaos of pillage and rape, stood a figure alone upon a gilded chariot. Lab'ayu had come into the city with the manly vigor of a hero from legend. He recited lines from the Epic of Ba'alu while he cut down the foe. *Your name, even yours, is Yagrush. Yagrush, drive Yam, drive Yam from the seat of his lordship. You will swoop from the hands of Ba'alu like an eagle from his fingers. Strike between the shoulders of prince Yam. May he sink and fall to the earth.*

In his delusion, he saw himself as the glorious hero of the gods, Ba'alu. He made mincemeat of the citizens of Muhazzu imagining them as the demonic thralls of Yam, the Tyrant king of the gods who in his sexual miscreancy raped his own mother. When he looked through the eyes of battle, he saw differently than what was there. He saw heroism, the courage of his men. He saw the scores he slayed both male and female as less than human. The clatter of weapons was the plucking of a harp, the howls of the dying was the choir of heaven.

Yet another sound would pierce the din of battle. In almost miraculous fashion it's quietness drowned out the cacophony in the ear of Lab'ayu. Heroism and cruelty are manifestations of perception. Lab'ayu found the shocking sound that drew his eye to the site that changed his perception. A young, plain faced woman knelt, infant in her arm. She placated the heaven, calling on Ba'alu to save her. Her veiled head she lifted upwards in supplication to the sky. Lab'ayu heard her

137

prayer, and looked upon her. He looked around. Where he once saw a glorious contest between good and evil, he now saw how his actions have harmed the innocent. A cry of pain was now a cry of pain. The slaughter of the innocent lost its glory. Lab'ayu had fantasized about war his whole life. His mother, father, and Priest told tales of battle. Ba'alu's battle with Yam, 'Anat's battle with Mot, Durusha's rebellion against Pharaoh.

It was all a lie, or at least incomplete. Real war wasn't heroes wielding legendary weapons against the forces of evil. Lab'ayu sickened; he had no stomach for what he saw. There was no fight in him to pull the men off from their conquest. He just stood from his chariot, feeling the blood of those he had slain drip off his sword and lance onto his sandaled feet. He thought, "How can I make my war good, how can I take the evil I bring and make a good result?" As Muhazzu burned, Lab'ayu awoke. It was as if he had eaten from the Tree of the Knowledge of Good and Evil. In wisdom, he found his tragic sin. If only all sinners but realized their sins, and those that did ever deigned to put a stop to them.

If only it were so easy.

23

Chapter 23: Reunion of the Road

Yapahu and his reserve troops marched again along the back roads, using hidden paths as his conveyance and ancient caves as shelter. These ways he knew like the back of his hands (which he plucked daily with little gold tweezers). Now it was not hope of victory but fear of annihilation that motivated their stealth. Yapahu gathered information from local villagers, and found that the town of Muhazzu had fallen to the Ḫabiru and Lab'ayu. The breadth of the land was abounding in Ḫabiru and Shechemite warriors, if the villagers were to be trusted. Thanking the informants, Yapahu gave them each a gold nugget as big as a chickpea. He loved giving gold to the poor. A little gold could turn a dismal life into a prosperous one for these honest folks. Despite his charitable mood, he still warned them, "If you turn us in to Lab'ayu for a greater reward, Milkilu will find out and have you and your loved ones burned alive as an offering to God and send your daughters to be bed-slaves in Egypt. He's not as kind as me."

When a rambunctious kid asked "How will Milkilu know we turned you in! You won't be there to tell him."

Yapahu looked him deep into the boy's eyes, and told him, "Through Nubian blood magic…. Siaspiqa, Shabaka, Shebiku…".

The boy ran and hid behind his mother. The words that were, in fact, no more than the names of random soldiers that Yapahu had befriended, had the effect of deadly sorcery. Even though the Canaanites feared the Ḥabiru, it was the Nubian Pitati that they feared most. Milkilu traded on his status as a half-Nubian to intimidate when he needed to. Lightening the mood, Yapahu purchased at a generous cost humble garments akin to what the Ḥabiru wore. Each man was outfitted in a white, blue and orange kilt. The villagers were greatly pleased with the profit they made. Carrot and stick, thought Yapahu, is how you train a donkey.

Addadanu had been doing his own interrogations as he beat his randy strut home to Gezer. He had on him the garb of a general of Gezer, with shining armor, powerful bow and a carnelian and lapis lazuli studded Akinakes of Elamite make. He cut an imposing figure, stately and handsome, and mighty in appearance. This was a part he played well until he opened his mouth and words came out. However, not long into his traveling orgy, his head was struck by a slight pebble of worry. The worrisome detail that he came by after vigorously questioning other men's wives and daughters was this; a band of Ḥabiru, well armed and coming from the direction of Ginti was taking the back roads making excellent time going in the same direction Addadanu was. He then spent the war gold appropriated from the stores of Muhazzu to raise a peasant militia. He had figured out by now that the less he said, the more he could convince men to follow him. He gave the same quantity of gold to men who fought for him as he gave for girls he screwed. A small grain about the size of a lentil. Sometimes, when he was feeling cheeky, he'd steal back the gold he gave them while they slept. If caught, he would take it in jest, and give them extra. He was usually not caught.

The militia was armed with simple farming implements, hunting bows and slings. He made some effort to drill them, but soon realized the more they trained the more their inadequacy was revealed, and morale was hit. At least, besides one noticeable exception. The men were able slingers, having used the simple weapon for fending off wild beasts from their goats and sheep. Addadanu decided that if they could successfully ambush the enemy, they could deal a crushing defeat to the Ḥabiru, and win himself a stunning military reputation. If he can win a victory with mere peasants his status would be raised above his brother, and he would get the respect he knew he deserved.

Addadanu and his spindly serf slingers waited in ambush along a particularly choice ambush location. Yapahu would have recognized the danger, and delayed the march to reconnoiter. This always irked his impatient and lazy brother. While now he saw the value of his brother's foresight, he relished the opportunity to make the decisions on his own. Hidden behind rocks and dry brush, Addadanu and the peasants waited for their time to pounce. When night fell, a dust cloud appeared along the horizon, and men obscured by it marched through the ravine. He was so focused on the men ahead, that he did not notice the scout sneaking behind him until called by his name. He leapt to his feet and started brutally stabbing the boy with his akinakes; a thrust to the shoulder, scraping the front of the boy's scapula, then several quick stabs to the guts, leaving blood and viscera all over the bejeweled weapon.

"Why are you killing me, I am a man of Gezer come to..."

"A spy! Gag his mouth so he can't call out to his fellows!"

The peasants gagged him, and even after he breathed no more Addadanu had at him. Thrusting was a skill Addadanu had acquired in the bedchamber, but he put it to use in this bloody contest. After he was done, the ignorant peasants had a go at it too. This scout, scarcely fourteen years old, was killed by the brother of his own king. Food for the eagles, Addadanu thought. His thoughts turned from how to cover up his crime to how to obscure it in glory.

Then the army passing through halted, waiting to hear back from the scout. Addadanu hesitated, then thought of a cunning plan, and outfitted one of his peasant boy's in the garments of the recently dispatched scout. *They'll never know the difference!* The boy, now dressed in the blood stained kilt, went out, somewhat apprehensively. When he arrived at the camp, he declared the information Addadanu had bid him to tell to the troops below.

142

"Path completely clear, absolutely no ambush!"

"Why are your garments covered in blood?" asked Yapahu.

"I shot a rabbit," replied the boy.

"Where's the rabbit?"

"It got away."

"Where is your bow?"

"I used a sling."

"We have no slingers, arrest him. He is a Ḥabiru spy"

"I thought we all were Ḥabiru..."

"What!?"

Yapahu looked at the boy. This was not the boy he sent out to scout. That boy had a pretty face and refined speech. Not this lad. This lad was missing too many teeth. But there was something that looked familiar about him.

"I remember you! Your sister was among the maidens we sent to Pharaoh some five years hence!"

"You... you are Yapahu! Not Ḥabiru at all!"

"And I'll take it you're not either, you're just a lad of the

143

Shephelah, brave and loyal to Gezer!"

"I am, lord, and Addadanu would be glad to see you! He
thought you were all Ḥabiru so he laid a little ambush for you!
My gods, that scout you sent out! He must have been one of
yours! We did him in, poor bugger! Pity!" The boy mimed
out the frenzied jabs of Addadanu. He laughed, but restrained
it before he got himself done in by the boy's brothers and
cousins.

"We'll have to strip off our Ḥabiru clothing here, men. We are
in friendly territory now. Get your native garb on!" Yapahu
led the way by undoing his belt and letting his kilt fall to the
ground.

Then all the men and boys stripped naked and changed into
Gezerite clothes. Meanwhile, Addadanu's spies reported
back to their leader that the enemy was stripping and putting
on Gezerite garb to confuse them into lowering their guard.
"That would never fool a clever man like me!" shouted
Addadanu, "We'll catch them with their kilts down! Then
we'll have them, right up their bottoms!"

Thinking of themselves as lions and tigers and other manly,
vicious and cruel beasts, Addadanu and his ignorant peasants
fell upon the true warriors of Gezer, who were both nude
and defenceless. Slingstones flew, cracking skulls and arrows
loosed, landing sometimes in most unfortunate places. A
handsome lad by the name of Damu-Addi wound up with an
arrow piercing right through his scrotum. He had just been
married before the war to a great beauty, the love of his life.

Now an arrow had pierced his manhood; it may as well have pierced his heart. He would now bid farewell to his dream of fatherhood.

Yapahu, hiding behind a shield, kept peeking out from behind his protection to reveal his face and get Addadanu's attention.

"Yoo hoo! Addadanu! We are from Gezer!"

"And I'm a donkey-headed-snake-tailed-chimera-monkey! Men, keep shooting, let them have it!"

"Brother, I am Yapahu!" He pushed his way forward past his beleaguered men, and by a sheer stroke of dumb luck, his naked body was not hit by any missiles. "As you can see brother I have nothing to hide!"

Addadanu halted the shooting. If this was a trick it was utterly convincing. That man was the spitting image of Yapahu. His bald head, his bulbous nose, his hairy and circumsized organ, all exactly the same as those of Addadanu's brother. In fact, the circumcision was a dead give away. It was a custom of Egypt. No Ḥabiru Addadanu knew of would have a circumcised member.

"If I am to let you go free of my trap, Pseudo-Yapahu, you will be my footman. You will obey my every command, and not nag me, or interrupt me as I speak. I am to give the commands, and you to meekly obey, and if you refuse, I'll have your head as a Ḥabiru spy."

145

"If I were to be willing and confident to go ahead with that, I would be no true Yapahu. I know you well brother, and commanding is not your strong right hand. I've missed you terribly brother, and both you and I know there can't be in all Canaan another man as fetching as I."

He approached his brother boldly, kissed both of his cheeks, and patted his back.

"If you had been Ḫabiru, I'd have done well." stated Addadanu.

"If we had been Ḫabiru, you'd have been dead. Men, finish getting your clothes on. We must move hastily."

"What about the wounded?" chirped the new-made eunuch Damu-Addi.

"They," sneered Addadanu, "will keep up, or get left behind."

Damu-Addi wrenched the arrow from his testicles.

"Well that's a sight!" chortled Addadanu, "blood and fishies!"

Only Addadanu could have mirth at such a misfortune, thought Yapahu. He was wrong. Only Yapahu could love a stranger enough not to laugh at Addadanu's infantile joke. Morale was lifted among the soldiers. At least, besides for Damu-Addi. He would have to suffer the pain of his wound and the humiliation of raunchy songs all the way back to Gezer.

24

Chapter 24: Love is Like a Game

The Pharaoh's seal was passed back and forth, rolling over documents to leave the indelible mark of the Pharaoh's assent. This was not done at his behest. The man was bedridden. It was his wife, and her... friend... who carried out the work of state.

"Have you heard from the 'Lady of the Lions'?" asked Ay.

"Oh, almost forgot about her. Pardon me." Tiye coughed, then lifted a well laid-out tablet onto her writing desk, "She says... needs more troops, dissent in the ranks... chaos in Canaan... that's not good. How about this? I've been reading Gilukhepa's correspondence..."

"She can't be trusted." said Ay.

"I KNOW THAT. But at least she can be trusted not to be trusted. Now I've heard king Shuttarna of Mitanni has a problem with his bastard prince, Etakkama."

"Bastards are always a problem." Ay laughed, "We should know…"

"Oh you…" Tiye pinched his cheek, "He needs to deal with his treacherous son, but doesn't wish to deal with… you know what I mean. Let's put this Mitannian to use. Sutarna the king of Qadesh lacks an heir. He has three perfectly good daughters, but he lacks an heir." Tiye sighed.

"Why are you looking at me? I didn't set the law for these Asiatic savages!"

"Let's give this Etakkama an opportunity. He will prove his mettle, and his loyalty to us, and thereby win himself an honored seat."

"And a beautiful bride…" Ay hummed the wedding hymn, jokingly.

"And all that nonsense. I rule the world and still I have to kowtow to these vile Asiatic customs."

"Enough of those damned Canaanites. Let's deal with the matters of Egypt!" Ay sneered, "As we all know, your *husband* can't control his own bowel movements, much less Egypt."

"He's dealt with. It's my son I'm concerned with now." Tiye recollected the events that transpired on the day of rest.

On the tenth and final day of the week, Amenhotep the

Younger and some of his followers gathered outside the largest and most important temple in all Egypt, the temple of Karnak. They each had in one hand a torch, and in their other a stout chisel. The operation was long-planned in utter secrecy, so even Tiye didn't know about it until it was too late. Like a long line of pilgrims, singing and loudly shuffling their feet as they walked, they entered the temple. Amenhotep led them through the dark and grandly decorated halls. Amidst pillars seventy feet high, Amenhotep pointed out where to begin his sacred work. With fierce clacks of metal on stone, he chipped away at hieroglyphic texts mentioning Amun. Dust from chipped stone and paint filled the moist air of the temple, turning to mud in the lungs of the devotees of the two gods. At first, the Priests of Amun were polite, asking them to leave and to respect the sanctuary of the holiest of gods. The prince ignored them at first, continuing his sacrilegious work, paying them no heed. Eventually, they decided to call the Medjay, those skillful Nubians who served as police in Egypt, to peacefully remove the Prince and his cultists of Aten from the sanctuary. Being led into the sanctuary, the Medjay, in the bluster of policemen throughout time, talked big game about all the nasty things they would do to these heretical intruders.

"We shall feed his balls to the crocodiles!" boasted Mahu, "And his liver to the ibis!"

The fearful priests didn't inform the Medjay that it was the Co-Pharaoh of Egypt that violated their shrine and that it was a quite sensitive situation. If the axe was to fall on someone for dealing with the heretic Pharaoh, better it was some common Medjay. When the Medjay arrived, the cultists were still diligently and studiously vandalizing.

"God knows why these fool priests put the confines of their sanctum in complete darkness! A temple to a sun god must be kept open air, to let the soft rays land on our skin, and bless us with its mark." preached Akhenaten.

"Who is it that disturbs and disrespects the holy precincts of the god Amun!" said Mahu, chief of the Medjay. He clacked the metal tip of his arrow against the bone and sinew bow on his shoulder.

"It is I, Pharaoh Amenhotep, fourth of my name, vile as it is, and prophet of the true sun. The radiant Aten blesses us all, from the hairy Asiatic to the handsome sons of Kush."

"My lord… I mean no disrespect. It is just… a great inequity you be doing at the temple, a great sin!"

"I think, Medjay, that it is these priests who sinned. Would you, a Kushite, a Nubian, ever be allowed into the Temple to worship? No, they hold that their god is exclusive for them alone, and the better part of the produce of the land they take, steal even, as tithes. Egypt and the world have no need of this oppressive cabal, taking the fat of the land, letting the peasants toil yet starve."

The Medjay who were often treated as mere muscle were now being treated as human beings and by the Pharaoh no

150

less. And his words were convincing too, no doubt about it.

"Don't listen to his heresy. Do as Medjay are meant to do and get him out of here. He is no true Pharaoh as long as his father still lives!"

"He is a Pharaoh. You are a priest. We have no place in your quarrel. Please sirs, we are just Medjay."

And those Kushite warriors retreated the way they came. Meanwhile, the word got out that Amenhotep was vandalizing the sanctum of Karnak, and clashes broke out between traditionalists and cultists on the streets. Stones and potsherds were thrown as projectiles, and many on both sides were horrifically maimed. This is not to mention the innocents, women, children, and the elderly that were pelted and trampled merely for standing on the wrong side of the street. There could only be one group of people this chaos could be good for. Egypt's enemies. Gilukhepa, the Mitanni spy, was a serious risk of information getting out of Thebes. If thye found Egypt was weak, Shuttarna's sons may take advantage to go past the border at the Euphrates and seize some Egyptian vassal cities in Syria. That was a threat, but the bigger threat was Hatti. If the Hatti prince Shuppiluliuma found out Egypt was consumed by strife, he could storm through Syria to Egypt; no one was safe. She knew that a few centuries before, the Ancestors of Shuppiluliuma had invaded Babylon, the mightiest kingdom in the world, sacked it's capital, toppling the prestigious Amorite dynasty of Hammurabi. The idol of Marduk was taken to Hattusha and only through diplomatic overtures was the New Kassite

151

Dynasty of Babylon able to restore it to its temple, the Esagila. Egypt could all too easily share the same fate. Tiye resolved to restrain her son's impulsive urges. She will yoke his wild bull spirit with the bonds of matrimony, with a girl of such beauty and charms that love will ensue. Many had been the times when Tiye had restrained her husband in their youth. Surely the same could be done with the Younger Pharaoh.

There was only one real choice for a wife for her son, someone she could count on to act as her loyal puppet. The girl in question had beauty and charms that were legendary despite her young age. Furthermore, she had sufficient social status to be a Great Royal Wife. She was Nefertiti, the daughter of Ay, the high priest of Min at Akhmim. Ay's family had deep ties to Tiye's. Tiye was raised in Akhmim, her father Yuya was the high priest of Min there. Yuya had taken the boy Ay into his care and made him a prodigy, teaching him all the sacred texts of Min. Ay was said to have his appearance and was made High Priest of Min as a successor to Yuya, as Yuya's son Ineb was made a high priest of Amun, a more prestigious position. Tiye was meant to marry Ay, and the two were lovers and close confidants for nearly their whole lives. Of course, Tiye was destined for greater things, being married off to the Pharaoh Amenhotep III, but there were some, including the pharaoh who suspected that his younger son, the hideous Amenhotep IV was sired by Ay. But Tiye and Ay had become too powerful to act against, so nothing came of the elder Pharaoh's suspicions besides his ire for the young Co-Pharaoh.

Now, the time came for the Queen to meet her Princess-to-be, and for her to ascertain the skills that must calm the stormy heart of the Prince, so filled with violence. Tiye went to the young woman, and what she saw moved her to sapphic pangs, such was the beauty of this maiden. Her neck was long and elegant, her lips perfectly formed into the right size and shape. Her jawbone was pronounced and strong, formed into a triangle shape. Her body, slender and willowy, yet womanly and comely. She had large eyes that shone like the morning star, beckoning the hearts of men and even women to stare longingly.

"What do you think of my maiden daughter, Nefertiti, is she suitable for our ends?" asked the proud father, Ay.

"She has all of your best features, Ay. And a few more. For the eyes, she is suited. But does she have the training in the arts of wedcraft?"

"It would spoil her chastity" rebuffed Ay, "She is perfectly innocent I assure you!" He lifted up the translucent linen garment that concealed her young nethermouth. The slit was as narrow as a blade of wheat, and only as long as a honey bee.

"That will not do. That will not do at all. You know, Ay, that there are ways of training a girl by which her chastity, if not her innocence, is maintained."

"If you have such a method, I leave it to you to train her. You will find her as quick to learn as any girl you'll see."

"I'll need to work with her. She must be ready. Beauties are seductive in themselves, but if they lack skill they are used and thrown away like plucked flowers. With a little training, under the care and supervision of a mistress of the art, she will be ready to be a Great Royal Wife, beloved concubine, and slave girl all in one. She shall ever have his ear, and her words shall be ours. He will have her ear, and his plans will be forewarned to us."

Tiye led the innocent and pure girl off to the Queen's quarters. Once the door was sufficiently blocked, she laid the innocent beauty on the bed and asked her to disrobe. The obedient Nefertiti was astonishingly willing, showing she had been at least somewhat trained before. Tiye took a polished granite phallus from the ivory box where she kept it. Tiye demonstrated a few exercises and techniques, explaining fellation with precision and detail. "The only thing more important than the action of the lips and the tongue in the simulation of the glans is the avoidance of using the teeth in most circumstances. The man's phallus is often portrayed as a symbol of masculinity, but it is more advantageous to treat it like something sensitive and thin-skinned like an infant, especially when it is in your mouth. A slight nibble can cause agony for even the most virile men, and that will spoil your power over them."

"How do you know such things, my queen?" asked Nefertiti.

"The woman who desires power and influence requires such knowledge. I have some secret papyri that outline the theory, but experience is gained by practice alone."

154

Nefertiti enjoyed the feeling of these lessons, and learned happily, respecting Tiye for her skill and care. Nefertiti was sure a man's phallus was not something cold and lifeless like the granite phallus Tiye possessed, and Nefertiti wished to try her skill on an organ of flesh. What she did astonished Tiye, almost as much as it aroused her.

"What you are doing Nefertiti," moaned Tiye, "Is something vile and unnatural. But I enjoy it, and it may be good practice, so please continue."

She was not really an innocent girl it seemed. She was a talented power-monger, in the feminine tradition, a mistress of manipulation. She was exactly what Tiye wanted. Or so she thought. The power, the learning, the application, the manipulation: the ways of Egypt.

25

Chapter 25: The Vanquished Heroes Return

One week before the arrival of Lab'ayu at the outskirts of Gezer, Yapahu and Addadanu entered the gate of the city. To assuage any sense of foreboding for the populace, Milkilu ordered that his two brothers be greeted with the pomp and ceremony of victorious heroes, however contrary the truth may be. The drums coughed their heavy penetrating rhythm in pulsing pounding beats. The castanets clacked the piercing, inspiring clatter that moves men to clap, and the women to shake their hips. Reed pipes squeaked their sunny, intricate, lilting melody from the mouths of breathy blowers. In the first chariot stood the blissful ignoramus. Addadanu was caught up in the festive atmosphere, believing the gambit. He was all too happy to be the conquering hero, already forgetting about the odious situation he had abandoned Muhazzu to. He waved, raised his weapons high, and blew kisses to all the pretty girls he saw. Compared to that backwater Muhazzu, Gezer was like a Serengeti of abundant maidens for hunting. Addadanu's hunger was like that of a lion.

In the second chariot was one who understood the true nature of this pseudo-celebration. Yapahu was trying to conceal his fear and anguish behind faltering smiles. No one would have been convinced by his performance. But that being said, everyone was focused on his majestic and beautiful brother Addadanu, who was in every way like their perception of a true hero. Yapahu knew better. Yapahu's men, unlike their leader, were not in any mood to conceal their joy at their return to their city. They had made terrible sacrifices to defend and protect it, and the people of the city welcomed them as they thought they deserved. The wounded would receive medical attention, the weary a soft bed, the lonesome; warmth of family. This was home.

Yapahu and Addadanu were escorted into the palace, and great cedar doors with big brass bars were shut behind them. As the sound of the crowds faded an ominous silence made Yapahu's hair stand on end. Milkilu was waiting for them. One look at his face would tell what he had in store for his brothers.

"How, my brothers, could you have mucked this up so badly? Are you men or are you swine, fit only to wallow in filth?" Milkilu's hand grasped the grip of his sword. He drew it, almost as if to kill his brothers. He looked at the blade, then put it back in its scabbard. "Yapahu, I gave you an army of three thousand. You come home with less than one thousand. How can this be? And you, Addadanu, your one task was to safeguard Muhazzu. Now, I find it has fallen, its population put to the sword and the ravisher's spear. Lab'ayu has wrested control of our fertile lands, our granaries, and our supply depots. I suspect Ginti won't have long before it goes over to the Ḥabiru. Now, what do you have to say!"

"If I may question the strategy we were given at the outset…" blustered the surprised and bitter Addadanu.

"No! You may not! It was the best possible strategy we had. You both had very simple tasks to fulfill and you both failed spectacularly!"

"It was a fine plan, no doubt" Yapahu consciously looked Milkilu right into his eye to give no outward appearance of lying, "but then again, no plan survives contact with the enemy. As for my side of the war, it went thus. I arrived at the site of the battle, just outside Ginti. I snuck a messenger into the city to request aid for a sudden sally out to fight the enemy. I was to attack the Ḥabiru, pinning them, and then the men from the city of Ginti would sally out, and the enemy would be trapped between a hammer and an anvil as it were. Tagi sent a message to me, now lost sadly in the fray, that gave every indication he assented to my bold and clever action. When finally the time for the attack came, I made good my plan and charged headway into the Ḥabiru and the Shechemites. Our forces fought with grit and determination under my leadership, and though the enemy outnumbered us and fought like ferocious Apsu demons, we held firm. Then, we gave the signal for the garrison of the city to sally out and run to our aid. A second, a third time we gave the signal, but the cowards in their city, no doubt misguided by your jealous father-in-law, did not open the gates, did not rush to our aid but mocked and impugned us as if they hated Gezer far more than they feared Shechem." Yapahu caught his breath.

"Those two-faced dust suckers!" said Addadanu.

"Please continue." Milkilu added.

"Once it became known that no aid was coming, many of my men took off fleeing. This then turned into a mass rout. I was resolved, in the thick of it, to fight until the last, till I was persuaded by my loyal charioteer, that I would be more of use to you, my beloved brother, king of Gezer, alive than dead beneath the wall of some fatuous and ungrateful city. I just barely escaped with my life, regrouped those who were near at hand, and set off back to Gezer. I met Addadanu on the road, and returned to you as you now see."Yapahu wiped the sweat from his brow. He was relieved to have remembered the words he had written along the way. He hoped that his literary style would not sound unnaturally verbose.

"Yapahu, I commend you, for you acted honorably. When I lay my hands on Tagi again, he will have hell to pay. Until then, I'll be content with his whore daughter. As for your craven men, they must be disciplined. Let them draw lots, so one man in ten will be whipped, and one man in one hundred shall be crucified. I will have no cowardice in the face of the enemy, no insubordination. As for you, Addadanu, what was the matter? Why have you lost the town of Muhazzu?"

"Those Muhazzites. Those lazy, good for nothing, piss

drinking, shoe licking Muhazzites. I put them to work, of course, fortifying the city. I was doing the backbreaking labor. Lifting stones, mixing mortar; thinking my exertions would inspire that rabble to put in their best work. Instead, they mocked me, calling me Addadanu the ox, even the donkey. Of course, I told them, 'How can I be an ox with loins like these', and lifted my kilt. Now they all saw my giant, gorgeous manhood, and they were ashamed, and in awe, but mostly jealous, and then they began to hate me!. They worked, grudgingly, and the wall rose high; like my manhood of course. We were ready just in time to hear word that Lab'ayu was coming, not waylaid by Yapahu at Ginti as he was meant to be. I told them all, 'This is our home. This is our land. We will fight and die defending it, to the last man if needs be'. This was not what they wanted to hear. They began plotting to surrender the city of the king almost immediately. Their plot was overheard, however, by a virtuous woman, Tamar bit Ammunapi, who forewarned me. She helped me escape by a secret path only she knew. Sweet woman, I hope to the gods nothing ill has befallen her. On the way, I recruited some peasant lads, and I even ambushed and scattered a much larger Ḥabiru army on the way home."

"You also have done admirably. And as a sort of divine justice, those cowards in Muhazzu have been dealt a harsh blow by the enemy, saving us the effort. I pray Tamar bit Ammunapi made her escape by the same way you have, and if she has, and she comes here, I believe she would be a suitable candidate for your marriage vow, Addadanu?"

160

"I'd be honored to wed her if you would allow me. Sweet woman she is, with a big heart!" said Addadanu, unwittingly miming the shape of her ample bosom.

"Now back to the matter at hand. Despite our best efforts, our numbers have been culled by half. We have lost strategic ground; Muhazzu and Ginti are out of the picture. Now we must begin a strategic defense, we must defeat Lab'ayu on our native soil, the countryside directly surrounding Gezer." said Milkilu.

"You may reconsider that. Why give up the advantage of a high-walled city on the hill, with ample food and water. Let them just try to take it."

"In normal circumstances, Yapahu, you'd be right. However, our food supply is more scarce than I anticipated. We were supposed to be able to resupply from Muhazzu, but that chicken has flown the coop, as it were."

"Maybe we could get reinforcements. Good, hardy, professional soldiers that scoff at mere Ḥabiru. I mean, of course, for us to go to Hanya, and request the Pitati. Let's see what our generous gifts to the Pharaoh earn us." said Addadanu.

"I understand your idea. I really don't want to use the Pitati. War is about more than just winning. Where would my reputation be among the kings of Canaan if I were to use the Pitati of Pharaoh to defend Gezer, the greatest and strongest city south of Megiddo? I'd be laughed at as a lap dog, and I'll never live it down." said Milkilu.

"I fear that if you do not heed his advice, we will all be dead, and from what I hear, being slaughtered by an enemy is horrible for one's reputation." said Yapahu.

"You counsel wisely. Addadanu, go to Hanya and Huy at Tjaru and request the Pitati with all haste. Bring rich gifts for Pharaoh, and personal bribes for his ministers; under the table and hushed of course."

"Addadanu will need me to come with him. We work best as a team. Let's learn from that mistake and not part us again."

"I would have liked that you'd stay, you are much more useful to me here. But Addadanu lacks the diplomatic touch, so, you two shall go as one, as has long been your way."

"Please, Milkilu, allow me one night of good rest in the palace of sweet sleep. I've too long known the dusty road as my bed, the rocks, my pillow." said Yapahu.

"Very well. Have not one, nor two, but three nights of good rest, and in the day you two shall aid me in my preparations for siegecraft."

That night, in the palace, Yapahu slept. Milkilu slept. But Addadanu only pretended to sleep, as was his way and hid a slave in his place in bed. He crept down to the queen's quarters, as was his way. He slipped in through the door and snuck in upon the queen who was weeping her eyes out and did not notice him until he gently put his hands over her mouth to prevent her from producing a startled yelp. She opened her eyes in terror, as was her way. She was accustomed to the abrupt appearance of her hated spouse, Milkilu. But as soon she saw the beautiful face and darling eyes of Addadanu she could not help but smile under his strong restraining hand. He let go of her face and went in for the kiss, an ability he was most skilled with and generous in giving, unlike her husband.

"Ramashtu, I adore you. Our parting is so hard. I can have no other woman in my heart but you!"

She was truly happy in his arms, an emotion she never felt around anyone else in this wicked city. He deepened the kiss, using his tongue on hers. Soon they were engaged in shameful acts of fornication. At the finish, Addadanu used the method of Onan to ensure no unwanted pregnancies would arise from their coupling. Milkilu had said that if a light-skinned child was produced by his wife, the child and its mother would be burned alive. It was a testament to the love Addadanu bore his brother's wife that he was able to exercise self-restraint in that regard. When they were done, the two lay together, smoking hashish from a silver shisha pipe.

"Addadanu, I fear my husband means to kill me"

"Have we been found out?" Whispered Addadanu.

"I don't think so. But he means to cut off my head and send it as a sort of trophy to my father, Tagi, for his betrayal."

163

"Cut off your head? I can think of far better things to do with it. Kiss it for example."

"Addadanu, you are sweet, too sweet for this evil world. I've been waiting for death for a long time, hoping that childbirth would kill me. But I don't want to die like this. My poor father would just die of grief, and between the two of us, that would be the end of our ancient line, going back to Enmerkar and Gilgamesh."

"I will not allow you to die, my Queen. I'm leaving for Tjaru in a few days. You'll come with us. I'll have you sent safely to the court of Amenhotep, where you'll be treated as an honored guest. I'll swap your clothes for that of a pretty slave girl. You will go with me, pretending to be my slave, while my actual slave will take your place and die if needs be. Your life is too precious to me, I'll not risk it, even for my brother."

She looked at him with both sadness and joy, love and fear in her eyes. He was a real man. No one could deny that Addadanu was the worthiest hero Gezer had ever known! In the morning, a servant girl was wearing royal clothes, and a Queen was setting off in slave's garb alongside Addadanu and Yapahu to the desert wastes of the Negev and Sinai, and her desired freedom. Ramashtu made sure that they took simple, common horses for their chariots. *Milkilu will not miss me, but he would miss his Steeds of Mitanni.*

26

Chapter 26: Turning Wheels, Galloping Time

"I heard Tushratta is plotting to kill you and take the throne." said Etakkama, to Artashumara. He walked around to the other side of the palace. "Tushratta! Artashumara is planning to have you killed when he becomes king."

When a king is old, such speech is made among his sons. At least in Washshukkanni.

Washshukkanni was a city of horses more than of men. Stables were as numerous as houses there. Mighty stallions, gorgeous mares, proud ponies, and foals in abundance. Horseflesh was the chief business of the city. Merchants and royal delegations from Hatti, Kassite Babylon, Elam, every Canaanite kingdom, and Egypt, even traders from as far as Ahhiyawa and Kush would purchase these priceless mounts. There was a saying, "There are horses, and then there are Steeds of Mitanni". These proud beasts were trained by the art of Kikkuli, the greatest horse-keeper who ever lived.

From his venerable manual of warhorse care and instruction, his name carried weight even in lands where they had no scribes to read the tablets his techniques were recorded on. Horses meant everything to the upper class. Horses were power, wealth, status, beauty, virility, war, pleasure, and protection. Mitanni, with its ties of kinship to the tribes of the northern steppe, always seemed to have the best horses.

As Etakkama heard the whinnies of horses, and smelt the characteristic sweet scent of the hay, he remembered his boyhood.

It was a sweltering day in the height of summertide. The princes and princess sat on bales of hay. Etakkama could almost smell the hay, the horse musk, the horse scat in his recollection. Tulish, their tutor, was speaking. His words seemed lost to time, until he addressed the boys directly. This lesson Etakkama could not shake from his memory.

"Behold, the chariots of Mitanni" Tulish pointed to the speeding vehicle driven by a proud Maryannu, "See how each horse works together. One horse could not pull a great war chariot, even if he were strong like stone and fast like the north wind. But see how two, or even four, horses work in tandem. That is the strength of Mitanni. The power of one man is null unless he rests his arm upon his brother. Likewise, where would be the power of the Maryannu if not for his subjects? The Hurrian and his plow, the Canaanite and his trade, the Assyrian and his wisdom? Regard how a chariot may roll on two wheels, a sturdy cart on four, but with one wheel, it is doomed."

166

"That may be so," the child Etakkama said, "But in chariotry, as with statecraft, is there not but one driver?" As a boy, Etakkama took excessive pride in his diction.

"One driver to hold the reins, one lancer to spear the foe, and a shieldman to guard his fellows." Tulish mimed out the action of the driver, lancer and shieldbearer to the youngest's, Biryawaza, delight, "You brothers must stand firm together. Artashumara, Tushratta, Etakkama, Biryawaza... even the girls like you, Gilukhepa, have your place. We can be a strong herd as Mitanni, or lone ponies, easy prey for the wolves."

Etakkama remembered another event that happened that day. That was the day he lost his sister. He remembered asking Tulish about why, why, why...

"Why is Gilukhepa being sent away?" said Etakkama, sobbing. He loved his elder sister like Indra loved his Indrani.

"She is to be given to the Pharaoh. To seal a formal alliance" Tulish rubbed Etakkama's head.

"Why can't Pharaoh send one of his daughters to marry father instead?"

"Oh, if only the world was so good. The Egyptians are haughty. The daughter of Pharaoh can marry no man but the Pharaoh himself."

"That's disgusting." Etakkama thought about his beloved sister forced to lay with such a disgusting pervert. He nearly

167

retched. Pain whinnied in both his stomach and his heart.

"There are reasons for us to send Gilukepa to Pharaoh. You are probably not old enough yet to understand..."

Etakkama remembered being frustrated by that remark, and extremely curious. Only years later did he realize that was Tulish's intent.

"I'm old enough! Tell me!"

"I told you our herd of horses is beset on all sides by wolves. It is a true fact. Egypt, Karduniash, Hatti..." he paused on that last word for emphasis, "Hatti. Sometimes we have to offer a mare to another herd to fend off the wolves. There was a day when Egypt was our foe. Now, Hatti..." he shuddered at the thought, "Is a threat. Let us band with Egypt. She may be a harsh mistress, but we have a common enemy. And... you would be amazed to know... Gilukhepa will be a hero in her own way."

Etakkama was amazed, "A hero how?"

"A hero of knowledge. She shall bring secrets from Egypt so we may know them. She may not bear a lance or shield, but she will save the lives of many in our country."

"I want to be a hero like Gilukhepa, teacher!"

"Heroism isn't about gaining great power, or destroying your enemies. Heroism is sacrifice. Gilukhepa will offer her

168

maidenhood to Pharaoh, but she will serve the general good. Are you ready to make what sacrifices you need to serve the general good?"

"I will. I will!"

Etakkama's thoughts turned from his past to his future. The king, his father, requested his presence. He didn't know if he would live another day. But like Tulish taught him, he was always willing to sacrifice himself (or others) for the general good.

The throne room of the Palace of Washshukkanni seemed to glow yellow with the light of the mid-morning sun. The king sat on his throne, cross legged on richly dyed purple, yellow and orange cushions. His body in youth once strapped with muscle and fat, but now his skin drooped with sag and jowls. His long white beard almost touched the floor. His floppy body jiggled as he waved to his son, bidding him to enter.

"Etakkama! My beloved foal!" said Shuttarna, king of Mitanni, "I am to assign you a task worthy of you."

"To keep me from the palace no doubt, and dissuade me from my dangerous intrigues! For you think of me as a danger to your heirs, your pure Maryannu born sons, my half brothers," replied Etakkama.

"I think you do well to have great ambitions. Your mastery over the ways of worldly wisdom is duly noted by me. But If you think I'll endanger the kingdom with your power

169

games, turning brother against brother, Tushratta against Artashumara, think again son. I am wise to your tricks. You want to achieve the circumstances where you are the only remaining heir and rule the kingdom. Then, you think, the world will follow."

"I really have no idea what you are talking about" Lied Etakkama, "I am content to live a humble life as an advisor, to whoever winds up on top, be it Tushratta or Artashumara."

"Your mother's country was Canaan, she was a native princess of Qadesh. Now you will go to aid your uncle, a man who was named in my honor. He has no sons and has given up on having such, so if you value kingship as your ambition, take up his cause and he will surely sing the betrothal hymn. From there, you can go any direction besides Mitanni. North and south and West are open to you."

"You show benevolence by giving me this opportunity," Etakkama lifted his hands to twirl his mustache, but realized he'd look too evil. He rubbed his belly instead. "You also see an opportunity to further your own ambitions I might add."

"You will also take your younger brother Biryawaza with you on your journey. I do love him, and I would not like to see any ill befall him as would surely happen when I die. He can play a minor part of your empire or a major one, I ask only that you protect him from danger as your flesh and blood."

"Even young Biryawaza will have a use in the game I will play. I will play the game of wars and brides."

170

"I'll grant you three centuries of chariots, with riders, archers, spears, suits of mail, and fine steeds. It is up to you to turn this into an empire."

"I'd be the master of the world with just a hundred chariots" boasted Etakkama, "Because one million chariot wheels turn in my head, going this way and that. And they will not stop till I achieve domination."

"My advice is thus: In Canaanite land, they value modesty over honesty. Speak restrainedly about yourself, and be ready for tricks, traps, and lies."

"They will have to be ready for my tricks, traps, and lies. Without delay for any cause, I'll harness my gallopers and make ready for whatever shall be, death or glory!"

With the wheels of a million chariots turning, cunning Etakkama hastily left the palace of Washshukkanni, taking care not to slip on the blood of those with whom he had played the game. *Don't be a horse*, thought Etakkama, *be the wolf.*

27

Chapter 27: Spite and Stones

"Addadanu will die for what he has done!" shouted Milkilu, to Shapiri-Ashtar, his captain of guard and advisor.

"He surely must, brother or otherwise, because how can a man let himself be cuckolded? I recommend beheading, as privately as possible."

"Beheading? The law demands stoning with stones, in the market by the citizens of the city. What I would give to see that pretty girlish face broken by hard stones!" Milkilu jerked his hands, spilling some wine on his hands. He licked it up. His father had taught him never to waste good wine. Milkilu liked the term 'stoning with stones'. It had a certain redundancy that struck him as official, and regal.

"As your loyal guardsman, I shall advise you truthfully. Addadanu has many friends among the citizens, especially among the women. If you asked the people to stone him, they might stone you instead. Wouldn't it feel much better to behead him yourself?" Shapiri-Ashtar reached for a collection of fine swords. He showed them to the king.

"You may have a point. What do you think I should do about the slave girl? Should I kill her?"

"I say you should have sex with her, leave her alive and pretend she is your wife. It would be a shameful thing to admit you were cuckolded especially at this critical moment."

"I've never laid with another woman besides my wife. I don't know if it's in my nature." puzzled Milkilu.

"Then all the better to start now, now that you have a good excuse. Addadanu should be fooled into thinking it's safe to return, then you can have his head. The most important lesson you can take from this debacle is you should never tell someone you will kill them before the blade falls. "

"Well... That's one thing I can learn. Let's drink some wine, and I'll see if I can stomach that slave girl."

"A good plan, as always, Lord Milkilu."

"I'll not forget your loyalty, Shapiri-Ashtar, you will no doubt prove an acceptable replacement for my brothers in my endeavors."

They drank and drank into the late hours. When Milkilu was black-out drunk, and most of his woes were forgotten under a veil of inebriation, Milkilu stumbled into his wife's room. The slave girl was having a grand old time, trying on all of lady Ramashtu's fine clothes and jewelry. Milkilu, who was far too intoxicated to see or think straight, walked right over to his pseudo-wife and gave her a wine-flavored kiss.

"My lady! My Queen! Indeed you are beautiful tonight, radiant and stunning!"

"Oh, you think so, Milkilu? That is so kind of you to say!"

"I've been thinking... I'm not going to kill you. It is not your fault your father betrayed me. How can I kill someone so lovely!" He brushed her face with his strong dark hands.

"Thanks for the compliment" the slave affectionately grasped Milkilu's hands, gently fingering it for rings she might steal, "And for agreeing not to kill me. I was wondering when was the last time I gave you the old suck-suck?"

Milkilu pondered it. "Never?"

"Well, that's got to change now! How can I be your wife and not do a wife's duty?"

Even though in the back of his intoxicated mind he knew the sorrows of the heart, he was able to feel happy in the mouth of this humble slave girl. *Is this what love is?* And all it cost him was a few rings.

Chapter 28: The Exiles

The night winds blew, the fires danced, and drink was poured. The raucous sounds of warriors at play filled the camps outside Ginti.

Concerning drink; milk is made in an instant. Should someone want to drink it, they have but to squeeze the teats of a cow, sheep or goat. But with wine, the process is long, involving arduous planting, pruning, and treading. Then the must must be allowed to ferment and age. Depending on the desired qualities, it could take from a few weeks to a lifetime, or more. Such is the case in the nature of warfare. A field battle is like the procurement of milk. It is done in a short while, but the result is ephemeral, and liable to spoil. A siege is much like the procurement of wine. It is a matter of waiting. But in the end, should it be done correctly, a precious result is produced, whose value is unquestionable and unperishable: the seizure of a city.

The men of Shechem and their Ḥabiru fellows set to their

beloved pastime; telling tales of self-aggrandizement. The commanders sat together. Like the men, they told tales of their past deeds.

"Regard, if you will, the state of the world some thirty years hence." Issuwa added some barley flour to the fire for a dramatic pyrokinetic display. Flames lit up, and flashed his bold face before the listeners. "War was waged, it seemed, between all good Canaanites and that thrice accursed Pharaoh. It came to pass that my brother, brave Ba'aluya, king of Shechem was besieged in Shechem. He said to me 'Oh, Issuwa, bravest of the brave, go forth from Shechem under cover of night. Go to the land of Bashan, across the Jordan, and beg, no, demand, aid of my kinfolk in Pihilu, and across the country of Bashan.' Now, the Pharaoh's men were ever vigilant. Like dreadful owls they sat upon their investments, ever eager to swoop upon any who dare go forth by night."

"And how did you do it?" asked Ayyabu.

"My brother lowered me down the back wall, where the view was partially obscured by a grove of Cypress trees. I was wearing not a shekel of armor on me... my stealth had to be complete. In my left hand, I held the precious seal of my brother, and in my right... this sword!" Issuwa flourished the sword through smoke and flame, creating a vibrant show of light and black in it's reflective blade. "I got no further than twenty paces from the walls, when to my dismay I saw them! An Egyptian captain and his ten loathsome Pitati, taking a virgin girl of Shechem to dishonor her... it is too horrible to

176

tell! So I plucked up what courage I had, and leapt at these curs of Kush, and their leader, the monkey of Misru. They were taken by surprise, but they were twenty and I was but one. Needless to say, I made kibbe of them. The girl, so taken by my valor and skill at arms, flung herself upon me. But I, bearing in mind my crucial mission, took my leave, not before allowing her to swear herself to be my bride... and she would be the mother of this one!" Issuwa grabbed his son Dadua's cheek and twisted it affectionately yet roughly. Dadua groaned. He waited with ire for the coming mockery from Yishaya. *After all, Yishaya is a Ḥabiru. They love making light of others' misfortunes.* Yishaya did not even chuckle.

"So kissing goodbye to my bride to be, I set off, northeast. I reached, as was my plan, a ford in the Jordan River. But the rains had set in early that year. The river was engorged, rushing with torrential vigor to the Dead Sea. I have, as you all know, always been an accomplished swimmer..."

"I did not know that." said Dadua, "and I'm your son."

"What I meant is it would be an accomplishment to get me to go in any water! I scorn even the bathtub."

"We are aware." Dadua clutched his nose in mock disgust.

"I knew if I were to hazard such a journey across the river, I would be swept away by the current. I would wound up washed up, drowned, earning the Dead Sea his name. So I undertook to contrive a plan as to how to cross the river safely. I resolved to fell a tree over the river as a sort of makeshift bridge. However, I knew not how far across the river was, so I might fell a tree of at least equal height. I did not have much time to waste felling trees of insufficient length. Not to mention, my labors would have given rise to suspicion in the locals, who may well have forewarned the Pharaoh's ministers of my intent. However, as a lad, I had been well versed in the study of mathematics. I was able to take my rope, and mark it with equal units. Then I cast the rope, weighted by a small log, to the opposite bank. However, the current sent the measure a ways down the stream. No matter, I thought. I took note of how long the distance was from myself at the bank to the end of the rope. Then, I measured the distance the log traveled laterally from me. I then constructed in my head a right triangle. Knowing the hypotenuse C, and a side length B, I was able to write the problem algebraically as $A = \sqrt{(C^2 - B^2)}$. Now I knew the distance across the river, so it was only a matter of measuring the trees, and eventually, I found one to the exact specifications. I felled the tree, and crossed the river."

"Wouldn't it have been easier to just get an eye for how tall the tree is to the river?" asked Yishaya.

"But what would be the fun in that?" Issuwa winked. "Anyway, looks can be deceiving. So, I continue into the country of Bashan. I soon encountered the city of Pihilu. I showed them my precious seal, that of my brother Ba'aluya. To my astonishment, instead of welcoming me as the brother of their liege, they clapped chains on me and brought me to the residence of the Egyptian governor. It happened that when King Ba'aluya gave the call to rebel, and to dispatch the

178

Egyptian garrison, the cowards in Pihilu instead hid their persecutors in a meek attempt to bargain for clemency. In recompense for their 'chivalrous' act, the Egyptian governor meted out the most severe repressions in their country. So, when I was handed over to the Governor, he resolved to have me put to death come the morrow. However, my wits were still about me. So I told the governor that I had an especially virulent plague; harmless to others as long as I live, but deadly in the case of death or the spillage of my blood. Horrified by the prospect of such a misfortune, he instead cast me into a dungeon to sit all alone. There I languished, until my beloved..."

"That you had just met a few days before..." said Dadua.

"It seems to me no peculiar thing, to fall in love like that, especially considering the antiquity of the times..." Ayyabu scratched his bald chin.

"You would know, with the quantity of 'loves' that come and go around your tent." Dadua laughed at his own joke.

"He said this story was supposed to be thirty years ago," said Yishaya, "Scarcely ancient history. I still remember keenly what I was doing thirty years ago."

"Then regale us, oh Yishaya. My father's drivel is annoying and dull in equal measure."

"It gets better, I assure you." Issuwa gestured his hand as if grasping the smoke in his claws.

179

Yishaya nodded. "It's already pretty good. Better than mine, for certain."

"You are gracious, Yishaya. We must hear your story, just as soon as I finish with mine."

"We will be hearing Yishaya's story when the rooster crows, " Dadua said. "No matter. It is probably as dull as yours, but unrefined and uncultured, as befits a Ḥabiru. Now if your cousin was here…"

"My bastard 'cousin' had better stay far away from here!" Yishaya roared in anger, and almost jumped over the fire to tackle the pipsqueak.

"Why do you hate him so?" asked Ayyabu, "Mutba'alu always speaks so fondly of him. 'A man with a heart of gold, gold teeth, and a golden tongue."

"If he ever had a heart of gold, he must have sold it to devils years ago. As for his tongue, I can tell you there is more shit about it than gold. As for his gold teeth, ever wonder why he needed them?" Yishaya brandished his fists like a pugilist.

"Why do you hate him?" asked Issuwa. "It seems an awful shame to hate one's cousin."

"An awful shame to do what he did." Yishaya spat into the fire. It hissed and sizzled a little. "Now when I was a small boy…."

"A puppy" jeered Dadua.

Yishaya restrained his anger, and closed his eyes. "As you say, a puppy, I had a sister, she was scarce thirteen years of age. So, my parents decided it would be a good thing to marry her off. There was a man in the village, homely, old, fat, a baker; he had some means. He was also a widower. So my parents got it into their head that she'd marry the baker, that louse. She looked so beautiful that day." Yishaya sighed with regret, "My grandmother, may she rest with Ba'alu, had sewn her a beautiful white gown, white to match her chastity. She was, after all, a virgin, scarcely met the red king, and all that. We had a fine wedding, food, gifts, the works, and then the louse takes her into his chamber to lie with her. So, naturally, my cousin, Abneru, like the pervert that he is, hid under the bed while they... you know what they did. So either as some twisted joke, or some vendetta, he absconded with the sheet."

"Oh gods." said Issuwa, "What happened next?"

"So the groom invents this nonsense that my sister is not a virgin, and that he has been swindled. My family vigorously denies it. But where was the sheet with the evidence of her chastity? The baker showed a sheet, white and pure as snow. So he takes his claim to the Egyptian Governor in Pihilu."

"You say this was thirty years ago? I recall there being a homely fat man with a sheet when I was detained, and I knew not why."

"Now you know. So the governor, he looks at his tablets, and he pulls out the most wicked ancient nonsense I have heard in my days. He says, 'for the crime of not being a virgin at marriage, the girl is to be stoned to death with stones.' So they take her to the village square, and she is bound, and sobbing her damn eyes out. One after another, the villagers throw stones. Most throw them to intentionally miss. They know she is innocent. This angers the baker. He takes a large and jagged stone," Yishaya grasped his muscular fist to keep himself from crying, "And aims right for her beautiful, innocent face. It bashed into her right eye…"

"Ruining her beauty," said Ayyabu, "What a pity."

"So my cousin, Abneru, starts cackling like a jackal. I ask him, 'why are you laughing' and he shows me the sheet with her maiden blood on it. Needless to say, I snatch the damn thing and stand in front of my sister, holding it, daring anyone who wants to throw stones to throw at me first. Now that Abneru, that swine, throws a stone at me! And he laughed as I took the sheet and cleaned the blood from my sister's eye. She lost it by the way."

"The sheet?" asked Dadua.

"The eye." Yishaya pinched the bridge of his nose. Tears were flowing. "And he only got worse from there, that bastard. So when I came of age, I got out of that village and became a Ḥabiru. Though, sure enough, that bastard would follow me. And he never stopped being a bastard since. So, Issuwa, finish your story. Give it a happy ending. I don't care how

182

you have to lie, prattle or bullshit to get there."

"It obviously doesn't have a happy ending in real life. Since we lost the war, and my brother died, as you know. But I'll leave you on a hopeful note, dear Yishaya." Issuwa gently stroked Yishaya's long, black hair. "So my beloved had heard I was in distress, so she had hastened to my aid."

"How did she cross the river?" asked Dadua, "Did she have to rely on astrological charts? Or did she recite the multiplication table to the river god?"

"No, to her credit, she knew her geography, and that a wooden bridge across the river existed in Bitsanu. So, she hastened to my aid, and found me, huddled and cold in the cell wherein I was kept. So she went among the citizens there in Pihilu, and roused to action and to shame by her courage, they flung open the door to my cell, and those of the other prisoners who were kept therein for their love of liberty. So we all, armed with whatever we could find, stormed the governor's headquarters, and I say we did justice by the tyrant."

"Meaning you and a violent mob murdered him in cold blood, along with his guards." said Dadua.

"Serves him right." Yishaya drank a swig of pilfered strong wine, "If only I was there to see it myself! Perhaps join in..."

"It was a sight to behold. So I organized five troops of infantry, three of archers, two of slingers, and a company of

Maryannu. Each company contained a hundred twenty men, and each troop had the equivalent of four companies. That made the total force equal to..."

"4920 men. Which is impossible. I figure the whole city and adjacent countryside of Pihilu today contains less than ten thousand souls, of which only about a third could be able bodied men. And any city requires food for its populace, even more so to support a war effort..." Dadua counted on his fingers as he did the calculations in his head.

"You are indeed your father's son," said Issuwa, rubbing his son's hair. "So I sent the troops from Pihilu forth to Shechem, and continued onwards into the heart of the land. Green vegetation became brown dirt, which became white sand. I was told by all who I met that there was a town far out in the desert called Qanu, wherein great warriors could be found."

"Ḥabiru warriors." said Yishaya, "I'm very familiar with Qanu. It is a haunt for us bandits, plunderers and mercenaries. To imagine a nobleman like you, a paragon of virtue, in a place like that is enough to give me pause. I would think we would take one look at your haughty face and hold you for ransom."

"No, they took one look at my haughty face and treated me with utmost hospitality." Issuwa mimed out the exchange of gold, "I had in my possession some gold taken from the Governor of Pihilu. Their chief told me that Ḥabiru would fight with me, for my cause was noble and good, just as they had for the vagabond prince Idrimi of Alalakh in days of yore. He said that tales of Idrimi and his heroic Ḥabiru and their

184

exploits are often told with a melancholic longing, and the desire of all Ḥabiru is to find a righteous cause again."

"I can't speak for all Ḥabiru," said Yishaya, "But I've never heard of the name Idrimi before today. And I've yet to find a Ḥabiru wanting to fight in some righteous cause. Gold before glory, we say."

"Ah, really? I wonder, has it ever crossed your mind, oh greedy Ḥabiru, that you could be paid far more gold in the employ of Milkilu and his brothers than you can make serving my nephew, Lab'ayu?" asked Issuwa.

"Ah, you see, gold is the life-blood of pimps and kings." said Yishaya, "They can spare a little on the hire, but cut them open," he mimed the butchery of a belly, "and what they kept hidden is for grabs."

"There is heroism in you Ḥabiru, mark my words," said Issuwa, "Even if you are too stubborn to admit it. If not, do you think Lab'ayu would ever consider you for his cause?"

"So you have some Pihilites and some 'Honorable Ḥabiru'. How does this story end?" asked Ayyabu.

"With a battle, of course!" Dadua laughed, "the Battle of the Concentric Eyes, as it was called. Which, if I remember correctly, you were defeated handily."

"Shut your yap!" Yishaya couldn't restrain his anger anymore. He flew into a mad rage and punched the boy across his jaw.

Only the sound of the ram's horn stayed the brawl which was soon to break out. The men around the camp stood up, at attention. The man, who was wearing a Ganakku kilt, presented a burlap bag. He removed the gifts. It was the bloody head of Apapa, chief of the Lionmen. Then, he removed the seal of Shisita, Lady of the Lions.

"King Tagi begs your presence for breakfast. There is much to discuss."

29

Chapter 29: The Desert Winds

The thundering chariots of the Gezerites rolled through the barren deserts of the Negev at breakneck speed. Yapahu and Addadanu whipped their horses, cheap but hardy steeds from Qedar, into a frenzied frolic of furious galloping. The sun beat down, shooting fiery arrows of sunbeams on the backs of the charioteers, reddening and blistering the skin. Sand grains whipped up by the wheels flung themselves, pelting the riders like a volley of sling bullets. They had many miles yet to go, and the rocky Sinai desert to cross. To go all the way to Tjaru was dangerous, but it was far superior to the alternative. There was a far nearer Egyptian fort at Sharuhen, just outside of Gaza. But Yapahu and Addadanu knew to stay well away. It was the den of the Extorter, Yanhamu. It suffices to say that Yanhamu and Milkilu had a history. A history of extortion, and threatening to kill Milkilu's children. No, it would be Tjaru for the brothers.

"Addadanu, can we rest, slow down, something, soon? The sun is making me feel hazy. I think I see water up ahead"

Ramashtu coughed.

"Silence, slave-girl!" said Yapahu, "We need to focus! Unless you want us to hit a rock and shatter to a thousand pieces."

"There is no water, it is but a mirage. Just another few days' ride and we will be in Tjaru and there will be water and beer, sweetened with date syrup." said Addadanu, reassuring his lover.

They rode on, galloping like the Gemar beasts of myth. By the time the fortress of Tjaru rose on the horizon above the rocky sandy crags of Sinai, Ramashtu genuinely could pass for a slave girl to the untrained eye. Her lips, once so beautiful, were dry and peeling. Her eyes were bloodshot from rubbing sand out of them. They approached the high mudbrick walls and towers of the fort. Ramashtu was awed by the size of those high yellow walls, a sight she never saw in her life. She thought it must be like Uruk, the city of her heritage.

"Who would enter the fortress Tjaru through the gates of Seth!?!" inquired the tall, snub-nosed, and fearsome-looking Nubian gatekeeper.

"Yapahu and Addadanu! We are the emissaries of Gezer, and we commend your presence. Very intimidating. No one would ever dare attack Tjaru when you are here." replied Yapahu.

"No one would even think about attacking Tjaru when I am here! I put an arrow in them before the thought even crossed their mind."

"No doubt! We have important information to declare to Hanya and Huy, so if you could open the gate??

"Right away lords Yapahu and Addadanu. Make yourselves at home."

The gate was open, and the eleven men and one woman, Yapahu, Addadanu, nine armed guards, and Ramashtu were escorted into the premises. They passed barracks and training grounds where the apparatus for the subjugation of Canaan was located. The nut-tough and lion-fierce Pitati, the ebony-skinned fighters in the service of Pharaoh spent every single day hours perfecting their craft. Archery was their specialty, and they had superior range and accuracy than archers from any other country. They would practice shooting on mannequins dressed up in the motley garb of the Canaanite, be it the striped kilt of a peasant or the rich robes of a noble. They would fill these unfortunate mannequins with obsidian-tipped arrows. These pincushions stood as a warning for any Asiatic who passed by, that they were in the land of their masters. In war times they would even crucify prisoners of war, men, even women and children, and practice on living targets. It was for reasons like these that everyone in Canaan hated and feared the dark-skinned Nubians. But, unbeknownst to most Canaanites, their brethren were used in much the same way to keep order and crush rebellions in Nubia, as slingers and heavy infantry.

189

The old adage in Egypt — divide and rule!

Yapahu and Addadanu were led into the inner sanctum of the commissariat. Shelves around the room were filled with clay tablets, papyrus scrolls, and treasured materials; lapis lazuli, gold, silver, copper, tin, carnelian, even Baltic amber. Hanya was reading a tablet and translating its content diligently onto a papyrus roll in neat, well-drawn hieroglyphs. Hanya took pride in his work and was promoted based on merit alone to the important position of Commissioner of Archers. As such, he was firmly ensconced in both the military and bureaucratic affairs of Egypt's Canaanite empire. Hanya enjoyed his job. In meeting new people, traveling, he had cultivated genuine heartfelt friendships with the kings of the various cities he went to on business. Hanya was a well-liked man, honest and generous. There was always mutual respect between Hanya and his Pitati, as he was full of vigor and many of his men were impressed that the fourth son of a humble peasant could rise to such lofty heights. They were inspired. Not so for Huy.

Huy was the opposite of Hanya in every conceivable way. While Hanya was promoted on merit, Huy was the son of the Vizier, Aperel, and was promoted on the basis of nepotism. He thought his lofty station was far beneath him. His older brothers had lofty perches indeed in Egypt. Seny was a steward of the palace and Hatiay was a priest of Nefertem. Instead of a cushy job in a palace or temple eating fine food and being surrounded by beautiful maidens, Huy was in the desert living the rough life of a soldier, inhaling clay dust and coughing phlegm. He hated Nubians, he hated

190

Canaanites, and he especially hated Hanya. He exhausted his noble mind conceiving methods to get Hanya discharged. At that moment, he was studiously examining a papyrus that was confiscated from one of his charioteers. In lurid detail, it portrayed the queen Tiye engaged in lewd acts with a she-goat. As the messengers from Gezer arrived, Huy hastily scrambled to hide the pornography under a pile of official documents. Huy was a disciplinarian with his troops and a hypocrite. The man he took the shameful papyrus from had been harshly flogged, and then left to the elements until dead. Now Huy alone could enjoy the pleasures of the papyrus.

"Yapahu, Addadanu, It's my pleasure, please come in! Enjoy the amenities of the Nile!" chirped Hanya gaily, handing each of them a piece of barley bread and a date, "What business brings you here to Tjaru?"

"Your hospitality is ever welcome my friend!" buttered Yapahu, "Though our business is rather grave."

"We've heard. You two and your brother have made a muck of the situation in Retenu. Now we have a rebellion on our hands thanks to you fools!" hissed Huy.

"Thanks to us! We were only servicing the Pharaoh's needs. If that is a sin — I don't know what's gotten into your head!" blurted Addadanu.

"Don't antagonize them, Addadanu. Causes aside, the situation is bad and getting worse in Retenu. Now is the time to send in the Pitati, to restore order before this rebellion

191

gets out of hand." counseled Yapahu.

"Yapahu, you are indeed right that the Pitati are needed to stabilize the situation. You are astute and wise, and supremely diplomatic, and that's why I must give you this regrettable order from Pharaoh himself. As much as I, and the Pharaoh himself for that matter, value and love Milkilu, he is now proving a destabilizing influence and has outlived his usefulness. We are aware that you have brought his wife to us, and we think it is for the best. Him killing her would be an absolute disaster for our control of the situation in Retenu, and in Canaan more broadly." Hanya lifted his head momentarily from his writing, and smiled.

"So you will protect her, keep her safe and comfortable?" asked Addadanu.

"We'll do our best to accommodate." said Hanya.

"My question is what do you mean to do to Milkilu? He has been a loyal servant of Pharaoh since he was a child, and while he may have erred in one way or the other from time to time, he always had the best intentions at heart." said Yapahu.

"He intended to get rich and amass power. His corrupt ways made him an enemy in Lab'ayu and unfairly represented Egypt, and as a result, it's been decided that we'll do away with him at the first opportunity. The two bastards' heads can sit side by side on stakes." gloated Huy.

"Is this true Hanya, that Milkilu is a marked man?" asked

Yapahu.

"Regrettably, that is our order. But there is good news along with the bad. Yapahu, you've been chosen to act as regent until Milkilu's sons Zimredda and Tagi come of age. To maintain the good relations between Ginti and Gezer, you will also be married to Milkilu's widow Ramashtu as is the custom among Asiatics."

"The savages." Added Huy.

Addadanu went from merely miffed, hearing about the pending fate of Milkilu to sorrow, distress, and rage at the fate of his beloved. In his head he screamed, "Shouldn't she have some say in the matter?" but for the first time in his life he held his tongue.

"This is a great honor. I had never thought I would ever have my own kingdom or a beautiful bride. But my heart breaks at the fate in store for my beloved brother." said Yapahu.

"Now I, Hanya, will show you three to the choicest quarters available in this fortress. Now you, Ramashtu, shall be taken to the very chambers reserved on most accounts solely for the Pharaoh himself. We will serve you the best food, provide the best wine! You are our honored guest!"

"Thank you, and I will also require clothes worthy of my station, make-up, jewelry, and slaves." said Ramashtu, "And a bath. I smell worse than my damn husband. That curr."

"These you will have!"

Ramashtu was lead into her new room: spacious, comfortable, costly. She drank wine, ale, and water, and ate dates, figs, sweetmeats, and roasted honeyed quail. All the while, pretty Nubian slave boys waited on her every whim. Meanwhile, Yapahu and Addadanu ate with the Pitati. Their food was for a rougher palate: barley beer, hard bread, and stewed ibex with onion, garlic, and cumin. The pimps were respected among the men; they ate and drank the same as they, and were eager to engage in a little roughhousing, wrestling, and the like. They even held their own! They slept among the soldiers, on animal pelts on the barracks floors. None of this was required, but Yapahu knew it was invaluable. And when on the morrow the Pitati set out, Yapahu and Addadanu walked with the men. *Chariots! Those're for softies!*

30

Chapter 30: Chariots of the Mind — Part One

The past few days had been a strange few for Sutarna's northern coalition. Scouts had gone missing with no explanation and were later found buried with honors on the road ahead. What was going on? Then a band of Sherdens, heavily armed mercenary soldiers from the far-off western island of Shardana. They offered their services, which was normal enough, armies would often hire Sherdens as mercenaries for hire, but they did so in a stunningly odd way. They requested a completely unrealistic sum for their swords, and when Sutarna attempted to haggle with them, they were offended and appalled at it.

"What are we, hocks of meat, artichokes, tubs of wine? If you want us to fight and die for you, pay us what we ask."

"We never asked for you to fight for us." chided Shisita, "We have more than enough men already, though if you make a reasonable offer we will add you to our ranks. However, this is not a campaign of plunder."

"You insult us, and we shall surely find our terms willingly met by some other warlord or king."

"I wish you well and hope you do. But if you rape or pillage in Canaan you'll have an enemy in us." Sutarna shook his fists, until a ring fell off his hand and he stopped pretending to be angry to pick it up.

After the Sherden captains left the camp, the leadership was abuzz with active discussion.

"I don't like them one bit" said Akizzi, "I smell a trap."

"Akizzi, why is your nose so big? You smell danger everywhere!" asked Sutarna.

"He is right, Father. They have an air about them that doesn't sit well with me. We should double the night guard and try to leave this place as soon as possible. We are trapped between any potential enemy and the sea, and there is no easy escape." advised Shisita, "Which is why I spoke against marching by way of the coast."

"What do you think, Yassib?"

"Why ask me, I'm just a nobody. You have a host of chiefs and kings and princes and you ask me, a mere warrior?"

"The reason is that I trust you. You have everything to lose and nothing to gain if we fail. And you know the mercenary business. Is this typical of Sherdens?"

"Being proud and very costly is quite believable. But that is not what we are noticing is amiss. Sherdens do not come to you looking for work like common laborers. They keep to their camps, and those willing to pay their fee to come to them."

"If so, I'll provide more men to keep watch over our camp just as a precaution. Personally, I prefer to keep to the shore so we can be easily supplied from Gubla by ship." Sutarna stuck removed his helmet to let the sea breeze run through his hair. He smiled meekly, "I trust Rib-Hadda to keep his word. King's honor."

Akizzi walked off and whispered into the ear of his father Idanda king of Qaṭna, "Why Sutarna is at our head, I'll never know. His head is soft like cheese. Sooner or later, he'll get us all killed."

"If I die, son, you must preserve Qaṭna. Do not make an enemy in Qadesh. Sutarna may seem weak and pathetic to you but his blood is fire, his bones bronze. Qadesh is mighty, pay heed, my boy, and listen much and speak little, as I do." Idanda, put his hand on Akizzi's shoulder.

"I myself will stand watch with the men tonight," asserted Akizzi, "If I am going to die, I want to die with my sword in my hand and other mens' blood on my chest"

197

"I'll sleep well knowing I'm in good hands." salved Idanda, rubbing his adult son's hair like he was a child again. Idanda was good natured, but pragmatic. His son was just pragmatic.

That night, Idanda supped with a group of common soldiers. Among them, there was no one past the age of twenty-four. None there could remember those days of his youth. He never spoke of those times, even though it was the happening of those days that pushed him on the path he took like the fast current of the Orontes. It was not from shame. The unwritten rule of kings was never to speak of those days before they assumed the rule of their city. "What king ever is made in good times?" was the saying, "In treachery, defeat, tragedy, and usurpation are kings made."

Idanda remembered the days when his hair was still black, not silver and white.

"Idanda, tell me, what do you think of this plan?" asked the sonless King Addu-Nirari, "Is the reward sufficient for the sacrifice, Vizier?"

"I am honored by such an offer, oh good, oh wise king" said Idanda as graciously as his heart would allow. "But it is a dear, dear cost."

"I chose you Idanda," the king stroked his thinning snowy beard, "There is no one in this city who is loyal like Idanda, no one in Qaṭna who loves Qaṭna like Idanda. He would give up his life a thousand times for the city."

198

"But this life is not mine to give." said Idanda, restraining his tears.

"One life... your eldest's, shall be sacrificed." Addu-Nirari made the sign of one finger, then ten, "for the many, many lives of Qaṭna. I know your son well, that Amut-Pi'el. He'd gladly give his life for the city."

Idanda remembered the meeting with his sons Amut-Pi'el and Akizzi with even greater sorrow.

"So you want to sacrifice Amut-Pi'el so you can gain the kingdom?" Akizzi was at once confused, shocked, angry and deeply sad, "Do not go brother! I do not want to be a prince for the sake of your end!"

"It's the command of the king," said the eldest, stroking the hair of his agitated brother. "I would sooner die for my city than grow white bearded and fat as a coward."

"Take this sword," said Idanda dolefully, "if your spying is discovered, use it to take your own life, and if possible kill any rebel leader you can."

"If it is the word of the king that I must act against the Canaanites, I will do it." said Amut-Pi'el.

"Why are we against the Canaanites?" asked Akizzi. "We are Canaanites."

"If Egypt's power wanes, we will have no protector against

Hatti. Recall the fate of Aleppo to the northern hordes."
Idanda shuddered. "When the time comes, I expect you to
sacrifice everything for Egypt, Akizzi. Your life, my life, the
life of thousands. For the rule of Hatti is hateful to all; man,
beast and god."

"He will be a good king," said Amut-Pi'el, "Qaṭna will not fall
in his time. Remember this truth, brother, save the many
at the cost of the few. Save the gods at the cost of a man.
Remain vigilant, and do always what is necessary without
remorse."

In the present, Idanda smiled tearfully. His son learned the
lesson well.

31

Chapter 31 Chariots of the Mind — Part Two

That night Akizzi stood with the watchmen. The others were often lax at their posts, trying to sneak off for naps. This night would be different from all others, and not just from the full lunar eclipse. The eagle-eyed Akizzi let no man derelict his duty. As for himself, he seemed never even to blink. The men, yawning, heavy-eyed proved to be no precaution. It was Akizzi who sighted the attack when it came; exactly as he had expected. He saw small movements in the dark. With a black moon in the sky and only starlight to illuminate the enemy, even the eagle-eyed Akizzi had to squint to see them. Akizzi alerted his men to the shadows, the snap of twigs, the rustle of gravel in the distance. They didn't believe him at first, but then one of the guardsmen saw the horned helm of a Sherden; there could be no doubt. The silence was broken by cries of alarm, and Akizzi blew his horn, an ancient keepsake made from the sinewy horn of a bull aurochs. The resounding blast awoke the men from the tents. Shisita was hardly sleeping. Her duck-billed ax and shield were soon taken into her calloused and muscular hands. She raised a cry like the war scream of virgin 'Anat, the goddess of battle and bloodshed, and charged into the fray with her men.

When the battle cry was raised and the horn blared, Sutarna was asleep, but in his dream battle raged. His father, brothers, and uncles massacred, now his daughters, his beloved Yassib, struck down... not by a Ḥabiru, not by Pharaoh, but by Mot; the god of death himself. Sutarna jolted awake. The sound of carnage and battle blurred with his nightmare vision. Sutarna called out for his men, rallied them. He rushed to find his weapons. His lance, his sword, his javelins of Qitta, he gathered them all and rushed in boldly without his bronze scale mail cuirass and his shield. He saw Yassib in danger and he acted accordingly. He threw the javelin, twisting its leather strap so it spun as it flew. It flew hard, fast, and crucially accurately. It was as if Ba'alu's love guided the the trajectory of the missile. It smote the man who was brandishing his massive Sherden sword at Yassib, Sutarna's lover. After being saved, Yassib rushed to Sutarna's side and defended him from attack with his spear. Though the Syrians proved their courage and skill at arms, the night attack by the Sherdens was proving effective.

"What's the point of being a Na'arun if we don't have time to put on our damn armor!" shouted a noble man. He retreated, tripped over the dead body of his own younger brother, and was soon stabbed through the gut by a Sherden's sword. Many mothers lost sons that night.

202

"To the beach!" said a peasant who was trying his best to hold his own in the fight with a spit used for cooking meat.

Suddenly, as the men at the shore started contemplating their mistake in never learning to swim, the resounding clatter of the horse jaw rattle was heard. The chariots of Mitanni, firing swift arrows as they galloped, smashed right into the rear of the Sherdens. Some were kicked in the face by the horses, others impaled on lances, some were cut down by the scythes on the chariots' wheels, brutally maimed and hobbled. Others still were trampled outright. Hemmed in on the front and the back the Sherdens were squeezed out on both sides. Almost as if the charioteers had bid the darkness to give way, the eclipse ended. The Moon's brilliant light shone on the armor of the heroes.

As the men of Syria were too exhausted to pursue the attackers, they praised the gods for their salvation. "Oh mighty Ba'alu, you have brought us salvation this night" and the like. Coughs and wheezes filled the air along with the screams of joy and death.

Lance in one hand and reins in the other, the *Architect of Victory* rode up. He was glorious in full bronze scale and a gilded and bejeweled helmet. Then he spoke in a voice that was full of the heady pride of a true Maryannu, saying, "I am Etakkama. Your salvation rests with me, me, and my brother Biryawaza. I have heeded Pharaoh's call to come to your aid, and it seems I managed to come in the hour of your need."

"Hail to Etakkama of Mitanni" Sutarna caught his breath,

then raised his javelins, "and to the salvation, he has brought to my army, and Canaan, almost single-handedly."

When noon broke, the men, who had slept like corpses on the corpses, were ordered to prepare the burials for the slain. "Syrians and Sherdens both" Sutarna proclaimed, "deserve honorable burial. Let us not dishonor our enemies in our moment of triumph."

Sutarna then called the council of war, with his commanders in his big blue tent. Etakkama and Biryawaza were made to enter the tent, and were treated like guests of honor. Honeyed wine was served in golden rhytons.

"If you do not mind me asking, Sutarna, what is your plan to defeat the Ḥabiru and Lab'ayu? Surely you men must have thought this through." said Etakkama.

The majority of the commanders blushed wine red, their eyes going this way and that. Akizzi smirked and gloated a little. Etakkama put in words what he dared not say.

"We will march south to Retenu, increasing our numbers along the way, then meet Lab'ayu in battle and soundly defeat him." Confidently proclaimed Sutarna. His voice did not conceal the lack of confidence in his mind. Had he been a leader of confidence, such a simple plan would be accepted, even praised. However, in his faltering oration, Sutarna could not help but cause alarm, and increase the lack of faith in him.

"That... is your plan? That is all?" Etakkama chuckled a little but covered his mouth.

"What is wrong with that? We'll have the numbers, especially when we get troops from Hazor and Megiddo..."

"If you have the numbers, why do you think Lab'ayu will fight you?"

"We'll pursue him until he is forced to fight, or surrenders." Sutarna waved his javelin this way and that, smiting armies in the air.

"You are too slow. Ḫabiru soldiers move fast, they don't delay like you seem intent to do. I set off long after you did, and with more ground to cover, yet I quickly caught your tail. If you try to pursue them, you will never catch them. They will dance around you, harassing your flank and rear, whittling down your numbers and only then fighting you, once they know they'll win."

"Then we will divide our forces and send them after individual bands."

"So they can be corralled by the enemy and defeated in detail?"

"Exactly! You took the words right out of my mouth!" asserted Akizzi. Akizzi was most pleased that someone was entering the fray that seemed to know what he was doing.

"If those words were in your mouth, Akizzi, why did you not let Sutarna hear them long ago?" said Biryawaza.

"I did. He called it *cowardice and pessimism.*"

"There you go, Sutarna. You have an honest and wise man among your number, but I suspect you give ear to sycophants. I suspect you have a maiden in your tent every night to warm your bed? To lay is no great shame, but to heed? You should know; it is folly to give heed to the weaker sex." Etakkama beat his knees, laughing.

"Strangely, he does not keep a mistress. Unless you count Yassib here as a maiden; beard and all!" said Sharrupshi. He regretted his words almost immediately. Sutarna was a weakling, but he was malleable. Sharrupshi gave arrows to Etakkama's quiver... and he didn't know what sort of man Etakkama was. Knowing better than Sharrupshi, the other Syrians concealed any reaction they might have had from Sharrupshi's comment. They hoped if they didn't talk about it, the problem would go away.

"Sutarna. You have undertaken to lead a coalition to make war. Every waking moment of your time should be spent in preparation; logistics, strategy, and keeping abreast of who you can trust to advise you on these matters." said Biryawaza.

"You speak wisely, Biryawaza. And my father would do well to pay heed." said Shisita.

"Who is this woman, your daughter it seems, to speak in the

206

company of commanders and kings?" Etakkama didn't know whether to laugh or frown.

"She is Shisita, the Lady of the Lions…" said Sutarna.

"She boldly says what you must hear. I would not let a daughter do the same to me, but at the same time, I like that she does so to you! If you Canaanite men acted more like your maiden daughters then you'd be man enough to fight a war!" Etakkama clapped the butt of his spear against the platform of his chariot. "Even so. Restrain your women's tongues. They have no use in a council of war."

Shisita clenched her ax in her hand. If she squeezed it's handle any harder, the wood would be crushed into splinters. Before she could raise her voice in anger, Akizzi spoke.

"There is the question, Etakkama, of why the Sherdens attacked us. We may have enemies we know not of, or our main quarry may be forewarned." said Akizzi.

"That is a matter of importance, Akizzi, and I'm glad you mentioned it!" said Etakkama, "It must be Rib-Hadda of Gubla that sent the Sherdens. He has been known to use the services of Sherden mercenaries before. Did you not give him recourse to anger?"

"Why would the pitiable king of Gubla, that wretch, ever take such aggressive action against us?" asked Sutarna. "Has he not enough arms against him in Amurru?"

"Supplies! He thinks if he thins your number he will have more of your precious grain to feed his war effort. He badly wants to retake Ampi and Shigata and will do whatever it takes to achieve it. I assure you, he is no honorable man, however, purple his blood, his belly is yellow. I suggest you order your supplies to come through the land route, by way of Amqu, or better yet, let your army requisition some supplies as needed as they make their way through to Retenu. That way, our movements will be unrestrained and speedy, and you need not worry about storms on the sea."

All the while Etakkama spoke, his cunning plan became elaborate, and no one suspected it was indeed he who hired the Sherdens. Etakkama was a man of war, and the Syrians were like kids to the slaughter. On the night of the black moon, the goat-headed spinner of fate, Ashima, worked her loom. Red, red, was the linen, and black the wool.

32

Chapter 32: Freedom by the Sword

A new day rose over the town of Muhazzu. In the sky turned dull violet by ash and smoke, a gray sun rose. It surmounted ruins of burnt houses, the remains of vagabond dead. The heat of flames gave way to cinderous cold. In the square Lab'ayu, at the head of Shechemite troops but noticeably not Ḥabiru mercenaries, decided to speak to the populace. He affected the smile and charm of a liberator. In his right hand he held a sword, in the left, rattling chains. The meaning of his pantomime was clear for all to see. He offered freedom by the sword, or bondage. Like a singer who begins to raise her voice to song, he started to speak, at first softly and tenderly, then thunderous, gaining volume like a bull spurred to anger.

"I understand you think ill of me. You say I have entered your city by treachery and did rapine and pillage in your town. I pray you to forgive me, for it was not my intent. I intend to restore your burnt homes! I cannot resurrect your dead, nor restore the chastity of your violated maidens. But what I shall do is avenge you upon those truly responsible; Milkilu,

Addadanu, Yapahu, and all of Pharaoh's minions!"

He stood down, and all the men of Shechem cheered and whooped their jubilant cries. The men of Muhazzu were confused, to say the least. At last, a forty-year-old woman voiced what the body politique was thinking.

"So, you do not intend to sell us as slaves?" said a survivor.

"I certainly do not! I mean to liberate you. Before I came you were slaves, Pharaoh's chattel. But now you are sons and daughters of a free Canaan!"

"So you will make us your foot-soldiers and use us for your power game as fodder for your rebellion against Pharaoh?"

"I will force none to fight unless he, or she, wills it."

"You may be lying. You probably are. But between you, and that vermin Addadanu and that Nubian whore-monger Milkilu you are the lesser evil."

At that moment, dogs barking and howling strolled into the square at the head of a formation of Ḥabiru, Shechemites, and surprisingly troops from Ginti, which included provocatively dressed prostitutes. Some were well-armed in the equipment of the Lions of Anat. Those ill fated lions' heads were impaled on lances.

"So Ginti has fallen, eh, Yishaya?" asked Mutba'alu.

"Ginti came over to our side! Those bull asses put up a hard fight, but ultimately Milkilu's letter opened the gate better than hunger, rams, or a saboteur." Explained Yishaya, "May God bless Milkilu. He is kinder as an enemy than as a friend!"

"Milkilu is a fatuous lord. He sought to punish me when I did my part in his war far better than his brothers. When word reached me my daughter was out of his clutches and in the custody of Hanya and Huy, what joy I felt! Now, Milkilu shall fall, and I shall take back what was once mine!" said Tagi. "And so for all Canaan!"

"Well said, Tagi!" praised Lab'ayu," You shall be a hero of Canaan now, not a downtrodden vassal of Milkilu's crumbling dominion! Men of Muhazzu, women too, let your weapons rise against your petulant protector! We will cut out his heart, and send it to Pharaoh on a golden platter. That shall be the last of our tribute!"

Lab'ayu was like the prophet at the sea. When he spoke, the water moved. He thought it was he that moved the tide. Does not the tide move itself at its appointed hour? Woe to the children of God!

211

33

Chapter 33: The Qualities of a True King

Amenhotep III, the old pharaoh, rose from his sickbed at long last. What he had suspected proved true. His wife was putting something in his medicine and his food that was decidedly not making him better. It was positively making him worse! Naturally, he used his last ounce of breath, his last breath of life to refuse food that had been prepared behind his back. He had his loyal cupbearer Emminat prepare him simple food, grown and prepared before his eyes. Naturally, he started to recover his strength, throwing Tiye's plans into disarray. She started sending in pretty girls to slip her drugs into the new food, but Amenhotep was vigilant. He was not a man easy to trick; he wasted many pots of otherwise good food. Tiye of course kept up the act that she was innocent, instead, blaming his foreign wives Gilukhepa, and the newly arrived Tadukhepa, Gilukhepa's niece, and especially Emminat, who she called the power-hungry harlot of Canaan.

While Amenhotep was always wary of Gilukhepa, he now saw Tiye as his biggest threat. She had made many disagreeable decisions without his consent. She had sent the order to kill Milkilu, one of Amenhotep's most trusted and beloved Vassals to Hanya using his seal. She ordered the armies of the Syrian vassals to move south, weakening the Empire's northern border with Hatti. *A house is only as strong as its pillars, a family only as strong as its father.* Egypt faltered under the infirmity of her Pharaoh. *If only I could send away my poisoning wife,* Pharaoh thought. But he couldn't deny she was the strength of Egypt now. For all his flaws, Amenhotep III loved Egypt more than he loved life itself. He would not destroy the pillar of his house.

Tiye was right about Emminat being malicious. Emminat was sending letters to Mutba'alu and Lab'ayu and providing information for Gilukhepa to send to Mitanni. Mutba'alu would send letters to her as well, painted with ink on potsherds, hidden inside jars of oil and wine. Tiye could present all the proof she liked of the guilt of Emminat. Her guilt made Emminat as innocent as a virgin lamb in Amenhotep's eyes. Aware that his correspondence was being read, Mutba'alu coded his message in the vagueries of poetry.

To the ears of my beloved.
It is to the benefit of the gazelle that the lion's den is in consternation.
Let the lions battle over the does, and trouble the lioness with the roar of her mate.
May the old lion be strong, and the lioness in their den,

213

and make them claw at their beards
and let the ibex and the leaping hare play in the summer sun.

Emminat played her game, letting Amenhotep get strong enough to stymie his wife, but never so strong that he would fully dispatch with the rule of Tiye. In this way, Egypt was rendered headless, or at least two-faced, which was exactly what Mutba'alu wanted. Emminat still obeyed her distant lover but also had grown attached to the old man. She wanted her son, Smenkhare to know his father, and in time rule the Empire. She would raise her son to be friendly to her people, so Egypt and Canaan would be tied with bonds of trade and amity, not blood and fetters.

As for Nefertiti, she was wed as was planned to the prince, and she set to work moderating the impulses of her husband so Tiye could rule in his stead. The whole truth was that Egypt's empire was many spinning plates, as Amenhotep III often said. But the plates in Canaan were now in a death whirl, almost set to collapse. That was no concern for Amenhotep IV. When you tell a man who the world calls ugly about how beautiful he is, tell an extremist about how right he is about religion, and add a side of sex to boot; you will have him eating right out of your hand. Especially so if you are beautiful beyond compare. Nefertiti was the servant who was mistress, as all great royal wives strive to be.

Amenhotep the Elder had one last deed he wished to carry through to prevent the whole system from falling permanently into anarchy. A message was prepared and given to the fastest racer in the whole chariot corps. The messenger's

214

chariot sent with Pharaoh's order to save Milkilu's life sped ahead, through the desert sands on the road to Gezer. The fate of Pharaoh's pimp hung in the balance. The fate of Egypt and Canaan rested on the spokes of Pharaoh's swiftest chariot.

34

Chapter 34: Entrance of the Archers

When the Pitati entered the city of Gezer through the great Ilu Gate, loud fanfare was in the air, but Atlanersa the Pitati champion could tell it was false pageantry. He had been feted and fed by many Canaanite kings before. Behind their smiles and hospitality lurked hate, and all too often a dagger. Atlanersa had learned to be vigilant. While Hanya could be fooled by the gallant gaiety, the world-weary and war-wise Atlanersa, the falcon of Napata, could not be deceived. He whispered to his friend and lover Shabaqo, "They make these efforts to convince us they welcome us. But with the Canaanites, a smile hides a dagger; an embrace of the cruel spear. They resent us Nuba, don't let anyone fool you. Keep your knife at your belt and go nowhere without bow and quiver."

"Why do you fear these Canaanites so!? They are mice men, and we are the lions of Kush. We are warriors, and they are fit only to tend the vine and the olive bough, and trade in the surplus of better peoples."

"Heed me Shabaqo, for I am the veteran of many battles. The Canaanites are not mice, they are the waiting crocodile. Trust not the light-skinned ones, especially in their generosity."

The Pitati were brought into the courtyard of the and were fed sumptuously; wine with honey, roasted nuts, sweetmeats of figs and dates, cakes of honeyed spelt, and fine delicacies made of the carob pod. Then stews and roasts; lambs, goats, hares, cows, chickens, ducks, and camels. The Pitati were well fed and intoxicated with sweets and wine. Finally, the host, Milkilu, rose and spoke to them in their native tongue, the language of Kush.

"Welcome, men of my own kin! It is honorable to be seated in the midst of the great warriors, the mighty Pitati, whose arrows fell lions!"

The Nubian Pitati who were eating hungrily and chatting gregariously, now stopped and paid heed to their benefactor. Their silence lasted some thirty seconds, before one among them spoke brazenly. He shot his sharp words like an arrow in the direction of Milkilu.

"Milkilu is not a name among us Nuba. You are of the Canaanites. Do not speak to us as brothers in our tongue. You do not speak it well, and you are not of us. We cannot but be insulted!" scolded Shebaqo. Atlanersa grasped the shoulder of his impetuous lover, to retrain him from leaping to his feet. Every Pitati in the room felt agreement with Shebaqo. Their faces told that story, even if their tongues

217

did not. Hanya grimaced. The love of Milkilu still choked his heart like a copper garrote. He recalled the teaching of Amenemope, *Associate not with a passionate man, Nor approach him for conversation; Leap not to cleave to such an one; That terror carry thee not away.* Another teaching of the same Amenemope always ripped at his side, no matter how he strove to silence it. *Beware of robbing the poor, and oppressing the afflicted.* Hanya was torn apart by the wild beasts of compassion and duty. *Milkilu my friend, I kill my self to harm you. Forgive me my obedience to evil.*

Embarrassed and secretly infuriated by the disrespect he was shown by these common soldiers, men he had done his utmost to honor and please, Milkilu retired to his chamber, sending along the Pitati to their barracks. But the drunk Pitati did not stay there, but went out into the city, entered houses, and did what they wilt with the women. The reputation of the Pitati was feared in all Canaan. Now, the citizens of Gezer would be reminded why. The children born by these nocturnal activities would ever more be known as: 'Children of Milkilu'.

Meanwhile, in the palace, Milkilu was too vexed to sleep. He found his dove-down cushions unusually rough. His head never found a comfortable resting place. As he shook back and forth in his bed, thoughts clashed in his mind. *Betrayal, revenge, slaughter, destruction.* He was losing the war, and it seemed there was no way out for him. He nodded off to sleep for about half an hour, then jolted awake when he found his dreams just as tiresome as his waking thoughts. He bid Shapiri-Ashtar join him, and they drank undiluted

Arak. Shapiri-Ashtar was the last person Milkilu trusted in the world. Beautiful, intelligent, and loyally accommodating, Milkilu wished his brothers would take after his Vizier.

"I had my spies investigate Hanya," informed Shapiri-Ashtar, "And they found him in sorrow, melancholy and dread."

"Of what?" replied Milkilu, "He is a man of great mirth and cheer, one who is a friend to all men."

"It has been revealed that the Pharaoh has ordered your death…"

"No. Impossible. Amenhotep would never do that. Not after all I've done for him!"

"The order Hanya received, with Pharaoh's seal upon it, was that you must die, and Yapahu should take Gezer."

"This is not the work of Amenhotep. He must be dying. The beloved friend of my entire life would not betray me, lest he was betrayed. Tiye! It was his scheming malicious wife that made use of his seal. Surely Hanya must realize that!"

"Be that as it may, the order was sealed with the seal of the Pharaoh, and Hanya must obey. I do not see the Pitati hesitating to carry out that order. Best betray the world before the world betrays you."

"You are the only friend by my side, Shapiri-Ashtar. But I cannot do harm unto Hanya, the Commissioner of Archers.

I alone can not even beat Lab'ayu! How can I beat Lab'ayu, my Brothers, and all of Egypt? It seems all is lost."

"You were put in this loathsome situation, my King, by serving Egypt. Your fate is alike unto that of Rib-Hadda, humbled by Amurru. Meanwhile the disloyal prospers. See how strong Lab'ayu becomes as a rebel! Make common cause with Lab'ayu, and in pillage enrich yourself among kings, yea, even in battle proclaim your name, not as a pimp and a lackey to Pharaoh but as a hero and a warrior!"

"As for Hanya, Yapahu, Addadanu, and the Pitati, what of their fate? And whom can I trust to convey my message to Lab'ayu?"

"Among them slay all, all but one, Addadanu. Make him your heir, above Yapahu, and he will be beholden to you. For him nothing is more hated than serving Yapahu. I'll convey the message. Soon Hanya will rest with his ancestors, along with the loathsome Pitati."

"What a bold path I shall follow, what a sad fate is mine." lamented Milkilu, "I pray to the gods to forgive me."

"Ilu and Ba'alu will not trouble you; destiny is non-existent. The path we choose in life determines our fate. Proceed with wisdom, open eyes, and cocked ears to hear the whispers, and in all ways, your life will be glorious and long."

220

35

Chapter 35: He Went Before the Assembly

"Addadanu, I know your secret." said Shapiri-Ashtar.

"What secret!?" Addadanu grimaced in jealousy and consternation.

"Your plans with Yapahu." Shapiri-Ashtar grinned, "No secret escapes me."

"What of it!" Addadanu crashed his fist into a cedar wood beam. He shook his injured hand and kissed it.

"I have a proposition for you..."

"What's a proposition?"

"I have an offer for you. Let's say you went through with the plan and betrayed Milkilu to Hanya and the Egyptians. What would you stand to gain?"

"Ummmm..." Addadanu went silent.

"You see, no one thinks about you! You are a worthy man, a good man, Milkilu's right hand!" Shapiri-Ashtar put his hands on Addadanu's shoulders, "Yapahu thinks he is better than you, that he is the brains of the whole operation, and you are but a pretty baby. Do you really want Yapahu's ugly fingers to caress the nethermouth of your beloved?"

"Damn no! But Hanya said..."

"To hell with Hanya! My word carries weight with Milkilu. Perhaps I can arrange some arcane procedure to allow your hearts desire to come to pass... Gold, garments, girls... perhaps Ramashtu can be..."

"Shapiri-Ashtar, you are talking so nice." Addadanu blushed, "Even she..."

"Can be yours."

"Tell me what task you need from me. I'm going to do it, or my name is not Addadanu."

Addadanu didn't have to ride far to find the army of Lab'ayu. They were nearly at the gates of Gezer, ready to besiege, to sack, pillage, slaughter, and rape. Needless to say, they were all in good spirits. They were astonished to see Addadanu arrive under the flag of truce. When the Peacock began to speak, their astonishment turned to awe.

222

"In the maelstrom of war, we all strive for victory, in order to secure multitudinous blessings upon our nation, but in the course of events when defeat becomes inevitable, and our erstwhile friends are offering us as a fatling to a holocaust, bonds mus be made and unmade. In light of current events, Milkilu and I have deigned to offer unto you Gezer, her arms at your disposal, her gold to pay your arm-bearers and without the carnage and loss of a battle or the depredation of siege." said Addadanu, affecting the highest register he could muster.

"Rayy!" cheered Abneru, laughing heartily, and clapping sarcastically, "You composed that little piece all by yourself, and memorized it too, for our sorry ears! Bravo!"

Addadanu rushed to pull down the sleeves of his robe, concealing the barely legible scrawl of Shapiri-Ashtar's words inked on his arm.

"The long and short of it is that Milkilu is in hot water with Egypt, and he wants to throw his lots in with you. That is why I think he sent me..."

"Addadanu, you show meritorious courage in coming to us with no guard, to ask us for forgiveness on behalf of your brother." complimented Lab'ayu. "But..."

"What does meritorious mean?" asked the tedious Addadanu.

"It means good, worthy of merit" Chided Mutba'alu, "You ignorant dust-sucking shoe licker."

223

"Oh, I thought it meant something like handsome, or gorgeous. I get those sorts of words a lot. Women like calling me nice things in big words. I'd rather a woman have big breasts, huge backsides than know big words. A woman's mouth is for sucking, not for speaking."

"What I was trying to say, Addadanu, was that you and your brothers were our primary objective in the war. No offense, but we don't like you. No one who has any sort of decency likes you, and we rebelled to utterly destroy you and raze Gezer to the ground as the pit of sin and debauchery it is. Why should we hear you out?" asked Lab'ayu.

"Give him a chance," said Abneru, "I believe I can speak for all the Ḥabiru here. Our goal in this whole business was to get paid. If we can do so without the tiresome boredom and troublesome risk of a siege, then all the better. I, for one, suggest we combine forces... Shechem and Gezer, and we shake down all the cities of Retenu. None would be strong enough to resist our combined might. There are so many ripe fruits to pluck, such as Lachish, Akko, Jerusalem, Gath... We could even shake down Megiddo, or mighty Hazor."

"Exactly, and who wouldn't consent to a deal where you, me, everyone involved would get incredibly rich?" asked Addadanu.

"It has merit." said the conflicted Lab'ayu, "But I don't mean to swindle Canaan, but to free it. One united Canaanite nation, with one King of Kings over it all: But your troops, your city, are truly invaluable. It would be a dear loss to Pharaoh

224

if we had it. It would cut off the line from North to South, splitting off what is beyond Gezer from the subjugation of Pharaoh."

"Lab'ayu, will you honor our terms? We ask only that you enter our city by night, slay those black devils, the Pitati, expunge Hanya, and make his head an offering at Tjaru." asked Addadanu.

"Before we can make you our friend, Addadanu, I hope you will accept our hospitality, and enjoy a delicacy I have prepared specifically with you in mind." sniveled Mutba'alu.

"Well, I'd be honored to taste whatever delicacy you think is worthy to pass my perfect lips."

"Slave girl, come, bring the platter"

Two large, fatty, round lumps of meat were served to Addadanu on a silver platter. The aroma was absolutely delicious, both unique from any other flesh he had tasted, but at the same time uncannily familiar in a very pleasant way. Ravenously, he tore into the succulent, fatty flesh with his fingers. Soon he ate every last bite, and licked his fingers.

"It is a little bit like camel hump, fatty, but it is tender and mild like a fatling calf. A most interesting meal I must say, and I would love to see the type of beast the meat belonged to. The epicures of Gezer would just gobble this up, and if I had a herd of them, I could make a killing!"

"You are looking at the 'beast' now!" Milkilu pulled the veil off his slave girl, revealing her to be Addadanu's old lover, Tamar bit Ammunapi. A few minutes of awkward silence went by, with Mutba'alu waiting for him to have a horrified or devastated reaction. Even a retch, a dry heave, would suffice. Addadanu was not that sort of man. For him, it was more pleasurable than distasteful. He had long been curious what human meat would taste like. He was curious what part of her they used to make his meal. He looked at the girl's face, then down, to where her large handsome bosoms once hung. Now, there was nothing but boyish flatness. He was not tempted to remove the dark cloth that covered her scarred flesh.

"It is a pity you cut off her breasts," said Addadanu nonchalantly, "because it was the only thing of value about her. I'm sure you'd have enjoyed squeezing them more. Now you made a valuable girl utterly worthless. But… I am grateful to have tasted such a rare delicacy. My compliments to the chef."

Now while Addadanu wasn't truly shocked by Mutba'alu's behavior, Tamar certainly was by Addadanu's. This man who she had laid with, loved, and trusted was now shown to literally see her as a piece of meat. She slapped him and spat at his face.

"Addadanu, you are scum! I'd choose even Mutba'alu as a lover over you! You are worth less than donkey excrement mixed with bull semen and chicken piss!"

Addadanu, not used to being mocked and insulted by a woman, punched her in the face with all his strength. It was not a wrathful strike, more of an instinctual, callous one. He reacted like he would have had a man said what she said. As for Tamar, she was thrown about five feet backwards to the ground. Her skull broke against a rock and she died almost immediately.

"Well done!" Abneru clapped his hands in amazement and admiration, "You have the makings of a true Ḥabiru!"

Addadanu, having shown his colors, embraced the Ḥabiru one by one. They hugged him, kissed his cheek. He was now their brother. Such a deed as his was worthy of a Ḥabiru of the highest order. They feasted and ate meat, and he was presented with weapons and kilts in the Ḥabiru fashion. He was no longer Addadanu the Peacock, he was Addadanu the Devourer.

36

Chapter 36: Exit of the Archers

In the dead of the black night, men hastened and hurried. Milkilu's servants opened the gates of Ilu inconspicuously, allowing the Ḥabiru to enter as silently as shadows. Milkilu was with his men hurrying towards the gate at the appointed hour. With the moon shining behind him, no one hastened faster than Shapiri-Ashtar. He hastened to the Pitati, to Hanya, to declare a message. He beat upon the gates and relayed there was dire news to be declared to Hanya. To Hanya, he was brought, and Shapiri-Ashtar spoke, "Hanya, I have dire news. Evil is to be attempted on your life, yea even the lives of your soldiers. Milkilu believes you mean to depose him, and while I gave him countless reasons not to think so, he has resolved to make common cause with Lab'ayu and open the city of Gezer to him. Therein, there shall be little means of defense for your men. So I say, hasten to escape by a hidden way. My slave will guide you!"

"How did Milkilu come to believe we meant him harm? Who revealed it?"

"I suspect it was Addadanu, seeking personal gain. I would have smitten him dead but there is no time, the Ḥabiru are upon us. Make good your escape, I shall remain by Milkilu's side and for you, I shall be eyes and ears. Now go!"

To his credit, Hanya took upon himself the task of rousing the archers. When Hanya came into the barracks banging a big copper pot, Atlanersa and Shabaqo were cuddled up like two puppies dreaming sweet dreams about stewed beef from their hometown of Edfu. Needless to say, they were upset about being awoken at 2 AM by Hanya, screaming and thumping cookware.

"Hasten, Oh Pitati! For the love of Amun take up the bow and let's be out of here! The enemy is upon us!"

The yawning, groaning, grumbling Pitati each took into their hands their fine composite bows and obsidian-tipped arrows. Or, it's fairer to say that they fumbled about in the dark, finding any bow and arrow they could get as best they could. They tripped and bumped into each other; they couldn't see each other in the dark. Hanya led his men into the street. The darkness was at first blinding, but it was miraculously lifted. The clouds that had covered the moon parted, and the shining celestial orb illuminated the streets. The sharp-eyed Pitati could see the enemy coming, and they began their fighting retreat.

The Ḥabiru and troops from Shechem and Ginti were sneaking into the city, preparing to take the Pitati by surprise. Milkilu and Addadanu were among them, leading them to

229

where the troopers were to be stationed. It was Addadanu, and the whores of Ginti, who were accustomed to nocturnal activity, that first noticed the Nubian archers escaping the barracks. Addadanu gave the first effective battle order of his entire military career up to that point. He had the men raise their shields. It was a lucky thing too, for the whistling arrows soon rained down among Lab'ayu's army. Had the men been caught off guard the casualties would have been catastrophic. They were instead merely devastating. Arrows pierced feet and shins instead of hearts and faces. Spurred to action by his foes' missile barrage, Lab'ayu from his chariot led the charge. The Maryannu charioteers thundered through the streets, followed by infantrymen, archers and slingers. Knowing they did not want to be trampled under hooves, the Pitati climbed the facades of the houses onto the roofs. There, they would be able to shoot their arrows with a height advantage and be safe from the charioteers and the infantrymen. They would retreat slowly, only giving up ground piecemeal, and at great cost to the attackers.

"Set fire to the houses!" said Abneru, "They are making pincushions of us!"

Lab'ayu thought quickly. Mutba'alu, Tagi, Dadua, and Yishaya all shared the same sentiments. Alone Issuwa raised his objection.

"Are you mad! We can't burn the city! It has come over to our side peacefully. Let's find another way to deal with the Pitati."

"What do you have in mind, Issuwa? I am loath to burn the city as well, but I fail to see any other way." said Lab'ayu.

"I will need three things. Ladders, of course, to scale the roofs. Secondly, I need archers and slingers of my own, and finally, those swift chariot runners, those youths who keep pace with the chariot troops."

"Take them! And go quickly!"

Issuwa led the men up the ladders. With the missile troops of Lab'ayu now at equal height to the Pitati, they could trade shots more equally. But it was the runners who were the bane of the Pitati. The fast-moving runners chased the Pitati from building to building, not allowing them to rest long enough to shoot many arrows. Those who were not swift were caught up to and ran through with spears. Hanya, courageous though he was, was not the equal of his archers at running. He was surrounded. His first instinct was to bargain for his life, he believed he would be a valuable hostage and would therefore not be slain. But when the youths set upon him, jabbing him here and there with their spears, he lifted his weapons to fight a hopeless battle. He was fortunate to have strong bronze scale armor, but that alone would not save him. He brandished his khopesh at the enemy, using the hook masterfully to disarm many attackers before slaying them with the blade or the backspike. But the youths soon learned the most valuable truth in war. When outclassed, rush the enemy all at once so he is unable to defend. Hanya was overwhelmed, and his body was pierced with about twenty-seven different wounds. He fought on to his last breath, praying to escape the fate of Senqenenre Ta'a, the much-lamented Pharaoh slain by the Canaanites.

It was in vain. He dropped dead, his fine linen tunic stained with his own blood. Issuwa beheaded the corpse, in disrespect for Egyptian customs. He hoisted the head atop his spear and called out a great cry of victory. Soon his victory cry was muffled into a whimper of death. The Pitati, in their last act of anger and defiance, shot about fourteen arrows into the body of Issuwa, before fleeing the city for good. Issuwa, who was sixty-four years old, met his end, toppling off the roof onto the hard street below. His son, Dadua, hearing Issuwa's cry, hastened to the side of his father. Taking his father by the hand, Dadua wept. He took Hanya's head off the lance that bore it, and kicked it into a latrine. Instead of resting in the land of reeds, the courageous Commissioner of Archers would rest in urine and feces.

The battle was at last won as the sun rose over the bloody scene. Lab'ayu was now the master of Gezer. He had vanquished the hated Pitati, and slain Hanya. It would be a victory worth celebrating. The cooks of Milkilu who had not so long ago prepared a feast for the Pitati would now prepare food for the Ḥabiru. And Lab'ayu looked down from the roof of Milkilu's palace. This was true victory and liberation. Canaan would be free. All paths were open, north, south, east, west. Lab'ayu smelled the meat roasting in the ovens. Ba'alu must have been smiling that day.

"As a calf returned to his mother, is Canaan to my hand." he

232

said.

He went to the halls of Milkilu, to greet his eternal enemy with words of amity and friendship. Sometimes, cooks do God's work!

II

TABLET TWO: BONDS FORGED, BONDS BROKEN

37

Letter of Abdi-Heba, King of Jerusalem, to Amenhotep III:

"Say to the king, my lord: Message of Abdi-Heba, your servant. I fall at the feet of my lord seven times and seven times. Consider the entire affair. Milkilu and Tagi brought troops into Qiltu against me. May the king know that all the lands are at peace with one another, but I am at war. May the king provide for his land. Consider the lands of Gezer, Ashkeluna, and Lachish. They have given my enemies food, oil, and any other requirement. So may the king provide for archers and send the archers against men that commit crimes against the king, my lord. If this year there are archers, then the lands and the vassals will belong to the king, my lord. But if there are no archers, then the king will have neither lands nor vassals. Consider Jerusalem! This neither my father nor my mother gave to me. The strong hand of the king gave it to me. Consider the deed! This is the deed of Milkilu and

the deed of the sons of Lab'ayu, who have given the land of the king to the Ḥabiru. Consider, O king, my lord! I am in the right!"

38

Chapter 38: Bread and Oil

Lachish was an old city, one of the oldest in the south. It's walls had stood for almost two thousand years. The people trusted in the walls, and its strong gates. They had forgotten why they stood so long. The king, Zimredda, was not under the same illusion. The walls of Lachish stood from acquiescing. A king that has no enemies suffers no defeats. A gate that is always open is never broken. Or so Zimredda thought.

Zimredda and his son, Shipti-Ba'alu had watched the war unfold with great relish. Neither of them were fond of Milkilu. When his power was broken at Ginti and at Muhazzu, they rejoiced. Lab'ayu was doing what no king dared before. He stood up to the corrupt prince of pimps and put him in his place. It was, to Zimredda and Shipti-Ba'alu, a reaffirmation of the Gods' favor for the ancient elite over the upstart rabble. But then, the situation changed.

"Father, I have grave news." Shipti-Ba'alu glanced directly at his father.

"Grave news! Do you want to give me a heart attack?" Zimredda looked this way and that.

"It is bad indeed! Lab'ayu has entered the city of Gezer."

"Why, that's great news! Serves those buggering brothers right! I can't wait to see their heads on spikes!" Zimredda shook his fist angrily. That made him tired. He walked over to a couch and lied on it.

"Their heads are not on spikes. They're at the head of an army. You see, what I meant to say is that Milkilu opened the gates to Lab'ayu, and now they're allies."

"Now... now... now! That's a grave matter indeed!" Zimredda jumped up, startled.

"They are moving south, towards us. Should I rally the Maryannu and harness the chariots?"

"What! Are you mad? Do you think we can take Lab'ayu and Milkilu at the same time?!"

"What are we supposed to do! They intend to make war and take the land of all the Kings under Pharaoh!"

"We open the gates to them, plain and simple."

"So we aid rebels now! What will we do when Egypt sends

240

forces against them?" Shipti-Ba'alu's nostrils blared.

"We open our gates to them too!"

"What kind of king do you get to be by acquiescing to every threat?"

"A very old one." Zimredda stroked his silvery beard.

It came to pass that when Lab'ayu and Milkilu and the rest of their forces came to Lachish, they found the gates wide open, and a smiling king waiting for them. In one hand he held a large loaf of bread, and in the other, a bowl of good quality olive oil.

"It seems the king of Lachish hastens to meet us with open arms and not spears." said Lab'ayu.

"A pity." said Milkilu, under his breath.

"Welcome! My honored guests, please eat of this bread and oil and partake of my hospitality!" said Zimredda of Lachish.

Lab'ayu tore off a piece of bread, and dipped it deep into the oil, swirling it around. Then he plucked it into his mouth and masticated. "This oil," he said, "Is very good. Almost as good as the oil of Gerizim!"

"All of you, good men, taste my oil! It is the finest around, I assure you!" said Zimredda, "Besides that of Gerizim, of course."

Mutba'alu ate, and Dadua, Yishaya, Abneru, Ayyabu, and even Addadanu all ate. At last, Milkilu alone had not tasted the sweet oil.

"Why the reluctance, Milkilu?" asked Mutba'alu.

"It's because it's been poisoned!" joked Abneru, pretending to choke and fall down dead.

Milkilu looked at the brown bread, then at the yellow oil. It might as well have been excrement and urine, coming from Zimredda of Lachish. Seeing the impatient looks on his new allies' faces as he delayed to complete the ritual, he tore off a piece of bread, albeit a small one, and brushed the surface of the oil with it.

"Lab'ayu spoke true, the oil of Gerizim IS better." said Milkilu, talking as he chewed. He had no respect for the weak-kneed king of Lachish. "But the oil of Gezer has no equal."

Into the palace, the kings of Gezer and Shechem were inducted. The walls were richly painted in the style of the long-lost kingdom of Mari. Antique paintings were a clue for Milkilu's suspicions. The palace had not been destroyed for a inordinately long time, unlike the palaces of Gezer or Shechem. This could only be the mark of a city that was an enemy to no one, at least no one strong. Milkilu knew Zimredda could not be trusted. Lab'ayu, on the other hand, was ever forgiving and trusting. It's what saved Milkilu's life. Now Milkilu feared it would seal his fate.

242

"Now, let us, all men of action, decide upon the course of action for our war." said Lab'ayu.

"There is not much treasure here in the south, I'm afraid." Zimredda glanced at his feet. "So, I recommend that you instead go north. The riches of Megiddo, Taanach, and Akko await there. And I'll be more than happy to guard your rear against Yanhamu and whatever feeble attack he can muster from Sharuhen."

"I have a much better idea, Lab'ayu, if you would give ear to it." said Milkilu, "I say we stay here in the south, and take some of the low-hanging fruit. Qiltu, Gath, even Jerusalem would not be too much for us to handle." Milkilu did not like the idea of Zimredda 'guarding his rear'.

"A good idea, Milkilu. But as for Zimredda's idea, it too has merit. I have decided. Milkilu, why don't you, Addadanu and Mutba'alu secure the south, while I go, with Ayyab, Abneru, and Yishaya to the north. As for Dadua, he shall stay to guard Shechem."

"I assure you, there isn't much here in the south worth conquering." said Zimredda. "Jerusalem is a tough nut to crack, and it's barely worth it. When I am thinking of cities hardly worth the land they are built on, I think Jerusalem."

"Why are you defending Abdi-Heba?" asked Mutba'alu, "Is he your ally?"

"I'm not defending him! I just don't want you to waste your

243

time and men on him. He's not worth it. No glory to be gained fighting the son of a footsoldier."

Milkilu stooped to the side and whispered something in Lab'ayu's ear.

"So it's decided. Milkilu and Mutba'alu will stay in the south, while I go north and liberate Megiddo. Zimredda, I expect you to obey and honor Milkilu and Mutba'alu, just as if they were me. I will give them my seal." Lab'ayu reached for his seal. "It must be in here somewhere... Aha!"

And soon, Zimredda would learn that some gates are better left unopened.

39

Chapter 39: The Fox of the Hills

"Abdi-Heba's career spoke for itself. The son of a humble footsoldier in the service of Pharaoh, his wit and skill at arms soon won the admiration of Amenhotep III. The boy exceeded all others it seemed, no matter what he tried his hands at. By the age of ten, he had mastered Egyptian Hieroglyphic writing and could read, write and speak fluent Akkadian. He was a skilled archer, could wrestle boys twice his size, and could drive a chariot like no one Amenhotep had ever seen. Had this boy been born a royal prince of Egypt, he would have been another Tuthmose III. Instead, as the son of a common foot soldier, he was by merit alone promoted to be king of Jerusalem. From a minor city of little importance, he transformed the hill town into the center of a powerful state dominating the hill country of Southeastern Retenu Valley. Those who dared resist him were masterfully subdued by the greatest of Kings."

"That," said Abdi Heba, to his chief scribe, "was pure poetry. One little matter to correct, and I hope you'll indulge me.

I, Abdi-Heba, am a Mayor, no king; merely Pharaoh's loyal servant."

"Certainly," said the Scribe, "I'll have the diorite carved to your specifications. King or no king, your merit is ostentatious."

"What does this word 'ostentatious' mean?" Abdi-Heba asked.

"Pardon me, oh king... oh mayor... oh servant of Pharaoh. I mean to say your merit is apparent."

"And that so-called noble King of Gath better remember that. Or else I'll lick her again."

"Surely you will. Defeat her I mean. Now, Abdi-Heba, I would suggest that in her company, perhaps you could refrain from colloquialisms and adopt a more... for lack of a better word... kingly persona."

"Good advice as always. Send her in. I will use my 'Kingly' register. Ma mê mi mô mu... Ma mê mi mô mu..."

"As you command, Abdi-Heba. Also, good improvement on your vowels."

A surly-looking female king was led into the throne room, sniveling as she looked at the plunder placed without care for what would enhance the mise en place of the room. It was a vulgar display of ill-gotten wealth. Shuwardata had no love for the King of Jerusalem. She gazed around, regarding

246

with jealousy and repudiation his possession of her former property. That was the cost of weakness among kings. If you cannot win the battle with swords, you must pay tribute. Shuwardata paid dearly to Abdi-Heba.

"Welcome, honored guest" said Abdi-Heba, reveling in the irony and discomfort for his beleaguered hostage, "I have been informed you have a matter which concerns me, the loyal servant of Pharaoh."

"I commit myself and my cities into your hands for you to save me from Milkilu and the sons of Lab'ayu." Shuwardata gestured with open hands.

"King Shuwardata, my lady, have no fear! Have no apprehension! Abdi-Heba your liege shall deal with these rebels. Even as great Hebat and Teshub have delivered into my hands Jerusalem, so too shall be delivered these rebel traitors. Beat not your breasts!"

The affected, refined speech of Abdi Heba made Shuwardata groan and grunt with inequity. Brought up with aristocratic pomp, Shuwardata had been treated as a superior individual her whole life. Her lot was to be genuflected to by lesser souls. Had she been dealt with so condescendingly by any mere footsoldier's son, she would have ordered him beaten with a knotted olive bough. Now the tables were turned. The common man now sat above her like a judging god, and it would have to be her that would submit to him. "How I pray, shall I... I mean you, pardon me, deal with these rebellious Kings?" She tripped over her words. In her mind, angry fire and calming water met. No wonder then that she would blow steam.

"We shall create a binding treaty with Ṣurata of Akko and his brothers Biridiya of Megiddo and Yaṣdata of Taanach. With our combined forces encircling the territory of the rebels, we shall put into action a strategy of mobile warfare. When the enemy dares attack any one of our cities, the others shall render chariots to his aid. The city walls shall be the mortar and the chariotry shall be the pestle. Using such a strategy, we can grind down the enemy like corn to flour!"

The efficacy of the plan was apparent to even this blue-blooded lady. Though it was hatred that governed her opinion of Abdi-Heba, she could not but respect the strategic mind of her erstwhile foe. Now the "Base Cunning" that broke the back of her kingdom shall be turned to her aid. Could she allow herself to be taken in by the son of a footsoldier? He had the mind of a King, a great one. No matter, she thought. If the opportune moment would present itself, she could always switch sides. Milkilu was a son of nobody, but Lab'ayu? His family was an ancient one, one that by virtue of nobility was worthy of respect. She would only stay loyal to Egypt as long as it was convenient.

"How do I know that when I am attacked by the sons of Lab'ayu and the pimp, you will hasten to my aid?" asked Shuwardata, breaching the rules of etiquette.

"I could ask the same of you! But what matters in this situation, is, as always, are practicalities. You will aid me for the same reason I will graciously lend my strong hand to you; for our own self-preservation. We have no other alternative."

Shuwardata was fed and set on her way. Despite achieving what she desired from this diplomatic mission, she could not help but feel violated, as if nature itself was offended by her submission to a commoner. Abdi-Heba was again alone in his throne room, chatting with his loyal scribe.

"What really gets to me about these aristocratic fools is this!" Abdi-Heba cackled, "Don't they know that any dynasty, however time-honored, has a founder? They honor their esteemed founder yet revile me as an upstart. Were not even ancient Alulim and great Dumuzid but shepherds before kingship passed to them!?"

"An astute point as always." said the scribe.

"It is GREATNESS that makes a man great, not birth! For we are all descended from men who work the hoe. When I defeat the sons of Lab'ayu, that proud fool better respect me or I'll not show her such mercy when I raid her lands. Now scribe, it is the time to recruit Ḥabiru. If Milkilu and Lab'ayu want to play with fire, they should know my heart is full of kindling too!"

"I'll send for the captains of the Ḥabiru at once!"

"In two thousand years, even three thousand years time, it will be Jerusalem that will be first among cities. Even mighty

249

Hazor will be forgotten and lay in ruin, but Jerusalem will forever be strong."

"Keep dreaming, master!" said the scribe, "Greatness is built on mighty aspirations, no matter how impossible."

"Nothing is impossible!" Abdi-Heba slammed his large fist into his muscular chest.

"Well, you may be right. Abdi-Tirshi is running Hazor into the ground." The scribe looked over the letters he had been writing to the Pharaoh in Abdi-Heba's name.

"Shows what good noble birth does you! Abdi-Tirshi, Lab'ayu, Sutarna. *I'm Sutarna, son of Abdi-Ḫimaru, son of Idiot, son of Shoe-Licker, son of Piss-Drinker, son of Lickspittle, son of Curr, son of Durusha...*" He held his head high in mock reverence for Durusha, before lowering his hands to his knees to laugh.

"Sometimes a mule is birthed from a fine mare."

"Sometimes a horse is!" Abdi-Heba laughed, "When the donkeys are away at war."

40

Chapter 40: The Wolf Leads the Sheep

The Army of Syria marched a faster pace ever since Etakkama and Biryawaza joined with them. True, instead of aiding villages that they passed along the way, the Army looted them, took what they needed and moved on, but this is war! So thought Shisita. Etakkama was a worthy man. Anyone who can spur on her father Sutarna to bold action was alright in her book. Sutarna was beginning to take to the warlike spirit. The ambush on the beach gave Sutarna no choice but to reveal his true colors as a warrior. When danger faced him, he could no longer cower behind his men. He fought with javelin and spear like the best of them. As Shisita could plainly see, it was for Sutarna like a weighty chain and collar had been removed from his neck. He was no longer a slave to fear. She wondered what other bonds he broke.

It was not long before the army entered the Kingdom of Hazor. The city of Hazor, which controlled the region around the lake of Kinneret, was one of the most ancient, strong, and proud cities in all of Canaan. That was to say nothing of its wealth. It's mighty walls stood taller than any the Syrians had ever seen. Compared to the walls of Hazor, those of Qadesh, Qaṭna, and Ukalzat were like mere piles of stone. It was as if the builders of the wall had set out to rival Mount Hermon itself due northeast of the city.

"What a magnificent wall!" said Sharrupshi, "I dare say no one could ever take it!"

"Who would even try?" asked Idanda, "If only Qaṭna had walls like this, then, Hatti would never trouble us."

"Qaṭna's walls are her brave men." said Akizzi, "Because walls alone are no good. Walls without men are like a fine bow with no arrows."

"I would say Hazor has men in abundance! I've never seen so many houses in one place!" said Biryawaza, "If one in five can be counted on to soldier, Hazor could repel even Hatti."

"And what of its king." asked Etakkama, "That is what matters."

"He… is a very certain sort of man." said Sutarna, "Not a man to be trifled with. Respect is due to any who rule a city as great as Hazor, and have as noble a birth as Abdi-Tirshi."

"Do you know him?" asked Shisita.

"We all will before long. I'm certain he will treat us graciously

252

as befits royal guests." replied Sutarna, "His pedigree is long, and prestigious."

"So you do not know him." said Shisita, "What you say is true in one regard. He is no man to be trifled with. It is best to avoid his company altogether in fact. We will have a far warmer welcome in Megiddo."

"This is when you should strike her. A daughter should be beaten when she speaks nonsense." said Etakkama.

"What is nonsense about what I said? I know these lands and their peoples better than anyone here. I say Hazor is best avoided."

"If you regard the word of your daughter above a prince of Mitanni, I don't know what it says about your manhood, Sutarna." said Etakkama. He made a pinching gesture with his finger, demonstrating the assumed size of Sutarna's manparts. Then, the Maryannu for Mitanni started to copy the gesture, mocking the King.

"We'll enter Hazor. It's a strong city by all accounts. Let's make a pact with Abdi-Tirshi. We need all the troops we can get after how many we lost in the ambush." said Sutarna, giving in to the pressure of the mockery.

"Then you men must get accustomed to the taste of other men's bottoms. Although I will admit this may prove less challenging to some than others." said Shisita.

Hazor proved a fairly easy mistress to enter. The gate was opened to the men of Syria with little need to argue or haggle. However, as the men entered the city, they had to hand over their weapons to the guardsmen of the city. This, the guardsmen said, was to uphold law and custom in the great city. No foreigner could be armed in the city, it was a standard precaution. Sutarna agreed readily; his intent was peaceful and diplomatic. What had he to fear from a man he had no quarrel with?

In a town as important as Hazor, it was not difficult to secure comfortable lodgings for the troops. The trade in tin (the lifeblood of all nations at the time) was brisk in Hazor, and the people were accustomed to letting rooms to those with the ability to pay. While the private residences of common citizens would suffice for the soldiery, the needs of royalty could only be serviced by royalty, in the comfort of a palace. Messengers were sent to Abdi-Tirshi. His residence was easy enough to find. There was no palace like it in all of Canaan. Only Malkata at Thebes, the residence of the Pharaoh, proved a match for it in the imagination of the Syrian kings. However, when the messengers reached the palace gates, they were sent away by the guards for not having the proper seals to show for certain that they indeed represented the royalty they purported to. The Syrian leaders, slightly miffed at the requirement, sent the servants again with the proper seals. When the servants arrived, they gave the seals to the guards. The guards then took the seals in, saying they would examine them. One hour passed, then two, then three. Finally, sick of waiting, the leaders went to the servants at the gate.

254

"What have you been doing, twiddling your thumbs! It's nearly dinner time and still, you haven't secured our room and board!" said Sharrupshi. Then he, and many other kings and princes began thrashing their servants, who tried in vain to protest, "Sire, the guardsmen of the palace have left to examine the royal seals, and they haven't returned." If it were not for the confiscation of the weapons by the Hazorites earlier, there would have been a bloodbath at the very gates of the palace. Finally, a voice came from the balcony above. It was Abdi-Tirshi.

"What is all this rancorous racket! I'm trying to eat my supper!"

At that moment, the guardsman of the palace bearing the royal seals arrived at the location of the King Abdi-Tirshi. He attempted to hand off the seals to the King.

"What am I to do with these!"

"These are the royal seals of the kings and princes who have come to greet you at the palace."

"Kings and princes eh? Kings and princes are as base as lowly chamberpot-emptiers these days. Abdi-Heba is the son of a footsoldier! A BLOODY FOOTSOLDIER! And Milkilu and his damned brothers are just glorified whore mongers."

"Sire, these are real kings and princes. From Syria. Qadesh, Qaṭna, Nuhhashe…"

"Why didn't you tell me they are Syrian! Have them come in at once!" Abdi-Tirshi leaned his proud head out over the balustrade, "Oh, kings, I beg your pardon! I bid you lay off striking your servants! My servants shall take up that task for you!"

With the changing of the guard, as it were, for the servant thrashing, the Syrian Rulers were escorted through the labyrinthine maze of rooms, colonnades, halls, and stairs. Finally, after much gawking at the fine artworks of Kaphtor, which featured griffins, dolphins, and nearly nude men and women, the kings were shown to a lavish room for feasting. The food was laid out in concentric semicircles, as if emanating from the place of the King, Abdi-Tirshi. In fact, all the food was set to be conveniently in reach of the king and not anyone else. The Syrians, with their stomachs all grumbling, were shown to seats directly opposite the king of Hazor, and thus, the food. When they sat, Abdi Tirshi dug back into the food on his table, eating like a wild beast. First leg of lamb, then fried prawns, then raw minced beef he sucked down, licking the grease off his fingers. The Syrians, who had not tasted food since their morning meal, looked in horror as the food was devoured by the King, disappearing down his royal gullet. Finally, Abdi-Tirshi spoke.

"I've been remiss as a host, I must admit. Servants, bring these gentlemen bread and oil!" He said, clapping three times.

The servants arrived and placed the daintiest, tiniest loaves of bread in front of each guest. A small quantity of poor-quality olive oil was poured into a communal bowl in front

256

of the men. They looked confused, almost like sad puppies. Finally, because they had little choice but to eat what was given them, they tore pieces off the bread and dipped them into the oil. The bread was dry and old, and the oil was bitter, tasting more like grape seed oil than true olive oil. Yet the hungry men (and Shisita) finished their bread.

Abdi-Tirshi poured a bowl of honey into his mouth, then yawned a mighty yawn and raised his arms high. "That," He said, "Was a supper worthy of any king. Best let's get some sleep."

Realizing now that the customary bread of guest right would be the only food he would be getting, Sharrupshi spoke up, "You have fed yourself fully and heartily, King Tirshi, but what of us, your noble guests? Would you put away the spread before we can sample your fine delicacies?"

"In Hazor, we have a custom. We say there is no such thing as a free lunch. All amenities are available here and are sold according to their value. Seeing as you are worthies who come from distant lands, we have generously supplied you with the necessities of bread and oil. Should you wish to sample our delightful viands, on the other hand, you must pay us according to the value of each item, either in kind or in bullion."

"You must think us to be common merchants, to ask us to pay for food as such!" said Etakkama, "I am Etakkama, a son of the king of Mitanni!"

257

"Even if you were the son of Pharaoh or the son of Ba'alu, the custom stands."

"You must understand," said Sutarna, "That we are not wealthy merchants laden with fine goods to barter for your wares. We are a party of war."

"War! What is it good for?" said Abdi-Tirshi, "Absolutely nothing. It is trade that is the engine of the world. The exchange of one commodity for another, to the enrichment of all."

"Then, Abdi-Tirshi, let's trade what we have in abundance for what we have in dearth." said Sutarna, "We shall use our army at your behest, in exchange for feeding and quartering us and our men."

"A most excellent idea. Now it has come to pass that in some territories of mine, notably, the cities of Leshem, Kedesh, and Kinneret, have seen fit to expel my governors, saying "We will join with the Ḥabiru". I ask merely that you return those cities to my hand, and I shall supply your army amply as it enters into enemy territory."

As the Syrians heartily devoured what would be the costliest meal of their lives, Shisita stared at a plate of lentils with grim realization. The relief to Canaan would be delayed, for gods know how long. Her warning unheeded by the men, she ate a plate of kibbe with all the delight as if she had been eating the minced remains of her own soldiers. Men and women would suffer and die to pay for a few dinners.

41

Chapter 41: Alone in the Wasteland

"The life of a dynasty is like unto the life of a man." said Shuwardata's father, "It begins with a moment of passion, a nativity. It discovers the world, grows, prospers, expands. It reaches its zenith, and comes to think it will last forever. But in the end, all dynasties and all men perish from the earth."

Shuwardata recalled her father's dying words. If its intent was to soothe her aggrieved heart, it did just the opposite. As time passed, she found the words of her father cut deeper. She believed in her heritage, the noble line that stretched back to the ancient giant 'Anaqu, through his descendants Erum, Abiyamimu, and Akirum. The Lady-King of Gath was taught in her youth to recite the names of her ancestors back to Anaqu when in danger; her prestigious ancestry would ward off evil men. She had long taken up the practice to ward off the evils in her heart: doubt, fear, grief, and shame. But it failed to stay any evil, either internal or external. The vultures and eagles picked apart Shuwardata's proud empire, both in the material and in her spirit.

There was a time, long ago, when Shuwardata was happy. At least, one could say, distracted from the ravages of worry. As a girl of fourteen, the regent who, in her minority, was ruling the city of Gath, arranged for young Shuwardata to be wed. She, like all prospective brides, was apprehensive about the matter. Would she be given to some upstart merchant to renew the treasury with his bridal Tirkhu? Would he be an old man, an ugly man, fat, loathsome and stupid? Her fears were cast away as she met the man she was to be offered to. He was tall, broad-shouldered, narrow waisted. His face was light, his features subtle. When she was told his name, all fears vanished. For he was Anish-Ḫurpe, brother of Abdi-Shahru of Jerusalem. They took to each other from the moment they met. For a while, all was good, until the war began.

"Please, oh wife, oh dearest Shuwardata" said Anish-Ḫurpe, "Allow me to take the troops and go to the aid of my brother in Jerusalem."

Remembering her husband's plea still brought sorrow to her, even as a grey woman. If she could bring back that day, that hour, she would have done all he asked and more.

"It is impossible. To go against Pharaoh in his might is folly. Let us remain loyal to our master. When the war is done, and the spoils are divided, our domain will increase, and our proud lines will remain strong in our times."

"You take pride in the honor of being a descendant of 'Anaqu the Giant. But regard him! It is not from inordinate size

260

'Anaqu is revered, and called 'Giant'. It is from the scale of his feats, the grandiosity of his courage. The strength of a vine is not in the span of its extent, nor in the bounty of its fruit. It is in stalwartness of it's boughs."

"I can not afford to risk it," said Shuwardata, "Nor risk the life of you my love."

She remembered the kiss she gave him that day, the last taste of his living lips she would ever know. Somehow the taste lingered, though time made it grow ever bitterer. Shuwardata bit her lip to draw blood. The taste was to remind her of the task at hand. She was leading soldiers. *I've earned the right to be called king,* she thought. *How many women of sixty-three years can lead armies into battle?* Indeed, her own troops called her 'Grandmother Death' for her fearsomeness in combat. She never let the accident of her birth as a woman, or her age restrain her from acts of courage in pursuit of revenge. For in revenge, she thought, lay the only hope of her salvation, if not the restoration of her fortune. Yet now it was to the aid of her enemy she rode, to fight with a threat she did not yet understand. She remembered those days that turned her heart into charcoal.

The Pharaoh was given repose in the city of Gath. Shuwardata ensured that every comfort would be afforded to him. The best food, the finest bed. She even procured (to her shame and embarrassment) girls of her city for him to lay with. Pharaoh's word was the highest law in the lands ruled by Egypt. With no oversight, he could make or break any person, no matter how lowly or how lofty. Shuwardata hoped by her courtesy to win the favor of the Pharaoh and cover the damage done by her late husband's hopeless deed.

"Shuwardata, you are a lady of refinement" said the Pharaoh, "I have not dined so sumptuously in all of Retenu."

"It is your graciousness to our city that has brought forth this bounty" said Shuwardata, "You have spared our lands the ravages of war."

"Loyalty has its rewards," said Pharaoh.

"Loyalty is its own reward." Shuwardata gritted her teeth.

"You are wise indeed, for a woman." Pharaoh stuck his finger into his mouth to wriggle loose a piece of gristle lodged between his molars, "Your husband said as much, how he regretted ignoring your advice. He was full of praise for you, until the end."

"He was a rebel. I give him no regard. Now, as to his claim on the city of Jerusalem."

"Yes, indeed, the seat has become vacant," said Pharaoh, "And you should know I have the most worthy pick in mind."

"I'd be honored..."

The Pharaoh interrupted Shuwardata's speech with cacophonous laughter "You! Goodness! You are a woman, for Amun's sake! How can I entrust you with such a city

262

as that! And the widow of a traitor!" Amenhotep coughed, choking on his own mirth. "I will give the city to a man of merit. He has no standing, as of yet, but he is a man of loyalty. After all, how can he not be loyal to me, when he owes everything to me? He is a man on the make."

"Perhaps," Shuwardata restrained her stomach's contents' uplift, "I may be able to do something that demonstrates my unswerving loyalty, and the virtue of my womanhood." She placed her hand on Pharaoh's.

Pharaoh clasped his other hand over hers, chuckling, "Old. You are far too old for me."

"I'm a woman but twenty-five years," said Shuwardata, "scarcely an old maid."

"Perhaps if you had a daughter..." Pharaoh jerked his fist, "I have forgotten you are barren. My apologies."

"Perhaps," Shuwardata gritted her teeth in anger behind her smile, "You can do me a favor. I do not think of myself as a barren woman, as my husband the rebel was a meek and timid man, unlike you. Your seed could plant a nation. Perhaps, if you give me your seed... if it is a girl, I will send her to you to be a comfort to you. And if it's a boy, think of it as giving your son a proud seat and proud heritage, the greatest in Canaan."

"Forgive me for saying this," the Pharaoh spat to get the unpleasant taste of stomach acid out of his mouth, "But you are not my sort. Here's an idea; why don't you wed Abdi-Heba. He is to be my new pick for the city of Jerusalem. As far as vigor goes, he is the son of a footsoldier! And after he is dead and gone, your sons can rule both Gath and Jerusalem."

"Oh my…" Shuwardata heaved, "Pardon me. I must have an attack of the vapors. It's a feminine thing… I must go away to my chambers…"

Shuwardata rode her chariot into battle, and each wound she received and dealt was softer on her than the memory of that night.

42

Chapter 42: Hills and Valleys

"Enjoy your meal!" said Biridiya. For him, it was more than a gesture of goodwill of hospitality. It was a threat, even a battle cry.

Dinnertime, lunchtime, breakfast-time, all were the domain of the king of Megiddo. King Biridiya was a hungry man; both for viands, and for power. Whether by war or by what he called his "Roasted Diplomacy", he ever sought to increase the domains and power of his family. Whether the dish was served hot or cold, roasted or fried, baked or boiled, Biridiya ensured it was seasoned to his demands. Food was ever abundant in the fertile Jezreel valley wherein was Biridiya's holding. Through the politics of the stomach, and the occasional discrete poisoning, Biridiya had graciously established royal seats for his beloved brothers. His middle brother, Yaṣdata, was given the prosperous town of Taanach five miles southeast of Megiddo.

The brothers had been quite successful in dealing with its

king, a former rival. Biridiya had invited the king into their city to create a formal alliance against Lab'ayu. Fearing Lab'ayu more than Biridiya, he instead lost his kingship and his life over a plate of boiled chicken with jute leaves and stuffed innards. As for the youngest brother, Ṣuraṭa, he was given an especially valuable prize, the coastal city of Akko. It was through marriage he obtained this maritime prize. Biridiya had his (relatively) attractive younger brother wed to the daughter of the King of Akko. Through a series of planned misfortunes and accidents, the King and his sons were soon eating dust in the tomb or drinking saltwater in the bottom of the Mediterranean. Ṣuraṭa was, of course, the only heir remaining outside of Sheol. From Akko, he would bring fresh seafood and a navy to Biridiya's richly stocked tables.

A rich table, set with all types of food, attracts the eyes of beggars and beasts. And Lab'ayu was indeed a hungry creature. Biridiya's lands were like a nude virgin, with open legs stretching to each horizon. Lab'ayu's armies were, needless to say, eager to partake in the bounty. Once Lab'ayu had returned from his conquest of Lachish, he led his armies on devastating raids into the Jezreel. What he could not take, he burnt as to deny the enemy supplies for the coming siege. Soon, refugees from the countryside came flooding into the cities. Now the cities would have more mouths to feed, and less food to stuff them with. Not that Biridiya would halt his feasting. No, it is his people who would suffer pangs of hunger, not the King. But that is not to say Biridiya would not fight.

266

It was a fine spring morning when the chariots were harnessed. The whistling of the wind through the trees was inaudible. The whinnies of the horses drowned out all sounds of nature. One by one, each horse was attached two to a vehicle, and fitted with the accouterments of battle. Biridiya and Yaṣdata oversaw the work, barking orders to hasten the process. The chariotry was ready. With a great heave of the reins, the brothers led the Maryannu charioteers in galloping through the streets and the gates, into the valley. It was a perfectly ordinary chariot raid that Biridiya and Yaṣdata had been throwing at the enemy since the war with Lab'ayu began. Chariot raids by day, guarding the walls by night; this was their war. The wind in their hair, the fluttering of banners in the wind, and the sweet carnage; all gave pleasure to the kings.

"War is sweeter than love." said Yaṣdata, "There is much good in subduing men, a little joy in subduing women. For when a woman cries out in pain, it is most piteous, but when a man screams out, his breast pierced by bow or lance, it is like heaven above."

"Battle is a great joy, it is true. I'd sooner spear a footman than a thousand comely maidens!" Biridiya ran a man through the neck with his lance, "Lab'ayu should have brought chariots. Killing his men is almost too easy!"

The sound of pillage was heard on the horizon. A village was being ransacked by Ḥabiru. Piteous screams of women were heard. More than grain and gold was being seized in this village, it seemed. Biridiya and Yaṣdata cracked the whips on their fast steeds, spurring them to an even faster gallop. The whinnies of the horses sounded like the cries of women being abused, and the sounds of women being abused sounded like horses' whinnies. Nearing the target of their rage, the kings passed the reins to the hands of their drivers, and drew their powerful recurve bows, and loosed their furious arrows onto the enemy ahead. The enemy likewise took up arms and prepared to be struck down by lances and arrows. It would have proved a fruitful carnage for the Megiddites had Yishaya not been there. He was atop a roof and was ready for the charging foe. He grabbed a hawk feather arrow in his right hand and strung it to his bowstring. He pulled it back, and loosed, and it flew true to its target. It struck Yaṣdaṭa through his Adam's apple.

"Arrghhaqaaaaqaaagha'aqa!" Choked Yaṣdata, coughing up blood.

"Brother, you must speak clearly! I can not hear you over the din of battle!"

Yaṣdaṭa collapsed. If not for the dexterity and quick thinking of his chariot driver, he would have toppled off the fast-moving chariot to be picked apart by the enemy.

After dispatching not a few Ḥabiru with his lance, Biridiya took a quick glance at his brother's chariot. Only then did he notice the grievous wound that his brother had suffered at the hands of Yishaya.

"It seems the wide-bellied king of Taanach has something

stuck in his throat!" mocked Abneru, nudging his cousin Yishaya, "He should chew what he's served before gorging his mouth with seconds!"

"Get down from that roof you dog-headed snake!" Biridiya spat on the ground, "And see who will be mocking who!"

"Oh, are you hungry! We will feed you heartily until you drop! Come taste our delicacies!"

Abneru and Yishaya then began shooting at Biridiya with their hawk-feathered arrows. Catching about five of them in his bronze-bossed shield, Biridiya soon realized he was in real danger of being struck. Killing enemy soldiers as they retreated, the chariot corps soon returned to the city of Taanach. Yaṣdaṭa was placed upon his royal bed. He was bleeding profusely. A physician from Sidon dressed the wound, carefully cutting off much of the shaft. Then, very gently, he wrenched the arrowhead out of the throat, applying pressure with linen bandages to curb the bleeding. A salve made of honey, garlic, and coriander leaf was applied to the wound to prevent infection. Yaṣdaṭa, in great pain from the sting of garlic on his fresh wound, attempted to claw at his bandages and had to be restrained by soldiers and slaves. He was then given a potion of willow bark for the pain. Yaṣdaṭa was loathe to drink it on account of it's bitter taste, but it was forced down his mouth regardless, irritating his fresh wound from the inside. It was not long before Yaṣdaṭa had lost consciousness from the blood loss and shock.

"His life is in the hands of Eshmun now," said the Sidonian, "For we are at the extent of the medical art. Burn two fatted rams at midday and three at vespers. Then seethe the flesh of a newborn kid in its mother's milk to feed him with, with oregano, coriander, garlic, and honey. Do not give him wine to drink, give him only clear water. He must also not engage in sexual intercourse for two months hence, for it inflames the blood."

"If he does not live," said Biridiya, "I'd take it as a failure of your skill. Be not lax in your prayers to Rashpu the healer, for your life hangs in the balance even as his."

"My prayers are readily for the King, your brother. Do as I instructed, and gods willing, he will recover. Pay me no heed, and he will surely die."

Angered by the proud and haughty attitude of the Sidonian physician, Biridiya took his bronze-bladed khopesh and struck his head off with a single blow. The Sidonian's head flew through the air, landing on the plaster floor with a sickening crunch. Naturally, the man's body similarly crumpled into a heap, oozing blood all over.

"The sacrifice has been made." said Biridiya, "I pray Rashpu accepts this haughty ram!"

The soldiers, men of action all, applauded their king. To not have done so would be suicide.

"I will have my revenge on Lab'ayu and his Ḥabiru even if it costs me my life and the lives of my kin!" shouted Biridiya, "Send word to the emissaries of Abdi-Heba! I will take his alliance."

43

Chapter 43: Deception and Betrayal

The chaos of war breeds odd bedfellows. Milkilu, King of Gezer found at his right side Mutba'alu son of Lab'ayu, the man who had not long ago returned Milkilu's royal seal to him, shoved up the rectum of his trusted servant. At his left side stood Zimredda of Lachish, an obsequious coward whom neither Mutba'alu nor Milkilu trusted. *Where am I now,* thought Milkilu, *that I fight alongside my worst enemies while my erstwhile friends now chaff at their bits for my blood.* But war gives rise to queer situations. Abdi-Heba proved to be a worthy adversary. When Milkilu led forces against Gath, Abdi Heba was soon enveloping Milkilu's forces from the rear. When Jerusalem was attacked, Shuwardata would come to Abdi Heba's aid. To the credit of Milkilu and Mutba'alu, their maneuvering of troops was such that they were never forced to fight a battle on two fronts. However, they were likewise unable to besiege the enemy cities, turning what was supposed to be a lightning campaign into a protracted quagmire of attrition.

"Defeat in detail! This is how we must subdue our enemies!" said Milkilu, "We need only to fight them separately and our numbers will prevail."

"A most excellent plan, Milkilu!" said Zimredda, "Shall we make for the north towards Gath or the East towards Jerusalem by way of Qiltu?"

Milkilu had thought a lot about the nature of the enemy. The enemy seemed aware of each step he was taking, and coordinated each step they took to best stymie him. Yes, someone was leaking information to the enemy. Who could it be but Zimredda? While Mutba'alu was no man of honor, he was bound to his father and his cause like a dutiful son, and thus could have no motive. Milkilu decided he must dispose of Zimredda without arousing suspicion.

"You shall have a discrete task. You shall assault the town of Qiltu and act as bait for Mutba'alu and I. Our troops shall hide in the ruins of Hebron, and while Abdi-Heba and Shuwardata converge on you from opposite directions, we will have them in their rear."

"I suppose I must hasten to raise the armies of Lachish at once."

"Go with God, brave Zimredda. Our plan depends on you!" Milkilu heartily patted his 'ally' on the back. Zimredda flinched. Thinking it humorous, Mutba'alu joined in.

Zimredda left the hall clenching his aching back and set off towards the east with his picked men.

"So now Milkilu, what is the real plan?" asked Mutba'alu.

"I wonder, if it may be so that the enemy is as plagued by internal conflict, even as we are?"

"I would say even more so!" Laughed Mutba'alu, "Shuwardata hates Abdi Heba's guts for being an upstart."

"Shuwardata might find common cause with you, on account of your royal heritage. Perhaps too, will I be able to tempt Abdi-Heba with the respect he desires. With each turned against the other, they will be annihilated without us having to lift a spear." said Milkilu.

"I have a plan for Zimredda as well. Once we use him to ensnare the enemy, we must capture him and his son Shipti-Ba'alu. We will offer their heads to the Egyptians at Tjaru!" Added Mutba'alu.

"Once Zimredda proves his true colors, then we can dispose of him. Your father takes a shine to him. If I only knew he turned an ear to sycophants when he was fighting me."

"Milkilu, my father is a gullible man. Worse, he is a good man. But he is a great man. I would let you know, Milkilu, that I never bore you ill will. Now that you are with us and not against us, you will find respect and justice of a sort no Pharaoh can endow."

274

"I have one desire, now that I am against Pharaoh. Yanhamu must be destroyed."

"The walls of Sharuhen will not protect him. Once we defeat Abdi-Heba and Shuwardata, I swear to you, we will destroy the Extorter Yanhamu. His is the corruption that my Father most wishes to destroy."

Milkilu looked at the Prince of Shechem. The youth seemed sincere, honest, and good-natured. Milkilu was no fool though. No matter how convincing an act was, he could still see through it instantly. He could trust Mutba'alu no more than he could trust Zimredda. But Lab'ayu, he was a straight arrow. In wrath and love, his heart was straightforward. What he wore on his face hid no treachery, no secrets. How can a man with no guise produce such treacherous dam? Good, Thought Milkilu. I will use his treachery as my weapon, but never lose sight of where the blade turns. If it turns on me, I will bring my blade upon him first.

And now, having considered the battle in his head with his friends, Milkilu turned to the task of battling his enemies.

To Abdi Heba, he wrote,

> *Message of Milkilu, King of Gezer, servant of the Pharaoh,*
> *to Abdi-Heba, that great man.*
> *Though circumstances of fortune have made us enemies,*
> *I would sooner have you as an ally.*
> *Though you have served the Pharaoh well,*
> *You have become execrated by many you call friends.*

I hereby warn you, as a friend, that Shuwardata has designs on
you.
She intends to betray you to the hand of Mutba'alu son of
Lab'ayu.
Instead of coming to our side a prisoner,
Is it not better to come over as a friend?
I despise the betrayal you shall befall at the hand of Shuwardata.
Heed our welcome and join our side,
For in our arms lie all Retenu,
And in the hands of Shuwardata, all that lies is a sharp iron
dagger to cut your throat.

As for Mutba'alu, he wrote in the same way to Shuwardata.

44

Chapter 44: Division

Shuwardata was vindicated, but being proved right was no comfort to her. The letter sent to her confirmed what she feared and expected most. Abdi Heba would make common cause with the pimp Milkilu and carve out more territory at the expense of the legitimate Kings of Retenu. Mutba'alu was a legitimate prince after all, and Lab'ayu's deeds now seemed less a rebellion against Pharaoh but as a restoration of the rightful order. What was Lab'ayu's crime anyway? He entered Gezer, the city of the pimp, whom all despised, and made war upon Abdi-Heba, the upstart, whom all despised. If Lab'ayu could proffer terms of amity with Gath, who am I to spurn it, thought Shuwardata. Mutba'alu was the picture of a perfect prince, polite, generous, he had the air of a noble spirit. Was there even in his letter the hint of a flirtation, the inkling of an offer of marriage? Lacking a husband ever since the death of her late Anish-Ḫurpe, her loins longed for a man of her station to restore her vitality.

What to do about Abdi-Heba's treachery was given in no

uncertain terms by Mutba'alu. "Abdi-Heba, who is in cahoots with Milkilu, shall seem to do nothing while your town of Qiltu is taken by Zimredda. When you come to the defense of your city, he will lay in wait like the crocodile, and when your men are committed to the struggle he will fall upon you from behind, in the guise of friendship. I pray you to be ready to fight him when he comes, for I shall fall upon him from his rear and make quick work of his troops."

It was a scorching day when Zimredda reached the town of Qiltu. The wind seemed to blow hot from the southeast from the direction of the Wilderness of Ziph. Zimredda's banners fluttered in the hot air like furious Bashmu dragons, ready to spit their venom on any who crossed their path. A token force guarded the town, just enough to delay any attacker until reinforcements could arrive. They gripped their spears in fear, trembling like almond boughs in the wind. Zimredda and Shipti-Ba'alu stood atop chariots unmarred by the slightest scratch or dink; their vehicles had never been used in battle before. Zimredda had no wish to go to battle now. Danger did not excite him, loud noises alarmed him and often caused him to soil his robes. His son cut a more martial figure. Shipti-Ba'alu was like a true Canaanite prince. Bedecked like his father in gilded bronze scale armor, he looked more like a dragon girded in scales than a fat fish as his father did. Shipti-Ba'alu, to no one's surprise, rallied the men for the attack instead of Zimredda.

"To arms, men!" shouted Shipti-Ba'alu, "These weak-kneed boys guarding that poor excuse for a town are just meat, ready to be butchered! Let the god of death rejoice in blood

278

spilled on this day!" He raised his martial weapons in bloody-minded gestures. This was what he craved his whole life. Glorious war could no longer be restrained by the "wisdom" of Zimredda.

While not inspired to battle by the rancorous speech of their prince, the men of Lachish rushed ahead, driven by the most base of principles; the desire for plunder. The town's defenders, though experienced at arms, ducked behind what could only be described as a four-foot fence, shooting arrows at the advancing ranks. This light hail of projectiles could have been well nullified by the Lachishites merely lifting their shields ahead of them as they charged, but the green boys in Zimredda's army had never truly fought a battle. Their only exposure to combat in fact was the pantomime fights performed at rituals to honor the goddess 'Anat. There, the performers would flail their weapons and shield wildly with great aggression but little defense. With the war dance in their minds, the soldiers twirled and gesticulated their weapons and did pirouettes. As a result, many men were pierced here and there by arrows. An arrow in the foot could be a grievous wound, but an arrow in the eye, heart, liver? These wounds were always fatal, yet almost always preventable. Zimredda in his inexperience could not but groan and cringe as his men were struck down. Many of the fallen were well known by the king, and yet others he indeed loved. To see them spent and lost could not but wrench his soft soul.

Once the Lachishites reached the sorry excuse for a city wall, they tried very feebly to surmount it. Had they been warriors of merit and experience, such as the Pitati of Pharaoh, the Na'arun of Milkilu or the Ḥabiru of Lab'ayu, such a low wall would have served as a negligible obstacle. They would have merely lept over the short wall with one mighty leap, engaging the defenders in a mighty slaughter. But these Lachishites bumbled, pawing the low ledge of the wall before comically trying to drag their unfit bodies up over it and onto the other side. With the push of their comrades behind them, many Lachishites were pinned in behind the wall, neither able to gain purchase on it nor able to retreat, so squeezed were they. The men guarding the wall then engaged with their spears those who attempted to or indeed did pass over the wall. Spears entered countless orifices and invented new ones. The men pushing forward were toppled back onto their fellows, bearing countless mortal and superficial wounds. Soon, the obstacle of the wall was overcome for the Lachishites by a ramp of their own dead and wounded. The air was shrill with the cries of the dead and dying, so Zimredda ducked his head and stuck a finger in each ear. Hear no evil, see no evil. Shipti-Ba'alu encouraged his men to attack with his typical stodgy dribble, "The rewards of the gods shall be upon the heroes who give their lives in this valiant struggle! Sell your souls at a great cost!"

Shuwardata was not surprised to see that the state of the battle was exactly how Mutba'alu described it would be. From a hill just behind the assembled forces of Zimredda, she watched eagle-eyed. She thanked the gods for the honor of Mutba'alu, and like a woman possessed, threw her chariots and infantry into the massed rear of Zimredda's men. There was something steely in her sixty-three-year-old soul, the

280

type of grit that is found in women who refuse to bend to the unfair constraints of a patriarchal world. Like a man, she rode a chariot, like a man, she flung javelins, loosed arrows, and wielded lance and sword. She was, however, despite her immediately aggressive charge into the enemy, quite careful to leave her reserves to her rear. Mutba'alu's admonition about Abdi-Heba and Milkilu was taken very seriously.

For now, the battle went remarkably well for Shuwardata. Her chariotry cut through the infantry of Zimredda almost as easily as a knife through lard. "Kill these piggies that would take our land!" shouted Shuwardata, "Send them home to mother sow squealing!"

Shuwardata turned her high-helmed head to the right, seeing King Zimredda cowering in his chariot like a serpent in its hole. Recognizing a chance to win glory and the battle in one fatal swoop, Shuwardata ordered her driver to make straight for the beleaguered King, killing Lachishites as she went. Zimredda, lost in anxious panic, did not even notice Shuwardata slaughtering her way towards his person. The same could not be said for his courageous son Shipti-Ba'alu. He rode off to intercept her, willingly trampling his own men in the process. They clashed about twenty paces ahead of King Zimredda. With a scream like a rabid harpy, Shuwardata jabbed forward her heavy bronze-tipped lance aiming straight for Shipti-Ba'alu's unprotected jaw. With great effort, Shipti-Ba'alu raised his shield just in the nick of time, pushing the spear out of Shuwardata's hands and into the mass of infantry below.

281

Eager to land a blow on his father's assailant, Shipti-Ba'alu brought down the back-spike of his khopesh to where he judged the forehead of Shuwardata would be. He was almost dead-on in his aim, had he managed to swing it but a few inches to the left he would have buried a sharp metal spike in Shuwardata's thick brow. Instead, it glanced off her gilded bronze helmet, causing only minor damage and pain instead of instant death. A slight trickle of blood dripped down her wrinkled cheek. She then sped on ahead past Shipti-Ba'alu, closing the distance between her and Zimredda far too fast for Shipti-Ba'alu's liking. He wrenched the reins from his driver and then attempted a desperate reversal of direction. The driver was almost flung from the chariot by the slinging motion of his chariot, but he grasped the front rail as the chariot was swung like a rag doll by the rapid turn of the two strong horses. Infantrymen struggled to get out of the way of the hairpin-turning chariot. Some were unlucky and were thrown with great force. Their bodies were broken by the hard ground along with the sturdy chariot frame.

Now on track and luckily still alive, the reckless prince made for the Queen of Gath. His horses were trained in Mitanni by the art of Kikkuli, so their speed and skill were second to none. Shipti-Ba'alu raised his bow, taking little time to aim, and loosed an arrow intended for the back of Shuwardata's unprotected neck. Unfortunately, a distraction modified his aim just a few degrees. Instead of finding Shuwardata's neck, the arrow penetrated deep into the neck of her driver. Thinking quickly, she grasped the reins of the speeding chariot before all control could be lost. The driver, a youth of twenty-three of great amity and breeding, and much beloved by Shuwardata, fell mortally wounded, toppling off the back of the chariot. It somehow caught in the spokes of Shipti-Ba'alu's chariot. The vehicle wrenched sideways, throwing Shipti-Ba'alu and his own hapless driver into the rough embrace of the scrubby ground. Luckily for Shipti-Ba'alu, it was his driver that caught the full hardness of the earth, breaking his neck and leaving a soft impotent cushion for the prince to land atop.

Bloodied and bruised, Shipti-Ba'alu rose to his feet, sword in hand, and immediately turned his attention to the distraction that turned his arrow from its mark. Banners rose from the horizon with able men bearing arms. The Blue, White, and Orange of the Ḫabiru and the Yellow, Purple, and Scarlet of Gezer told all that gazed that Mutba'alu and Milkilu were here to take part in the battle. Shuwardata noticed expectantly. She had decided that it was best to set up a defensive perimeter in front of the troops set to attack her. Still trusting in the word of Mutba'alu, she sent only a token force to secure the portion of the line facing him. She figured he would soon be switching sides and fighting Milkilu along with her. To the side facing Milkilu, she put her best troops, her Na'arun, along with plenty of ranged troops behind them to skirmish and shoot the enemy. She set her charioteers to harass the forces of Shipti-Ba'alu and Zimredda to prevent them from attempting to surround her forces from two sides.

"Do you see, Milkilu, that the enemy is well and truly deceived! Shuwardata put such faith in me that her left flank lies entirely prone." said Mutba'alu.

"If she is wont to open her legs to you, I say give it to her hard and fierce like a bull in heat."

"I say that instead of that, we allow her to think I am on her side. You engage her troops directly, while I hold back. Trusting in me, she shall take away what little she has guarding my flank. Thereupon, I shall attack her from her rear and make short work of her. We shall have her as a prisoner and then all that will be left for us is to deal with Abdi Heba."

"Do not worry about Abdi-Heba. He is well and truly taken care of."

"Sometimes the reed stylus is mightier than the sword." said Mutba'alu, "Or at least it gives strength to arms."

Milkilu sent his chariots first. Firm but flexible, lightweight yet forceful, the vehicles kicked up dust as they thundered ahead towards Shuwardata's infantry. Their column divided in two as they approached the arrow range of the enemy. After turning, the skilled troops on the chariots unleashed a deadly barrage of missiles at the enemy. Shuwardata's troops did what they could, attempting to intercept the fast-moving projectiles with their heavy shields. Still, arrows pierced eyes, cheeks, necks, shins, feet, hands. Anywhere uncovered by armor could be pierced by the "Thorns of Maryannu". Even arrows that did not pierce flesh found their way to harm the hard men of Shuwardata. Arrows deeply embedded caused the shields to become unwieldy in their hands, rendering the men vulnerable to further assaults.

The chariots sped around making loops, passing by the massed soldiers and spewing death and injury from their bowstrings. Shuwardata had archers, slingers and javelin-men of her own as well. They made a gallant attempt at returning a salvo at the charioteers, but the speed and armor of their targets made successful shots uncommon. Instead, it was the missile troops who were made vulnerable by their attempts to return fire at their enemy. Unlike the infantry, the skirmishers had little in the way of defensive equipment to stymie the enemy's barrage. Terrible wounds were inflicted and young men died by the scores. Eventually, these light-armed troops cowered behind the infantry and did not dare to shoot anymore, even when bid to by Shuwardata and her captains.

Seeing that the chariotry had admirably weakened the infantry of the Gittites, Milkilu now saw fit to dispatch his infantry into the battle. Under cover of missile support, Milkilu himself advanced with his infantry. The phalanx of the Gezerites was formidable. The men marched in perfect order, rank behind rank displaying their long spears. Sturdy bronze-bossed shields presented, a faceless wall of painted wood and shining metal advanced at the Gittites. It was like the ravage of time; slow-moving but inevitably fatal.

Shuwardata understood the overwhelming force of Milkilu's army would be tough to overcome alone. Yet, she had a plan that she felt would grant her an inevitable victory. "Present spears!" She shouted, causing her infantry to level its own row of deadly spears just as the enemy forces arrived.

The first stage of the clash was almost dance-like. The two sides looked each other over and occasionally threw swift blows at the opposing side, mostly glancing harmlessly off the shields of their adversaries. As the battle continued, and the commanders egged on the men to courage and aggression, the battle entered the second stage. Each side courageously pushed towards each other, in a line dance of advance and retreat. Casualties began in earnest, as a careless moment could allow a spear to dart past one's hard shield and armor and enter into something soft and vulnerable. That being said, it was hardly a bloodbath. That sort of carnage was for later stages. Shuwardata gave her command to begin the third stage of the battle. It was a coded order she had coached her men ahead of time, simply, "Wing". This time, when the Gezerites made their attack, the Gittite center simply gave way, forcing the Gezerites into a salient. Then, Shuwardata sent her troops on Mutba'alu's side to fall in on the Gezerite right flank. This side, of course, was the most vulnerable because it lacked the defense of shields which were invariably held in the left hand. Shuwardata then rode her chariot out to inform Mutba'alu that now would be the perfect time to attack Milkilu and completely surround him.

"Ah, Shuwardata, you have come to me!"

"Hasten Mutba'alu, send your forces in and we'll wipe out this duplicitous Milkilu!"

"Shadraha, take this daughter of 'Anat prisoner. Now we go, men. We shall annihilate Gath!"

Shuwardata was stunned. She couldn't imagine how a highborn prince like Mutba'alu could have betrayed her with such duplicity. She was ready to fight, to die in spiteful resistance, riding her chariot like Shapash the sun goddess, but the Ḥabiru footmen had already seized her reins. They unyoked her horse, then Shadraha came. He was a powerful mountain of a man, almost seven feet tall and muscled like a bull. She raised her sword to smite him, but his khopesh caught the hook of hers and he flung her weapon far away. He lifted her off the chariot with no more effort than it would take for a common man to lift a baby. He undid her armor and tied her in bonds, careful to not harm her with excessive tightness nor enable her to escape with laxness. Knot tying was a skill he had mastered in boyhood.

She was held over his broad shoulder. Looking at the battlefield upside down she saw the Ḥabiru surround her forces and cut them down instead of Milkilu's. The battle was over. Her Gittites were captured or slain, and the forces of Milkilu, Mutba'alu, and Zimredda had taken the city. There would be little to stand in the way of them taking Gath itself. Shuwardata would have taken her own life at this point, but she was denied even this. Her defeat was complete, testament to the power of diplomacy over arms. Shame was heaped upon her like bones upon an altar. Like the bones of offering, she was burning up. Let the gods smell the smoke, and take pity on Canaan, for surely the Canaanites will not.

45

Chapter 45: Tribute Bearers — Part 1

"A little detour, what will it cost us?" Sutarna wasn't asking. "After all, we can't have hostile forces in our rear, can we?"

In Canaan, there were always those who went Ḥabiru. The poor, crushed underfoot, often had little recourse but to take to the dusty and bloody path of mercenary life. Sometimes, in times of great crisis and tumult, whole cities would rebel from their lord and go Ḥabiru. Such was the decision taken by the cities of Galilee. They turned from their lord, king Abdi-Tirshi of Hazor. They didn't necessarily join with the forces of Lab'ayu, but they rejected the power of those arbitrarily put over them. Now, Sutarna and his army would be co-opted into Abdi-Tirshi's war. Sutarna was gullible enough to believe what Abdi-Tirshi claimed, that the cities had or at least would make common cause with the Ḥabiru of Lab'ayu. *After all, a Ḥabiru is a Ḥabiru, no?* He didn't realize the irony.

Shisita had no such illusions. She had warned the army

against getting involved with the affairs of Abdi-Tirshi. "His every word is poison, his every deed a dagger in the heart" she said. But Shisita had little influence now. Etakkama grasped the power in his eagle's claws and would let go for no man or woman. He had the air of a military man. He could create stratagems that seemed so admirable in their complexity. As for Sutarna, he had no knowledge of war. He did not know that complexity is poison to battle strategy while simplicity is firm stone. Regardless, by Etakkama's beard, seeming experience and cunning, and of course his sex, he captured the hearts and minds of the Syrian kings.

"We shall each set for ourselves a city to take. Sutarna, you and Sharrupshi should take the city of Kedesh of Galilee. I could not pass up the pun of a Qadeshite taking Kedesh. Idanda and Akizzi, you should take the forces of Qaṭna southward and take the city of Kinneret. I have full faith in you to defeat these rebels, as even Hatti doesn't dare to match you. As for me, and my brother, Biryawaza, I shall set myself to the most difficult task. The great walled city of Leshem shall be my quarry."

The kings and princes all nodded, satisfied with their lot. But Shisita burned with anger. "What shall be my task, oh great Etakkama?"

"You insist on taking part in martial combat? I should think you would be better suited to the laundry. We should marry her off, Sutarna. Women thrive in the marital, not the martial."

"Do you see, Etakkama, that I bear the seal of Queen Tiye, and it was I, even I, that set the forces to march together. It is I, even I, that am the Lady of the Lions. And what are you? Some illegitimate son of a dead king of a second-rate empire?"

The men looked aghast at Shisita's declaration. Certainly, all she said was truthful. No one could deny it; it was as apparent as the sun and the moon. But nonetheless, no one wished to be shamed by a woman, a virgin.

"I would examine that seal of yours. To be aware of its authenticity." said Etakkama.

"Be my guest." said Shisita. She handed him the seal without a moment's hesitation, expecting it to work its magic on him, just as with all other men.

Etakkama looked over the seal, hoping to find one discrepancy, one excuse to dismiss it. But it was undeniable to any who looked upon it that it was indeed Queen Tiye's seal. Shisita's confidence was not ill-founded. Etakkama decided to make a Gordian knot of it.

"Here's what I think of it." Taunted Etakkama. He threw it on the ground and then stamped it's fine alabaster with the bronze butt of his lance. "I am no slave to any woman, be she a Lady of Lions or Queen of Egypt."

Like water set over a hot cooking stone, Shisita's blood boiled and hissed. Her anger at Etakkama was the same as if he had slaughtered her own child. She rushed at him, a dagger in her right hand, a knife in her left hand, like Ba'alu, dodging those set on keeping her away from him. She was ready to carve out his heart and eat it, but just as her weapons were ready to meet his flesh, her arms were restrained from behind. Sutarna grasped her left arm, Yassib her right.

"Perhaps, my daughter, you can use this willful anger against our enemies! Come with me, Shisita, and we will make short work of the city of Kedesh." soothed Sutarna.

"Do not restrain me father, or I shall make the gray hair of your beard drip with blood."

"So you are quoting 'Anat, oh Shisita." Yassib broke into laughter, "Do not spill your father's blood this day. Spill Ḥabiru blood! Do not spill the blood of Etakkama. No matter how comic it may be!"

Shisita calmed down, restraining her anger into a silent urge. She ordered her men to pick up the pieces of the broken seal; she could not allow herself to look weak by picking them up herself. She would have it mended with gold seams. Mere glue would not suffice. Her men would obtain that gold by absconding the jewelry of Etakkama. No man dared stop them, for they knew better than to get involved in this quarrel.

"Someday, Etakkama, you will regret having angered the daughter of 'Anat." said one of Shisita's lionmen, as he carried a box full of Etakkama's golden earrings.

"And the day that happens, I will eat my hat."

The armies of Syria set forth in their various directions. Akizzi and his Father Idanda were the first to reach their quarry. The city of Kinneret stood on a medium-sized tel overlooking the plains of Genesaret, and the large lake which took its name from the town. The land was covered in prosperous farms, and as Akizzi and Idanda took the city by surprise, the abundant food would be used by the besiegers, not the besieged. Nonetheless, the difficulty in besieging the city became apparent soon enough. While not the finest walls in Canaan, they were strong enough and amply guarded enough to discourage a direct assault. That usually wouldn't be much of a problem, as most cities would open their gates to an invader as soon as hunger set in. But a few weeks into the siege, it was clear that the defenders had no lack of food and supplies. The city was being resupplied from across the lake by merchants coming in small boats.

"Akizzi," Idanda began, "I fear that their city is being resupplied from the outside by way of boats. The task of besieging this city seems to be as futile as filling a pierced waterskin."

"Father, I have solved this problem. Their greatest advantage is their greatest weakness. Their city's walls do not protect their city on the lake-ward side. I shall take two hundred picked men, and find those merchants who sell to the city of Kinneret. I will bribe them, and they will ferry our troops into the city. Plug the gaps, as it were."

Before long, merchants loyal to no man but to gold alone

292

were ferrying Akizzi and his best troops to the port of the city. Expecting to trade, the elders of the city did not bring arms to meet the merchants. Akizzi seized upon the elders and they, fearful and hopeless, opened the gates and accepted Abdi-Tirshi's rule entirely bloodlessly. The elders of course begged the prince of Qaṭna to take the city for himself instead of the hated Hazorite king, but he refused, his steely eagle eyes betraying no emotion as he turned over the citizens of Kinneret to a terrible fate under Abdi-Tirshi. For him, honor was in obedience, not empathy.

Sutarna's army and Etakkama's set off to the northeast, taking alternative paths. Etakkama's army naturally moved much faster than Sutarna's due to Etakkama's fierce discipline. He and Biryawaza arrived at Leshem several days before Sutarna, Shisita and Sharrupshi arrived at Kedesh.

Leshem was, unlike Kinneret and Kedesh, a quite substantial fortress on it's own merits. There were no obvious vulnerabilities. The citizens of Leshem had heard well in advance about Etakkama's advance on their city from peasants fleeing the cruelty of Etakkama's arms. Therefore, Leshem had ample time to fortify and secure supplies for a long siege. They had plenty of time to hold out, and excellent walls to defend them. They were high and thick, with a foundation of strong stone topped with red mudbrick. Such was the color of the walls that Leshem was called 'Damu' the bloody. The citizens trusted in their walls; their structure dated back over seven hundred years, before even the time of Hammurabi and Shamshi-Adad. Their triple-arched gates had never been seized in anger by any invader, and Leshem was resolved to resist. They dared to earn the title 'Bloody'. They had even sent messages to the king of Damascus, requesting aid. The old man joined forces with his vassal Arsawuya of Ruhizza and marched southwest to meet Etakkama and his forces in battle and relieve the siege.

"Brother, the scouts have reported that the King of Damascus has sallied out with 1200 men to relieve the city." said Biryawaza, "What's the plan, clever boy."

"Well. Welly well well. Starving them is off the table, clearly. I have already tried bribery and infiltration, as you can see; dear old Tulish's head and entrails dangle from their walls."

"Oh no! You let them kill Tulish!" Wept Biryawaza, "He was like a father to us, taught us Akkadian and Ethics."

"Now he taught us how not to subdue a city." replied Etakkama.

"So what's next?"

"Tulish taught me something else that you may not know. This is a certain device of Assyrian design that they call a Yashibu."

"A Yashibu? What is the nature of such a device?"

"It is the most ingenious design. There is, to begin with, a wooden structure on wheels, bearing a heavy wooden post with a strong bronze beak on the end dangling from strong hemp ropes. Then the whole structure is covered over with a convex roof that is covered in animal hides to prevent the device from being inflamed and to protect its operators. The device is then rolled up to the gates of the city, whereupon it can be used as a ram to break into the city." Etakkama gasped for air after he finished the speech. The description of the machine was verbatim, memorized from an Assyrian treatise he had read.

"And this you think will allow us to enter the city before the reinforcements are upon us?"

"That is exactly what I have in mind for it."

"And who shall construct it, Oh Etakkama, with our dear Tulish resting in pieces?"

"This shall be my charge, Biryawaza, and I shall leave to you the maintenance of the siege. Now, this construction must proceed with utter secrecy. Should the Leshemites discover our plans they may well make a sally to destroy my device."

"Only you and I know of the device, Etakkama. I recommend removing suspicion by acting out an illness. Thus, we deceive the enemy into believing it is normal that I shall lead our forces."

"You are a brother of mine, Biryawaza, to share in your mind the same thought as I!"

From the perspective of the citizens of Leshem, it seemed as though little had changed. Etakkama had assumed that an elaborate spy system was universal to all in the art of war. His agents moved in all camps. However, the citizens of Leshem were not organized as such. Lacking a strong central figure to rally around and organize their military and political affairs, the Leshemites had no vulnerability in the form of a leader's personality. Etakkama played the game of war like it was the game of twenty squares; every move he made was calculated to contend with a singular opponent. Leshem was unified only by a thorough rejection of Abdi-Tirshi's rule and would resist with a united front any who would return them into his hated hands. However, the republican politics of the city made their moves incongruous at best, and illogical at worst. In incompetence they found their salvation.

46

Chapter 46: Tribute Bearers — Part 2

While Etakkama toiled with a few hand-picked servants on his secret weapon, Sutarna, Sharrupshi, and Shisita began laying siege to the city of Kedesh of Galilee. This came as a dreadful shock to the inhabitants of the city, who had thought the peaceful approach of the Qadeshites proved that they were not hostile to their cause. They actually thought that the Qadeshites were the forces from Damascus sent to fight Etakkama! Settling in for a siege, the three commanders had, like their peers at Leshem and Kinneret, strategized how to seize the city. It must be said that only Sutarna regarded the taking of Kedesh as a matter of any importance. Shisita had warned the Syrians to avoid any dealings with the ignominious King Abdi-Tirshi. As for Sharrupshi, he had been co-opted into this war against his will. He had long followed the path of Yasmah-Adad, loving more the pleasures of the flesh than 'Manly Pursuits'. This campaign proved manlier than he had a taste for. He longed every hour for his comfortable duck-down cushions, his rich foods, his sweet wines, his lascivious concubines. The thought of taking a city had no luster to him.

Sutarna was not accustomed to thinking for himself. In the world that he lived in, scribes, officials, and advisors were the spring of ideas, ideas for which, ultimately, the king was always credited with if they succeeded, and excused from if they failed. But now, Sutarna had a problem in his mind, how to take the city. There was no one to tell him how it must be done, no pillar to hold his house; he must stand on his own or fall. Sutarna puzzled at the problem, considering the situation with a freshness of mind those who were versed in military affairs simply didn't have. And the solution was as simple and as gentle as the King's soul. Calling his distracted comrades to meet in his tent, he laid bare his plan.

"So, what if we find out what they want in exchange for their surrender, and give it to them?"

Shisita and Sharrupshi, slightly taken aback by the idea, remained silent for a while. Finally, it was Sharrupshi who spoke.

"It was Abdi-Tirshi, the Rat King, that sent us on this fool's errand. If he had wished to make terms with his rebellious vassals he would not have sent us."

"Perhaps, this is our way to make good of our detour," said Shisita, "We can act as intercessors."

"Shisita, I've heard it said that your name carries great respect in Retenu. Maybe you can negotiate."

298

"Respect is what I earned from *never* shying away from battle. But, this siege is wasting our time. Every week it goes on innocents are slain by the wretched Lab'ayu and his sons. I'll resolve this the cowards' way so we may fight the *real* war."

Not wasting the least time, and with the grace and vigor of battle-hardened 'Anat, Shisita grabbed a white cloth and a spear. She made from it a white flag of truce, and barged out of the tent, requisitioning Sutarna's royal chariot. She drove her father's chariot with full battle fury until she was twenty yards from the gates of the city of Kedesh in Galilee. After she dismounted the vehicle, she planted the spear six inches in the ground with all the fiercesomeness of finishing a wounded foe. The guards saw her and sent word to the elders of the city to meet with her.

"Say to the city of Kedesh of the Galilee." Shisita twisted her martial spear into the ground. "In the name of Queen Tiye, lady of the Two Lands, I, Shisita, Lady of the Lands demand your complete acquiescence to the rule of Abdi-Tirshi! Or you shall know the kiss of spear and the embrace of the ax!"

"But, my lady!" pleaded the eldest elder,"Abdi-Tirshi does what is hateful in our eyes! He takes and takes, and never gives, he uses and uses, but never replenishes! He is a son of Yam!"

"Pu!" Shisita spat at the old man's feet, "He is your king. He may do as he will with you! He may oppress, may tax, may rob you blind, but a king is a king is a king."

"Lady Shisita?" the grandson of the old man stepped forward, shiny eyed, six years old, "My grandpapa always told tales of you, how you fight for justice, and destroy the enemy that robs the people. We are not Ḥabiru! Abdi-Tirshi is like a Ḥabiru."

Shisita was moved by the words of the boy. He was right, in her opinion. She hid that. "Ciitizens of Kedesh. I am Shisita, known throughout the land as the bringer of justice. I will bring your complaints to the king of Hazor. He will listen to me, as I speak with the voice of Tiye, Lady of the Two Lands. Your grievances will be redressed."

As they knew the reputation of Shisita, they acquiesced to her demands. The forces of Qadesh on the Orontes had subdued Kedesh of the Galilee with the power of performance; that is, the power of lies.

In the camp of the Mitanni princes, Etakkama tirelessly worked on his siege engine. However, without the guiding skill of Tulish, his tutor, the engineering problem proved difficult to overcome. Etakkama, it should be said, had the idea of a battering ram in his head, but replicating his idea into a physical machine proved... fraught. Even before the construction began, finding adequate material proved challenging. Trees in the region were mostly fruit-bearing ones in the orchards of local farmers and landowners. Pistachios, Mulberries, Olives, and Figs were grown in the region. Etakkama had to obtain the wood while maintaining absolute secrecy. Thus, he sent raiding parties to secure wood and silence.

300

The sun was beating down overhead like a carpenter's hammer when a humble farmer, Abdi-Milkutti, was pruning the branches of his olive tree. Looking out into the distance from the canopy of his sturdy olive tree, he noticed men in the distance. Merchants, he thought. It was not unusual for merchants from Naḥarin to pass through his land on their way to Egypt. He would earn a pretty penny giving them food and board, and selling them high-quality olive oil. He climbed down from his olive tree and shouted for his wife to fetch the visitors bread and oil to offer them guest-right. She came bearing the bread and oil, young children following her. Each were filled with curiosity about the foreign merchants, hoping to hear about their travels in distant lands. There were three boys and two girls, none older than eight because Abdi-Milkutti was yet only a youth of twenty three.

Etakkama looked upon the family of peasants, trying to hide his disdain for them in his proud eyes. "What price would you give me for your olive trees?"

"My land is not for sale, sir, for it is the livelihood of my family and the heirloom of my fathers."

"I need not the land, but the lumber."

"Lumber from olives? Surely you are mistaken. You should go to the Golan Heights and purchase fine lumber, oak, and cedar."

"This is a license I can't afford. I need lumber, and you will sell me yours, or I'll have it all the same."

"Are you threatening me, merchant!? After I gave you oil and bread, and the hospitality of my home?"

"You will sell, and you will speak of it to no man."

"Children, run inside. Ascend the roof and pull up the ladder. We have a madman on our hands."

As the children were about to escape, Etakkama sent his guards to seize them, along with their mother and father.

"I really hate to have to do this, farmer, but you leave me no choice."

"Burn to ashes, Binu Ḥimari!" Abdi-Milkutti spat at Etakkama's feet. He knew from prior experience that begging for his life would do no good. At least the gods would recognize his defiance.

Etakkama took from the folds of his robes a sharp iron dagger with a gold handle inlaid with carnelian. He slit the family's throats one by one, letting them bleed out before burning their remains. His servants then set to cutting down the precious olive trees. This was a typical occurrence in Etakkama's quest for lumber. Soon stumps and corpses littered the Galilee. Only the mingling of sap with the blood of victims made these raids novel.

With time spent between raiding and constructing, time passed quickly, but the ram did not materialize. Each iteration of the machine was lacking in some way, and it always broke down or was too difficult to push. Etakkama had almost finished his fourth version when Biryawaza gave word to him of the approach of the kings of Damascus and Ruhizza. Etakkama was so eager to run off to battle that he tripped on a broad beam of wood and twisted his ankle.

"Aaaaaaaa!" Screamed Etakkama, grasping his twisted foot.

"I shall go and fight them in your place, Etakkama," said Biryawaza. He had never fought a battle on his own before. Etakkama, Tushratta, or Artashumara had always commanded. Biryawaza now had to find the confidence to fight on his own.

"Take my armor..." groaned Etakkama. He was hoping he could trick his brother into being mistaken for himself, bringing the glory to his own name. Biryawaza did not accept it.

"My armor will suffice. Any victory I will win shall add to my fame, any defeat shall accrue to my infamy."

"Fight well!" demanded Etakkama.

Biryawaza had studied the surroundings of the city of Leshem. In the northeast, from where the enemy was coming, stood the high mount, Hermon. He decided his best chance in battle would be to use the mountain as a mortar and his chariots as a pestle to grind the enemy into flour. To manage this feat, he would have to move quickly. To that end, He decided to forgo the use of infantry. He divided his chariotry into three groups, each to attack the Damascenes from a different side. The Mitannians rode through the night, obscuring the stars and moon in a bridal-veil of dust. Biryawaza could not have picked a better time to strike than when he did. Far from being ready to fight, when the enemy was reached they were still snoring in their tents. The watchmen were efficiently dispatched by a few arrows, allowing the orgy of chaos and slaughter to begin in haste.

With the mountain looming in the background, and the whole scene filled with an eerie silver haze, the charioteers rampaged through the camp slaughtering and taking prisoners. While the lower classes were expected to die in battle, the elites often didn't face the same danger. They were thought to have plenty of wealth to barter for their release, so it was more economical to spare the lives of the enemy nobles. Horses too were almost never killed. In war, it was more honorable to kill a fourteen-year-old peasant boy than to kill a horse. The king of Damascus was sleeping soundly when he heard the din of slaughter outside his royal tent. His ransom would have been quite high, as a king's ransom would be, but there is no ransom for kings who die in battle not by wounds but by a stroke. Arsawuya on the other hand was taken prisoner. Biryawaza had claimed victory at nearly no cost to himself. It was almost too easy. The spoils, ah the spoils. The men were gay that night, drinking wine and eating the bread and meat of the defeated.

As Biryawaza rode his chariot at the head of his victorious force, the Maryannu captains took turns riding up to him. They praised him for his victory and encouraged him to take

304

from Etakkama the command of the army. "It should be him that takes the city of Leshem, and who knows, perhaps on to Ruhizza and Damascus? Why trouble yourself with fruitless struggle against Lab'ayu?"

Biryawaza planned his next move in his head. What he thought was known only to him.

When Biryawaza entered his brother's camp, Etakkama stood beaming with pride in front of his 'invention'. He was dressed in his fine gilded armor and his orange robes and addressed his troops with passion and intensity.

"We see before us the red-walled city which no man has ever despoiled. No man before me, that is. You shall follow me through their hereto never broken gates, and dye their walls a darker shade of red. Let's give them a reason to be called 'The bloody'! We shall crush them beneath our boots and take from them all they adore. Their property shall become ours, their boys shall be our slaves, and their girls offered to the spear!"

"Hail, Etakkama!"

"What news Biryawaza?"

"Complete victory!"

"You can see that we are on the cusp of a great victory here too."

"Forget that old ram. I have a much better plan. I take it you've heard of the stratagem of Djehuti?"

"How will you pull that off? The tale is probably apocryphal anyway. After all, it defies basic common sense..."

"They do not know we vanquished the Damascenes. Indeed, we can deceive them into thinking we were fully defeated. Then they will surely accept our 'tribute.'"

"And when I burn my precious ram, they will know of our defeat." said Etakkama, attempting to maintain his charade of cunning.

On the city walls of Leshem, the guards witnessed a curious ritual. A strange wooden vehicle was brought out and lit on fire. It was like nothing they had seen before. Then, wagons bearing... well, gods only knew what they bore. Things in sacks. Perhaps hocks of meat? There was gold in there too, from what they could see. They were taken to the front of the city gates, and a figure dressed in sackcloth approached. They didn't recognize him till he spoke.

"I, Etakkama, prince of Mitanni, offer your city a fine tribute as a solemnity. Gold, silver, myrrh, lapis lazuli, ebony wood, and linen garments. For I am thy slave."

The figure went back. They could not see the malicious grin on his face as he was facing the other direction. The men on the wall deliberated. Those who counseled caution were overruled. Such riches could not be passed up.

"Our victory is great! See, even a prince of Mitanni is humbled before the might of Leshem!" said a man who would live long enough to regret his optimism, but not long enough to regret a long life wasted on vain pleasures. His mother would be as surprised at that as he. But, not for long.

They hauled in the 'great hoard of treasure' right through their great arched gates. They brought it into the courtyard of the temple, ready to place each piece of treasure before the god's altar. That was when the Mitannians burst forth, with Biryawaza at their head. Sixty picked men, each in heavy armor and with akinakes swords, set upon the Leshemites. It didn't matter if man or woman, layperson or priest, adult or child if any person stood between the Mitannians and the gates they set to open; they were slaughtered wholesale. Calls were made for soldiers to come to kill the intruders, but they were ill-prepared and ill-equipped for the fight. Finally, the Mitannians cut their way through to the gate and opened it. Soon their fellows were swarming the city. It was no longer a slaughter. It was pillage, rape, and inferno. Etakkama had no mercy in his heart for any who crossed him. He took the sprained ankle as a great injury done him by the enemy, and he was avenged of it. Not a thousandfold, not a millionfold, but a fold of such a number no word had yet existed for it in Etakkama's language. He would invent a word for billion in his language to express the magnitude of his revenge. Writers are so cunning in their inventions!

The bloodsoaked streets gave way the next day to an impromptu slave market. All those who did not perish by flame or sword were sold at fair prices to Abdi-Tirshi's merchants.

Etakkama and Biryawaza became heroes through bathing in the blood and tears of the innocent. Soon, Biryawaza marched on Damascus, taking it as his own personal fief. The young prince became the mighty king. Etakkama and Biryawaza were men of their own kind!

47

Chapter 47: Epistles of Ambition

FATHER AND SON

Say to my son, Huy, Commissioner of Archers,
Message of Aperel, Vizier, Commander of Chariots, and God's
Father,
Oh, how I beam with pride when addressing you with that august
title!
It would fill any father's heart with mirth
To see his beloved son getting along in the world.
I recall how, with each letter you sent, you accounted for the
indignities suffered
At the hands of that base curr, Hanya.
I had been lobbying without end to see him removed, and you
instated
Now, almost as if a reward for our prayers,
The Asiatics he so revered did God's work
And put him out of his — and our — misery.

Say to the father, Aperel, Vizier, God's Father, Commander of
Chariots
Message of Huy, Commissioner of Archers, Commander of Tjaru
Perhaps you are hasty to offer congratulations.
The Asiatics, like the lice-covered vermin they are,
Have risen up against our power.
It seems that every war we win but sows the seeds for another.
I have been dutiful about reporting on doings here in Tjaru, and
in Retenu
Why do you not do what I asked and say what is going on in
Egypt?
I have gathered that Amenhotep, whom the the Asiatics call
Nimureya,
Is ailing, but as to the state of his kha I can not say.
Can you fill me in?
As for Hatiay and Seny, are they thriving?
What of my mother, Tawaret?
Your letters are all that give me solace in this blasted wasteland.

— — — — — — — — — — — — — — — — — — — —

Say to my son, Huy, Commissioner of Archers,
Message of Aperel, Vizier, Commander of Chariots, and God's
Father,
You write that I did not speak of matters concerning Egypt
I may be remiss in not telling you, but I wish not to worry you.
It is a natural and normal thing for a father to die before a son.
I have prepared a family tomb for us, by the cliffs of Bubastis.
Why, you ask do I count on dying soon?
As you noted the Pharaoh is ailing. His health fails by the day.
The great royal wife, Queen Tiye, has been grasping at power.

310

I did try to get on her good side.
But she has a favorite, let's not be coy, a lover
From her hometown, his name is Ay
He means, and she aids him, in becoming Vizier
What place does that leave me but the grave?
As for your mother and brothers' they are hale.
But as for me, can I say the same?
Stay in Retenu, become invaluable
The real war is brewing in Egypt.

———————————————————

Say to my son, Huy, Commissioner of Archers,
Message of Aperel, Vizier, Commander of Chariots, and God's
Father,
I will heed your advice and remain here,
Though it burdens my heart to be away
You are kind to not cause a fuss about Ay's usurpation
You know what it means for Hatiay, Seny, and myself.
I will one day be Vizier like you, father,
And the name of Ay will be erased.
And the name of Aperel will endure.

————————————-

MOTHER AND DAUGHTER

Message of Shisita, Lady of the Lions
Say to my mother, Sura'ata, Lady of Qadesh
Do not say I have not been a dutiful daughter in not writing to
you!
I have a war to fight.

311

———————————————————————————-

Message of Sura'ata, Lady of Qadesh
To Shisita, daughter of my heart.
Do you count me among the ignorants?
War is not a game of sport, like wrestling or boxing.
War is a game of thought, planning, speech, and deception.
What keeps you from writing from your mother?
I'm not near planting, nor harvest.
My mind is a sound instrument.
If there is a problem of war, let me know.
Let my wisdom instruct you.

———————————————————————

Message of Shisita, Lady of the Lions
Say to my mother, Sura'ata, Lady of Qadesh
How do you handle the foolishness and ignorance of men?
Sutarna has been giving ear to bad council.
I dare not speak names on account of his espionage.
My war is no longer with the Ḫabiru
It is a war within our own ranks.

———————————————————-

Message of Sura'ata, Lady of Qadesh
To Shisita, daughter of my heart.
Don't tell me you've let internal division fester in the forces!
How I handle men, and how you should:
Allow them to think they think
Allow them to decide to decide.
Quietly be the source of ideas.
There is no glory in womanhood
This is a man's world.
You cannot be seemed to want.
You cannot be seemed to rage.

312

Be restrained in your speech.
Praise your enemy.
Be not a threat
Seize power from under their noses.
Is this not the way of Tiye, of Hatshepsut, even Ilatu?
Does not the comic poem say we are
"A sharp iron dagger to cut a man's throat"?
Be not a crude ax.
Be as subtle as a dagger.

48

Chapter 48: The Silence and the Speech

The people of Taanach did not know whether their king was alive or dead. Rumor carried its story, as twisted as a snake and as many-headed as a hydra. In a world where neighbor informs neighbor, and on and on, the truth is obscured in a dense fog of contradictory stories. It wasn't even universally known that Yaṣdaṭa was struck by an arrow. Some said he was smitten by a javelin, a sling-stone, a spear, an ax. Others still said that he was not wounded at all but using an excuse to carry out an incestuous homosexual love affair with his two brothers. Such license of speech would not have been possible with a king in town. In a sea of speech, it was only the authorities that remained silent. When the voice of the powerful grows faint, and those of the weak and humble grow loud, who is powerful and who is humble?

What truth the people of Taanach knew, and was subject to no distortion, was that Lab'ayu was upon their city, and he was strong. His rivals could cry up to high heaven, even to the Pharaoh, that Lab'ayu had given himself over to the Ḥabiru and set to himself the task of pillage. But like the heavens themselves, Pharaoh remained ever silent. There came a time when Pharaoh was no longer feared more than Lab'ayu, and in the hearts of God-fearing men, fear brought love in equal measure. While the talk of the rich was of the depravity of the Ḥabiru, the destruction of property, the insubordination against Pharaoh, the speech of the poor took a different timbre.

"Heed my words, Lab'ayu is a new Durusha, come to set us free of the bondage of Pharaoh!"

"Is it not true that the descendant of Durusha rides south, with the arms of Mitanni, to give strength to Lab'ayu?"

The people spoke and were engrossed in the living legend of Lab'ayu. To the chagrin of the rich and powerful, the commoners started expressing hope. The hope of liberation accomplished exactly what the elites feared. Lab'ayu was welcomed into the city of Taanach.

Lab'ayu stood on his gleaming, if worn, chariot hailing the people and looking the part of liberator as best he could. The cheers filled his heart with joy. Is it not the desire of all men to be acclaimed by all, to be held in eternal fame? Lab'ayu's name was proclaimed as exalted in the streets, in the markets, and in the temples. And for now, Lab'ayu did nothing to sully his reputation among these people. He was no butcher. With his son gone to the south, the north could welcome Lab'ayu like a vaunted saint.

Abneru and Yishaya followed the King, neither hailed nor regarded by the people assembled. They could not be more irrelevant to the legend of Lab'ayu in the eyes of the common man. Hero worship fell without fail on royalty after all. What could be said for those who fought, who gambled their lives for the cause? Of course, Abneru did not have any real regard for the cause. His cause was personal enrichment, and he had hoped to take great spoils from the city of Taanach. He had counted on it, to pay his gambling debt if nothing else, if not to pay the soldiery. Who was Lab'ayu to play at war, to put the myth of herodom above the truth of war? War is not about liberty, independence, fraternity, gods no! War is business, an engine that runs on theft justified only by the fact that war is the sport of kings. Soldiers cannot be paid in inspiration, cannot be fed on hope, he thought. We will take our due. If the king dares to chastise me, what can he do? We can always take our leave and give our arms to the enemy! Abneru remembered his dear friend Mutba'alu. There was fraternity in war, even for the unidealistic Abneru. He would leave to be with his friend. *Let Yishaya stay with the king!*

The palace was like a hive of bees agitated by the paw of a thieving bear. The servants and slaves were rushing each to their post, to complete tasks left undone since the disappearance of King Yaṣḍaṭa. Hastily, rooms were cleaned, bread baked, tablets put in order. The crown of Taanach was taken from the reliquary where it was stored. Priests brought sacred oil, holy water, and all accouterments of coronation. It was clear Taanach had a new king.

Lab'ayu entered the palace of Taanach, and could not help

but gawk at the comfort and luxury therein. Dove-down cushions, Kaphtorite murals, embroidered carpets, silver Hittite rhytons, and Aḫḫiyawan pottery filled each room with color and ostentation. And this was not to mention the gold and gems. Lab'ayu was now so accustomed to the rough life of soldiering and war that comfort was as alien to him as the forest is to fish. He was set to be crowned king of Taanach, after all, the people demanded it, but he had other plans. He had his own city, and he looked upon the wealth of the palace and the poverty of the commons and he saw that the people needed a king to focus on them specifically. Dadua, the son of the great hero Issuwa should be given the city as a sort of posthumous reward to the father's shade. Dadua was crowned, but Lab'ayu could not prevent those gathered from showing obeisance to himself and not to Dadua.

After a long and uneventful feast, Lab'ayu retired to the quarters assigned to him. In his bed, the person who greeted him was the person he least expected. It was his wife, Zarwatu. Her earthly facade was as common and plain as a peasant. She wore dull colors, greens and reds so faded they were almost brown. Her hair was embraced by her woolen veil. She was the picture of a common Amorite woman.

"So, Husband, you have achieved your ambition of taking a lordly seat. Now, you shall take the pearls and cast them before swine. I suspect you will take your share first."

"Issuwa was a worthy man. What better way to honor the father than to reward his firstborn?"

"Were you so deprived in Shechem, that you needed to take Gezer and Gath, Taanach and Megiddo?"

"You are greatly mistaken if you think I did it for myself. I could live my days quietly in your embrace; even as a private citizen. I would be a farmer who works the earth, or a potter, or a baker. But one detail must change. Canaan must be free."

"You are so much like your father. He spoke of freedom for Canaan, but he lived to pillage. In the end, Shechem itself was pillaged, Shechem lost its freedom."

"The Pharaoh was a young man then. Now? He is a bedridden old lout and his son prefers glancing at the sun to ruling Egypt."

"The fallacy of Kings, Lab'ayu. Pharaoh is not Egypt. You are not Shechem. Do you think Tiye lacks power? Your son's spy reports on what occurs at Thebes, yes, but have you heard what has been happening in Kush?"

"What difference does it make what happens in Kush. Should I update myself on doings in Elam? Ahhiyawa? Gog and Magog?"

"You would do well to update yourself on doings in Kush. They, much like you, thought the Pharaoh old and his son feeble. They had their fun, rebelling, denying Pharaoh his gold. But Tiye had a man for them. *HOREMHEB*. This name should be ever on your mind. Do not play games of war. I

318

will not have my womb penetrated, my sons ripped apart by wild beasts. When you wake up from your dream of Empire, you will not find me to accompany you to the scaffold."

"Sutarna, the Descendant of Durusha, is said to be coming to my aid."

"It doesn't matter. Even Durusha himself was defeated by Egypt."

"By simple luck."

"You think you'll be luckier? Do you think of yourself as Ba'alu, prevailing over even death? You may win a hundred battles against vassals, but you will never defeat Egypt."

"Go, run away, throw yourself at the feet of Queen Tiye and beg for mercy! Turn your back on your husband, your sons, your very people!"

"No, I will not betray you and our sons to them. I will go to my kinsmen in the land of Amurru. Perhaps with them on our side, we can resist Horemheb. And if you fall, I will take my sons and go into the mountains."

"You are the best of women, Zarwatu."

"I'm a woman with a head, a rarity, I know." she rolled her eyes, making fun of the nonsense she uttered, "I'd need a good one since you and your lot seem so lacking in it. Besides Mutba'alu. Who'd believe he is your son?"

319

"He is my son. He has my courage, my wit, my honor!"

"Honor? Courage he has, but honor? Wit? You mean low cunning." she tapped her head.

"No wonder he is your favorite." Lab'ayu grinned, showing his decaying teeth.

"Between him and that piece of mushy cheese Ayyabu, I'd pick him any day. Maybe it will be him that will win your war for you."

"Ayyabu will contribute, in his own way. If not through battle then through marriage." Lab'ayu tapped his fingers on the seat.

"I feel pity for the lucky lady."

"And you don't feel enough pity for yourself, being married to me?" Lab'ayu kissed her cheek.

"The moment I feel pity for myself I'll lose what little power I have. You should know, under my direct rule, Shechem is prospering like it never did in a hundred years."

"I think my victories might have a little to do with that." said Lab'ayu. His wife raised her eyebrows.

"Shechem is a great city now. Perhaps we should count our blessings and pay tribute?" She tickled her husband. When he refused to laugh, she started scratching him. She made her point.

"Let's make them pay tribute to us. It's far more profitable."

"Well, you always had a head for business. I will make offerings in the temples for your victory. If you don't win, you'll have the gods to blame."

"If I don't win, let the gods blame me."

"They surely will." Zarwatu left the room.

"Take a speedy chariot…" Lab'ayu called after her.

"Of course, because I have a death wish." Zarwatu called back, "My black soles can alone carry me to the mean land of Amurru and my father. My feet, and my ears."

She set off to the mountainous lands of Amurru. The queen of Shechem disappeared into the forest like a Ḥabiru, never to see, but to hear alone. In in her hearing, she cast her lot to the wind.

49

Chapter 49: An Offering

Tjaru was a dusty place. Tears could not be shed without turning into acrid clay in the eyes of the weeper. The mud of grief ran down Yapahu's cheeks daily. In all the days of his life, he never expected his brothers to turn Ḥabiru. He never expected to be sundered from his kin, torn apart like garments in the ravisher's hands. Yapahu was a wise man. He knew what fate awaited those who dared to take up arms against Pharaoh. He could not bear it happening to his dear Milkilu, his precious Addadanu. Like a maiden separated from her vicious lover by war, Yapahu could only remember the good parts of his relationship with his brothers. Their childhood so fraught with peril and suffering became a golden age in his memory. The days they spent stealing the virgin girls of Canaan he remembered in smiles and not screams.

Tjaru was abuzz with action every day. The death of Hanya could not be ignored by the Egyptian authorities. Canaanite lives could be destroyed without the authorities batting a painted eyelid, but Egyptian lives mattered. Huy, who had been promoted in the interim to Commissioner of Archers, now set his men to work and train at a breakneck pace. No matter that he always despised Hanya, they were deeply beloved comrades if the speeches were to be believed. The Pitati, who always despised Canaanites, had more reason now to spur them to new heights of hate. From time to time, merchants who regularly passed from Canaan into Egypt by way of Tjaru were imprisoned on trumped-up charges. Then the Pitati would use the poor souls for target practice. The commissioner did nothing to discourage this barbarism, as he was eager both to present himself as a strong leader and to accrue the wealth of the merchants for himself. Yapahu could see what he had been blind to his whole life; the Egyptians were at least as bad as the Ḥabiru.

In the desert outside of Tjaru, three men walked with muddy eyes. But unlike Yapahu their bondage was literal. Three men in bondage, three men their binders. Zimredda of Lachish, his Vizier Turbazu, and his vassal Yaptiḥ-Ḥadda. They were all found to be complicit: Complicit in a plot to divulge secret information. Milkilu, Mutba'alu, and Addadanu discovered the tablets of Shuwardata, and under torture, her slaves revealed what Milkilu had suspected all along; Zimredda was a traitor. With little time to act, Zimredda warned his son. Shipti-Ba'alu thus did not cry muddy tears in the desert with his father's men. He was hidden in a secret cave, with a few slaves to care for his medical, sanitary and culinary needs. He had their tongues cut out so they could speak of his whereabouts to no one. The slaves, already eunuchs before thier latest tasks, were accustomed to having their body mutilated by their masters. At least this time they were promised freedom and gold for their suffering.

It was almost midday when the condemned men reached their destination. The gate of Tjaru stood tall and imposing like a mountain before the condemned and their adversaries. Milkilu took his sheep's horn, gnarled, twisted, and hollow. To attract the attention of the Egyptians, he blew seven deafening blasts. His soldiers stamped their spears and clashed their swords and shields together to create a haunting, savage rhythm. The Pitati, the scribes, Huy, and Yapahu climbed atop the wall to witness it. Yapahu gasped when he saw his two brothers. He held out a forlorn hope they were there to surrender, while their surrender may still be accepted.

"These currs, these swine, these rats" began Milkilu, gesturing at Zimredda and his lot, "Have come to suckle with their mother-sow, great Egypt."

Mutba'alu and Addadanu led the prisoners forward.

"Oh please, Huy," they pleaded, "Pay our ransom so we may serve our father the Pharaoh."

"See how modestly they plead at the foot of your fortress." said Milkilu, "Give us a hundred Deben of gold for them, and two hundred of silver."

Huy looked down upon the assembled mass of Canaanites. They were far too numerous to fight with his Pitati alone. He spoke.

324

"Give you gold and silver too for mere rats? I would not lift a finger to save some Zimredda of Lachish, much less a Turbazu or Yaptiḥ-Ḥadda. They are children of asses, as are all Canaanites!"

"I had prayed it would come to this." Milkilu took his meteoric iron akinakes. It gleamed with silver anger in the fierce noon sun. Mutba'alu and Addadanu pushed each hostage onto their hands and knees. With anger guiding his hand more than skill at arms, Milkilu set to beheading his captives. It was a grotesque affair. Rather than severing the head in one fatal but merciful blow, each of the captives suffered at least nine strikes of the sword to the neck before at last their head was severed from their chest. Their cries of pain and anguish filled the air with a cruel heat, even more than the sun itself. Yapahu could not bear to watch it. With the deed at last done, Milkilu collected each man's head by their hair and lifted the three high into the air. Then, with a fearsome jerk, he threw them before the gates of Tjaru.

"Thus to those who betray me." Milkilu said finally. He glanced at that moment at his brother, Yapahu, on the wall. Their eyes briefly met. Yapahu had never seen eyes so terrifying. Then, as suddenly as they arrived, the Canaanites returned into the desert sands from whence they came. The bloody bodies laid there, headless and smelly, for quite a long time, until their bodies were picked apart by hyenas and Pitati. Why let good meat, garments and gold go to waste?

The ravages of hunger are known to all who suffer through war, as the citizens of Megiddo knew only too well.

325

50

Chapter 50: The Stratagems of War

King Sutarna and his Syrian coalition entered the city of Megiddo through the Northern Ḥaddu gate. The sound of ten-stringed lyres rang out, heralding the procession of the Syrians. The Lyre was the symbol of the city, emblazoned on shields, displayed on banners, and embroidered on clothing. The denizens of Megiddo, the high-walled and populous city, were hesitant in jubilation, for they knew an army must eat, and in this day of shortage, little would be had by the common man. Biridiya their king, and his brother, Ṣurata, feasted on the fat of the land like corpulent pigs. Meanwhile, due to the Ḥabiru of Lab'ayu raiding, the grain was less abundant and more paltry in the dole. They affected the smiles of the liberated, but in their hearts contention reigned. Now, Biridiya is secure from our wrath, they posited, but so too may we be from the forces of Lab'ayu. Fate would decide if the men of Syria would be a godsend or a tribulation.

As the citizens knew of and were displeased by, Biridiya had laid a feast for his honored guests. Grilled meats marinated in yogurt, sweet biscuits stuffed with almond or date paste, fried chickpea fritters, and bread made from flour so refined and finely milled it was almost white were served on the table. The generousness of Biridiya contrasted harshly with the stinginess of Abdi-Tirshi.

"Welcome to my domain" said King Biridiya, "Megiddo is at your service. Since time immemorial Megiddo and Qadesh have been like two brothers, allies in war and trading partners in peace. We'll never forget the greatness of your ancestor Durusha."

"Nor will we forget the sumptuousness of your vittles. You have our thanks." Sutarna raised both sides of his smile to his ears. Food was a great pleasure for him, as with all men.

"With luxury like this on offer, Biridiya, surely you must have plentiful food for both citizens and soldiery?" asked Yassib.

"That is a matter I must discuss. Since Lab'ayu's Ḥabiru have come before us, it has become impossible to leave the city to do business. The fields are untended, the sheep unshorn. Because we have no fodder for our animals, farmers have sold their livestock to the butchers. The price of meat is now lower than the cost of bread. Lab'ayu's northern army has taken our port city of Yapu, meanwhile, the land routes of trade are blocked. Gezer and Milkilu control the middle route, while the Shechemite city of Pihilu blocks the eastern route. Grain from Egypt cannot reach us, and our economy is equally starved from lack of trade. With your manpower, gods willing, we must defeat Lab'ayu in battle."

"A successful battle is a risk for the men of Lab'ayu, but less so for Lab'ayu himself. His men are replaceable, but the man is not. My orders from Tiye are to capture Lab'ayu and bring him to Egypt alive." Shisita said.

"How is that possible?" asked Sutarna.

"With your previous familiarity," replied Shisita, "He will think of you as an ally. You may send word to him that you have captured Megiddo for the rebellion. You are therefore willing to offer up Megiddo as a dowry for his son, his eldest Ayyabu, to marry your beautiful virgin daughter, me. Then when the wedding music plays, you will have Lab'ayu and his heir, and if we are lucky, his high command, delivered up like a holocaust before the gods!"

"That is a clever plan indeed! I could not have made it better myself. Well, maybe." proclaimed Etakkama. He decided it was better not to sow division in the table of their allies.

"It is treacherous and dishonorable. Despicable and simply disgusting. If I did that my reputation would be ruined." Cried Sutarna.

"Perhaps Sutarna; you may not have to have your name sullied. Have Biridiya be the betrayer, you the betrayed, and have yourself and Lab'ayu delivered together as accomplices, with secret correspondence detailing the truth to Pharaoh, of course." Etakkama said.

"Even so, I dislike this plan." Sutarna moaned, "But as Shisita

328

has Tiye's seal, and as it will be more humane, saving life, I feel compelled to go along with it."

"Let's drink! To Pharaoh, Baalu, and the future peace!" said Biridiya, rejoicing in their deceits.

"To peace!" toasted everyone. Not only in the room, but throughout Canaan. But toasting to peace does not bring peace, just as greeting with health does not heal the sick.

Chapter 51: Suckling Babe

"To health!" toasted Amenhotep III.

It was a pleasant evening in the gardens of Malkata. The perfume of the lotus disguised the scent of sweat. The Pharaoh had, after a long bout of illness, finally recovered his strength. To celebrate, he had gathered his entire clan for food and drinks, and to enjoy a spectacular thing. This thing was the singer, Urhiya. Amenhotep had written to the king of Mitanni concerning his illness, and, like a true friend, King Tushratta had sent him the finest of all his court musicians. Urhiya was a prodigy on the lyre, and a master of song, though he spent scarcely twelve years outside of his mother's womb. Now, his lilting melody in Hurrian filled the air.

I sing of him, Silver the fine
Wise men once told me of the fatherless, yet divine
Long ago, Silver's sire had disappeared
And as for where he did go?

They do not know.

Silver struck an orphan with a stick,
To which the boy spoke an evil word
Why, oh Silver, do I you lick,
For you are an orphan like I, have you heard?

His mother snatched the stick away,
To him she turned the other way,
Said to him: Your father is Kumarbi, lord of Urkesh,
Teshub and Shaushka your siblings
Fear only Kumarbi, who stirs up beasts, enemy lands
Fear him who delivers men into hostile hands.

As Urhiya released his pleasant melody from his throat and
fingers, a young woman stood by the opening of the doorway.
At her breast, a small babe suckled. While to Amenhotep the
Father, the lyrics may as well have been in the tongue of far
off Kaphtor or Ahhiyawa, to Tiye, they were fully intelligible.
In her spying on her rival Gilukhepa, over the years, she had
become proficient in the language of the Hurrians. Urhiya's
song of a boy, a lonely orphan that did not know his father,
moved the heart of queen Tiye. At first, naturally, she thought
of her own son, Amenhotep, so neglected by his powerful
father that he may as well be an orphan. But as she glanced
this way and that, she noticed Emminat and her suckling
babe, Smenkhare. The boy would never know the love of
a father, thought Tiye. Like Silver in the song, he would
stand in the shadow of a mighty brother; a brother who
may wrathfully swat him like a fly at any moment. Tiye was
moved to pity, and shed a single tear.

"I told you, Tiye, the singer is good," said the old Pharaoh.

"Must be, to thaw a heart as cold as mine." Tiye put her hand affectionately on her husband's arm, "Do you regard the son of your concubine, that suckling babe?"

"Young Smenkhare, what of him?" Amenhotep gritted his teeth. "Perhaps you mean to taunt me about what you will do with my last remaining son."

"On the contrary, Husband and Master, I will ensure that he is well treated and taken care of, even as my own boy."

"And why, pray tell, Tiye, would you do so? Does he serve your plans?"

"My plans!" Tiye laughed, "I've given up on plans and plots. Far too often they bring harm to my person as much as anyone. My only scheme now is the maintenance of mother Egypt, and her power. And what is the power of Egypt outside of *Maat*?"

"The songs of Urhiya cures all ills, just as my brother Tushratta said," Amenhotep grinned at his wife with the love he again bore her, "Now I remember, my dear, that you are the cane I stand on."

"And you, my love, are the foundation of my house." She kissed him. A love long lost was restored by the crooning of a Hurrian and the plucking of sheep gut. *I can go to the Field of Reeds knowing Egypt is in good hands,* thought the Pharaoh.

332

52

Chapter 52: A Prisoner Delivered

Bound in fetters, given up by his own father, Mutba'alu was marched as a prisoner on the rough and desolate road to Gaza. Strange as it seemed, this was his plan. Information was shady in Egypt about what was going on in Canaan. In all his letters Lab'ayu made sure he was portrayed as the perfect loyal servant and vassal. The seed of doubt had been planted so no one could know what was going on. It was a dark haze of contradictions and confusion written in incoherent cuneiform. And that was exactly what Mutba'alu and Lab'ayu wanted, to be unknown to an enemy they knew well.

All along the way, Mutba'alu played up his innocence, manipulating his guards with his charm and affecting good nature. Manipulation was a game Mutba'alu played splendidly. In fact, as he made no effort to escape and was in every way kind and friendly to his guards, they soon put him up on a donkey. They would not see this noble and sweet prince forced to walk in the cruel summer heat! Mutba'alu was gracious, praising each person who met him and giving each their share in donatives. When a gracious person hands you gifts of gold and silver, do you question the source of such treasure?

When the towers of the fort of Sharuhen appeared on the horizon, like a mirage, guarding the port city of Gaza, Mutba'alu praised the make and beauty of the fort. He was taken into the quarters of a noble hostage, not the rough prison of bonded men. This was partially because he was not seen as a threat, and to a larger extent because he made sure the right palms were always greased. The generous prince won the love of the fort's commissioners, Addaya and Yanhamu. While Addaya was an honest bureaucrat who fulfilled his tasks with competence, his commanding officer, his colleague was a beast of a different color. He was known as Yanhamu the Extorter; a reputation he had earned as a scurrilous tribute farmer. His favorite target, possibly because of a grudge, or because of the riches to be gained, and certainly because the ease at which it was possible to extract, was none other than Milkilu of Gezer. There was a time when his extortion got so bad Milkilu had to appeal directly to the Pharaoh for redress, writing "May the king, my lord, know the deeds that *Yanhamu* keeps doing to me since I left the king, my lord. He indeed wants two thousand shekels of silver from me, and he says to me, "Hand over your wife and your sons, or I will kill you."

Yanhamu hated Milkilu as his social inferior, raised to un-deserved heights, and it took little convincing for Yanhamu to buy all of Mutba'alu and Lab'ayu's stories with regards to him. Whether or not Addaya was convinced was another

334

matter, but not one of importance, because of the simple fact of lofty birth, the belief of Yanhamu the Extorter had more weight than that of Addaya, the honest man. This intel was not far from being consistent with the information discovered by Hanya before Gezer was entered. In short, Lab'ayu was an offended party, rightfully angered at the aggression and defamation of Milkilu, and merely asserted his dominance by rightful strength of arms. The fact that Lab'ayu had transgressed Milkilu at any point was missed entirely.

With the guard of the commissioners lowered, Mutba'alu was largely free to go his ways unmolested, and it was not long before Mutba'alu ascertained the weakness of the fortress. Like all human habitations, Sharuhen required a way to deal with human waste. In the case of Sharuhen, their latrine was in the form of a discrete room jutting out from the wall. It bore seats with holes dropping precipitously to the bottom of the high wall. Those who needed to relieve themselves would sit, and their dung would drop into a revolting heap below. This was just the sort of hatch Mutba'alu could escape from by just moving the stone cover that blocked a hole just wide enough for a human body. Slipping out of the fortress by way of a hemp rope dangled out the poop shaft, he rendezvoused with forces of Milkilu and the Ḥabiru captain Abneru and showed them the portal of access.

"That hole will be a tight fit, not to mention covered in dung. Well, it will be like sodomizing a young virgin girl who seldom bathes. Nothing we haven't done before a thousand times over!" Abneru grinned.

In the dead of the night, Ḥabiru youths entered Sharuhen by way of the poop shafts and ladders. They emerged atop the wall, stinking of feces but ready to attack. They quietly subdued the guards at the gate, allowing Milkilu and his Gezerite heavy infantry to enter Sharuhen. Lit only by a faint crescent moon, the Ḥabiru and Gezerites fell upon the hated Pitati. Before the Pitati could be roused to draw an arrow to a bow, swords cut their flesh and spears skewered their muscular bodies. Some held their hands open and knelt to surrender to the enemy. Their surrender cost them their hands. Though, these amputees were not long to suffer disfigurement, for their heads were soon to join their disembodied hands on the dusty floor.

"Oh Milkilu, we are your brother Nubians! Spare us our lives and we will never again take up arms against you! We did not wish to be sent here to this gods-forsaken land!"

"Oh you Pitati, when I was in your hands, did you call me a brother!? Gods no! You spat on me as a "Canaanite". Now you shall find yourself in the hands of a CANAANITE, no brother to you."

Addaya, the honest man, was courageous enough to fight for a while, briefly holding his own against the onslaught. However, no such honor existed in Yanhamu the Extorter, the Fleecer of Canaan. He did not have a heroic death in battle. He was found cowering in a hiding hole prepared just in case such a need would arise. He was brought before Milkilu, his greatest enemy. The mutual enmity was palpable in the breathing of the foes.

"Yanhamu, you would kill me, and take my family as slaves. How many like me have been threatened, fleeced, and bad-mouthed by you? You are the enemy of honor! But your days of tyranny are over. Canaan shall be for the Canaanites, our wealth for our own benefit. Not for Egyptian parasites. Not for the greedy tribute farmer who is tasked to collect five hundred shekels but takes two thousand, and keeps the difference."

"Spare him his life," pleaded Mutba'alu, "he may have done you injury, but is it not more godly to repay injury with kindness?"

"I will spare him his life, but instead I shall take from him what all men treasure most."

"If so, spare me and take my gold, it is what all men treasure most!" proclaimed Yanhamu.

"You Egyptians have a custom of counting our dead by our uncircumcised members. Now I shall count you, scribe, by your circumcised part, and make it a gift you may present to Pharaoh personally."

"Do not do this Milkilu! I will give you gold, and ivory! I will make your name sweet to Pharaoh again!" pleaded Yanhamu.

Milkilu reached under Yanhamu's kilt, and with a swift and clean movement of his dagger, collected a trophy from the Commissioner's pelvis. Milkilu then forced the agonized Exhorter to put it in his mouth. Then Milkilu threw the severed member into the dust. Milkilu ripped from the Commissioner his vitality, crushed his Kha. Yanhamu would speak to Pharaoh about the treachery of Milkilu, the nobility of Mutba'alu. Confusion and chaos were rendered. With Sharuhen taken, Gaza was entered easily without bloodshed. The South had fallen in line. It was not long before a treaty of neutrality was drawn up between Abdi-Heba and Lab'ayu's men. It looked, for now, like a free and unified Canaan would be born.

53

Chapter 53: A Steep Bride Price

In the air, the smell of incense, roast meat and flowers perfumed the air in a way distinct to royal weddings. The musicians from far and wide had come to Megiddo to play music, and more importantly beg for tips. Each separate troupe would have sounded gorgeous on their own, but in competing with each other, their dischord contrasted with the harmony of the smells in the same way the sudden bite on a prick could ruin a bit of fellatio. The slight discomfort of the guests in their beeswax earplugs was pleasurable by comparison, even if it caused their ears to sting and ring for days hence. Canaanite weddings are a sight to behold, not a sound to hear.

The game is won, thought Lab'ayu. Mutba'alu had cunningly seized Sharuhen and Gaza, leaving the Egyptian administration bereft of its most important center of power. *Now, My old friend Sutarna has taken the greatest of prizes, Megiddo, seemingly effortlessly, and offers marriage between his daughter and my eldest, sealing a permanent familial alliance. This was* a match more than worthy of his soft-spoken and coy son Ayyabu, and with the promise of the entire might of Syria to back his campaign, Lab'ayu's hopes seemed well-founded. He would negotiate a Tirkhu, a bride price to be paid to Sutarna, the father and owner of the bride. With a woman of great status, the cost would be hefty, but the war more than paid for itself. Lab'ayu had gone from a King of an impoverished city to the richest man in the south. Disobedience has its rewards.

Lab'ayu and Ayyabu both were welcomed into the halls of Megiddo, and Sutarna hailed him, just as any old friend would, and they kissed each other graciously on the cheek.

"Sutarna! Did I not say our paths would cross again..." Lab'ayu said, counting years on his fingers, "many... years ago!"

"It is joy itself, Lab'ayu, to be reunited. Even you cannot know the depths of love I've always felt for you! And this is the boy... I should say, young man! Your Ayyabu is handsome like his father! I hope he has as much wisdom in his heart as his father. Surely then, my daughter will be pleased beyond measure!"

"I never found myself a man of beauty, and as for worldly wisdom, I fear my brother Mutba'alu possesses more than I" Ayyabu blushed red. His natural coloration was concealed however, with the excessive red blush painted on his pale face.

"And modesty! Such a rare virtue in men these days! You should meet my daughter, under supervision, of course, you little lady killer! Meanwhile, leave it to us fathers to discuss the dull and gritty details of the Tirkhu and wedding expenditures."

Ayyabu went into the room where his beautiful bride-to-be waited for him, dressed; unusually for her, in beautiful and feminine regalia. Her long and flowing robes covered her strapping unwomanly muscles and battle scars.

"Am I, as your father says, desirable in your eyes?" asked Ayyabu, "I wish to be pleasing to you, for when we are wed, I want you to be happy, and us to be of one mind, happy together and in love. If that is possible."

"Love is a curious thing" Shisita played with the curls of her hair, as if she was a coy girl, "You can love someone, and he can reciprocate or not, and not for reasons that make sense, but for his own, mysterious heart-reasons, ones no one understand but him. You can even be married, a couple of twenty years, bear him his children, yet he may neglect you, choosing a lover among the pageboys to grope and sodomize, and yet even in the disgusting sanguinity of his sexuality, he still thinks it noble and the greatest good. This is the nature of love. I wish I could not love, I wish my will and heart would be forever my own, not to be faced with the cruel assaults that love lays upon the soul. But that is regrettably impossible, man or woman must love or not love based on powers they do not control; I pray you treat me well and do me honor, and I will endeavor to love you as much as you deserve."

"You speak at length against love, the force that cannot be tamed, yet I feel I can make myself love you, in fact, it comes easily to me. In you, I see a woman's heart, one who fawns over the pretty boys and is helpless to their whims. I would like to make it easy for you to love me. I want to treat you kindly and gently, keeping you comfortable and protected in the palace. It must be a rough life for a woman, being dragged along onto a campaign by her father, to be sold off like cattle to an absolute stranger, and never see her old life, her beloved mother and native home ever again."

Meanwhile, in another room, Lab'ayu sat on cushions on the floor next to Sutarna and their respective guards. The two men were holding hands, as a token of a long and loving friendship. Sutarna almost let himself be fooled that the amity was real. He longed for the love of his friend far more than for victory. If he thought about the plans to betray his friend, his eyes could not help but well up in tears, and that would give the game away.

"What I am stunned by" stated Lab'ayu, "Is how low the price you are willing to give your daughter for. Is she not valued in your eyes, Sutarna? Or am I seen as a pauper?" Lab'ayu jabbed Sutarna's side, playfully.

"Not valued as you are, my friend, my love" said Sutarna, "and I am not a man who values the accumulation of things as much as I value matters of the heart. I found for my daughter a bridegroom from an excellent family, with a

342

wonderful father-in-law. My desire is that she be wed as soon as possible, here in Megiddo, for the war needs your attention more than the wedding needs my extended family."

"Rightly said. But with your men from Syria, nothing will stand in the way of the total liberation of Canaan from the scourge of Egypt!"

The preparations were made, the Tirkhu was paid and the feast at the temple was laid. In the courtyard of the temple of Ba'alu, the canopy was held high above the bride and groom, and the Priest Benel began the marriage chant.

> *Let songs of love be sung in the shade of fig trees*
> *Let the sound of mirth run from the lips like honey*
> *Yarikh, the son of Dagon is betrothed*
> *Nikkal-wa-Ib is wed*
> *By the light of the moon, let love be joined*
> *By the fragrance of fruit, let love be made*
> *The tirkhu is paid, the groom will take the bride*
> *The threshold they will cross,*
> *The boundary of the husband's home will they pass.*
> *May she bear him seven, even eight sons.*
> *May she produce seven, even eight daughters.*
> *Praise be to the gods who have brought them together in matrimony.*
> *Praise be to the deities who taught us to be bonded.*

The two, bride and groom were bonded, and it was the time to eat a feast and imbibe copious quantities of wine. Lab'ayu sat with his guardsman, the Ḥabiru champion Shadrahu. The champion was under orders from Lab'ayu not to take off his armor nor be without his mighty sword, the khopesh he called Hand-Smiter. Shadrahu was a warrior without peer among the Ḥabiru and was unlike most of them loyal both to Lab'ayu the man and his noble cause.

"Shadrahu, why do men like you go Ḥabiru?" asked Sutarna.

"Being a peasant in Canaan," replied Shadrahu, "is half a slave, half in the grave. You are to work the land, suffer the pain of labor only to have the first fruits claimed by some king or chief or official. We are not treated like people, we are beasts of burden. The fruits of our labor are stolen from our very mouths. Now, many of us are drafted to fight in some petty war when one king covets his neighbors land. In this way, many of us learned how to fight. Why fight as a slave for your master, when you can be your own master richly rewarded in golden plunder?"

"But you Ḥabiru terrorize the peasants in the lands you raid, raping and murdering those of a station you once belonged to!" Shisita took another swig of honeyed wine. She had already had too much.

"Not all of us do that. A few among our numbers get drunk on power and indeed commit atrocities, but the true victim of our wrath is the parasitic merchant and the greedy landowner."

Lab'ayu wasn't usually much of a drinker but now he was lost in his cups. His friendship, the frivolity of a wedding,

344

the enticing flavor of the wine, all caused him to lower his guard. He grew sleepy, and his eyes turned towards his knees. He even began to nod off a little. That was when Biridiya, his brother Ṣurata, and his chosen Maryannu entered, with swords, bronze armor, and war bows of horn and sinew.

"LAB'AYU, KING OF SHECHEM, SUTARNA KING OF QADESH, YOU HAVE BEEN REBELLIOUS AGAINST PHARAOH!!!" commanded Biridiya, "You shall be apprehended to the court of Pharaoh so that judgement can be done by his hand!"

"Biridiya of Megiddo, you wretched traitor! You would give over your country to her enemies!" Bellowed Lab'ayu.

"I would give over my enemies to my master! If I had known Sutarna had meant to make common cause with rebel kings and Ḥabiru, I would never have let him pass my gate! Ṣurata, to Akko hasten! There, board a ship to Thebes, and with our prisoners sail; these traitors, Sutarna, Lab'ayu, Ayyabu, and take the virgin too, my gift to Pharaoh."

With fetters of strong hemp rope, Ṣurata led out the heroes into the throes of bondage. It was a dream, a nightmare. One Lab'ayu could not wake up from. By the light of the wedding moon, the bride and groom and their fathers ambled to a fate blacker than the sky.

345

54

Chapter 54: Unity

If there was something Tiye and her husband Amenhotep could agree on, it was this. An attack on the fort of Sharuhen, and on Pharaoh's own minister, could not go unpunished. Who was to blame was however a matter for discussion. Amenhotep asserted that the message had reached Milkilu in time and that he was still loyal. Mutba'alu was to blame, and under Lab'ayu's orders. Tiye, as all wives claim to, knew better. It was Milkilu who was to blame, as he had the motive to attack Yanhamu, unlike Mutba'alu. She had received word from Yanhamu himself to that effect, that it was Milkilu who disfigured him so painfully and shamefully. Yanhamu almost died in Canaan, with no one to preserve his body for the afterlife. Amenhotep was a lover of Canaanites, she thought; he cared more for his beloved pimp than royal officials of proud Egyptian stock.

"He was a jackal, in truth. A real son of Sutekh. But he was Egyptian. I must lead the attack. We will call up the levies, raise the Meshwesh, the Sherdens, and Pitati. Such aggression can not stand!" said Amenhotep.

"How can you lead an attack when you can barely stand?" Tiye replied to her husband, "We have generals for this. Send Horemheb to deal with the rebellious vassals."

"What does Horemheb know of Canaan and its customs?" Amenhotep beat his breast, "I saw what work he did in Nubia. If he behaves similarly in Canaan, with butchery and savagery, that will turn even the loyal kings against us. Which is the last thing we want. When I go out by day, as all men do, what will be left for our son? He will know chaos in the lands."

"All the more reason to use Horemheb. When you and I are long gone, Horemheb will remain, ready to serve our son and his progeny."

"And why do you think he will remain loyal to our family? He surely harbors *aspirations*."

"It is out of the question that a mere commoner like Horemheb could hope to aspire to anything higher than General. This is Egypt, not Canaan. Everyone knows their place." said Tiye.

"I think it is out of the question for a commoner promoted to General would be willing to stop there. Just look at Milkilu." Amenhotep beamed with pride, mentioning his friend.

347

"Well, if he asserts more power, that won't be your problem, will it, old man?" said Ay. He knew that as soon as the Pharaoh died, the office of Vizier would be wide open. He could take advantage of his connections with Tiye and Nefertiti to seize power.

"Do not take that jeering and disrespectful tone to your pharaoh!" shouted Aperel, the current Vizier. He was as aware of Ay's aspirations as Ay was, and hoped to have him killed before he himself could be done in.

"What are you two going to do, beat me to death with your canes?" said Ay.

"That's enough, Ay." chided Tiye, "You've made your point."

"When I die, I pray there will still be an Egypt. That will be up to you, Tiye, and your son. Ach…" Amenhotep winced in pain from his abscessed tooth.

"Either way, Horemheb will be sent to deal with Milkilu's rebellion and the Ḥabiru. Let it be known that each Nome will provide one hundred men, equalling 4200 soldiers, and we'll supplement that number with Meshwesh, Sherdens, and Pitati. We will retake Sharuhen, put Yapahu on the throne of Gezer, and deal with Lab'ayu and his sons."

"Agreed," said the four.

Blood would flow from the hand of Egypt like sweet water from the Nile to the sea.

55

Chapter 55: The Corvée of Blood

The recruitment boats sailed up the Nile from Thebes. Mighty Horemheb looked with pride on his growing prestige. The young man was of common birth, the son of humble farmers like the men who made up his army. But he was a clever one and caught the attention of a Nomarch, who paid for him to be sent to scribal school. But the belligerent boy was the terror of his schoolyard enemies, as skilled in beating his mates as in the painting of hieroglyphs. His intent was to be a royal scribe of the Egyptian military and earn his keep, but he never knew it would go so far. He impressed his superiors in the military after saving his commanding officer from a barrage of arrows, using a shield with dexterity and good instinct. He then charged headlong into a unit of archers with the fighting men and using only his ceremonial dagger, dispatched many. After climbing the greasy pole of military life, he was sent in to deal with a fresh revolt in the lands of Nubia and Kush. He utterly disregarded the pleas of the governors to act moderately, and slaughtered the Nubians and Kushites in the rebellious regions, men, women, and children, and sent the children of many prominent families to be slaves in Egypt. Those were the lucky ones. As for the ring leaders of the revolt, he made a big show of how clemency would be shown if their families would be sent as hostages.

When the rebellious Nubians brought their families, expecting them to be treated nobly, the opposite occurred. Horemheb had them bound, then forced them to watch as he inflicted horrible torturous deaths on their wives and children. Babies were impaled on spikes and then roasted like meat. Wives would have their breasts and noses removed, then would be penetrated deeply into all of their orifices by red hot pokers, their sizzling tongues and colons and vaginal canals providing a savory if not pleasant aroma to perfume the choir of screams and lamentation. Young boys would be fed to crocodiles, and virgin girls would be raped and then have molten copper poured into their anuses, vaginas, eyes, mouths, nostrils, ears. In short, it was an orgy of torment. And when the rebellious men who had come to surrender witnessed this destruction of what they loved, they begged for death, but Horemheb reserved deaths for the innocents. For the guilty among the Nubians and Kushites, their fates were far worse, too terrible to be recorded in any work that wishes not to offend the sensibilities of even the hardest-hearted men. From his deeds, Horemheb earned the moniker *The Crocodile that Lies in Wait.*

It was a fiery hot summer day in the sparsely populated Ibis Nome. The peasants had gathered from all around the Nome to witness the spectacle, and to potentially be called upon for military service. On a slight incline hill overlooking the scattered farms, homesteads, and impromptu markets, two powerful, 'strapping bulls' engaged in a wrestling contest fit to be recorded on the walls of a temple. Atlanersa and Shabaqo were pitted against each other. Thick layers of manly muscle were brought to bear in a contest that excited the peasants gathered and brought out their bloodlust. These Pitati champions were used as both muscle and attraction in this recruitment operation. This was needed as the Native Egyptian peasantry often had little will to fight. In their religion, if they died outside of Egypt, they would be doomed to wander in a world of monsters and never reach the Field of Reeds. Most never left their village of origin in their life. With two exceptions, the first being the Corvée. Laborers would be called from across the country to work on the renowned structures for which Egypt rightly earned her fame. While the work was arduous and dangerous, the workers were richly rewarded. The other exception was military service. For this, however, the people often needed a little propaganda to get them hungry for Asiatic blood.

"See these warriors, these manly bulls!" boasted Rensi to his younger brother Khudjem, "They will be nothing compared to us! When we volunteer to go to war, our deeds will be noted as worthy of praise! They'll make me a General; and as for you, I'll make you my chief officer."

"I'm frightened. Mother told me that if we die in a foreign land, our souls will not go to the Field of Reeds."

"Nonsense! No chance you'll die with me by your side! We'll

raise a spear or ax, and dispatch Asiatic vermin like toads beneath our feet!"

"I'm frightened by the Asiatics. I saw one once. He looked so wicked with all that disgusting hair on his head and face. In Retenu they say water drips from the sky, and that they live on raw meat like savages."

"Asiatics are nothing to be afraid of. They are mice-people, living in their cities like rat holes to protect them from real men. Like us!" Rensi flexed his fifteen-year-old muscle.

"And who among you, strong people of Ibis Nome, will be among us and the great general Horemheb as we crush the Asiatic mice beneath our sandals!" Proclaimed mighty Atlanersa. Out of the quiet, came Rensi's reply;

"I, Rensi of Ibis nome and my brother Khudjem shall fight for Egypt and Pharaoh as befits warriors!"

"Scribes note their names! They are the braves of Ibis Nome, and see to it they get the honors recorded, and get additional pay and rations!"

As if prodded by an unknown force, many peasants jumped up and jostled to be recorded as one of the hundred from Ibis Nome. War fever raged, men hungered to slaughter their wretched and vile enemy and have their way with nubile maidens. Wives and mothers gave prayers to Sekhmet in order to see their men come home. Sekhmet did not always oblige. Even in proud Egypt can the wailing of widows be heard. The wail of widows, and mothers.

But so too can kings wail!

56

Chapter 56: The Wandering Words

Wallowing in defeat and disgrace, shame and fury filled the powerless Lab'ayu. He had been trapped by a curr and scoundrel, and now he and his old dear friend were beating the path to death. Yet the path seemed strangely long. They covered far more ground than the distance from Megiddo to Yapu would be. The way was west to find the ship that would take them to their doom, but the roundabout path serpentined east and south and west and north in no semblance of order. Ṣurata was a cruel taskmaster, and worse, he had a taste for the flesh of man. He left Shisita, the beauty, untouched and virginal as a gift to the Pharaoh's carnal lusts, but not so the men: he relished Sutarna's backsides and made Lab'ayu watch as his eldest, his beloved heir was made to lay on his belly and be scourged with sodomy and secretions. Lab'ayu was unwilling to be used thus. "If your manparts dare go near my lips" he threatened, "then they will be promptly bitten off". It was a lucky break; they feared him too much to attempt coition. No one sodomizes a lion.

"Oh what a pity," Lab'ayu beat his brow, "Oh what a *lamentable* pity. From all my labor to achieve wealth, it will not avail to me now! My captors are stern men, they prefer to obey Pharaoh's command and let the many *talents* of gold, indeed, untold shekels I possess, slip through their fingers."

"What will the Pharaoh give us if we deliver Lab'ayu to him?" asked one of Ṣurata's soldiers.

"Short-shrift I'd bet. If you ask me, Ṣurata would be a fool not to ransom Lab'ayu to his kinsmen. I mean, does he really want to live in the shadow of Biridiya his whole life?"

Ṣurata listened to his men. *I'm incorruptible*, he thought. But as the startling amounts of gold Lab'ayu possessed became clear, his imagination ran wild. He loved his brother Biridiya, but jealousy crept into the abscess of his ears. His men were right, why should he take orders from his brother? With the gold of Lab'ayu, he could set himself up as more than a mere puppet. He could build a kingdom, even take Megiddo and perhaps Hazor! Gold brings soldiers. The Sodomite of Akka noticed each time he did the roll count of soldiers in his detachment, more soldiers were there than last. Since word got out about Lab'ayu's gold, more troops were joining up than defecting. He went from a man who could want for nothing to a man who wanted everything. The path of Ṣurata's wanderings turned decisively to the east... towards Shechem.

"Have you heard the news!" said a Ḥabiru to his fellow, "Ṣurata has Lab'ayu in his hands! There will be big, big, gold

355

in his ransom! Let's join up with Ṣuraṭa, get a little piece of the action!"

Word passed from Ḥabiru to Ḥabiru, until it came to the attention of Yishaya.

"Captain Yishaya! Big action to be had with Ṣuraṭa, lots of shinies. They has the king of Sikum, Labyua!"

"You mean, Lab'ayu?" Yishaya tapped his fingers on his forehead with annoyance.

"Maybe, maybo! Gold is to be had in his ransom! They also have his son Abayyu and his ally Suparba"

This was the first Yishaya had heard of his boss's capture. Had the Dog-Lover been a common Ḥabiru, his mercenary loyalties would have caused him to switch sides and join Ṣuraṭa. Had he been a man of loyalty and honor, he would have alerted Dadua's command about the predicament right away. He was neither. He was Yishaya, and a third way was apparent to him.

"And how will the keepers of Lab'ayu's gold pay the ransom if they do not know he is taken? I shall do the honors and inform Dadua, but you must have the other Ḥabiru save for me a captain's share of the ransom. I was, after all, the man who brought the gold to you! Make sure you all cease spreading news of this capture. Let's not spread the gold around more than we have to."

356

Yishaya quickly availed himself to Dadua, who was holding court in his new won city of Taanach.

"Oh, Yishaya. Dog man. Do you have any idea what is taking Lab'ayu so long? He told me to prepare the Tirkhu for his son's bride, but I haven't heard from him since."

"That's just the matter I wished to discuss. Lab'ayu, Ayyabu, and the bride and her father, whatshisname, Suparba? Sutarna! They've been captured by Ṣurata who is holding them for ransom."

"You!" Dadua bit his lip so hard it started bleeding, "Yishaya! You surprised me. But I shouldn't have been surprised. The truth has been apparent since we met. You are a good, honest, and wise man. I've misjudged you too much." Dadua started weeping, "but you, in our moment of need, showed your true colors. When other men would be jostling for riches, you stay loyal. You are a dog-man, but do not take it as an insult! You are a loyal, just, and good person, you keep in your heart all the virtues of that oft-derided animal! I will take you as my example. If even a Ḥabiru can be a virtuous man, what excuse do I have! I will change my ways! I'll reject my pride, my greed, I will be a man after the fashion of a dog!"

Yishaya stood awkwardly still as Dadua hugged him, bleeding out humane tears from his once so haughty eyes. Yishaya then found it in his interests to play the role, and he embraced Dadua.

"Let us make haste, Dadua. Do not spare any expense getting

Lab'ayu back to us. He is our leader, and we cannot do without him."

"Of course, Yishaya. Lab'ayu is the greatest hero of our time. I will follow your example and serve him loyally to the bitter end."

The two men set off, with carts full of gold and treasure, and a full complement of guards. Even Ḥabiru knew to be wary of Ḥabiru.

Upon hearing that a ransomary force was in the vicinity, Ṣuraṭa met with Lab'ayu's generals at once. It was time for the men to do business. Now it was in the head of Dadua that he could negotiate the price of the prisoners to about half of what they asked for. After all, everyone in the known world who wasn't a sap knew that.

"You'll pay the full ransom for all four prisoners," said Ṣuraṭa, "or I'll myself kill them here."

"Do that and you'll earn the ire of your brother king Biridiya and the Pharaoh both while being left shekel-less for the bother." said Yishaya. He whispered to Dadua, "Accept his terms, even if they seem a little steep."

"I see that King Lab'ayu spoke falsely of his endless wealth. I will take as ransom what you have brought, but with the added condition I will take that yon town Gina to my personal domain. So that I may do with it as I will."

358

"You drive a tough bargain! Gina is one of the most prosperous and unaffected towns in these days of strife." replied Dadua, "

"Wealth enough indeed! Fit even for a king. Will you take the bargain?"

"We must do so, or the king is lost. We *will* recover him at the cost you've set." said Dadua.

And the deal was sealed. Gina was at the beck and call of Ṣuraṭa. Dadua and Yishaya had thought he merely wished to use the town as a tax farm and a power base independent of his brother. However, his intent was far worse. As gold and silver were handed over to the Akkite army under Ṣuraṭa, and Lab'ayu, Ayyabu, Sutarna, and Shisita were released, Ṣuraṭa entered the town. He made sure that the exchange was theater for the citizens, their king's life for theirs.

"Citizens, for the life of your king, Lab'ayu, whom you have loved and esteemed, your life is forfeit. He gladly sold you by the multitudes to me for the cowardly desire to save his own skin! So much for the liberator king Lab'ayu! Now for all the trespasses your king has done in the land of Megiddo, Tanaach, and throughout the Jezreel you shall suffer thricefold!"

And it was no vague threat, no empty promise. Ṣuraṭa and the Akkite men fulfilled their carnal lusts on whoever they chose, both for pleasure and to exercise power. Children as young as five, both male and female were deflowered,

Men were made cuckolds watching their wives get sheathed before themselves being made humble before Megiddite spears. "If they resist your advances, chastise them with the rod" was the maxim of Ṣurata with regards to the men, women, and children who fought their carnal subjugation and their financial one. The fruits of many years of labor were seized, the people made no better than slaves for the avarice of a foreign king. Without Egypt's tributary burden they had gotten rich and fat. Now under Ṣurata's yoke, they were destitute and hungry. Many were impregnated with the bastardry of oppression. Ṣurata's ploy had worked. They decided that this was the fault not of Ṣurata, their oppressor, but their prior king. Lab'ayu, whose duty lay in protecting them, traded their property, their freedom, their very lives for his very own. It was a deed not worthy of a King of Shechem. Word would leak to the four corners. Lab'ayu's reputation was forever sullied. He was yet to know the extent of it.

Lab'ayu, Sutarna, Shisita, and Ayyabu were taken to the army, camped on a hill near the city of Shechem. It wasn't long before they heard the fate of the town of Gina. All were distraught at what happened there. Furthermore, worse news came from Emminat, Lab'ayu's spy in Egypt. Horemheb, the cruel and ruthless general of the Pharaoh had been sent to pacify Lab'ayu's revolt. Emminat further confirmed that in the mind of Horemheb, pacification was more of a by-word for brutal extermination and depredation. To redeem his reputation after the humiliating capture, Lab'ayu needed to act quickly. "We shall make haste to recapture Gina! The men, women, and children shall be redeemed by my avenging sword!" cried Lab'ayu.

Sutarna was becoming further enamored of Lab'ayu, and he was deathly afraid for the fate of Canaan. Shisita did not share the feelings for Lab'ayu but shared the feelings for the land. The genie was now out of the bottle. It would be hard to stop the flames of death and destruction Horemheb's army promised to bring. Sutarna had agreed to crush his beloved friend to prevent an invasion by Amenhotep III. Now, regardless of his efforts, Horemheb was coming. If the Pharaoh was a demon, Horemheb was the mother of all devils. Tiye was now pulling the strings, and her puppet would be unleashed on the rain-fed lands like an unfed dog. Sutarna and Shisita needed to get away from Lab'ayu and his army, reunite with their own force and kill the sacred bull, the beloved of Canaan before Egypt could reach the heart of Canaan. Meanwhile, they needed to maintain the trust of the hero they strove to slay. After being counseled by his daughter in hushed tones, Sutarna spoke. "I have just heard a word from my captains. My troops have fought their way out of that trap at Megiddo. Let me go to them so I can put them to use in your cause."

"Surely it is better for you to send them here. Then we can go in force to liberate Gina."

"Time is of the essence, Lab'ayu." said Shisita. "By the time our troops have reunited with you, you will have lost time, the time you desperately need to face Pharaoh's Crocodile, Horemheb." said Shisita.

"Parting is such sorrow. Let's meet again in a free Canaan. Rally your men to the groves to the north of the city of Gezer. Conceal your men there, and while Horemheb besieges Milkilu therein, you and he must coordinate a surprise pincer movement. You will hit his forces from the sides with the Mitanni chariots and your courageous Syrian heavy infantry. Milkilu will furthermore make a sally to meet them through the middle, and in the melee, Egypt will be vanquished. I shall send in my men then, to regroup with you, Milkilu and Mutba'alu to assault Tjaru, and seize the Delta of the Nile as our ancestor Yakbim did so long ago. The Egyptians will know the bitterness of what it is to be a subject people. They will taste the pain they visited on us for three hundred years!"

Knowing the battle plans of their beloved enemy, Lab'ayu, Sutarna and Shisita rode off in his fastest chariots towards Megiddo. Like the eagle of Aesop, Lab'ayu provided the means of his own destruction. Lab'ayu had never forgotten the truth of war. If he failed, not only would he die, but the angel of death would fall on all those under him. The innocent, swept in with the guilty would die by the thousands. The fate of kings is the fate of their people. The sins of the father will be visited on the sons. The King is the father of the whole Kingdom.

Shisita and Lab'ayu were poised like two bulls fighting over a cow. They both wanted to protect the people of Canaan from the fury of Horemheb. Should not one triumph fast enough, the crocodile would seize the heifer and drag her to the depths of hell. Neither could back down. Neither would retreat. Horns would lock.

362

57

Chapter 57: The Reunion

Sutarna and Shisita rolled into camp gallantly riding the finest Shechemite Chariots. The high walls of Megiddo, the Armageddon City, towered like sheer cliffs over the camp. Bright tents with majestic colors were illuminated by the full moon and dancing yellow campfires. The scent of ovens wafting from the evening bread filled the camp with more than just the smell of human and horse excrement. The majestic sight of the king and his warrior daughter lifted the spirits of the men. The guardsmen hastened to call a convocation of the leading commanders. The news bearers found the commanders in the midst of a game of strategy. Sharrupshi of Nuhhashe was playing the game of twenty squares and getting handily beaten by Etakkama. Akizzi was glad to win the bet he had made with his father Idanda. Idanda didn't trust or like the ambitious and cunning Etakkama, but Akizzi was enraptured. Since Shisita and Sutarna had departed, Etakkama, Idanda, and Biridiya shared command of the forces. Idanda was soft-spoken, modest, and cautious, while Etakkama was loud, reckless, and arrogant.

Biridiya was like a coquette, turning one way then another to arguments of the other commanders. He was happy to play them off eachother. The factions canceled each other out in a way that was hurting discipline in the wider army. However, the return of Sutarna and more importantly, Shisita, would truly set the house in order!

Shisita spoke at length about the testy predicament they had come from, about the betrayal of Ṣurata in taking ransom, and furthermore the plans Lab'ayu intended to undertake.

"I suspect" Stated Etakkama, "That Lab'ayu knows you are not with him. And furthermore, intends to make a trap for us at Gezer. No offense to you, but your love of men, him especially, has blinded you to his manipulation and cunning. For the sake of the army, I put it to you that full control over the coalition should be given over to me. I am unblinded by the passions the heart gives, and my mind is sharp and as wily as Lab'ayu's at least."

"A good idea!" shouted Akizzi, "Give the command to he who merits it! Etakkama, the Magnificent Maryannu!"

"You are forgetting that Sutarna is not in truth the commander of this expedition." Informed Idanda, "For it is not he, but his daughter Shisita, Lady of the Lions that bears Tiye's seal and scarab. She is the cleverest of women, and she will prove more than a match in wisdom and wiles for even Lab'ayu."

"I am honored you think so of me, Idanda. But this mission cannot be led by one person, much less a woman like me.

All of us have our strengths and weaknesses. Etakkama has cunning, but he lacks subtlety. Sutarna may seem weak-willed, but he is a proven warrior and a shrewd diplomat. Akizzi is sour, but his intentions are good and his courage and devotion are exemplary. I have my virtues, but I am a woman, and though women may counsel or guide, it is hard for us to be taken seriously as leaders. We must all work together as one to overcome the enemy. In our unity, we have our advantage. Our enemies are united only by greed and ambition and hate each other far more than they hate us. Milkilu is a friend of Lab'ayu only out of circumstance. He too is hated by Tagi, whose daughter he abused, and Addadanu is only loyal to the whims of his member. Mutba'alu son of Lab'ayu is a wretched and cruel man who is only using Lab'ayu's campaign as an excuse to rape and pillage. Only the power of Lab'ayu's name keeps the factions in check. We need not to just defeat Lab'ayu, but to defeat the idea of Lab'ayu. We need to attack his reputation and his success so that those who follow him either by inspiration or by greed will lament their loyalty to him. Defeating Milkilu will be of no matter once Lab'ayu falls; leave him to Horemheb. But for Lab'ayu, I know the perfect place to strike is Gina. I have cultivated for myself a reputation there, with good contacts. We close Lab'ayu into the town from all sides, and there will be no escape in those narrow streets. I know from experience it is the perfect spot for an ambush."

All the men were moved in admiration of the magnificent woman whose mind was as sharp as the cleverest men. Biryawaza was sent off to get news of Lab'ayu's plan to

Horemheb, and all the host retired to their tents to rest for the march tomorrow. But Sutarna was not among those to retire to a fine embroidered tent. Instead, he came to the paltry tent of Yassib, his lover.

"You cannot know how much I missed you, Yassib." Sutarna sighed.

"How can I not know", said Yassib "When the feeling is so mutual!"

"How did the time keep you, my love?"

"In bitterness and lonesome tears. From all three eyes." said Yassib. They both laughed.

"I'll silence your heart's pangs with sweet kisses."

"I've waited too long to hesitate any longer. I'll kiss you by my own volition!"

Yassib forced his lips on his lover with passion, and their lips met in a fiery embrace. Like swordplay, the tongues of the lovers clashed, with manly vigor in each other's mouths. This was an expression of the purest love, albeit one that resulted in the rising of manly spears. Yassib was an aggressive lover. He grasped under Sutarna's heavy woolen frock, attacking his erect phallus with hard strokes. Sutarna then lifted the youth over his shoulder and laid him upon the goatskin that Yassib used as a bed. He undressed the handsome youth from his girdle and tunic, folding them neatly. Then he licked

366

Yassib's phallus with long and gentle strokes.

Yassib moaned in pleasure as Sutarna swallowed the shaft with his full and lascivious lips. The goatee on Sutarna's chin tickled the bald testicles of Yassib's youthful crotch. Yassib let the king enjoy his manly taste in his mouth, the taste of a body that has endured the roughage of journeying far and wide. Yassib was never going to last very long, having gone for so much time without the sweet embraces of his lover. The seed of Yassib spurted into Sutarna's mouth. It's warmth and sour-salty taste reminded him of the buttermilk he drank when he was a boy. He loved it, swallowing every drop. But now it was Sutarna's turn to take his pleasure. A beautiful boy of nineteen, still youthful enough to not have much body hair is particularly suitable for thigh humping. Yassib lay prone on his back, legs up in the air, and Sutarna stuck his fertile piece between the youth's thighs and humped him.

"Sutarna, I'm willing and ready. Damned be the consequences and these false airs of morality. I know what you want, and I want it too, I want to give you my back-hole, so you may know it."

"You've never been willing to offer this up to now, my love. It is noted as a great sin, and now that I've suffered it, I can tell you it is a great agony for those who receive it."

"It is my first time so take me gently. I'm sure I'll enjoy it if you are doing it."

Sutarna spat on his male member, lubricating it for a hard

sheathing. He pushed his index finger inside the hole to stretch it a little. Yassib moaned. Then Sutarna sniffed his finger, expecting a fecal smell. But Yassib, knowing Sutarna had returned, had meticulously cleaned his rectal canal, and anointed it with sweet-smelling oils. Not to mention the shameful things Yassib had a habit of doing with his back entrance.

"Take me now, I'm ready" Teased Yassib, "I'm yours."

Sutarna took his large, dark pillar, and slowly inserted it into the smooth and fragrant crevasse of his amorous partner, gradually filling the back of Yassib's body with tingling and a little bit of stretching pain.

"Aaaaaaa AAAAA aaaahhh!"

Sutarna then moved into a rhythm of penetration, push, release, push, release. He never felt something as lovely or as pleasurable as Yassib's now gaping hole. Yassib was overcome by the pleasure of it, moaning loudly in a way that both woke up all the neighboring tent-denizens of the camp and aroused Sutarna, forcing him onwards, faster, harder. Sutarna thought about his wife's hairy vagina, now with disgust. What need have men for the lesser sex? He was enjoying a far greater joy, a better love than some arranged marriage that only reminded him of it's maker, his dead father. He was at last at his middle age to experience the youthful joy of loving and being loved in return. The thought of that love more so than the pleasure even brought him to climax inside the anus of his beloved, emitting so far into the youth that it tickled his stomach.

"What good is life without love?" asked Sutarna.

"I don't remember a life without love, before you I was nothing."

"I know what loveless life is. It is death itself, the walking that gets nowhere, the eating with no taste, the sleeping with no rest."

Outside the tent, foot soldiers joked at the expense of the king and his lover. But what was the shame in mockery compared to love?

While Yassib was pining for his lover, all the while, Yapahu was pining for his brother. Love cuts both ways, it severs and it mends.

58

Chapter 58: The Lamentation

Yapahu was drinking. He always drank in mirth since the day he was circumcised, at the age of thirteen. But now he drank with sorrow and not mirth. *I have betrayed my brothers,* he thought, *for no great gain on my end. If I take Gezer as my personal fief, it would bring me no joy. For what joy is it to be king over the ashes of your home and the bones of your brothers?*

The beer he drank in the desolate lands of Gaza was warm and it tasted like goat urine. He did not care about the taste. He wanted to forget. He wanted to fade into the blackness and erase his pain. But Yapahu was too smart to forget. His mind was always at work, never at rest. He was cursed to be a curr with a conscience.

"Yapahu, just the man I want to see!" Called out Horemheb, with Huy flanking him, "I hope you do not overindulge in this thirsty desert. We may need your brilliant mind to take the city. I want you to know, Yapahu, that the accident of your partial Canaanite birth is no cause of dismay for us. To us, you are a true Egyptian."

A week ago, the city of Gaza had fallen. Knowing the strength of the Egyptian army at hand, and the lack of supplies in Sharuhen, Mutba'alu, Abneru, and Milkilu abandoned Gaza to its fate. Yahtiri, king of Gaza, always the milksop, dared not to resist the Egyptian entry any more than he resisted that of the Ḥabiru. He was rewarded for his cowardly compliance with torture by Horemheb. They seared his flesh with hot rods and scourged his back with leather whips. Salt and natron were poured into his wounds as if he were a corpse to be mummified. He expired in the grossest agony. Only days later did Horemheb, at last, concede that he knew nothing of Milkilu and Lab'ayu's plans.

"Hark, I'm a messenger!" called a charioteer rolling in from the north. He was Biryawaza, son of Shuttarna II of Mitanni. His voice seemed to shift in pitch as he quickly approached the General.

"Who is this? Refuse of the Khabur by the looks of him" said Horemheb.

"I am Biryawaza, son of Shuttarna II, the late king of Mitanni, and brother of Tushratta, king of Mitanni. I come from the army of Syria, to offer aid from the loyal Canaanites of the North. I also bear a letter, describing in detail the plans of the enemy"

"Why should I trust you, Yiriababa? Men, fetch the instruments. Let's make this Naḥarin Nightingale sing."

Horemheb's large, childlike eyes lit up like a lion that caught a gazelle.

"You mustn't do that, Horemheb!" Yapahu slammed his fist into his open hand.

"Who are you, Yapahu, to question my orders!"

"It would cause a diplomatic incident of great harm to torture a Mitannian. If king Tushratta found out you tortured his younger brother, that could cause all sorts of problems. It may even stymie your career." Yapahu let his words twist the knife in. He knew what Horemheb was after.

"I doubt it. Tushratta himself killed his own brother Artashu-mara to take the throne." Horemheb looked at the ground. He knew he had been bested.

"Be that as it may, he did what he did for his own reasons. Mitanni is an ally of Egypt. Tiye would have your balls on a platter if you made Mitanni an ally of Hatti by your choices."

"Yapahu, you have a good head on your shoulders, even if you are a drunkard and a harlot-hounder. As of now, I will heed your advice, but mark my words, you are to beg for death if your admonition is ill-placed." Horemheb gave Yapahu a hearty pat on the back. Yapahu flinched.

"I will read you the tablet he bears. Any conclusion you make thereof is your own business."

And as the words written by Shisita were read in the blistering sun of Gaza, the independence of Canaan withered like the corn in drought. Ignorance was the sole weakness of the Egyptian enemy, and it was wiped away in one fatal blow. Two daggers of knowledge and force struck at the heart of the Scorpion of Shechem. He would die in the desert, and never know the promised land.

59

Chapter 59: The Marching Ants

Milkilu and Addadanu looked down from the battlements of Gezer upon the Egyptian camp below the hill. Like little ants, Pharaoh's warriors walked this way and that, in seemingly meaningless activity. Nobles gleaming in coats of gilded bronze mail and shining bejeweled pectorals, Pitati with their stout bows and ebony skin, Sherdens with their almost comically long straight swords, Meshwesh Libyans with their hide shields and javelins, and the massed peasantry with spears, clubs, axes, and bows. Many Canaanite Kings since ancient times were fooled into a false sense of security by how small the ants beneath their wall seemed to them atop the stalwart heights of their fortifications. Milkilu was no such fool. Walls prevented an assault, but not starvation or treachery. They kept the enemy out for now, but also kept its defenders in. The Egyptians were determined, and they would have the city and Milkilu's head. It would be only a matter of time before the orgy of destruction would begin.

"How did it come to this, brother, that we, the ever-loyal

servants of Pharaoh, are to be slaughtered like rebels? Such a turn would have been unthinkable five years ago." said Milkilu, resigning himself to his tragic fate. He scratched his beard. It was getting long, and gray hairs peppered its blackness. War made him age before his time.

"Is it certain we'll be killed? I'm sure someone clever like you can think of a way out of this. If Yapahu was here he certainly would."

"Please, don't speak of that curr in front of me!" Milkilu said. He changed his tone, "If we sally out to attack we'll be outnumbered. We'll be wiped out in the field and forced to retreat into the city, with the same predicament; only fewer men. We can attempt to hold the city, but then we'll start starving, and there will always be that one treacherous soul who betrays the city to save his own skin. I am not so naive to believe that I am loved here. To them, I'll always be the Nubian, the Kushite, the Pitati. I'll always be marked as an alien by my black skin."

"We possess food and water for many months. That gives Lab'ayu plenty of time to come here and relieve the siege. We have his son Mutba'alu here, our little hostage. Surely he will send aid."

"Do you remember that dispatch we received from Lab'ayu? He seemed to think Sutarna, king of Qadesh was going to come and lift the siege. If only he knew that Sutarna was Pharaoh's man, sent to destroy him, not render aid. If only we could give the guards the slip and get the news to Lab'ayu, our situation would not be hopeless."

"See those Meshwesh down there, with their dreadlocks and cloaks? Aren't they the spitting image of me, with my fair skin? They are my kin on my mother's side. I can outfit myself as one of them and pass through the lines if luck is on my side. I can then deliver your message on a tablet to Lab'ayu." Addadanu was tired of running from danger. He resolved to use his swift feet to save more than just himself.

"A tablet is too risky. Having you merely memorize the plan will not suffice. You might not be believed, and you may be tortured by the enemy." Milkilu scratched his scalp. His braids were tight, and they irritated him. "I have a cunning plan. We shall shave your hair and carve the message onto your scalp. Then once the hair grows enough to hide it, you wear a wig and escape. You can then shave your head again to reveal your message."

Later in the barracks, Mutba'alu and Abneru were discussing matters as well.

"I suppose Gezer is as good a grave as any." Abneru sat back in his seat, "With rich grave goods, and many beautiful maidens to accompany us to the land of Sheol."

"Let's not resign ourselves to the grave, brave Abneru. I for one intend to live a long and fruitful life."

"By all means, if you have a plan, tell me. If it is good, it will merit action. If it's not, at least it will be worth a laugh."

376

"I suggest that we propose a plan to king Milkilu. We must encourage him to make a sally from the south gate, with his heavy infantry. With his wall of spears, shields, and bronze armor he shall hold the line and force the guards on the east gate to abandon their post. Then, we can slip through there and hit the Egyptians on their right flank. That's what we tell Milkilu. What we really do is exit Gezer and make a run for it. Better Milkilu is buried than us, right?"

"That is the move to make, but how will we persuade Milkilu to go along with this?"

"We must wait for the right moment. He'll surely send his brother on a mission to secure Lab'ayu's aid. After a time, we disguise one of our Ḥabiru as a messenger and he'll inform Milkilu that Lab'ayu is ready to attack when Milkilu sallies forth. This is how we escape. He shall take our plan as his own."

When night fell on the day of the black moon, Milkilu lowered down his brother Addadanu on a makeshift rope made from linen garments tied together. He was attired in Libyan garb, a doubled cloak that opened in the sides, a dread-locked wig, and an ostrich feather on top. He made his way slowly, sneakily, to the east. He passed through the camp of the sleeping guards of the east side, drawing little attention to himself. But one man was out, still wearing armor, with a spear in one hand and a wineskin in the other. Addadanu grasped his dagger. He would have to kill this guard if he wished to slip past without attracting attention.

He silently snuck up behind him when he heard the man speak.

"Addadanu, do not conceal yourself from me, I know you by your gait. I mean you no harm"

It was Yapahu. He turned around and kissed his brother.

"Quiet, don't give me away."

"What are you doing here? It is dangerous. Horemheb is bloodthirsty and he will provide a torturous death for any who try to escape."

"I cannot remain on a sinking ship brother. Milkilu is trying to render his escape too. You know as well as I do Milkilu never betrayed Pharaoh, it was Pharaoh that betrayed him."

"Go in peace brother, I'll not stop you or Milkilu from making your escape. The guards ahead I'll ply with drinks to aid you."

And away slunk the Devourer into the moonless night. Only owls and Addadanu could hazard a journey in such blackness.

60

Chapter 60: Journey by Night

Addadanu walked the main roads on feet that mostly knew not the earth, but the lofty chariot perch. All alone he wandered, nipples and spear chafing with the friction of his rough robe. Blisters formed on his soft feminine feet from the rough leather of his commoner's sandals. His wig fluttered in the dusty wind, irritating his freshly shaved and carved scalp. Every step took him but slightly closer to his salvation and his brother's. He had little water and the dust of the road made his throat bone dry. He coughed, heaved, and spat, belly aching from hunger and weary and worn from thirst. He had tried to run like messengers of yore, but his handsome body was not made for such work. He looked like the shades of the dead, his once neatly combed beard now wild and unruly with dirt-caked all around. But what pained him most was in his heart, pangs of heartbreak and even conscience. He had sheltered himself from the truth hiding behind a wall of stupidity and lust, but the consequences of his foolishness bit at his heart like a gnat on the ballsack.

He was alone in the darkness and woe with only his thoughts for company. They smote him one after another like a Pharaoh's mace on the head of a rebel. What have I done, by my deeds I brought harm to my beloveds and innocents alike! For my selfish desires all good falls, all green burns, all love suffers! I was not but willing to play the fool, to sacrifice wisdom and honor at the altar of pleasure. At least, had the thoughts come coherently as fine poetic words, it would be thus. But for a shallow man like Addadanu, he had no words for such ideas in his head, just pangs of deep emotion. His poetry was feeling; his heart sang a dirge.

As the sun began to rise in the east, a city was illuminated on the horizon. It was Ginti, the city of Tagi, father of the woman his brother owned, and Addadanu loved. Ramashtu.

That would be a friendly place to rest, find food, and drink. He was so thirsty he would even drink water! So he ambled the last miles and finally collapsed at the gate of Ginti.

When Addadanu awoke he was bound in fetters. King Tagi stood over him, watching him like a vulture eyes the carcass of a bull.

"Addadanu, we are thankful for your visit, now more than ever." said Tagi, grinning exactly how a crocodile does as it holds a gazelle in its jaws.

"Is this how you show your thanks, leaving me in a barren cell tied tight with a rope?"

"Consider the reason we are thankful; our gratitude is to God for delivering you into our hands. Let our soothing wine show that we are gracious hosts. Drink well for you seem parched in thirst."

Addadanu was given a draught of fine, strong, sweet wine. The taste of it uplifted his spirits, quenching the thirst of his dry tongue, and loosening it with every draught. He barely took notice that he was never given bread or oil.

"I have an important message to deliver to Lab'ayu that he must know immediately. It is a matter of life and death!"

"That being so is your value, indubitably. Your brother sent you hither no doubt to redeem Gezer of it's recent siege. Yes, I am most aware of that predicament. And as you know, between Gezer and Shechem is my little town, Ginti. So once Gezer is fallen, as we know it shall, whereto shall go the avenging Egyptians but to my humble city — and I dare say Horemheb is not known for his clemency! Alas, what is a man to do to save what he loves! And to speak the truth, I value Milkilu not in the least, as now my daughter reveals to me the depths of his wretched depravity! She deserved better than to be made to suffer at the hand of some vicious pimp, she deserves the love and tenderness that the gods themselves show to their beloveds! She has been treated as befits a royal Queen in the Land of Egypt, and she was given due comfort and care by Huy, that honorable man! I would gladly give her hand to him if he desired it, once Milkilu is out of the picture!" Tagi almost spat as he pronounced the name 'Milkilu'. He moistened the head of his prisoner with

381

his spittle.

"Did Ramashtu not write to you concerning me, and how it was I who risked everything to save her life?" said Addadanu. Tagi raised his eyebrow.

"She wrote concerning you, how you and she once had a foolish fling she now regrets. You are not worthy of her. I feel people have been too polite to you, not telling you the harsh truth that you must hear. That being, you are a boorish fool that causes untold suffering and trouble. Even Prince Yam would blush at your deeds." Tagi adjusted his clothes.

"You speak truthfully Tagi, if unflatteringly. My conscience rips at my liver like an eagle having a snack. Now it is my will only that those I love are preserved: Milkilu, Yapahu, Ramashtu; and they are hale. I care no longer for my flesh, my accursed beauty, and the demon of my prick." Addadanu writhed on the ground, beating his head against the wall.

"In the name of Ba'alu, how did Addadanu learn wisdom, even Addadanu learn shame!" Tagi placed his hands on Addadanu's shoulder. "Milkilu is doomed, you cannot save him. But you can save Ramashtu and Yapahu, and make them hale. I will deliver you into the hands of Horemheb to save my city, to spare my daughter, and then your fate will be in the hands of the gods. I have brought you holy images so you may make peace with them."

Servants carried in beautiful bronze, ivory, and alabaster statues of the gods. A Bronze Ba'alu smiting, an Ivory

382

Athiratu with her ample bosoms, and an alabaster carving of
Ashtartu blessing with her holy hands.

"You are merciful, oh lord Tagi. I shall pray not for myself,
but for you, your daughter who is the worthiest of women
and my brother Yapahu who has stood by me, corrected my
error, and been a truer brother than any man could hope to
have."

"In that case Addadanu, I in turn shall pray for you. Turn
your ways around so Ba'alu himself can greet you in the Land
of Freedom. It's never too late to change your heart."

Addadanu shivered with cold in the dark and drafty room.
He was truly alone, self-enlightened, and lubricated with
wine. Before long, an old itch stirred in him, the demon
itch, the stirring in his shaft. He stared at the idols of the
goddesses' smooth white carved bosoms with their shining
gold inlaid nipples. As he was desperate and not lacking in
dexterity, he wriggled his way out of his bonds and stripped
himself naked on the dusty ground. He rubbed his male
member like a monkey, making his insipid and disgusting
noises. He didn't notice there was a window to the street
well above his head, and passers-by were looking upon him
and started spreading rumors. The rumors of the guards
got to their housewives who brought it to their sons who
brought it to their whores. The whole calumny process took
about seventeen minutes before the whores found out about
Addadanu, their stallion, being held as a prisoner, made to
relieve himself to old idols! HE needs real women, real
madams of the Boudoir to satisfy themselves and him on

his manly piece! They agreed. They would arm themselves, and sally to rescue their prince.

There was nothing the guards could do as these dangerous war-veteran harlots burst into the compound, armed with kitchen knives, rolling pins, and brooms.

"We demand that the prisoner Addadanu be released from his cell. Until that point, we will be on strike from our sex work. If we are forced to do that, every man in the city will be forced to have sex with his own wife!"

"We are under strict orders from King Tagi to not release Addadanu under any circumstances!" The guard's loud voice did little to conceal his fear, and lack of confidence.

"King Tug-on-his-Balls has nothing on us! Release the prince or we will have at you!"

"NO! BACK AWAY! AHHHHHH!"

The horde of angry and horny harlots launched into a fearsome berserker rage, and the guards were either cut down, battered, or fled. The whores lowered the ladder into the basement where Addadanu was kept and went to him. He was still in there, beating his meat, as he was not quick to climax (his one virtue), so they went to him and each and every one of them took a turn. He was so aroused that he used them, one after another, and all of them were satisfied before he spilled hard inside the last of them. She counted herself blessed. A daughter born with the looks of Addadanu would pay dividends as a whore.

"We have come to rescue you, boss!" said the whores, after they all reached carnal satisfaction.

"We need to make an escape. I am in a rush to reach Lab'ayu, to save my brother Milkilu. We can still win this war and our freedom from Egypt! Does anyone have a chariot?"

"A chariot? Who do you think we are, Maryannu? We have an ox-drawn cart."

"So you shall disguise me as a maiden, and five of you shall go with me to the east, towards Gina, where we shall meet with Lab'ayu and I'll declare my information."

The ladies of the brothel shaved off Addadanu's beard, rouged his lips, and dressed him in fine female garb with a beautiful wig. He was so handsome a man, that even as a transvestite he was so alluring and convincing that passers-by catcalled him as they rolled out the city in the direction of Gina. Addadanu paid them no heed. He could take his time to satisfy the lusts of women, but men? That was not for the likes of him. Haste must be made!

61

Chapter 61: The House of No Door

Dawn rose on the warriors of freedom. Shahar's cool morning air blew the hair of the men making them look gallant in the sun's first lights. Sunbeams glittered on the scales of Lab'ayu's magnificent mail coat and gilded helm. With the certainty of victory in their hearts, the warriors beat the ground with the butts of their spear and sang their battle song.

> *Our fathers' fathers long ago*
> *Pharaoh's mace had struck their head*
> *And dealt them a crushing blow*
> *And scores of heroes bled*
> *By the hills of Megiddo*
> *When long ago Durusha failed*
> *And Pharaoh's treachery prevailed*
> *Beneath the high walls of Megiddo*
> *But what was the cause of us to fall*
> *It was that we stood alone*
> *So we must rise up one and all*

To topple Pharaoh's throne
For alone we are but insects small
But together we stand tall
Like the walls of Megiddo.

The men were ready to fight, in battle array, as proud as eagles. The town of Gina had no walls, it was held by those Megiddite traitors under Ṣurata, who had lead his men to the outskirts of town. But what was deeply unsettling to the Ḥabiru captain Yishaya was the enemy despite lesser numbers was standing confidently, not shaking with fear.

"I fear this may be a trap, Lab'ayu. See how the enemy forces are standing with courage against our greater numbers as if they have hidden plans."

"What you see is the courage of fools, oh Yishaya. Ṣurata has seen me humbled, he thinks me weak and unthreatening. When battle is joined you'll see his confidence turn to anguish, and he'll regret the evils done to me, my son, and my dearest friend."

"You know Ṣurata better than I.", said Yishaya, "At least, I pray you do."

Lab'ayu now raised his weapons high. In his left hand, a lance in his right, in the left, a khopesh made from bronze so well polished it shone almost like gold. In his chariot, standing high above his army, Lab'ayu seemed almost like Ba'alu, the rider of the clouds. In his own head, he was nothing less. He had forsaken the revelation that he had achieved at Muhazzu. He could no longer see past his own heroism. War, at least his, was a glorious struggle. The cost of the war could only be blamed on his enemies. His war was immaculate, a struggle of good against evil. As if he was possessed by Virgin 'Anat's own violent and haughty personality, his voice rose in supreme anger and confidence.

"MEN! Before us stands this town of Gina! This is a domain of the country of Shechem, so harm not, harry not the citizen! BUT AS FOR THE ENEMY SHOW NO MERCY AND NO QUARTER! DESTROY THEM WITH THE FURY OF A STORM OF FIRE!"

And with that, the ram's horn was blown. The skirmishers were first sent up to pepper the enemy with missiles. Javelins, arrows, and sling bullets were to be launched at the enemy. That was until the sound was heard, and the men laid eyes on the enemy shields. To each one of the shields, Ṣuraṭa strapped an infant or young child. The first hail of missiles had flown and struck the babes, wounding and killing many. A sorrowful din filled the air. No one could fail to be moved by the wretched cries of the innocents of Gina being horrifically killed and the wails and pleas of the city's mothers and fathers begging both sides to spare the little ones this wicked carnage.

"Lab'ayu is a wretch who values riches more than your infants. He would willingly have them killed to take this town. He values your children as less than dirt. If you wish to save your own children, stand in line before us and fight him! He is your true enemy and the enemy of all Canaan, for what can come of his rebellion other than the deaths of innocents?" said Ṣuraṭa, proving the old adage, *a truth deceives better than a thousand lies.*

"What shall we do? They are using infants as human shields!" Labayu squeezed the shaft of his lance, "It is as if he knows my love for the innocent is greater than my love of battle."

"You must push on, and destroy them. If these tactics defeat you, your reputation will be ruined!" Ayyabu beat the floor of his chariot with the butt of his spear.

"If I willingly allow my own people to be slaughtered, my reputation would again be ruined!"

"These people are evil. We must make any sacrifice, however dear, to defeat them" said Ayyabu, "This is what Mutba'alu would have said, and he is a master of victory!"

Lab'ayu sent his warriors into the fray, with the orders to preserve life if possible. But the Ḥabiru were not the sort to risk their own lives for the sake of others. They were not afraid to land blows that would wound the infants on the shields. The parents of the children could not just watch their children get hacked to pieces by fierce mercenaries; they joined in the fight. But all and all, the forces of Ṣuraṭa and the citizens of Gina were pushed deep into the town. Pursuing their foes, Lab'ayu and his men cut their way through to the town center. Casualties rose on both sides. This was not an organized line battle of Na'arun, nor the fleety skirmish of chariotry. This was a chaotic free-for-all melee. Limbs were hacked off, heads severed, skulls crushed, ribs broken, bellies pierced, guts spilled. For starters. This was the dance of the Ḥabiru.

It should not be missed that not all Ḥabiru in the battle served the King of Shechem. Ṣurata had, with Biridiya's wealth purchased more than a few mercenaries to throw into the meat grinder. Lab'ayu's Ḥabiru were at a loss. Why would their Ḥabiru colleagues throw themselves with such reckless abandon into a fight they stood no chance of winning? Yishaya, wise Yishaya who fought in more battles in his seventeen years a Ḥabiru than most do in their lifetime, he alone grasped that the jaws of death were soon to close around his comrades-in-arms. In the chaos of fighting, one could look directly forward, or to either side. Yishaya broke an unspoken rule; he looked behind him, and in the half of a second his face turned from the foe ahead he caught sight of the foe behind.

"Lab'ayu! The enemy has come for us from the rear!"

Lab'ayu looked out from his chariot, taking the reins from his driver and handing him the bloodied weapons of war. He turned the chariot around, riding through the streets with immense skill. He looked this way and that. Each of the few entrances to the town was blocked by well-armed soldiers. The banners of Sutarna, king of Qadesh, displaying the image of the maiden Ashtartu flew above troops to the north. Etakkama and Biryawaza's banners bore the eagle-winged sun of Mitanni, flanked by lions, coming like the rising sun from the east. Akizzi showed the three palms, symbolic of the city of Qaṭna, heralding troops from the west. And Sharrupshi's men of Nuhhashe bore banners emblazoned with stylized reed boats, sailing in, as it were, from the south.

All in all, the Syrians had blocked every entrance and exit to the town, holding the choke points like a cork cap on a jar of wine. The citizens of Gina ascended to the roofs of their houses and raised their ladders after them, pelting Lab'ayu's men with missiles. Ḥabiru and Shechemite fell all around. Then, on foot or on chariots, the Syrians advanced. The streets were choked with the dust of their action and the din of battle was overwhelmed by the magnitude of their battle cries and the rumble of chariot wheels on dusty walkways. The army of Syria fell upon the Shechemites and their Ḥabiru mercenaries. If the battle before was violent, this was carnage. Neither side was willing to give ground; men were thrown at the enemy, sacrificed to the blades and points that awaited them. In such a contest martial skill gave little purchase. Death came to all regardless of skill at arms. Only the fine armor of the leaders protected them from being cut down like peasantry.

Ayyabu was taken prisoner by Akizzi, after being swiftly disarmed. He had little martial skill after all, and little stomach for the blood he now saw spilling all around him. He proved wiser and luckier than most of his comrades on that day. His life was preserved. Lab'ayu, who was already stirred in his heart by the innocent babies being slaughtered, now witnessed emotional doom. His son, Ayyabu, was captured, and sure to be turned over to Horemheb for the worst kinds of torture. And the betrayal, the backstab by his most beloved friend! He saw Sutarna in a chariot, throwing javelins, javelins slaying men dear to his heart. To fight one's enemies is simple enough, but to destroy one's own friend? That would be a deed of anger, of sorrow, and disgust. Betrayal was not something anyone could take lightly, and Lab'ayu was not just anyone. Lab'ayu was a fire, he was not a man. Lab'ayu was anger. Lab'ayu was sorrow. Lab'ayu was courage, and the last hope to escape the slaughter.

"MEN, WITH ME, WE FORCE A WAY OUT! THE COW-ARDS HAVE BETRAYED US! THEY HAVE BETRAYED THEMSELVES, AND CANAAN, AND FREEDOM! GIVE OVER THEIR SOULS TO THE HARVESTER OF LIFE!"

And with the fury of a bull defending his cow, a cow her calf, Lab'ayu charged his chariot at the betrayers. His horses galloped; the beating of their hooves on the ground pounded like war drums. He loosed several volleys of arrows as he went, felling Syrians. His arrow struck the eye of the elderly Idanda, king of Qaṭna, and wounded Akizzi in the arm. He pushed forward, with a spear in his right hand, and a bronze khopesh in the left. His driver, the greatest of charioteers, threw him into the line where Sutarna was leading. His horses trampled men underfoot, his spear pierced them, his sword butchered them. Inspired by their king's courage, the men went forth into a fearless charge. These were the best veteran warriors of Canaan, who had fought in countless battles, contending against Syrians who were not as brave or experienced, though greater in number.

392

It would have been a matter of moments before Chariots collided. Lab'ayu was nearing Sutarna, who had set aside his javelins for a handy lance. Battle would have been joined, pitting friend against friend, Canaanite against Canaanite, North against south. Sutarna had made peace with the fact that he may soon be dead or even the killer of his friend. On his face, neither a frown nor a vacant look was born forward, but a serene look of stillness and peace. Sutarna was a warrior like Durusha in that instant. But such a duel was not to be. Instead...

Thwack!

A stone flew from a sling, a sling belonging to a citizen of Gina. Her name was Adashatu. She was a mother of twins. She was, at least before the battle. She had watched her two young boys die before her eyes. A mother's fury flung the stone harder than a mercenary with years of experience could. It bashed into Lab'ayu's helmet and cracked his skull like an earthen pot. Blood filled the abscess of his skull, choking his brain. He did not die right away. He was flung from his chariot; his bones were broken and he was trampled by his own men and the enemies. He was dying a slow death, being covered by corpses. Even in the strongest physical agony possible, his emotional fire was worse. It burned in him, carrying him to the blackness in the inferno of hate. He breathed his last, broken on the streets of Gina. Shisita, the heroine of the Syrians, dug him out of the pile, then cut off his head with a swift blow with her duckbill axe. She placed it high on Sutarna's lance.

"See, rebels, what becomes of you!" she yelled, or rather screamed, to the dismay of her enemy. Lab'ayu's head was a grisly reminder of the truth he was blind to in life.

At the death of Lab'ayu, the battle was essentially over. Lab'ayu's great army was either captured and dead, crushed beneath the boots of the Syrians. And Sutarna's mind was filled with a new vision, a new trauma. HE was the Pharaoh in his vision. He crushed the Canaanite rebels. He killed his own father, his uncles, and brothers. He was powerful. He was destroyed, torn down, built up anew. There was blood on his hands.

When Addadanu's cart arrived with the prostitutes a few days later, all they found were bones picked clean by the beasts of the field, and a town, almost wiped off the map. It was as empty as a dream.

62

Chapter 62: Sunset in Malkata

Amenhotep III was ailing. There was nothing anyone could
do. His tooth abscess had spread to his brain. In pain and
sorrow, he passed. Of course, his tomb was ready, and the
best embalmers were at hand. He was properly prepared for
the next world, everything had long been ready. His organs
were put in canopic jars, (apart from his heart, which was
left in the body). His brain was scrambled with a crook and
poured out through his nose. His body was dried out with
salt and natron, and wrapped in linen bandages. He was
placed in a golden sarcophagus and taken to the Valley of the
Kings for internment. Many condolences were sent by the
kings of the day. Tushratta, king of Mitanni, sent, "When I
heard that my brother Amenhotep had gone to his fate, on
that day I sat down and wept. On that day I took no food, I
took no water." Tushratta was lying. It didn't matter.

His last love, Emminat, was weeping. Many thought it was
for the pharaoh, and they comforted her, saying he was to
enter the next world, the better world. But she was not

crying for him, she was crying for herself. The harem would be gifted to the new Pharaoh. And she feared him, for all that the late Pharaoh had said he was.

The crowning of Amenhotep IV was a lavish affair. People from all around Egypt traveled to get a glimpse of their new ruler. He was unlike anything they had ever seen. And as strange as he looked, his queen was as unmatched in beauty as he was in deformity. The new Pharaoh spoke.

"You have come here to see me. I am a new Pharaoh. Many Pharaohs have come before me. Many Pharaohs have been content to carry on the old traditions. These traditions make you slaves. You are slaves in your souls to false gods. You are slaves in the fields to the Priests of false gods. I shall be the one to lighten your burden. I will be the Pharaoh that sets aside the lies and the old ways that make Egypt, with its verdant fields and rich grains, like a barren desert to the common man. I am the salvation. I am the new horizon. So I shall take a new name. I shall be now and forever known, as Akhenaten. "

And he sang, with his Queen Nefertiti, the hymn of the Aten,

"How manifold it is, what thou hast made!
They are hidden from the face of man.
O sole god, like whom there is no other!
Thou didst create the world according to thy desire,
Whilst thou wert alone: All men, cattle, and wild beasts,
Whatever is on earth, going upon its feet,
And what is on high, flying with its wings.

396

The countries of Syria and Nubia, the land of Egypt,
Thou settest every man in his place,
Thou suppliest their necessities:
Everyone has his food, and his time of life is reckoned.
Their tongues are separate in speech,
And their natures as well;
Their skins are distinguished,
As thou distinguishest the foreign peoples.
Thou makest a Nile in the underworld,
Thou bringest forth as thou desirest
To maintain the people of Egypt
According as thou madest them for thyself,
The lord of all of them, wearying himself with them,
The lord of every land, rising for them,
The Aten of the day, great of majesty."

And many watched him, and many wondered. *What is he on about?*

And others heard him and prayed.

And others knew. *This is the death of Egypt.*

Tiye stood, just to the side. She thought to herself, *what have I done?*

63

Chapter 63: The Hungry Hill

The siege had worn on for many months. No sight of Lab'ayu. No trace of Addadanu. Sutarna certainly was not at hand to aid them. Milkilu looked out over the crenellations dejected. He preferred to look outside of the city, for the true horror was inside the walls, not outside. The horror of a starving populace. People were eating dogs and cats, chasing rats to make what Abneru jokingly called "The renowned delicacy, Kebabs Gazri."

Milkilu was a king, so he had access to hidden stores of food that were unknown to his citizens, but even for him, the cruel claws of hunger pinched his belly. The Ḥabiru in the city were the worst. They would let the ordinary citizens chase the food, then muscled it from them with their strong arms. No matter, it was they who guarded the city. Shapiri-Ashtar, the king's closest advisor, kept Milkilu abreast of developments. Who was planning to betray the city? Shapiri-Ashtar made sure any attempt to surrender or escape was foiled. As for public order? Milkilu resorted to violence to maintain it. Earlier in the siege, a fight broke out in the square. A merchant who sold vegetables was robbed by an emaciated farm boy, not more than nine years of age. The merchant in his fury threw a javelin, slaying the boy who stole his onions. The boy's father cursed the man and called him a dog and a son of a donkey. The furious merchant beat the farmer. This infuriated many farmers in the city and they mobbed the greedy parasite. They had all sold him their produce for a low price before the siege, now he was ripping them off, profiteering.

Milkilu and his men rallied to the scene of the riot.

"Men of Gezer, sons of trade and the spade! I understand this siege is long, may be leaving you famished, but let's not turn against ourselves! For I have it on absolute authority, that outside our walls the enemy is withering from thirst! They are lacking in water, and furthermore, their grain and oil are running low! So speak, men of the city, and tell me who is to blame for this spat."

"THIS MAN CALLED ME A SON OF A DONKEY!" the merchant spat, spewing blood and spittle and a small piece of his tooth on Milkilu's sandals.

"Because he slew my son!" the farmer replied.

"As I was in my rights to do, he stole onions from me!"

"Onions we grew, and sold to you for a mere pittance, and you now expect pay in silver for it. SEE HOW THE PARASITIC

MERCHANTS RIP US OFF!"

"On the divine principle of the law, an eye for an eye, as God himself ordained, you shall be beheaded." proclaimed Milkilu. He lifted high his sword.

"I beg your forgiveness king, but I was only acting in defense of my property!"

"You resorted to violent measures, which if I had not stepped in would result in division and thus calamity. Your life is forfeit. Kneel, bend your head so I can do it painlessly!"

The weeping merchant bowed his head. His broken nose dripped blood onto the streets. He hoped with one swing it would be over. It took three hefty swings before the agonized Merchant's head was removed from his shoulders (Merchants are thick-necked people). His head fell to the ground, and blood spewed all over the ground and people's feet.

"Look at that nice, fat pig," said the farmer, "I think he would be nicely marbled too. He is free range."

"You will not eat the dead." said Milkilu, "There are still rats and cats and dogs to eat. We are civilized people in Gezer."

"Tell us where you is hiding the grain!"

"I will give you, farmer, today, a soldier's ration, in condolences for your son."

"No matter! We already et him!"

Milkilu retched. How did it come to this? It was not long ago that he fed his people roast beef, sheep, and goat! Now the people feed themselves on roast people. It was a fate worse than death for Milkilu. This was the annihilation of the soul. He had failed his people, failed Gezer, failed his father. Milkilu cursed himself. The body of the merchant was carried away, and his head was put on a spike atop the wall. It would be the first of many. There would have to come a time when the citizens would be forced to eat their dead. Maybe they would even be forced to surrender.

Those two thoughts made Milkilu shudder. He replaced them with two better ones. *I will win this*, he thought. *I will make Gezer great again.*

64

Chapter 64: Only the Innocent are Punished

Word reached Horemheb and his army about the death of Amenhotep III. There was much lamentation in the camp. He was a respected leader, a magnificent king, a father figure for all of Egypt. Most did not remember a time when he was not their Pharaoh. The new Pharaoh, who proclaimed himself Akhenaten, ordered that mercy should be shown to the Canaanites. Horemheb was not keen on that. Milkilu was guilty of the disfigurement of Yanhamu, and the death of Addaya, deeds worthy of the vile god of chaos, Seth. He could not escape justice. But be that as it may, he sent word to the city. The new Pharaoh shows mercy. *Open the gates and none will be harmed.* Past trespasses will be forgiven, and quarter would be shown. Peace would be restored. Milkilu believed him. In his heart, he still trusted Egypt. He had no choice. He quit the city with his nobles and his two young sons, Zimredda and Tagi. Then he bowed seven times and seven times before Horemheb.

"Horemheb, I confess I'd never wished to fight Egypt. The Pharaoh was like a father to me, and his son is wise to be merciful. I will do what I can to serve Egypt. Furthermore I will help you, by delivering Lab'ayu into your hands. He thinks I am his brother!"

"You need not do so. He is dead already. I alone shall march to take Shechem and destroy it so that man may not dwell there. Not even in two hundred years' time."

"What would you have of me?"

"I'd have you dead. But be that as it may, I have no right to take your life myself. Pharaoh forbade it. But you, Milkilu, shall not survive. Yapahu will have Gezer. He shall take your sons as his own. He shall take your wife as his own. Millkilu: take your own life, and die with honor, or live, watch your city burn, and I will slaughter your own children before your eyes."

"In life, only the innocent are punished," said Milkilu, "I shall die, so that Gezer may live."

"Take this dagger. It's sharp, so the business of dying will not be drawn out. Kindly kill yourself. That — Is more than you deserve."

"I have one request, Horemheb"

"What is it?" said Horemheb, slightly annoyed that a defeated rebel would make requests of him.

"Put my body in the tomb of my father, in Egypt, in the Egyptian fashion. I would like to see him in the next world." Milkilu's thoughts turned from saving his life, to what he would say to explain himself to his father in the afterlife.

"Very well. Do the deed." Horemheb threw the dagger onto the dusty ground before the erstwhile King. Milkilu had his servant grab it for him. He would bend to no man.

Milkilu lifted the scales of his armor, and stabbed himself through the gaps of his ribs, directly into his heart. He felt pain like none other in his life, but he did his duty. He pierced his heart, and despite his struggle to die standing, he fell, and lay dying on the ground.

"I don't see..."

He expired, and the blackness took him.

"Burn his body. He is not worth the effort or cost of an embalmer. Send him to oblivion. " said Horemheb, "Let there be damnation upon his memory. Let any who even utter his name be put to the sword."

Yapahu wept at the death of his brother. So too did Addadanu when he found out. Ramashtu did not, and was wed to Yapahu. Mutba'alu and Abneru and the Ḥabiru left to find Lab'ayu, but they would never find him in this life. They joined with Addadanu, Dadua and Yishaya, and like the Ḥabiru they were, set to another bout of raiding and warring. In the end, Death comes for all living beings. We may struggle against him, but we are not mighty gods. The tomb awaits the living.

A few years went by, and in a dilapidated house in Qaṭna the wife of a merchant and her daughter poured offerings to the shades of Abi Rashpu and Upuzu in the netherworld...

ANCILLARY MATERIALS: CHARACTERS, LOCATIONS

FIGURES REFERENCED IN THE STORY, BOTH REAL AND MYTHICAL

Abdi-Ashtirta

King of the Kingdom of Amurru. Engaged in a large-scale war with Rib-Hadda, king of Gubla. Father of Aziru.

Abdi-Heba

Mayor of the City of Jerusalem (Urushalim). Long-term rival of Shuwardata, king of Gath. Allied with Shuwardata, Ṣurata of Akko, and Endaruta of Achshaph against Lab'ayu's sons and Milkilu. The son of a common footsoldier.

Abdi-Milkutti

A humble olive farmer of the Galilee region. Killed by Etakkama, along with his family.

Abdi-Tirshi

The proud and haughty king of Hazor.

Abi Rashpu

A common merchant from Qaṭna. Father of Upuzu. Slain by Mutbaʾalu.

Abneru

A Ḫabiru captain known for his darkly witty remarks. A cousin to Yishaya.

Addadanu

A vain and foolish royal from Gezer. Brother of Milkilu, king of Gezer, and Yapahu.

Addaya

An Egyptian official who did business in Southern Canaan. Died heroically in the taking of Sharuhen.

Akizzi

The son of Idanda, king of Qaṭna. Known for his intense honor and loyalty to Egypt.

Alulim

The first Sumerian king in Eridu after the kingship descended from heaven. Ruled for 28800 years.

Amat-Sharrupat

A woman of Muhazzu and lover of Addadanu.

Amenhotep III

A great Pharaoh of the 18th dynasty, known as Amenhotep the Magnificent. A great builder and consummate diplomat. Husband to Queen Tiye and Gilukhepa (and many others), father to Amenhotep IV (Akhenaten) Tuthmose, and

Smenkhare (And 4 daughters).

Amenhotep IV

Also known as Akhenaten. A famous Pharaoh of the 18th dynasty. Tried to impose the monotheist cult of Aten. Husband to Nefertiti, and son of Amenhotep III and Queen Tiye. Suffers from a deformity that causes him to have unusual looks.

Ani

A scribe working for the Pharaoh and the tutor of Hanya. Also the writer of a book of sayings.

Aperel

Chief Vizier under Amenhotep III. Father of Huy.

Arsawuya

King of the minor Syrian city of Ruhizza. Vassal of Damascus.

Artashumara

Briefly king of the Kingdom of Mitanni. Deposed and killed by his brother Tushratta.

Atlanersa

A Pitati from the Garrison of Tjaru.

Ay

A Pharaoh of the 18th dynasty, Vizier under Akhenaten, and close confidant of Queen Tiye. Father of Nefertiti.

Aziru

A king of the Kingdom of Amurru. Continued his father, Abdi-Ashtirta's war against Rib-Hadda.

Biridiya

King of the city of Megiddo. Brother of Ṣurata of Akko and Yaṣdata of Taanach. Enemy of Lab'ayu.

Biryawaza

A minor prince of Mitanni, brother of Etakkama, and eventually king of Damascus.

Dadua

An important general of Shechem. Son of Issuwa and cousin of Lab'ayu.

Djehuti

A great general of Thutmose III, known for his strategy in the "Taking of Joppa" where he disguised soldiers as a tribute gift to take a city. This stratagem predates the Trojan horse by about 300 years.

Dumuzid

A humble Shepherd who becomes an Antediluvian Sumerian king and a lover to the Goddess Ishtar. Also known as Tammuz.

Durusha

A famous king of Qadesh; valiantly fought against Thutmose III at the battle of Megiddo.

SEVEN TIMES AND SEVEN TIMES I BOW

Emminat

A spy for Mutba'alu and a concubine of the Pharaoh Amenhotep III.

Enmerkar

A Sumerian king known for the construction of the city of Uruk and the conquest of the land of Aratta. Reigned for 420 years.

Etakkama

A minor Prince of Mitanni that becomes King of Qadesh. Known for his cunning and arrogance. Brother of Biryawaza.

Gilgamesh

The legendary Sumerian king of Uruk. Known for his friendship with Enkidu, his battle with Humbaba, and his quest to find immortality. Immortalized in the *Epic of Gilgamesh*.

Gilukhepa

Mitanni-born wife of the Pharaoh Amenhotep III. Sister to Tushratta, Artashumara, Etakkama and Biryawaza. Aunt to Tadukhepa.

Gulati

Daughter of Sutarna. Sister to Tiwati and Shisita.

Hammurabi

The famous king of Babylon. Known for his code of laws and his conquest of Mesopotamia.

410

Hanya

Egyptian Commissioner of Archers. Highest ranked civil and military official of Egypt's Asiatic territories. Known for his affable nature.

Horemheb

Egyptian general; known for brutally suppressing a rebellion in Nubia. Would later become the last Pharaoh of the 18th Dynasty.

Huy

Commissioner of Chariots. Second highest Military official of Egypt's Asiatic empire. A son to Aperel. Known for his capricious and vengeful nature.

Huzziwanda

A Ḥabiru officer in Lab'ayu's army. Slain during the siege of Muhazzu.

Huzziya

A Ḥabiru captain and brigand; known for raping infants. Interrogated and slain by Shisita and Yassib.

Idanda

A king of Qaṭna; known for his strong stand against the Hittites. The father of Akizzi.

Ineb

The son of Yuya and brother of Tiye, a Priest of Amun.

Irqati

A woman of Muhazzu and lover of Addadanu.

Issuwa

An important General of Shechem. A father to Dadua. Slain in the battle of Gezer by the Pitati.

Khudjem

A humble Egyptian peasant who volunteers for military service with his brother Rensi.

Kikkuli

A master horse trainer from the kingdom of Mitanni of Hurrian origin. Developed the best techniques for training horses for chariot warfare.

Kohan Benel

A priest from the city of Qadesh.

Lab'ayu

A legendary king of Shechem, who rebelled against Pharaoh and made war against his vassals in the hope to unify Canaan into a free nation. Father to Mutba'alu and Ayyabu. Known for his inspiring and charismatic personality.

Mahu

The chief of the Medjay, Egypt's police force of Nubian origin.

Milkilu

The conflicted and wrathful king of Gezer. The son of an Egyptian Official of Canaanite Origin and his Nubian lover,

Milkilu rose to the position of King of Gezer due to being a favorite of the Pharaoh Amenhotep III. He, with his brothers Yapahu and Addadanu provided the Pharaoh with beautiful virgins to be concubines. For this dirty work, he earned the moniker "The Pimp of Gezer"

Mutba'alu

Lab'ayu's vicious, cunning, and manipulative son. Known for consorting with the Ḥabiru and his love of violence. A brother to Ayyabu.

Nefertiti

Amenhotep IV's beautiful but crafty wife. The Daughter of Ay.

Onan

A figure from the bible known for being killed by God for pulling out after he made love with his wife to prevent childbirth. Gave rise to the term Onanism.

Ptahhotep

The writer of *The Maxims of Ptahhotep,* a work of ancient Egyptian Wisdom literature.

Qamarti

A woman of Muhazzu and a lover of Addadanu.

Qenna

A rival of Hanya's father, the son of Userkare.

Ramashtu

The dour and melancholic wife of Milkilu, king of Gezer. Daughter of king Tagi of Ginti and secret lover of Addadanu.

Reanap

A minor Egyptian Commissioner under Hanya.

Rensi

A humble Egyptian peasant who volunteered to fight in Canaan along with his brother Khudjem.

Rib-Hadda

The hapless and put-upon king of Gubla. The archenemy of Abdi-Ashtirta and Aziru of Amurru.

Seqenenre Ta'a

A much lamented Pharaoh of Egypt's 17th Dynasty. Captured and brutally killed by the Hyksos. The father of Ahmose I, who founded the 18th Dynasty and drove the Hyksos out of Egypt and pushed into Canaan and Nubia; establishing the groundwork for the Egyptian empire.

Shabaqo

A Pitati from the Egyptian garrison of Tjaru.

Shadrahu

A courageous champion of the Ḥabiru.

Shamshi-Adad

An Amorite chieftain who conquered much of Syria, Anatolia, and Mesopotamia forming the Old Assyrian Empire. The father of Ishme-Dagan and Yasmah-Adad.

Shapiri-Ashtar

The clever and manipulative chief advisor and confidant of Milkilu of Gezer.

Sharrupshi

A decadent and testy prince of the powerful Nuhashe kingdom in Syria.

Shipti-Ba'alu

The unusually courageous and competent son of King Zimredda of Lachish.

Shisita

The Lady of the Lions. Queen Tiye's direct representative in the affairs of Egypt's Asiatic empire. The Daughter of King Sutarna of Qadesh, known for her passionate beliefs, her love of fighting, her worldly wisdom, and her sometimes forceful, sometimes lenient nature. Eventually declared Queen Mother of Bet Shemesh.

Shuppiluliuma

The second son and brilliant general of the Hittite king Tudhaliya II. He restored Hittite fortunes, defeating the Kashkans and the Hayasa-Azzi. He would eventually become Great King of the Hittites by deposing his brother Tudhaliya III and leading a great campaign into Syria.

Shuttarna II

A king of the Kingdom of Mitanni, and the father of Tushratta, Artashumara, Etakkama, Biryawaza, and Gilukhepa, and the Grandfather of Mattiwaza, and

Tadukhepa.

Shuwardata

A female (Possibly) king of the city of Gath in Southern Canaan. A longtime rival of king Abdi-Heba, but allied with him to fight Lab'ayu's sons and Milkilu. Was captured in the battle of Qiltu.

Smenkhare

The son of the Pharaoh Amenhotep III and his concubine Emminat. A threat to the kingship of Amenhotep IV.

Sura'ata

The competent and strong-willed wife of King Sutarna of Qadesh. The mother of Tiwati, Shisita, and Gulati.

Ṣuraṭa

The corrupt and rapacious King of Akko. The brother of King Biridiya of Megiddo. Was tasked with taking Lab'ayu to his city to be sent to Pharaoh, but was bribed to let him escape.

Sutarna

The shell shocked and softhearted King of Qadesh. The father of Tiwati, Shisita, and Gulati. He is desperately in love with one of his captains, Yassib.

Tadukhepa

The daughter of King Tushratta of Mitanni. A foreign bride to Pharaoh Amenhotep III along with her crafty aunt Gilukhepa.

Tagi

The jealous and proud king of the city of Ginti. The father of Ramashtu and the Father-in-Law of Milkilu, whom he despises.

Tamar Bit Ammunapi

A powerful woman from the town of Muhazzu, the daughter of the Egyptian official Ammunapi. She is the main lover of Addadanu and is raped and mutilated by Mutba'alu during the siege of Muhazzu. She is finally slain by her own lover Addadanu.

Thutmose

The designated heir to Pharaoh Amenhotep III. His untimely death forces the Pharaoh to make his hated son Amenhotep IV heir.

Tiwati

The flamboyant daughter of King Sutarna of Qadesh. Later wife to Etakkama, and mayor of the city of Lapana. Mother of Ari-Teshub and Niqmaddu.

Tiye

The puppetmaster of all affairs in the Egyptian Empire. The chief wife of the Pharaoh Amenhotep III, and the mother of Amenhotep IV and Thutmose. She is the daughter of Yuya, priest of Min.

Tulish

Etakkama and Biryawaza's tutor of Hurrian origin. A scholar of Akkadian language and the sciences. Slain at the

417

siege of Leshem.

Turbazu

The Vizier of Zimredda of Lachish. Killed in the executions of Tjaru by Milkilu.

Tushratta

The King of Mitanni, son of Shuttarna II and brother to Artashumara, Etakkama, Biryawaza and Gilukepa. The Father of Mattiwaza and Tadukhepa.

Upuzu

The son of Abi-Rashpu, a common merchant from Qaṭna. Killed in a raid by Mutba'alu.

Userkare

The father of Qenna, who disfigured Hanya's father.

Yahtiri

The pusillanimous King of the City of Gaza. Tortured to death by Horemheb.

Yakbim

A Canaanite chief who founded the Canaanite 14th dynasty of Egypt. He was a predecessor of the Hyksos.

Yanhamu

The corrupt, greedy, and immoral Egyptian commissioner was most known for extorting kings such as Milkilu. Castrated by Milkilu during the taking of Sharuhen.

Yapahu

The thoughtful, kind, and wise brother of Milkilu and Addadanu. Loves his brothers despite how awful they are.

Yaptih-Hadda

A minor vassal of king Zimredda of Lachish. Killed before the gates of Tjaru.

Yaṣdaṭa

The king of Taanach and the brother of King Biridiya of Megiddo and king Ṣuraṭa of Akko. Mortally wounded by Abneru during a chariot raid against the invading Ḥabiru.

Yasmah-Adad

The son of the great Assyrian king Shamshi-Adad. He was given the city of Mari to rule. He lived a life of decadence and sexual depravity, much to the chagrin of his father and brother Ishme-Dagan. He was eventually deposed by Zimri-Lim, the rightful King of Mari.

Yassib

The comrade of Shisita, and male lover of her Father king Sutarna. He is known for his quick wit, good looks, and generosity as a lover. From Ugarit originally.

Yishaya

Known as the Dog-Lover. Humorless and practical, unlike his Cousin Abneru. Defeated Yapahu at the Battle of Ginti.

Yuya

The father of Queen Tiye and a priest of Min.

Zimredda

The cowardly and weak king of Lachish. Opens his gates to Lab'ayu and Milkilu. Is executed along with his allies at the gate of Tjaru. Father to Shipti-Ba'alu.

LANDS, CITIES, GEOGRAPHICAL ITEMS, AND PEOPLE GROUPS

Adonis River

A small river in Lebanon, said to run red with the blood of the dying and rising god Adon.

Ahhiyawa

The Akkadian term for mainland Greece and the Greek parts of Anatolia, cognate with Achaean. Home to the Mycenaean Civilization.

Akhmim

An Upper Egyptian city that was the hometown of Queen Tiye.

Akkad

A general term for central Mesopotamia, and the homeland of Sargon of Akkad and the Akkadians who promoted the Akkadian Language to the lingua franca of the Near East.

Akko

A coastal city in Northern Retenu, ruled by King Ṣurata.

Amorites

A powerful Canaanite people known for their nomadic lifestyle and skill at war. They reached their zenith in the Middle Bronze Age with rulers such as Shamshi-Adad, Yarim-Lim, and Hammurabi being among their ilk. In the Late Bronze Age, Amorite was a prestigious culture, and rulers would often take Amorite names.

'Ampi

A coastal town in Northern Lebanon contested between Rib-Hadda and the Kingdom of Amurru.

Amurru

A revolutionary Ḥabiru kingdom in inland Lebanon and Syria. Asserted its power at the expense of its local neighbors. Ruled by Abdi-Ashtirta and then his son Aziru.

Anti-Lebanon Mountains

A broad mountain range in northern Canaan running parallel to the Lebanon Mountain Range with the Amqu (Bekaa) Valley in between.

Arzawa

A Luwian-speaking kingdom in Western Anatolia that often warred with the Hittites.

Askhkeluna

Also known as Ashkelon, a powerful coastal city of southern Retenu ruled by King Yidya. Occupied by Lab'ayu.

Assyria

A powerful and warlike kingdom in Northern Mesopotamia nominally under the control of the Kingdom of Mitanni.

Avaris

A city in the Delta of Lower Egypt populated mainly by Canaanites and the capital of the Hyksos.

Babylon

An important city in Central Mesopotamia that was founded by the Amorites and made a great Empire by Hammurabi. Was sacked by the Hittites and eventually reoccupied by the Kassites.

Canaan

The land of the Canaanites, roughly composed of the modern nations of Israel, Palestine, Jordan, Lebanon, Syria, and the Hatay region of Turkey.

Cedars of Lebanon

A great cedar forest that contained precious cedarwood, one of the principal luxury goods of the Canaanite lands.

Damascus

An important city in Southern Syria. Ruled by King Biryawaza.

Egypt

A powerful land and Empire that was founded along the fertile Nile River. Composed of Upper Egypt and Lower Egypt. Conquered the lands of Nubia and Canaan.

Elam

A powerful kingdom in Southwestern Iran, with its capital at Susa. Known for its Ziggurats and its matrilineal succession. Often warred with the kingdoms of Mesopotamia.

Eridu

The Sumerian city where it was said the kingship descended from on high.

Euphrates River

Along with the Tigris, one of the two main rivers of Mesopotamia. Stretches into Syria and Anatolia.

Galilee

Region of far northern Retenu. Borders with Syria.

Gath

An important city in Southern Retenu, ruled by Shuwardata.

Gaza

A major city on the far Southern Coast of Retenu, ruled by Yahtiri. Also an administrative center of the Egyptian Empire.

Gezer

The most important and wealthy city of the Shephelah region in Retenu. Ruled by Milkilu.

Gina

A minor town in Shechem's orbit. The site of the Battle of

Gina, where Lab'ayu was killed and defeated.

Ginti

A minor city in Central Retenu ruled by Tagi, the Father-in-law of Milkilu. Also known as Ginti-Padalla.

Gog and Magog

Mythical descendents of Noah and the distant lands they inhabited.

Golan Heights

A plateau in southern Syria known for its timber.

Gubla

A very important city on the Lebanese Coast, wealthy from trade with Egypt. Ruled by king Rib-Hadda. Also known as Byblos and Gebal.

Gutium

A mountainous region in Northwestern Iran home to the Gutians. Known for its fine horses.

Ḥabiru

The designation for mainly lower-class Canaanites and Hurrians who gave up farming and herding for a life as bandits and mercenaries. Used by Lab'ayu of Shechem for manpower in his army.

Hatti

Central Anatolia. The heartland of the powerful Hittite Empire. Homeland of the Hattian peoples.

Hattusha

Capital of Hatti and the Hittite Empire. A great city known for its walls, palaces, and temples.

Hazor

The most powerful, ancient, and prestigious city in Northern Retenu. Exerts control over the Galilee region. Ruled by Abdi-Tirshi.

Hittites

An Indo-European-speaking people in Anatolia who founded the Hittite Empire.

Hurrians

Numerous people residing mainly in Anatolia, Syria, and Northern Mesopotamia. The main ethnic group of the Kingdom of Mitanni.

Hyksos

An Asiatic people probably of mixed Canaanite, Hurrian, and Mesopotamian origin who conquered Lower Egypt in the 17th century BCE before being driven out by Ahmose I.

Ibis Nome

An obscure and infertile region of Upper Egypt where Amenhotep IV would found his city of Akhetaten.

Jerusalem

A powerful but minor city of the Judean Highlands ruled by Abdi-Heba. Also known as Urushalim.

Jezreel Valley

A fertile region of Northern Retenu ruled from the city of Megiddo.

Kaphtor

The ancient name for the Island of Crete, home to the Minoans and known for skilled mural artists and fine pottery.

Karduniash

The name of the Kassite Kingdom of Babylon. A strong ally of the Egyptian Empire.

Karnak

The most important Temple of Amun in Egypt, later defaced by Amenhotep IV.

Kassite

A nomadic Iranian people who conquered Babylon. Master charioteers.

Kedesh

A minor town of the Galilee region.

Kinneret

The city that gave its name to Lake Kinneret, which is located on the shore of.

Kush

Synonymous with Nubia. A land located to the south of Egypt, home to the Nubians who are skilled as archers and cattle herders.

Lachish
An important city in Southern Retenu. Ruled by King Zimredda.

Lake of Kinneret
The ancient name for what is now known as the sea of Galilee. A large lake in northern Retenu.

Lebanon Mountains
A long mountain range running parallel to the Anti-Lebanon Mountains. Known for its abundant cedar wood.

Leshem
The most important and ancient Canaanite city of Galilee after Hazor. Known for its powerful red walls and arched gates. Known later as the city of Dan.

Libya
A sparsely populated desert region to the west of Egypt, populated by Berber tribes.

Malkata
The grand palace of the Pharaoh at Thebes.

Mediterranean Sea
Also known as the Upper Sea. The sea was used for maritime trade by the Canaanites, Greeks, Egyptians, and Anatolian Peoples.

Medjay
The Egyptian Police force, mostly of Nubian origin, named after a tribe in Nubia.

Megiddo
A powerful city in Northern Retenu best known for the famous Battle of Megiddo. Ruled by King Biridiya.

Meluhha
A term used to refer originally to the Indus Valley civilization in modern day Pakistan. Due to conventions of Archaism, Meluhha is used to refer to southern Nubia by the Late Bronze Age.

Meshwesh
A Libyan tribe used as Auxiliaries by the Egyptian Empire.

Mitanni
A powerful kingdom in Anatolia, Syria, and Northern Mesopotamia with an Indo-European speaking Elite and a mainly Hurrian population. A former enemy of Egypt forced into an alliance to counter the growing power of the Hittite Empire.

Mount Gerizim
A holy mountain located near the Canaanite city of Shechem.

Mount Hermon
A holy mountain located between Leshem and Damascus.

Mount Zapan

A holy mountain located north of Ugarit but south of Alalakh. Said to be the home of Ba'alu, the thunder god.

Muhazzu

A minor town in the orbit of Gezer, located in the Shephelah.

Naḫarin

Another term for the Kingdom of Mitanni, meaning *The Two Rivers*. Presumably referring to the Khabur and the Euphrates.

Negev

A barren desert south of Canaan where wild tribes such as the Shasu of Yahu dwell.

Nile River

The lifeblood of Egypt, the most fertile river in the world known for its predictable annual floods. Flows from Nubia into Egypt before dumping out into the Mediterranean in the Delta.

Nubia

A vice royalty of the Egyptian Empire, home to the warlike Nubians.

Nuhhashe

A kingdom located between the Orontes and Euphrates rivers of mixed Hurrian and Canaanite population. Its capital is Ukalzat. Ruled by king Adad-Nirari.

Orontes River

An important river in Syria, along which the cities of Qadesh, Ukalzat, and Qaṭna are located.

Pitati

The Elite Nubian archers used by the Egyptians to garrison their forts in Canaan.

Plains of Gennesaret

Flatlands adjacent to the lake of Kinneret.

Qadesh

A vital city of Syria located along the Orontes River near modern-day Homs. Coveted by the Hittite Empire. Ruled by King Sutarna.

Qaṭna

An ancient and proud city of Syria coveted by the Hittites. Ruled by King Idanda.

Qiltu

A minor city located between Gath, Jerusalem, and Lachish. The site of a battle between Shuwardata, Mutbaalu, and Milkilu.

Retenu

The Egyptian term for Southern Canaan. Encompasses modern Israel, Palestine, and Jordan.

Ruhizza

A minor city in Syria ruled by King Arsawuya. A vassal of

the city of Damascus.

Shardana
The ancient name for the island of Sardinia. The homeland of the Sherdens, one of the Sea Peoples.

Sharuhen
A Strong Egyptian fort outside the city of Gaza.

Shechem
A powerful city in Retenu and a traditional enemy of Egypt. Ruled by Lab'ayu.

Sheol
A dusty and grey place known as the Canaanite afterlife.

Sherdens
A people of Shardana (Sardinia), known for their work as expensive mercenaries.

Shigata
An inland city in Lebanon contested between Gubla and Amurru.

Sidon
A coastal city in Lebanon known as the homeland of the God of Medicine, Eshmun.

Sinai
A mountainous and deserted peninsula separating Egypt from Canaan.

SEVEN TIMES AND SEVEN TIMES I BOW

Sumer

An ancient and extinct civilization of Southern Mesopotamia, known for inventing writing. Sumerian language was still used as a prestigious language for religion, and Sumerograms were used often in the Cuneiform writing in Akkadian, Hittite, and Hurrian.

Sumur

An Egyptian fort on the northern coast of Lebanon that the Kingdom of Amurru is attempting to seize.

Susa

The capital of the Elamite Kingdom.

Syria

Northern Canaan, encompassing modern-day Lebanon, Syria, and the Hatay region of Turkey.

Taanach

The twin city of Megiddo in the fertile Jezreel Valley, ruled by King Yaṣdaṭa.

Thebes

Also known as Hundred-Gated-Thebes, to distinguish it from the Greek city of the same name. The Capital of the 18th Dynasty of Egypt. Home to the Malkata Palace and the Karnak temple, and near the Valley of the Kings where the tombs of Pharaohs are located. Known as Wawat in the Egyptian Language.

Tjaru

An Egyptian fortress in the Sinai. The gateway to Canaan. A major garrison of the Egyptian Army. Known as Silu to Canaanites.

Ugarit

A great city of the Northern Syrian Coast, near modern-day Latakia. Known for its music, literature, and art. Ruled by King Niqmaddu II.

Ukalzat

The capital of the kingdom of Nuhhashe, located in the northern reaches of the Orontes River. Hometown of Sharrupshi.

Uruk

An ancient city of Sumer founded by Enmerkar and brought to its apogee of power by Gilgamesh.

Washshukkanni

The capital of the Kingdom of Mitanni. Known for its horses.

Yamḫad

A powerful kingdom in Syria of the Middle Bronze Age centered in Aleppo. Eventually sacked and conquered by Hattusili I of the Hittite Empire.

MAPS OF THE REGIONS DEPICTED

CANAAN

THE NEAR-EAST

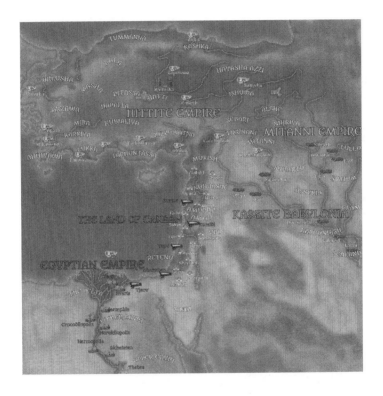

UNITS OF MEASUREMENT

Weight:

Deben: 91 grams, 3.2 ounces (New Kingdom)

Shekel: 11 grams, 0.39 ounces

Talent: 50 kg, 110 pounds

Mina: 660 grams, 23 ounces

Length:

Royal Cubit: 0.525 meters

Knet (Rod of Cord): 52.5 meters

Iteru: 10.5 kilometers

About the Author

Khn. Killetz is is known for his lifelong commitment to awakening the star of Ancient Canaan. His B.A. is in History and Middle Eastern studies, and has been studying Canaanite Culture, Religion, Language and History for 10 years. He knows that it is the stories of ancient cultures that awaken wisdom and love in the peoples of today. He made the film Qart Qadesh (2013), the series's Bronze (2016) and Baal (2019).

Also by Kohan Killetz

Printed in Great Britain
by Amazon